Raw Justice

By

Kerry Barnes

The trilogy

Ruthless

ISBN 978-84897-497-5

Ruby's Palace

ISBN 978 – 84897-801-0

Raw Justice

ISBN 978 –19997262—01--1

Dedication

I dedicated this book to my aunt Margaret who sadly passed away. She was such a sweet and beautiful woman who was loved by so many.

May you be dancing in heaven with the angels.

Acknowledgments

It is very rare that we experience the blessing of an angel. To have a complete stranger come into my life and offer their time, patience and vast knowledge, just to see me succeed, was the biggest gift of all. Therefore, if there are mistakes in this short paragraph it is because this was the only part he didn't edit for me.

My angel and my co- pilot - Robert Wood

During my journey writing novels, I have also met some great supporters. Deryl Easton has been my sidekick and sanity check through all the ups and downs, and a dear friend to cherish.

I would also like to acknowledge the members of the NotRights Book Club who have supported me tremendously.

Julie Simpson for her kind words and Shell Baker for her fantastic reviews.

My friends and family who have stood by me and encouraged me to continue writing, I am truly grateful.

I am blessed.

Raw Justice

by

Kerry Barnes

PROLOGUE

The steel door opened and in stepped the fat woman with the face resembling something out of a horror movie. Anya backed herself into the corner of the cell, away from her. Her body shook all over as the pain in her head was so unbearable she thought she would die – and she prayed fervently she would. She just could not take any more from these monsters. The fat woman snarled, curling her lip, and then like a twisted, sick madwoman, she smirked, "Get this dress on, whore!" She then threw the black evening gown, encrusted in crystals, onto the bed.

Anya despised the metal-framed bed with the grey mattress. Enduring night after night, in the depths of the huge mansion, her hands tied so tightly to the bedframe, and with ugly, brutal men abusing her body, she had no choice but to do as the fat lady said. The door slammed shut, and Anya, like a robot, picked up the beautiful dress and pulled it over her aching head. Her frail, thin body would once have filled this dress with ample bosom and a thicker waist, but now she barely had any fat to call her own. Her hair, once long and thick and so much admired by her mother, was thinning to nothing. She tried to do the zip up at the back, but how could she? Her right arm was now dislocated at the shoulder. So, in despair, she sat on the bed, held her head in her hands, and cried with no tears. The wet tears had run out. She thought of her mother back in Russia and her heart ached; if only she could hear her voice just one last time to say goodbye and to thank her for the fifteen years of happiness she had given her.

The door opened again, but Anya didn't move. It was strange, for she'd had a dream about this moment only a few days ago. But like so many of her dreams, she couldn't remember if it had ended well or not. She suspected the latter would be the case. So this was it: she was going to die. She was dressed ready for her grave. The fat woman roughly zipped up the back of her gown and then grabbed her face, pulling it to the light. A large bag was set down carelessly on the bed next to her, and the older woman pulled out a tube of foundation which she spread over the girl's face. Anya closed her eyes and allowed her to plaster on the make-up. She never gave it any thought; she couldn't imagine what they had in store for her and was now too tired and too despondent to care. All she hoped for was a quick death.

The cold air outside hit her and she took a deep breath. A tall man, dressed in black, holding a gun, whispered in her ear, "You have five minutes to escape, so run as fast as you can across the field and through the woods."

Anya, for a few moments, thought the man was on her side, and he was going to help her. As if all the adrenaline had hit her at once, she ran with the wind whistling through her hair and tore across the field. Although her feet were sore, and the ground was hard, nothing was going to stop her, for this was her chance to escape to save her own life and return to her mother. The cold air burned her lungs, but she was determined to keep going. She must never stop. Forgetting the pain in her head and the dislocated shoulder, she fought on with every ounce of strength she had. Then, she heard another whistling sound behind her. But this was not the wind; instead, she felt a thud as something hit her neck, and then there was this searing pain as if a wasp had stung her – except that it wasn't a wasp, it was a tranquilizer dart. She didn't stop until her legs began to feel numb and her eyed blurred.

"Oh no, God, please no!" she cried.

CHAPTER ONE

Alone in her cell, Gemma kept an anxious eye on the clock by her bed. She was on edge and had been really ever since the visiting order had been arranged. This visit was a culmination of many hours of hard thinking time. It had to be thinking time. There was no way she was committing her thoughts on paper.

Over and over in her mind, she had played out scenarios as to how she would get out of this dreadful nuthouse. It wasn't so much the usual violence – by inmates and some notable screws who had found out about her past – but the need to exact revenge on one particular family. She wanted them dead, but she also wanted their business empire too. But she couldn't achieve her objectives in a cell all cooped up 24/7 with no outside help to call on, or could she? She realised that the only person in the whole world who could help her would be her visitor today. She had the contacts, she had the resources through her family, and she was the one and only link to the person she really needed to see.

On first glance, the prison looked pleasant enough from the outside. HMP Bronzefield was modern and not at all imposing. It was built to house just over five hundred women inmates. Cassie looked at her watch. It was approaching two o'clock in the afternoon. The radio presenter had announced that this was going to be the hottest day of 2016, and he wasn't wrong. She wiped the sweat from her brow with the back of her hand and nervously fumbled inside her bag for the VO. There were so many things on her mind, but these would have to wait. She needed to get her thoughts around the person she was visiting.

She had almost forgotten what she looked like, it was so long ago. In a strange way, she was excited, but she was also nervous not knowing what this visit was really about. The visiting order had arrived out of the blue to her address, which at the time had stumped Cassie because she had no idea this woman even knew where she lived.

Once Cassie had gone through the gates, the security, and the search area, she slid onto the cold plastic chair and gazed around. The whole experience was new; the sound of the heavy metal doors sliding shut sent shivers up her spine. She thanked God she had stayed out of trouble. The visiting room was like a café but the bars at the windows and the burly female officers brought home the reality of it all. She pulled her cardigan tighter and crossed her arms under her breasts, which had ballooned in the last two months. Not moving her head, she scanned the room. Other visitors were seated, waiting for the door at the end to open, from where the inmates appeared. Of course, Cassie didn't know the drill, having never been inside a police station let alone a prison. Yet it could easily have been her. She had been brought up in the same system: foster care and children's homes. She'd also had a few naughty boyfriends; well, it was the done thing back then. As long as the social workers could tick the right boxes, no one really cared what you did and who you did it with.

The end door slid open and two officers dressed in thick blue uniforms called out names: Black, Smith … then Gemma's surname, Ruthers. Cassie took a deep breath and stared. With no expression on

14

her face, the scrawny pathetic waif of a woman walked towards her. She could have been a ghost – the wandering spirit of an inmate who'd passed over. Cassie bit her nail and waited for the skinny woman to sit down.

"Thanks for coming, Cass."

Gemma looked up and tried to smile, but her face was drenched in pain and anguish. Cassie was wide-eyed and silent; she hardly recognised Gemma.

"Look, Gemma, I shouldn't have come. Me ol' man don't know I'm here. I don't know what you want, but I can't help you."

Cassie was afraid but not of Gemma. Instead, she feared this woman's deathly look and the deep brown lifeless eyes which had sunk into their sockets. The gaunt and sour expression wasn't the Gemma she knew. The voluptuous blonde bombshell, who had oozed life, livened up a room, and captured an audience, was gone. All that was left of her was this shell of a woman.

"Cass, please help me? I can't do this." Even Gemma's voice was pathetic: it was like that of a scared child.

Now the shock had worn off, Cassie took a closer look. Gemma's hands were shaking, with her nails bitten down to the quick. Those hands were once soft, with long painted nails; bright red was her favourite colour. The scars up her arms were alarming. It took a few seconds for Cassie to take it all in. Gemma's once thick lustrous hair, which had tumbled down her back, was now dull and thin. With her head tilted in shame and her hair pulled back into a tight ponytail, Cassie could see just how fine it was. Gemma looked up at Cassie, begging with her eyes, which formed big round pools of sadness.

15

"Don't, Gem, I can't help you, babe. I know we were like sisters years ago … For fuck's sake, you were sixteen the last time I saw you. That's got to be almost twenty-four years ago now."

"I got no one else."

Reluctantly, Cassie nodded. "All right, listen. I can send you in a bit a poke but just a one-off … see, me husband don't know I'm here, and he wouldn't like it."

Gemma lowered her head again. "I don't want money. I need you to get me out of here."

Cassie sat back on her chair and laughed. "Yeah, right! I'll bake a fucking cake and line it with gunpowder, send it in as a treat, and you can blow your way out. Don't be stupid, Gemma. I can't get you out of here. I fucking lock meself outta me own house enough times."

Chewing the inside of her mouth, Gemma's eyes met Cassie's. "No, Cass, I mean with a lawyer."

It was then apparent that Gemma had got wind of her connections.

"I can't shit miracles, Gem. Look, you're in the system. They have legal processes, legal aid. You're entitled to those, aren't you?"

Gemma leaned forward. "They said it's not worth even appealing me sentence, so no one is bothering. Me own barrister, after the case, told me to just keep me head down, and in seven years, I'll be out. But I can't stay here, Cassie. It's not being locked up that bothers me. It's being inside with—"

She stopped dead and glanced over Cassie's shoulder at another inmate. She was walking towards her and smiling. Gemma froze and then shrunk her head into her shoulders. Cassie waited until the inmate had passed before whispering, "What's up? You look like you've just seen a ghost. Who was that woman?"

Gemma shook her head. "They call her the rapist."

With a deep frown, Cassie curled her lip. "What the fuck? A woman can't be a rapist."

"In here she can, and she is."

Cassie put her hands to her mouth. Vivid, sick ideas raced through her mind, and a sudden, empty sensation gripped her stomach. "What's going on, Gemma?" There, she had asked the question, but she wished she hadn't. She didn't want to get involved with Gemma – not now – and not after all these years.

They had lived in the same foster homes, on and off, from when they were four and six years old. Gemma had run away when she was about twelve and was then eventually brought back and that was it. Life was tough back then, and Cassie didn't want to revisit it. She had her own life now, her Dan, and the new baby on the way.

"I'm clean, no drugs, no drink, I don't even smoke."

"You could've fooled me. Look at the state of you, Gem! You've got scars all over you. Truthfully, love, I wouldn't have recognised you in the street. I don't know many scagheads now, but by Christ, you are the epitome of one. I have to say, mate, you look more going on sixty not forty. Anyway, what's being clean got to do with the price of eggs?"

"I don't get searched coming off a visit." She paused, taking a deep breath. "They want me to bring stuff in for them, and no excuses, or so they said."

"Well, don't think, for one minute, I'm getting caught up in all that bollocks. No way, matie," replied Cassie, her arms once more folded tightly under her breasts.

Gemma shook her head. "No, Cass, of course not. That's why I need to get out of here. They're cruel, Cass, really fucking wicked." Fat tears rolled down her cheeks.

With pursed lips, Cassie unfolded her arms and leaned forward again. "Look, love, we were close, you and me, but you got out the house when ya reached sixteen and left me with that fucking pervert, and to be honest, I hated ya for it. You could have taken me with you, but you didn't. I was in the way. You found your fella and went swanning off to his pad, big enough for me, too, but you left me behind …" She looked around her and sighed. "Don't get me wrong. I was gutted for ages, but then I got out and moved on with me life. I don't hate you anymore, but I don't owe you either." She looked at the resigned expression on Gemma's face and felt an overwhelming sadness for her.

"I know, Cass, I know. I really thought Bobby was everything … How stupid was I?"

A sympathetic expression covered Cassie's face; she knew in her heart she would have done the same – a gorgeous-looking bloke, a flash car, his own place. If she had been in Gemma's shoes, she would have run off and not given anyone a second thought.

"Nah, not stupid, just looking for an escape. I guess we all were, back then." She frowned when Gemma shook her head and the tears flowed. "What is it, mate?"

"Oh, Cass, he was an absolute cunt, but worst of it is, I knew he was." Her voice was low as she stared off into space.

Cassie rubbed her arm. "You were young, babe, so he was a bit naughty. We loved guys like that back then: fast cars, cocky bastards, it was part of the thrill."

"No, it was worse, so much worse ..." She bowed her head. "I'm sorry, Cass. You're right. I should never have asked you to come. It's best you go and forget you ever saw me." She got up to leave, but Cassie grabbed her arm.

"Look, babe, I can't promise, but I'll see what I can do. Send me a VO for two weeks' time, and I'll try to get you a brief in the meantime. I can't say fairer than that."

Gemma's face almost lit up, but Cass could see her grief was so deep. "What's really fucking going on here, Gem? You look like shit, and you're shaking like a pisshead."

One of the officers was glaring in their direction and it didn't go unnoticed by Cassie. "I don't like this, babe. Why is that screw behind you staring at me?" she whispered, lowering her face so the officer couldn't lip-read.

Gemma's eyes widened. "Is she fat, cropped black hair?"

Cassie nodded.

In despair, Gemma closed her eyes and slowly shook her head. "They're all in on it – the inmates and the fucking screws. I thought I was paranoid, but I ain't, Cass. That cunt has got to them. It's Bobby. I swear to God, he has spies everywhere."

Cassie shuffled uncomfortably in her chair. It was so hot in here. And what she was hearing and seeing seemed like a million miles away from her quiet and settled life with Dan.

She could feel the tension and it made her nervous. "What do you mean, *he's* got to them? For fuck's sake, he ain't one of the Mafioso … this is only Bobby we're talking about."

"No, Cass, it's the whole fucking lot of them."

"You've lost me. I thought you got locked up for stabbing your old man, Bobby? Least, that's what I heard," replied Cassie, frowning.

Gemma looked to the floor, biting on her nails. "I guess that's what everyone's saying. Yeah, I did, but I had no choice, he was—" She stopped and stared over Cassie's shoulder. The big dark-haired screw was now standing an inch away, and staring, in a menacing manner. Cassie turned her head and looked the officer up and down.

"Right, Ruthers, your visit's over. You can leave with me for a strip search."

"Hey, hold on a minute, love. Visiting hours are over at five fifteen. No one else has been asked to leave," snapped Cassie. A sharp pain shot up her leg. Gemma had just kicked her under the table.

A big grin spread across the officer's face. "If I suspect an inmate of taking contraband, I finish the visit. Now, I suggest you leave without a fuss, or I'll call in the police to have you searched – your choice." The smirk remained on her face and Cassie was livid. The anger was overwhelming; she so wanted to fly-kick the fat bitch out of this room, but she knew she had her unborn baby to think about. Cassie looked back and noticed the resigned expression on her old friend's face. She instantly stood up, towering above the officer and slowly turned to face Gemma. "Send me a VO, babe," she said firmly.

Gripped by fear, Gemma couldn't even look up; she knew she was going to return to a beating, or worse.

Cassie left the visiting room but glanced back before she slipped through the exit door to see the fat screw marching Gemma out. Her heart sank for many reasons. Firstly, she wished she had never agreed to the visit, and secondly, she suddenly felt close, like the old times, and had the urge to help.

The warm summer breeze blew her long chiffon dress, and the ugly stale smell of the prison wafted away. The odour had gone, but the vision remained. Cassie snapped out of her daze once she reached her new car and the unlock button bleeped. She opened the door and slid across the fresh suede seat, started the engine, and turned the radio up. The stifling heat inside the car, which had turned it into an oven in the baking sun, was causing her to sweat. She also had a severe migraine, following the visit. She just couldn't get out of her mind that evil stare from the screw, who had taken Gemma away from the visitors' room. She turned up the air conditioning for an instant cool relief.

She hated traffic; however, it was the summer holidays and so the roads were not chock-a-block. But the migraine wouldn't go away.

As she pulled up to her driveway, ready to click the security gates, she stopped for a second and felt overwhelmed by guilt. The sadness in Gemma's eyes haunted her. She was about to enter the driveway to her home, a house nearly as big as a mansion, her perfect life, leaving her sister abandoned in a stinking shithole. A rotting prison. She couldn't just walk away and do nothing: not now, not after seeing her in such a pitiful state. After taking a deep breath, Cassie clicked the automatic unlock and waited for the gates to open. She then drove up the tree-lined drive and stopped outside the pillared entrance.

Inside the house, a gentle humming sound was coming from the housekeeper; Maria always purred or sang when she worked. Cassie looked around the living room. Every day she admired the luxury of it all and was grateful that her life was so perfect – her handsome and loving husband, her designer clothes, and now their new baby on the way – but today she felt sickened. The huge cream sofas and marble fireplace, the enormous French windows dressed in all their finery, and the designer kitchen as big as a small pub, were so far removed from where she had come. How could she enjoy all of it when Gemma was sweating in prison? She sighed, wishing she had never gone to the nick. If only she had thrown the VO in the bin, she would have been none the wiser. She owed Gemma nothing, but it was too late now. The only way to live with it was to deal with the problem.

She pulled her iPhone from her new Chanel handbag and dialled a number; she was nervous because her husband had no idea she had gone on a prison visit. He would have dug into the whys and wherefores. Cassie had never gone into her past and that's how she liked it – no disturbing memories to come and bite her on the arse.

The international dialling tone continued for a few seconds and then a deep Italian voice answered. "Hello, who is calling?"

"Oh, hi, it's Cassie," she replied nervously.

Although Cassie had been a part of her husband's family for two years, she still felt awkward at times, as they were so tight-knit and powerful.

"Hello, Cassie, how are you?" Sergio's voice softened. He could be in the room next door, so clear was the connection.

"Yes, Sergio, I'm well, thank you. Is Francesca around?"

"She is. I will pass you over, and you have just saved the day. She is, as you say, picking on me for eating too many pancakes."

22

Cassie smiled. Her sister-in-law Francesca and her husband were the quintessence of a flawless marriage: they doted on each other.

"Hello, Cassie," said Francesca, her tone upbeat. "How are you feeling? Not long now, eh!"

"Four weeks to go and little bump will be here. I'm good, Fran, and yourself?"

"I'd be better if my husband stopped eating so much. He's becoming plump, shall we say," she said, giggling.

Cassie laughed with her, stalling for time. She was trying to work out how she could ask for Francesca's help, when really she didn't even know all the details herself. Luckily, her sister-in-law was so excited about the new baby, she rambled on about all the gifts she had purchased. The extravagant baby bits, which had been bought in the States, just kept increasing.

"So, I'll send over the photos of the cot and the mobile. Let me know what you think and I'll get them shipped over ..."

Cassie heard the voice falter and of course she knew why. She felt enormous sympathy for Francesca. She had watched over the years, before being part of the family, how Francesca spoilt her nieces and nephews because she couldn't have children of her own. The reason for it was so awful and disturbing that it would break anyone's heart.

"So, Fran, are you still up for helping out in the next few weeks? Dan's really excited, but he still has the clubs to run."

"I have my suitcases packed already and I can't wait!" replied Francesca.

Cassie didn't have a mother of her own. In fact, the only family she did have was Gemma, although it had been years since she'd last seen her before the prison visit. So her brothers-in-law all suggested that Fran should come to stay and help out. She knew, however, it was more for Francesca. That was how it was; the family made decisions together. She never minded because being part of the pack was what she had always wanted. Not having family herself, she longed to fit in. The Vincents were a no-nonsense family. It was her family versus the rest of the world, and now she was one of them. She enjoyed the same status, the respect, and of course the money. But that wasn't why she'd married Dan; she'd fallen in love with him long before he'd even noticed her. His brother had offered her a job in one of their clubs, and for years she'd watched and admired all four brothers, but Dan was the man of her dreams. When he'd asked her for a date, she'd grabbed it with both hands and prayed she wasn't going to be another one of his one-night stands. She suspected that Francesca had been instrumental in getting them together. As good-looking and charming as Dan was, and with girls falling at his feet, he eventually showed Cassie she was the one for him. Once that ring was on her finger, he treated her like a queen. Cassie worried that after his past history as a player, he would miss the excitement of dating a different girl each night, but he didn't. He was faithful and attentive. The family were kind, loving, and protective, and she fitted in. An easy transition because they had come to know her over the years, trusting her to manage the bars and the staff.

"Oh, listen to me rabbiting on. Sorry, Cass, did you call for any particular reason?"

There was silence for a second; how and what exactly was she going to ask?

"Fran, when you come over, could I ask some advice for a friend? Legal advice."

"Yes, of course. Are you okay?"

"Yeah, I'm fine. It's just a friend of mine is in some kind of trouble, but we can talk about it when you come over," replied Cassie.

"Okay. To be honest, I'm a little bored, so anything to keep my brain active."

Cassie sat back on the sofa. She was relieved that Francesca hadn't asked too many questions because she didn't have many answers. She wanted to talk privately with her and not have her husband worrying she was getting involved in something that really she should leave well alone. At least she could go back to the prison with some kind of assurance that Francesca would look into the matter.

An hour later, Dan strolled in to find Cassie dozing on the sofa. He stared for a while, admiring her soft skin and the silky auburn hair, which tumbled gently, framing her flawless features. A few years ago, he'd gone after brassy blondes with big tits, a ton of make-up, and half his age. Cassie was different: she was thirty-eight and not obviously pretty. She was more naturally attractive, with long legs and a sculptured face that was softened by her green eyes. The sun had tanned her cheeks, and she put him in mind of a rose bud. He loved her with all his heart; she was the only woman outside the family who truly meant anything to him. She never complained, was always there, and was full of beaming smiles. In fact, it was her coy smile that had melted his heart. With the punters from the club, she was brash and hard as nails, but when she looked at him, she blushed every time.

He slid next to her on the sofa and gently stroked her cheek. She slowly opened her eyes and smiled. Gently moving his hand over her swollen tummy, he felt his baby move.

"I think it's a boy, Dan," she whispered, cupping his hand with hers.

"I think it's a beautiful baby, just like its mum." She loved his raspy voice; it added to his sex appeal.

She leaned into him, resting her head on his chest, enjoying the tender moment. Her life was already more than perfect and soon when their new baby arrived it would be complete.

*

Alone in solitary confinement, lying on the hard bed, Gemma stared up at the ceiling. It was the only way to protect herself. Giving Sandra, the butch screw, a right hook in front of the number one governor, secured her the right to be put down the block. The strip search had been humiliating and aggressive. Sandra had taken great pleasure in manhandling her, and it had been far more coarse and invasive than was necessary. "You might think twice about sending out another visiting order," she had whispered, in a cold, intimidating tone. That was a warning, but Gemma would take what came just as long as she could eventually get out and finish what she'd started. Tears trickled down her face as she looked at the unsightly scars and the hundreds of slash marks – each one a product of innate depravity. How cruel could this man, who was supposed to love her, be? She had self-harmed when she was a kid in that ghastly home but only a few times. It was noted in her psychiatric records but that was over twenty-four years ago. If only the courts had believed her – but they hadn't. The cuts were from her husband; the evil bastard knew he could get away with it. Who would believe a woman with a history of drug abuse and a weekly prescription for antidepressants? The judge in the court case certainly hadn't but that had been no surprise. Perhaps it would have been better if her husband had killed her; after all, who would look at her now she was covered in scars? The only other man who had, had enough scars of his own, but where was he now? Anyway, that didn't matter; she never wanted another man again. She was sick of the sight of them, having been used and abused by every man she'd ever met. The Ruthers, every one of them, were the worst kind. Sick, vile bastards – even the mother, the controlling cunt, and the eldest sister was just as insane.

As she was falling asleep, the door swung open. Gemma didn't want to look, afraid of a scary apparition disguised as Sandra – or worse, the rapist.

"Here you are. I've brought your food," said Linda, another screw. Her tone was soft. She was firm but fair. She was so different from Sandra, the butch screw. Probably in her late thirties, she had startling blue eyes, a clear complexion, and an attractive face. She gave the impression of being trustworthy.

Gemma sat up and attempted to smile. "Thank you," she whispered.

Linda, a slight woman, sat next to Gemma, still carefully holding the tray of food. The bed was just a mattress on the floor. "So, how are you feeling?" she asked.

"Yeah, I'm okay, I suppose," she replied, surprised because no one had ever asked her that question before.

"She wasn't too rough, was she? I mean down below."

Gemma shook her head and stared at the blank blue brick wall.

"She is a bitch at times. I had to laugh when you clumped her one. She deserved it."

Curiously, Gemma turned her head to face Linda, finding it difficult to believe that another screw was on her side. At last, here was someone she could talk to. It was hard to find a friend in prison. Everyone was after something: fags, food, drugs, or just respect – none of which Gemma had to give. She was at the bottom of the pecking order and ergo an easy target.

"I only hit her to get put down here. I didn't want to hurt anyone really." She averted her gaze, hoping that the screw couldn't tell she was lying. She'd actually enjoyed punching Sandra in the face, but she wouldn't have done it without the number one governor being present. She was her guarantee that Sandra couldn't hit her back. The new number one was a no-nonsense woman and played strictly by the rules.

"Well, I reckon she needed a bashing. Too big for her boots. I can't stand her myself."

An unexpected giggle left Gemma's mouth. "Do you think she's got a black eye?"

"A right fucking shiner, and from you! Look at you, the size of a fag paper." She rubbed her arm. "Don't let that fat prat get you down. Anyway, enough about her. I heard you had a visit."

"Yeah, I haven't seen my sister since we were kids. It was really nice though," she said, matter-of-factly.

Linda raised her eyebrows. "So, is she all you have in the way of family? Only, that must be your first ever visit."

Gemma felt a little hot under the collar; had she said too much? Was Linda really on her side? She looked into her eyes and noticed the soft gentle smile radiate across her compassionate-looking face. Naïvely, she concluded Linda was a friend.

"Yeah. When I say sister, we grew up in care together, so I guess we refer to each other as that."

"It's a shame you didn't keep in touch. Still, I'm sure you'll rekindle your sisterly relationship and hopefully she'll come again, eh?" Linda smiled.

Gemma began to unwind from the stress of the visit and subsequent events. She felt more relaxed now and happy to talk. "Yeah, she said she would organise a lawyer for me. Gonna visit in a couple of weeks. She knows people in high places, see."

"Has a good job then, does she?"

"No, she's married to some big nightclub owner whose sister is a big shot lawyer. So Cassie will see to it that she gets me out of here."

"Well, let's hope she has good news for your next visit. Talking of good news, it's not long now until you get your A Level result. So what made you choose to study law?"

Gemma shrugged her shoulders. "I didn't get the chance to finish me school education, so I thought it a good idea to keep meself busy and me mind off being in here." The truth was Gemma had wanted to study law to use it on the outside. The more knowledge she had under her belt, then the more power she would have to run a business – her business.

Knowing that she couldn't squeeze any more information out of her, Linda got back on her feet. "You eat that and I best be off. I'm on lock-up tonight."

The child-like smile, Gemma gave the screw, had touched a nerve. Linda walked away, feeling guilty, but then she thought of the bung she was going to get, and her guilty feelings vanished as quickly as they had appeared. A few grand would sort her conservatory out and there would be enough left over for a week in Spain.

As she reached the end of the block, Sandra was there waiting. "Well?"

"She's expecting a visit from her sister, Cassie. She's married to a nightclub owner, but the sister-in-law's a lawyer, and apparently this Cassie is going to see to it that she gets Gemma out. So, when do I get my cash?"

Sandra, who was a hard-faced screw, in her mid-thirties, and who looked more like forty, frowned. "She has a sister? It doesn't say that on her records. The fucking bitch is lying."

"No, she's not a blood relative. She's a foster sister, but anyway, she's seeing to it that Gemma gets out. So when do I get my poke?"

Sandra glared through spiteful eyes. "Don't fucking sweat. You'll get yours, but next time, don't fuck up."

"I never fucked up!" spat Linda.

"When I tell you to keep the governor occupied and she strolls into the room where I'm conducting business, then you fucked up, lady."

When Sandra went to walk away, Linda, concerned she wouldn't get her money, called her back. "Look, San, I've got the info you wanted, and I tried my hardest to distract the governor, but I tell you, San, she smells a rat. So you'd better watch your back. They aint forgotten that you were brought in and questioned over that Gemma being poisoned. Ya know, I'd lay off her a bit, if I was you."

With a huff and a grunt, Sandra marched off up the corridor, mulling over the day's events. It wasn't normal for the boss to come into the search room. Maybe she had let a few things slip. She rubbed her bruised cheek; it was certainly reason enough to hate the girl and it eased her mind to continue with the plan. Plenty of money was heading her way. She consoled herself with the notion that the system wasn't paying her enough for all her hard work, so a little side-line was a perk of the job.

The harsh sounds of the banging and clinking doors were enough to have her biting her lip. If she got caught, she would also spend a hefty lump inside. It was a thought too disturbing to ponder over.

Scarlet, the so-called rapist, was leaning against the wall outside her cell. She whistled at Sandra to catch her attention. As Sandra looked over, her heart raced. She fancied Scarlet, or Scar for short. To keep up the professional pretence, she casually strolled over.

"So, San, when's the rat out? I want me puff."

"She ain't got any."

Scar stepped away from the wall and glared into the officer's eyes. "I told that cunt to organise a parcel for me and now you're telling me she ignored my request?"

Sandra nodded. "Yep, she must have bottled out, but watch yourself – the number one is acting strange. She came into the search room, she never does that ... lucky, really, because if she'd had your parcel stuffed up her crotch, the governor would have nicked her, and she'd have had her watched on future visits. Even if she'd had it, I couldn't have got it for you, not with her eyeballing."

"I'm still gonna bash the rat. I ain't letting my reputation go down the pan, or all the other gofers will think they can get one over on me," scowled Scarlet.

Sandra looked her up and down, admiring the gumption of the woman. The fire in her green eyes and the way her wild hair hung around her face was a real turn-on. "Wait till later, after lock-up, and I'll fetch some in. By all accounts, there's some in the amnesty bin. There's not a lot, but enough to see you over the weekend … but you'll owe me one." She winked.

Having the butch lesbian screw on her side was a bonus, but the sexual favours were sickening. So she just smiled, leading Sandra on. She had to keep up the pretence in order to feed her habit. Ten years for murdering her neighbour would have been a long old slog, but securing her reputation as someone you wouldn't want to fuck with eased the harshness and dispelled the fears. Far from being a lesbian, she had to swallow her pride and gulp back the revolting feeling to ensure her time behind bars was full of privileges, including the blind eye turned to her drugs and drink. A quick muff dive with Sandra was well worth the bottle of vodka for her troubles.

Once Scarlet stepped inside her cell, she looked over her shoulder and winked. Sandra almost blushed. Deep down, she knew Scarlet was only playing a game. She was prison-bent – doing what she had to, to get by. Wondering when this pretend love affair would be over, she smiled back. If it happened, she'd have to look out for another wannabe arse-licker. Maybe she should be more proactive? The predatory power over the new naïve inmates filled her with excitement.

CHAPTER TWO

The visiting order arrived a week later and much sooner than Cassie had expected. Luckily, Dan was still in bed and hadn't seen the post. After checking the date, she slid the envelope into her bag and headed for the kitchen to pour herself a cup of tea, as coffee now made her feel sick. Perched on the stool, sipping her new flavoured herbal concoction, she cradled her bump: *not long now, little one.*

Maria entered. "Good morning, Cassandra, how are you today?" Her Spanish accent was soothing.

"Yes, I'm good, thank you. Is the spare room ready for Francesca? She'll be here the day after tomorrow."

Maria laughed. "Yes, of course. You shouldn't worry so much. Francesca isn't fussy, she is a good person, and she will take you as she finds you."

"I know, she is lovely, but I want her to feel at home and happy to help out with the baby when it eventually arrives. I know she's my sister-in-law, but I still get nervous. It's not her fault, it's just me," replied Cassie.

"Perhaps you see Francesca and Dan as heads of your family? You worked for Dan for a long time, did you not? Maybe you find it difficult at times to see him as just your husband. Try not to think like this. After all, hasn't Francesca always been … easy-going with you? She loves you very much!"

Maria's occasional stilted English made Cassie smile inwardly and she loved her all the more for it.

"I know. Maybe this is the problem. She is this top lawyer and a multi-millionaire. Her brothers adore her and she's so kind. Perhaps I feel inferior. I guess I come from nothing. I'm not clever and certainly not clever like she is. In fact, I'm probably a bit boring." She looked out of the window and stared across the vast expanse of green landscaped garden.

Maria walked around the back of her, placing an arm around her shoulder. "Cassie, I have known the Vincents for many years. Francesca wants nothing more than for you to be close to her family, and you, you are part of them now. She loves you. And as for boring, you are not. So, I think, when she arrives, it will give you two time to become closer and maybe then you will see her as a sister, not a lawyer, or a rich woman. I am sure she would want that too."

Of course she was right; the time together would be a good thing.

Tomorrow was too soon to give Gemma any news. She knew this would not go down well and would fuel the despair that was there in Gemma's state of mind. She still couldn't get the image of that helpless expression out of her head. It wasn't even the way she appeared. It was that deathly look in her eyes – as if she was just surviving.

Maria returned to her cleaning and Dan joined Cassie in the kitchen. He looked as handsome as ever. His white shirt was loose and unbuttoned to the middle of his chest. Having just awoken, the waves of hair that were usually slicked back had fallen forward, lying

34

in a somewhat dishevelled state. Cassie smiled to herself. Even looking like this, she still got goose bumps. He was an extremely good-looking man and he was her husband. She couldn't have wished for anything more.

"So, my ray of sunshine, how are you and bump?" He cupped her face in his hands and cocked his head to the side. Cassie stared into his steely-blue eyes, absorbing the intensity of his doting look.

"I'm good and I think bump is contented," she said, as she blushed.

"Aw, Cassie, you're my angel, and I love you."

She felt her heart beat faster. He didn't say it every day out of habit. It was at those unexpected, precious moments, when he touched her face or held her tight, he whispered those words, and she knew he meant them.

"Are you still happy for my sister to come over and stay?"

"Of course I am. I'm really looking forward to it. I hope she offers to do the night shift." She giggled.

"If I know Francesca, she'll offer to do any shifts, just to have a few cuddles … Oh, by the way, did I mention that she's arriving tomorrow? The flights were changed."

"Oh, is she?" Cassie recalled the visiting order. "Only, I arranged to meet my friend tomorrow." She didn't say who but she wasn't exactly lying. Even so, she hated being economical with the truth with Dan.

"That's all right. She'll probably spend time with Mum and Dad and come over in the evening."

Although Cassie never wanted to keep secrets from her husband, in her heart she knew he wouldn't like the idea of her visiting someone in prison, especially in her condition. She thought it best to keep it to herself for now. The state of Gemma played on her mind and so she spent the afternoon shopping.

The next morning, Cassie got up, ready for the visit. She felt uneasy and unsure about the whole thing, but that vision of Gemma was nagging away at her. She had bought a few items of clothing to take in to her: a tracksuit, some jeans, and a variety of tops. From the previous visit, she assumed Gemma was a size 8 and that was on a fat day.

Cassie fanned herself as she sat in a traffic jam listening to Little Mix's 'Black Magic'. But she couldn't concentrate. The air conditioning was drying her throat, and try as she might, she couldn't get cool. The uncomfortable heat had caused her ankles to swell. Finally, she arrived and parked the car, which was five minutes away from the prison. The bag with the clothes was heavy but she was determined to carry them in. She knew the drill now and waited as the queue of visitors slowly trickled to just her and another visitor. Eventually, she was inside and went to the desk to hand over the clothes. Everything was checked and double checked and forms signed and signed again. Finally, the clothes were placed in an HM prison plastic bag and taken away.

"I'm sure Gemma will be pleased, designer labels no less," said the officer with a cheesy grin spread across her face. Cassie wasn't perturbed. She just wanted to get in the visiting room and make sure Gemma was all right.

She queued again, removing her shoes, watch, and bag, before going through the metal detector. At last, she sat waiting for the back door to slide open. The officer, a different one from the week before, called Gemma's name and the thin, pathetic sight of her sister appeared. Cassie shuddered as she watched Gemma's bony frame walk towards her. She smiled, a gesture of compassion. "Jesus, Gem, you need to eat!"

"I do, but the food is shit and it's hard to hold it down. Any news?" She was eager to hear something positive.

"Yes, well, I spoke to Francesca, my sister-in-law, and she said she'll talk to me when she arrives at mine. She lives in the States but is gonna stay with us for a while to help out with the baby."

Gemma was hoping for more, but at least Cassie hadn't let her down and was doing something to help.

"Do you think she can get me out of here?"

"I have no idea." Cassie chewed the inside of her mouth. "All I know is, she's a bloody good barrister. A clever woman. My Dan says she's the brains of the outfit, so if anyone can, she can, but to be honest, babe, I don't know how. I mean, you were caught bang to rights, by all accounts. Well, so the papers said."

Gemma looked over her shoulder and smiled. Cassie turned to see who was there and was surprised to see an officer smiling back. "That other bitch ain't here, then?"

"Nah," she replied, shaking her head. "She's kept away. After they marched me off to the strip search room, I punched her one, the horrible cow."

Looking at her frail sister, and recalling the size of the screw, she almost laughed. "What on earth did you do that for?"

Averting her gaze, Gemma whispered. "She's a nasty cunt, and I didn't want to go back on the wing and get beaten-up or worse by that nutter, the rapist. So I thought it best to get meself put down the block. I'll do it again. I like me own company."

The sick visions again shot through Cassie's mind and she swallowed hard. This was a nightmare. The sooner she could speak with Francesca and get her sister out of the nick, the easier she would sleep at night.

The stifling heat was taking its toll on Cassie. Her ankles were tight and she felt light-headed. She knew it wouldn't be long now before her baby arrived.

"Listen, babe, I'm gonna have to go. I'm really sorry. I feel a bit sick and the baby's due soon. You don't mind, do you?"

Gemma smiled and rubbed Cassie's hand. "Course not. I only wish I was the one helping you with the baby."

Cassie's heart sank; even though their bond was still there, she was relatively powerless at this stage to offer much more than moral support.

"I need time to talk to Francesca, so wait a few days, and then send a letter to Jamie Walker, our family's solicitor. Francesca works with him ... well, she set him up in business. He's a good guy and a close family friend. He'll probably take on the case. I'll tell her to expect the letter. I'm sure she won't mind. I don't know the address off the top of my head, but he's based in London."

Excited that someone was finally going to help, she nodded. "I'll find the address and phone number, don't worry." She had no intention of waiting, as she was so eager to move things along.

Linda, the officer who'd smiled at Gemma, sneaked out of the side door.

Getting up to leave, Cassie struggled with the chair as the baby was low down and heavy.

"Call me. I've sent you a letter with my phone number on. Hopefully, bump will be here soon, and I can update you on the legal stuff."

Gemma stood up to help her. "I really appreciate this. You have no idea how much this means to me, and I will find a way to pay you back."

"Remember, write to Jamie Walker. I can't promise anything just yet, but I'll do my best, babe," replied Cassie, meaning every word of it.

Linda was now face-to-face with Sandra. "You're fucking lucky I can lip-read," she said.

The bruise was still prominent under Sandra's eye. Her blood was boiling, having spent a week being humiliated by the shiner she'd got from a thin nobody – a wretched runt of a woman. She had to keep her cool and out of the way of the number one governor.

"Well, spit it out," she snapped.

"She's going to talk to a barrister, and she told Gemma to write to a law firm, Jamie something or other."

Daunted by unease, Sandra shuffled nervously. "So, what did the woman look like?"

Linda frowned. "Tall, auburn hair, and pregnant. Why?"

"What was she wearing?"

Linda's frown deepened. "A long white dress and sandals. For fuck's sake, San, you are a real perv, do you know that? Honestly, you make me wonder about you." She turned on her heels and left.

Sandra was in a rush; she needed to get to a phone and fast. Sasha, the number one governor's sidekick, was a nosy bitch and hanging around for some reason, so Sandra couldn't use the desk phone. Hers was in her locker. She marched down the corridor, being careful not to run and make a scene. Her locker was next to the staffroom. No one was around, so hastily she got her phone out and dialled the number.

"Tall, auburn hair, white dress, sandals, and a big bump in the front, so you can't miss her." She hung up the phone, placed it back in the locker, and leaned against the wall. Her heart beating like a jackhammer and her mouth dry, she knew the consequences of that call, but she consoled herself with the fact that what they did with that information was nothing to do with her. She was just the go-between and nothing more.

Outside, the air was still and Cassie looked forward to the cool breeze from the air conditioning inside the car. She had tried to park in the same spot as last time, in the visitors' car park. Today, however, there were no spaces, so she'd had to park a few streets away in a cul-de-sac with easy access to the prison entrance. It was just as well, for her ankles had now ballooned and she'd struggled with the walk. Sweat trickled down the back of her neck. She stopped to search her bag for a hairband to tie back her heavy locks – anything to keep cool. Unaware of the blacked-out BMW, idling at the kerb, she concentrated on the stroll ahead. The street was quiet; it was nearly three o'clock. The sun beat down and Cassie felt it burning her skin. Her mind drifted to Dan and the new baby and how wonderful it would be, sitting with their tiny bundle under a parasol in the garden by the pool.

Cassie heard a popping sound and an invisible hand punched her in the chest. She heard another pop and something hit her arm, and then, as her legs crumpled beneath her, she fell to the ground. In the hazy distance, the black car sped away.

As soon as Cassie put her hand to her chest, she looked in disbelief as it came away covered in blood. A sick realisation gripped her. She had been shot. Her white summer dress was turning a deep crimson, and she understood she had been hit badly. Breathing was almost impossible, and she felt her lungs closing up. Fear of death, and losing her baby, seized her. Her mobile had been flung from her bag and lay beside her on the pavement. *I have to get help*, she thought. *I have to save my baby*. With her last ounce of strength, she dialled 999 and managed to say where she was and she had been shot.

Moments later, a jogger spotted her, lying on the ground, with blood pooling beneath her and running into a nearby drain. As he knelt beside her, he could see she was alive, although her pained expression and the steady stream of blood told him everything he needed to know.

Her eyes were staring intently into his. "Please," she whispered, "call Dan."

The sounds of sirens were receding in the distance, along with the rest of the world, so Cassie knew medical help would be too late. She had to say goodbye.

The jogger prised her phone from her bloody fingers; he then scrolled down to 'Dan' and pressed 'dial'. He cradled the woman in his arms and held the phone to her ear. He felt numb, finding himself in a situation that was almost surreal. This jog had turned into a nightmare, as, horrified at the quantity of blood, all he could do for the poor dying woman was hold her and let her say goodbye to Dan.

What a tragic waste: before him lay a very pretty but damaged woman, and somewhere, probably not far away, a husband was about to lose both his wife and their baby.

The paramedics jumped from the ambulance and almost pushed the jogger aside. He held on tight to Cassie and kept the phone pressed to her ear. She was grateful to him; she knew it would be the last time she would hear her husband's voice.

Dan was with Sam, his younger brother, going over the accounts at *Dan's Palace* when his phone rang. "It's Cassie. Fuck me, she might have gone into labour," he said to Sam, with anticipation showing on his face.

"Hello, babe, is bump on its way?" he giggled.

There was an unearthly silence. Dan sensed something was gravely wrong, and then she spoke. "Dan, I love you. I've been shot, I may not—"

The blood drained from his face as he stared at the phone in disbelief.

A paramedic took the phone from the jogger as another strapped Cassie's unconscious form to a stretcher.

"Hello, this is Nicolas. I am a paramedic."

"What's happened to my wife?" His words were more of a whisper as his body shook all over.

"We're taking her to Saint Thomas' hospital, sir. Can you meet us there?"

"Yes." That one word was all he could say; the reality had just knocked him sideways.

The paramedics had just been informed that there was no way they would be able to drive to the local hospital in Ashford due to a major road accident. Nicolas prayed he would be able to get this woman to the London hospital alive.

Sam stopped what he was doing and stared at the deathly expression on his brother's face. Slowly, he got up from his chair and just managed to grab Dan before he wobbled.

"Cassie's been shot. They're taking her to Saint Thomas' hospital." He was white and ready to collapse.

Sam gasped, and then his mind kicked into action. He grabbed his car keys. "Come on, mate, I'll drive." He held his brother's arm and led him to the car, which was parked outside the club. So totally stunned by the news, Dan couldn't speak.

Ruby almost bumped into them on her way to the office. She could tell instantly something was critically wrong.

"Dad, what's going on?" she asked Sam.

"Cassie's been shot. Phone the others and tell them to get up to Saint Thomas'."

Wasting no time, he opened the front passenger door of his new white Jag and helped Dan inside; ignoring the speed limit, he tore away, heading for the hospital.

Dan was like a zombie, barely able to put two words together, but Sam was in the zone, with one objective in mind: to let his older brother comfort his wife.

"She's gonna be all right, mate, you'll see. She's a fighter, she'll be okay," urged Sam.

Dan could hear his brother's words, but all he could think of was the worst-case scenario. If Cassie died, his life would be over. She was everything to him. Dan heard a screaming sound, a deafening noise that seemed to come from nowhere, and then, as Sam grabbed his head and pulled him close, he realised the scream was coming from himself. Sam sped through the streets, swerving in and out of the cars, whilst holding onto his hysterical brother. "Come on, mate, it's gonna be all right," Sam repeated.

He had never heard his brother scream or seen him cry except when they'd been kids. It had been the time when their sister had to be sent away to live with their aunt. Dan stopped the screaming and sobbed uncontrollably.

"Please, God, don't let her die!" he shouted.

Sam pulled up outside the accident and emergency entrance. "You go in. I'll park," he said. Dan leapt from the car and ran into the hospital to find medical staff rushing around. Then, suddenly, a nurse grabbed him. "Sir, you cannot come in here. This is strictly off limits," she admonished.

Dan noticed the police buzzing around.

"My wife, she's here somewhere, she's been shot, and I need to see her."

The nurse nodded. She knew exactly who he was talking about. "Sir, can you wait over there, please? I'll get someone to see you right away." Her voice was calming, but Dan couldn't wait – he had to see Cassie. He shook off the woman's hand from his arm.

"Where is she? I have to see her." Dan was fraught with anxious fear and was pushing his way towards the double doors.

The petite Filipino nurse tried to hold him back. "She's in surgery. Please, sir, take a seat, and I'll get someone to talk to you."

However, Dan looked unstoppable; he pushed forward, focused on getting to his beloved Cassie. The tiny woman attempted to grab both his hands to restrain him but to no avail.

"Please, sir!" But he was away.

Dan scoured the room. All the cubicles were closed off and there was a sense of panic in the air. A police officer approached him and took over from the nurse.

"Are you Dan Vincent?" The officer was firm.

Dan anxiously nodded.

"Would you like to take a seat over here, sir." He pointed to the four plastic chairs bolted to the wall.

Sam raced into A&E, spotted Dan, and rushed over to him. "What's happened? Is she okay?" he asked, between gasps of breath. Yet he guessed his brother was none the wiser from the bewilderment showing over his face.

"I'm PC Markham," said the policeman. "May I ask a few questions?"

"Look, mate, is Cassie all right? We just got a call to say she's been shot. What's going on?" snapped Sam.

"She's in surgery," said Dan.

"Who are you, sir?" The officer was softly spoken.

"Sam Vincent, Dan's brother. So, can you tell me what the fuck is going on or not?"

"Mr Vincent, we got a call to attend an incident, and when we arrived at the scene, Cassandra was already in the ambulance, waiting to head here. All we knew then was that she had been shot twice, and a jogger had found her in the street. We still have no witnesses coming forward to inform us of what happened ... I am so sorry, sir. I need to inform you ..."

But Dan wasn't listening to the officer as he ran his hands through his hair. He looked at his brother with so much despair on his face. It was at this point that Sam knew he had to take charge. He grabbed the officer's arm and pulled him away, so he couldn't be overheard by Dan.

"Is she going to be all right?" he whispered.

The officer looked back at Dan and then he slowly turned to face Sam.

"I'm sorry, sir, she died in the ambulance on the way here. That's what I was about to tell you."

Sam gasped; his hands flew to his mouth, and he glared in horror. "But they said she was in surgery," he spluttered, in disbelief. The officer's rather clumsy way of informing Dan and him about Cassie's fatal injuries hadn't registered at all, as his brain couldn't seem to process information at present.

Markham bit his lip. "They're trying to save the baby. I'm so sorry ... I know this isn't the right time for any of you, but we need to find out who did this. Can I ask a few questions?" He stepped back, anticipating a backlash, and he was surprised to see Sam nod.

Sam was in total shock. This shouldn't have happened. Why? Someone had killed Dan's wife; how the hell was he going to break the news?

46

"Do you know if either Cassandra or your brother has any enemies or perhaps anyone who would want to harm either of them?"

Sam's eyes widened. "No. Look, do we have to do this now?" He barged past the officer and sat next to Dan and put his arm around his shoulder.

Markham let him go; there'd be time for questions later. With eighteen years in the force, he knew from experience that this was not the right time to intrude on the Vincent family's grief.

Sam tried to think how he was going to break the news. Suddenly, there was a commotion, and the pair looked up to see Francesca and Fred, their sister and brother, followed by their mum and dad, rushing towards them.

With tears tumbling down her face, Francesca was the first to reach Dan. "Jesus, Dan, what's happened?" He stood up and put his arms around her and sobbed into her shoulder. She looked over at Sam, who shook his head.

Unlike Fred, he stood silently, waiting for someone to speak. Bill, their father, was holding Mary, their mother.

"What's happened, son?" he said.

Before Sam had a chance to answer, a doctor appeared. "Mr Vincent?" He looked at the three brothers, waiting for one to answer.

Dan stepped forward; he knew already, but he had to ask. "Is she—"

The doctor's expression said it all. "I'm so sorry. We did everything we could, but the wounds were too severe. Blood loss ..."

Dan heard no more. With an anguished cry, his tall frame started to fall just like a collapsed tower block in free fall. Sam and Francesca managed to grab him before he fell onto the floor and they got him back to the seat. Just as she did when he was a child, Mary held him in her arms and rocked him.

The doctor waved his hand in Francesca's direction. With Dan safely in the arms of his mother, Francesca followed the surgeon to a side room. Dan assumed she had gone to identify the body.

"Why? Why?" cried Dan, as the tears poured from his red, swollen eyes.

"Come on, son, let's take you home," said Mary. She knew there were no words that could ever comfort him. Cassie had become his life; he doted on her and relished the idea of being a father. Now it was all gone, in a heartbeat.

"Who could have done this?" asked Fred. He was calm, which was completely out of character; normally an incident like this would have sent him over the edge – he'd be hopping mad and threatening to kill whoever had done it. This was different though; this had plunged them all to the depths of sadness. It was something none of them could get their heads around. Everyone's main concern now was for Dan and his overwhelming grief.

"Come on, Dan, let's get you out of here. There's nothing you can do now, son." Bill rubbed his shoulder.

"I can't just leave her here. I have to say goodbye."

Mary felt a huge lump in her throat and could feel his pain. "You do what's best, babe. If you want to say goodbye, then you do that, but if you want to get your thoughts together, then we can all come back tomorrow."

Still dazed, Dan looked at each member of his family in turn, searching for answers. But this was his call.

"Let's wait for Fran to come back. She'll know what's best," suggested Fred.

Dan nodded and sat back on the hard plastic chair. A nurse arrived and suggested they should wait in the family room away from the public in their moment of grief. They agreed and trooped after her into the side room; it was full of old people's comfy chairs.

"I'll bring some tea. Please, take a seat. The doctor will be back soon."

Still numb with shock, Dan almost fell onto the seat. Twenty minutes went by as they sat sipping tea in silence. Then the door opened and the nurse returned, holding the door open for someone else to step inside. They all assumed it was the doctor and gasped when they saw Francesca carefully holding a baby wrapped in a blue blanket.

Her face was full of compassion and sorrow but with a gentle smile. Mary jumped to her feet and helped Francesca inside.

"Dan, they saved your son!" she cried, as huge tears fell and tumbled down her face.

"Oh my God!" Dan gasped, as he leapt from his seat and took the baby from his sister. Then there was silence as he stared down at his precious bundle.

Mary gripped her son's arm. "There, my boy, you have something to go on for. You might not have Cassie, but she gave you a son, and it's my guess that she would want you to be strong for him."

The words merged into one as he gazed at the tiny pink-faced bundle with his mop of black hair.

"Is he all right?"

The nurse smiled. "Yes, Mr Vincent, your son is perfect and healthy. We want to keep him in overnight, just to make sure, but so far he seems fine."

Before the nurse could prise him away, they all took it in turns to hold and kiss the new family member.

"Ahh, bless him, dear little thing. He looks your double, Dan," swooned his mother, overcome with emotion.

Dan was staring out of the window to the next block, wondering what life had in store. How would he ever get over losing his wife? And how could he feel love for anyone when he felt so much grief?

As if Francesca had read his mind, she placed an arm around his shoulder. "You won't be alone. You have all of us," she said, quietly. "We'll help you get through this. It's gonna take time, but we'll be by your side, every step of the way. Now, let's go home and we can come back tomorrow."

The officer was outside the room, waiting; he didn't want to intrude. He had been told exactly who the Vincents were and had decided he needed to take a sensitive approach.

"Dan … may I call you Dan?" he asked, as they filed out of the room.

Still oblivious, Dan nodded.

"Do you think you're up to answering a few questions? You know how it works. The sooner we have a lead, the quicker we can nab the person who did this."

It was odd because it was the first time Dan had actually realised that someone had shot his wife. She hadn't just died; some bastard had killed her. His eyes widened and it was then the officer noticed that all the Vincents had the same cold expression behind those steel blue pools.

"Yes, of course. What do you want to know?"

"Well, actually, can we take this down the station?"

Fred was the first to jump in. "Nah, you fucking can't take him down the station. He's fucking traumatised."

Mary wanted to calm her son – he sounded so aggressive – but she knew he was right so remained quiet. No one was surprised by his outburst; as the youngest brother, and Francesca's twin, he was the most volatile and reckless Vincent.

Francesca spoke up. "I'll take my brother home and you can meet us there. I'd rather he be at home. As you can see, he's very upset and needs his family around him." She stared with eyes of steel and the officer realised there was no point in pushing the matter.

"All right, we'll call round later," confirmed PC Markham and with that he left.

Sam drove Dan home, followed by the others. Ruby, Sam's daughter, had contacted everyone, and by early evening they had all gathered at Dan's house. Maria poured brandies for everyone and left the family together whilst she made the baby's room ready for tomorrow. With a heavy heart, she tried not to cry in front of Dan.

It wasn't long before the police arrived. Markham had his sergeant with him and as they entered the house they wiped their feet on the mat. Markham gazed at the huge entrance hall, and then Maria led them into the lounge, where they were faced with the gawping eyes of the Vincent pack. Instantly, he noticed the close bond; it was so obvious he could almost taste it. He looked from one to the other and felt a tingle in the back of his neck. He sensed the rumours about this family were true.

"Mr Vincent, I'm Sergeant Sampson. I'm very sorry for your loss. May we ask a few questions? We'll then leave you in peace."

Francesca stood up. "Of course, please, take a seat. Would you like tea, coffee, or something stronger?"

The older policeman, Sampson, waved his hand. "No, we're fine, thank you."

"Do you have any idea who could have done this?" Dan asked, visibly shaken.

Sampson shook his head. "The only thing we have is CCTV footage of a few cars in that general area at roughly the right time, but that's no guarantee of anything. Unfortunately, the road your wife was found on doesn't have cameras, so we really don't have any clues. Do you know of anyone who would want to harm your wife, or—"

Dan's voice cracked as he went on. "No, no one would, she was a lovely ..." He bowed his head as the words stuck in his throat.

"This may sound harsh, but we have to ask these questions. Do you have any enemies yourself?"

Francesca took charge. "We own the *Vincents' Palaces*, but I assume you already know that. So, whilst we have no known enemies, we do get the odd customer escorted off the premises who makes ridiculous threats."

Sampson nodded; he was drawn in by Francesca's cool tone and the refined way she moved. Both he and Markham had been informed of the Vincents and were well aware of their reputation. However, he was almost intimidated by the sister. She seemed to take control so effortlessly, commanding attention, and the others listened intently; if there were such a thing as a pack leader, it would definitely be her. From the descriptions given to him back at the station, he was able to identify each person very easily. Fred stood leaning against the fireplace, tapping his foot like a coiled spring. Sam, the taller brother, was next to Dan with his arm around his shoulder. He had pure hate in his eyes; it was an anger that was deep-rooted. Joe was the muscle, a giant of a man, but his eyes were softer. The small blonde woman was obviously Belinda, Joe's wife, because she was clenching his arm as if she were on a white-knuckle ride. Sampson knew that this family was tight-knit; they ran a clean nightclub business called the *Palaces*, each one named after one of the Vincents. Then there were the nieces and nephews. Jack, the eldest, was a strapping lad, by all accounts a boxing champion, and he was a handsome young man without the boxer's flat nose. He sat next to their grandparents, teary-eyed. Standing by the window was Ruby, his younger sister, the image of Francesca. The tall tanned woman with long wavy black hair and a face fit for *Vogue* magazine was obviously Kizzy, Jack's girlfriend, because she was perched on the arm of the sofa with her hand rubbing the back of his neck.

"Where did you find Cassandra?" Francesca asked.

Her reputation as a successful barrister was not to be sniffed at. Sampson watched his words.

53

"In Ruggles-Brise Road, a short walk from HMP Bronzefield, the women's prison. Do you know it?"

Francesca shook her head.

"What the fuck was she doing there?" asked Fred, his tone aggressive.

"Well, we were hoping you could tell us that."

Maria, who had so far kept quiet, suddenly spoke up. "She was going to visit a friend this afternoon," she recalled.

"Did you know this?" He looked at Dan for answers.

Dan remembered the morning's conversation. "Yes, she mentioned it, but I didn't ask who."

"Was her friend in prison? Could she have gone there?"

"No, I shouldn't think so. She doesn't have friends in prison, and even if she did, I wouldn't imagine she would go there in her condition."

"It's possible, I suppose, that she visited someone in the street. She was found shortly before three pm and prison visits finish at around five fifteen pm," said Markham.

Francesca felt her chest tighten as she remembered the phone conversation she'd had with Cassie. She had asked Francesca if she could help with a legal matter for her friend. Francesca decided to keep this quiet and get to the bottom of it herself.

"Right, we're really sorry to have had to ask so many questions," said Sampson. "We'll leave you in peace and follow up what we have so far." With that they left.

The doctor had given Cassie's bag to Francesca at the hospital, but with everything else going on she'd forgotten about it. She retrieved it, snuck into the hallway, and looked inside for any clues. Her heart sank as she pulled out Cassie's purse and saw a wedding photo of her and Dan looking so happy. She searched around again and found a piece of paper; a quick look showed her it was the stub of a visiting order, for two fifteen this afternoon, and she saw the name 'Gemma Ruthers'. She popped it into her pocket, deciding to keep it to herself for now and allow Dan to get over the shock of Cassie's death before she told him.

The conversation turned to the baby; Dan had not mentioned him at all.

"Listen, son, bless your heart, I know you're grieving, but we'll have to organise our new baby coming home," said Mary, in her sweetest voice.

Dan looked up and nodded, his face red and swollen, knowing that he had to focus on immediate practicalities. His brothers were teary-eyed but less from the loss of their sister-in-law than the pain and anguish on Dan's face. None of them would be able to take that pain away from him.

"What are you going to call him?" asked Ruby.

There was silence as they all waited. Mary was concerned that he would reject the baby.

"Cass wanted to call him Billy, after you, Dad."

Bill's eyes widened and he felt a lump in his throat. "Aw, bless her, she was such a good girl ... who the fuck would do that to her? I mean, a pregnant woman an' all." A tear fell down his cheek and he couldn't speak anymore.

55

"I bet you she held on to life long enough to give me my son. She loved me so much, and I know that. She was every man's dream, never moaned or nagged, she was so—" Dan buried his head in his hands and sobbed. Instantly, Sam held him tight, rubbing his back.

"Come on, son, Cassie would want you to be strong. You're a dad now. She'd want you to be there for the baby," urged Mary, in her most compassionate tone.

Francesca darted a look at Fred and discreetly flicked her eyes for him to join her. Fred gazed around at the others; no one would notice him slip away. He met her in the entrance hall, and then he followed her up the stairs and into one of the guest rooms, out of earshot.

"What's up, sis?"

Francesca looked at her brother with compassion. He was still as handsome as ever, with a few grey wisps among the black waves, but he was also just as fit-looking now at forty-six as he'd been in his twenties. Fred hadn't settled down with a good woman, like Dan or Joe had; instead, he'd chosen to live the high life.

"Here, look at this." She handed over the torn part of the visiting order.

Fred's eyes widened. "Fuck me, sis, she did go to the prison! Who the fuck is Gemma Ruthers?"

"I have no idea, but I bet this Gemma has something to do with what happened."

"Are you gonna tell Dan?"

Francesca bit the inside of her lip. "Not sure what to do yet. The police have no clues, useless bunch of pricks, and I think it's best that no one says a word about poor Cassie. I don't want any rumours and our Dan hunting down the wrong person. Do you know anyone called Ruthers?"

Contemplating the name, he eventually nodded. "I do know a family called Ruthers, but they have no connection with us. They're from South West London, a big family, and nasty bastards by reputation. I don't know them personally … but Ruthers is a common name. This Gemma may not be linked to them at all."

"Well, Fred, I can soon find out. I'll run a check tomorrow and our Jamie can sort out a legal visit with this Gemma Ruthers."

In full agreement with his sister, he nodded. "Don't say anything to Dan just yet, then. Let's keep this to ourselves because I, for one, want whoever killed our Cassie dead and buried. That was a proper cunt stunt, killing a pregnant woman. I mean, who would stoop that low?"

"Would that Ruthers family be capable of such a thing?" asked Francesca fearfully.

"From what I've heard, yeah, they would."

"Right, tomorrow I'll make some inquiries," replied Francesca, in her business voice.

"What shall I do, sis?"

Francesca smiled. "Just be there for our Dan." She kissed him on the cheek and they headed back to the living room.

CHAPTER THREE

Violet Ruthers sat in her chair next to the fireplace. Her name was something of a misnomer, as it did not suit her personality; she was certainly no shrinking violet – the complete opposite. In fact, she was a big woman with a foul mouth. Violet didn't care what people thought as long as she ran the racket. She had five sons and two daughters, and when she would say 'Jump' her boys would ask, 'How high?'

She still lived in the same street in Streatham that she had when her eldest was born. Even when they had all left home and offered to buy her a large house, somewhere by the sea, she shook her head. She could have been living in luxury, but then she wouldn't have been the woman she was now. Running the estate was her forte, and she was extremely good at what she did. The neighbours, the local scallywags, all ran to her; she had her own business going and enjoyed the fear in people's eyes, if they dared to cross her. She lived on the excitement of being the queen bee in Streatham. No one messed with Violet Ruthers. The locals knew that if her boys didn't fuck you over, then she had enough men around her to do the job instead.

Even at seventy-two years of age, she ruled her kids with an iron rod. In addition, she thought nothing of jumping to her feet and giving any one of them a backhanded slap, if they so much as looked at her the wrong way. George, her eldest son, at fifty-two, the biggest one, was smart and always well dressed. He had to get his suits tailor-made as nothing off the peg would fit his chunky frame. She adored George; he was the apple of her eye and the image of her own brother. He called the shots and yet always listened to his mother's advice.

Violet was waiting until all her sons had arrived before she spoke of the incident. George, whose head was completely shaven, ran a handkerchief over his face; the beads of sweat kept accumulating and running down his nose. The fire was on low to take the chill off the summer evening; it was far hotter than he could handle, and yet he wouldn't complain to his mother. If she wanted it on, then so be it.

The cool expression on his mother's face caught his attention; he had never noticed before now how dark and beady her eyes actually were. Perhaps her age and lifestyle had cursed that spiteful look. Her hair, dyed jet black, didn't help to soften her features, but no one had the gumption or the nerve to tell her so.

Another annoying trickle of sweat was quickly mopped away. He'd had enough. He stood up to remove his dark grey suit jacket before rolling up his shirtsleeves.

Violet watched his moves with interest and smirked. "Don't let the others see you in that state. They'll think you've gone soft, boy!"

"Why should I be fucking worried? It ain't my mess. Bobby-silly-bollocks called this one in. He never even spoke to me first!"

Sharply pursing her lips, she shuffled her bulk forward in the chair. "Now, you listen to me. You are all in the shit!" she snapped, her voice harsh.

Riled up, George sat back down and breathed heavily. He was fuming that his youngest brother was getting too big for his boots. Bobby was riding on the back of his older brothers' reputation and had done for years. It was fine – and even encouraged – years ago, but now Bobby, at forty-five, was in shit up to his neck and behaving recklessly. Tired of cleaning up his fuck-ups, George wanted nothing more than to give Bobby a bashing to knock some sense into him.

"Tressa, you made that fucking tea yet? I'm gasping in here!" Violet called to her daughter and then mumbled under her breath, "Lazy cunt."

"I had to go next door for sugar!" Tressa shouted back breathlessly.

George heard a car pull up outside and stood to look out the window. He was nervous but had to pretend otherwise. The flash blue Jag had his brother Charlie's name written all over it, figuratively speaking that is. He rolled his eyes. "It's Chaz," he said, relieved it wasn't the police.

"Has he got Bobby and Lenny with him?" asked Violet.

"Nah, only Jim."

Violet tucked her large saggy arms under her breasts and tapped her foot. George knew his mother was annoyed. *Watch out for fireworks*, he thought. As he watched his brothers walk up the path, another car pulled up across the road. This one held his two younger brothers, Bobby and Lenny. The hairs on the back of his neck stood on end; he was wound up as he watched Bobby jump out of the car and walk with a cocky stride across the road.

"They're all here, Muvver."

"About fucking time," she growled.

Charlie walked up to his mother and kissed her on the cheek, followed by Jim. Her sour face softened as the corners of her mouth turned to form a half-smile. They both sat heavily on the other sofa, opposite George, and waited for Bobby and Lenny. Charlie could easily be mistaken for George, they were so alike – big men with deep folds and hands the size of shovels. They were only ten months apart in age. Jim, on the other hand, was smaller – still a big man, but shorter than his older brothers. He had been plagued with teenage acne, and now, at fifty, he had potholes all over his face. There was nothing appealing about him; he was the ugliest of the bunch and had a nasty sneer when he smiled. All three of the eldest boys had their mother's stern look and thick build. So, based on looks alone, it was something of a surprise to see that they were not short of girlfriends. However, they didn't trade in just looks but in reputation; they were hard men, successful at what they did, and money gave them status. Jimmy was too ugly to have a girlfriend; no amount of money could tempt a woman to kiss that face. He had a face that only his mother could love, and she did.

Bobby gingerly entered the room; he knew he was going to get both barrels from George. He walked over to Violet and kissed her on the cheek, and he was followed by Lenny, who was his younger brother and sidekick. He took a seat opposite his mother on the settee pressed against the wall. Violet glared at her two youngest boys. Bobby may have been seven years younger than George, but he was treated as though the gap was twenty years. Lenny, however, had no standing in the family; he was just an irritant, which was a view shared by all except Bobby.

"For fuck's sake, Tressa, where's the tea?" shouted Violet again. She was now beginning to get seriously angry with the useless slut.

62

Violet had no time for her youngest daughter. She had liked her once, but when Tressa had accused Jim of an unforgivable act, she'd turned on her. Her boys could do no wrong in her eyes, so she was treated like shit from then on.

Tressa came wobbling in, shaking, whilst trying to balance the tray with the large royal Worcester teapot and matching cups. Easing herself between the sofas and careful not to drop the heavy tray, she placed it on the coffee table and looked around at her brothers. As her gaze landed on Jim, she quickly looked up at her mother, who was glaring with contempt.

"Go and make us some ham rolls and don't take all fucking night. Me boys are starving."

Glad to leave the room, Tressa couldn't bear to be ogled by Jim, the creepy bastard. Still fuming, George wanted to leap from the seat and smash Lenny's and Bobby's heads together, but his mother was there and she would never let her boys fight each other.

"So, Bobby, wanna tell us what the fuck you were thinking?" George's tone was low and menacing.

"Look, bruv, it's all taken care of. No one saw us, as there are no cameras down that road. The car ain't even in our name and it's been burned out now, so no one can link us," smirked Bobby.

George was shaking his head. "You think that just because you have no links to the car the Ol' Bill won't be sniffing around? You stupid little shit, it's the motive they'll be looking for." His anger was rising and the redness in his eyes made him appear demonic.

Bobby bit his lip and sank deeper into the sofa. He didn't want a beating from George, but more importantly, he didn't want to look an idiot.

"You cranky cunt!" bellowed Charlie. "Who fucking shoots a pregnant woman in cold blood in the middle of the day without a damn good fucking reason? And to top it all, right by the prison! If you think that the Ol' Bill won't put two and two together, you are very much mistaken. Another thing ... who gave you the go-ahead? Because it sure weren't from us."

As Bobby looked from George to Charlie, he knew he was in serious trouble, and so he darted his eyes towards his mother for support. He was scared of his brothers; they were hard men and he had seen them in action at first-hand. He'd watched George get hit over the head with a hammer and he hadn't flinched, so he had every reason to fear him.

Violet remained silent; she needed to hear the facts before she could make any decisions.

"Oh, for fuck's sake, I had no choice. That Cassie was going to help Gemma get out. By all accounts, she was leaving the visiting room to see a hotshot lawyer."

Bobby ran his hands through his curly hair. "I can't have her singing like a fucking canary, or she'll drop us all in it. We may have got away with it before, but trust me, a good lawyer will have her out of there and ... who knows what."

George got to his feet and stepped towards Bobby. Towering over him, he rudely stabbed a finger into his chest. "You are nothing but a little shit of a man. If it weren't for your cock-up in the first place, we wouldn't be watching our backs now ... I mean, all you had to do was silence your missus for good. It weren't that hard, but, no, you couldn't even get that right! It was all planned. We fucking knew she was up to no good with that Russian cunt Alex and all you had to do was let her know she had left her phone behind in the

64

cottage, and then, when she turned up to collect it, to make it look like a suicide. Oh, but not you, ya cunt, you just had to go one step further and help yaself to a piece of her fanny that weren't part of the plan, ya numb nuts."

He poked at Bobby's chest again and said, "Jesus, you fucking knew she was shagging Alex and don't pretend you had no idea, 'cos ya did know, and what the fuck did you care? Your pathetic marriage was over years ago." He threw his hands in the air in pure frustration.

"George, you can't blame all this on me. It was your idea to let her get involved in the mansion in the first place, and you even had her working after she fucked-up with one of the punters. It ain't my fucking fault she was getting cosy-cosy with Alex. I tried to hang her when she turned up at the cottage, but then the bitch fucking stabbed me. She near-on killed me, remember!" spat Bobby, hoping to get the sympathy vote.

Violet jumped in. "What I wanna know is what you mean by 'accounts'? By whose accounts are you referring to?"

With wide eyes, he looked at his mother and realised he was in even more shit than he'd envisaged. So, nervously, he replied, "I have a couple of screws on the inside, making sure Gemma stays there, or worse, hangs herself. Honestly, it's all under control."

George spun around and grabbed Bobby by the throat. "You what?"

Like a wild cat, Lenny jumped up to try and prise away his eldest lump of a brother, but George slapped him, sending him sprawling to the floor. Bobby was choking and gripping George's hand with all his might to pull his fingers apart.

"Enough, George, let him go!" ordered Violet.

Instantly, George dropped Bobby like a hot brick. "You're lucky I don't fucking rip your throat out. I spent years building up the mansion business but not for you to go and fuck it up! Give you a piece of string, and you'll go and hang yourself, taking all of us with you. Well, boy, this is one fucked-up mess you can sort out. I ain't part of it. You are lucky that Alex thinks we have the situation under control 'cos otherwise we would all be fucking dead. By Christ, if he had any idea that Gemma was gonna squeal to the filth, to save her own arse, it would be us in the firing line. He is one dangerous bastard. He may have had a thing with your missus, but he tossed her away as soon as she was nicked. So bear that in mind. He sees everyone as disposable." He looked at Charlie and Jim. But they just sat there like two stone statues.

"Boys, boys, calm down!" shouted Violet. "We stick together in this family. Now, then, what I want to know is how much do these screws know?"

In frustration, George shook his head and plonked himself back on the sofa.

"They know nuffin'. I tell them to make sure they make her life hell, so that hopefully she'll slit her wrists, and to let me know if she has any visitors. Ya know, just generally keep their ear to the ground."

Next to have his say was Charlie. "I swear you was swapped at birth, 'cos by Christ, you are one thick muppet. Do you not realise that when those screws hear you've shot a pregnant woman they'll run straight to the Ol' Bill and tell them everything? Are you some kind of cunt?"

Hoping that his mother would defend him, Bobby gave her his little boy look, but she wasn't buying it. Instead, she was glaring like a volcano ready to erupt.

"Nah, they won't. Trust me, I bung them enough money to keep schtum, and they know there's plenty more where that came from. I ain't stupid."

Jim, a man of few words, who had been sitting quietly up until then, suddenly laughed out loud. "Fuck me, boy," he said, "you really are stupid if you think that little set-up is a smart move. You don't even have a decent hold over them. Some things just ain't worth the money and shooting a pregnant woman is too below the belt for most people to handle!"

Bobby glared at his brother, outraged that Jim was talking about morals, when, out of all the brothers, he had the least. Nothing was too below the belt for him.

Charlie stood up. "Well, Bobby big bollocks, you better be cocksure they won't grass, else you'll be serving a very long bird for that cunt stunt." He bent over the coffee table and poured the tea.

With a deep breath, Bobby bravely stated, "I got an alibi, anyway."

"Yeah, see, George? Bobby ain't stupid," taunted Lenny brazenly.

Lenny looked up to Bobby. They were always together, being just a year apart in age. Like him, Lenny lived off his older brothers' reputation, although he hated it when they had a go at Bobby. So he would defend him to the hilt when necessary. He and Bobby might be a good few years younger, but they could rule the manor now; they were old enough and had a reputation of their own, which Lenny was proud of.

"Shut it, Lenny, you're just as divvy as him," spat George.

"Go on, son, tell us what crackpot alibi you have now." Jim laughed.

Charlie handed out the tea; the cups were so dainty that they couldn't put their fat sausage fingers through the handles. Bobby looked at each one and wanted to laugh. It was like the mad hatter's tea party.

"Tommy and Jack were down in Margate doing a few break-ins, so I told them to drop my driving licence in one of the robberies. Nuffin' too major. It was only some old girl's house. They nicked an antique clock and a few bits of jewellery, turned a few cupboards over, but that's it. I have the antique clock in me bedroom with me prints all over it, so when I get nicked, I can't be in two places at once. Plus the old girl called the police straight away, and that was at three o'clock." A smug grin spread across his face. He was up there again, so George would be impressed.

Before anyone had a chance to speak, the front door flew open and in walked Rita, as bold as brass, and heavily built like the older brothers. She was forty-nine and looked so much like Jimmy they could have been twins. At the same time, Tressa appeared with a tray piled high with overloaded ham rolls. Rita almost knocked her out of the way, trying to grab one. Tressa tutted and went to leave. "Oi, skinny arse, what's your fucking problem?" hollered Rita.

"You! Keep calling me skinny arse. You wanna look at your own size before you comment on mine!" spat Tressa.

Rita put her roll down and spun around. "You little mouthy prat. I'll put you on your skinny arse if you talk to me like that. Fucking state of ya. You look like a cunting scaghead!" Rita was coming up to her fiftieth birthday; she was two years older than Tressa and twice

68

the size. She was used to putting Tressa in her place with the odd slap and vile words.

The boys were grinning at this diversion to the current argument; their sisters could not have been more different. Rita was a big woman with a fat belly and porky legs, narrowing down to her ankles. She was *a hard-faced bitch*, as George would say. However, Rita was right about Tressa, though – she'd let herself go and did resemble a junky.

As Rita flicked her dyed black hair over her shoulder and went back to the bread rolls, the men watched her grab another roll in her other hand as she plonked down next to George.

"All in order, girl?" asked Charlie.

"Yep, the girls are all fed, watered, and locked down. Igor's watching them tonight." She smiled.

"Oh, yeah, I bet he's taking his turn for a bit of free fanny." Jim laughed.

Rita stopped munching and glared at Jim. "You're a prick, Jim. My Igor don't touch the filthy whores. They're all too skinny and they're proper ugly an' all. It's a wonder anyone wants to pay for a piece of their arse."

"Lucky he likes fat birds then, sis, or he wouldn't be giving you one," replied Jim, with a creepy snarl.

"Fuck off, ugly. You're just jealous 'cos you don't get any unless you help yaself," she snapped back.

"All right, enough banter. We need to get down to business," protested Violet.

69

"I say we knock the next shipment on the head — at least for now, anyway," suggested Charlie.

Violet leaned forward and cleared her throat. "You two," she pointed to Bobby and Lenny. "Get your arses down the coast. Jaffa has a place down there. Stay away for a while, and take the antique clock with ya, before you get into any more shit … and speak to no one. Do nothing unless I fucking say so. Got it?" she snapped.

Both boys nodded.

There was silence as she stared at her two youngest who shuffled uncomfortably on their seats.

"Well, go on then, fuck off!" she yelled.

Bobby looked at the others who all glared back in silence. He couldn't believe he wasn't going to be present for the rest of the plan. Feeling unnerved and very insignificant, he grabbed Lenny's arm and they marched out of the house.

The others stared at Rita shoving the food in her mouth, as if she hadn't eaten for a month. George grunted, "Slow down, girl, you're gonna chew your fingers off."

Away from the madness, Tressa sat in the kitchen at the long table, sipping a coffee laced with brandy, which had now become her secret escape. She kept the bottle hidden behind the healthy food options in the far left cabinet. It was the one place her mother never went to. In the background, she could hear the planning and scheming, and once upon a time she would have been in there with them, giving her two penn'orth, but not now. She had learned to despise them although leaving was not an option. She was a psychological prisoner. Fleeing the nest would put her life in danger. She thought about Gemma and her stomach turned over; her own life was following the same path as Gemma's, and if she turned against them, her fate would be the same or perhaps worse. She had thought about it enough times but didn't have the bottle.

It was 1992 when Bobby met Gemma, a mere kid back then, but no sooner had she entered the family, and she was one of them. Her mother had initially got Gemma working the debt collecting business whilst Tressa was running the prostitution flats, which was an easy little earner. That all changed though when her brothers got involved in more sophisticated rackets, of which the sex trafficking game proved to be the most lucrative. They gave the flats to Gemma to run, which she did for a year, whilst she helped her older brothers with their new venture in London, running the serious business of the lock-up, or villa, as it was initially referred to. That had started in 1996, but by 1998 they had closed the villa and ploughed everything into a huge lock-up known as the mansion.

Her job in the villa, and subsequently the mansion, had been to make sure the girls were clean, fed, and looked their best for the punters. It had never bothered her then just how awful it really was because she'd been brainwashed, since she'd been very young, by her mother. "*They're nothing but whores over in the Eastern Bloc; at least you're giving them a decent life, and they ain't living in squalor with the pigs,*" she would say, without even flinching. The first trip, bringing over the refugees, landed them thirty grand. Once they'd hopped off the boat, the money was theirs. Three grand apiece was nothing to be scoffed at. George built up his contacts and was trusted. He went into business with Alex, a ruthless Russian, with no morals whatsoever. He was a huge man who would cut you in half as soon as look at you. Tressa was sucked into the thrill of it all: the money, the respect, and her family's status. George and Charlie trusted her and would often remark that she had the ability to have people eating out of her hand: her sharp wit, and quick thinking on her feet, gave her an edge. But that all changed when *Sick* Jim, after a few too many whiskies, thought he could help himself.

Her room was dark when she'd arrived home. She remembered it well because it was the eve of her birthday in 1998. Violet was next door, gossiping with the neighbour, old *Shitlegs* Sheila, an Irish brass. The house was silent. She kicked off her new Jimmy Choo black stilettos, and just as she pulled her tight figure-hugging tube dress over her head, she felt two enormous hands grab her. She attempted to scream, but her face was pushed into the pillow. As she tried desperately to wriggle free from the dress and escape the clutches of her attacker, a hard fist clumped her across the side of her face. It knocked her sideways and blurred her vision. Within seconds, her knickers were ripped away, and she was left almost naked and exposed to the awful rape. Before she saw who it was who had gripped her waist and forced her legs apart, she recognised the smell: Old Spice aftershave. There was only one man she knew who would wear such outdated cologne and that was Jim, her own brother. The terrifying feeling engulfed her, and she fought with all her might to stop him. But he was too powerful and with angry force he entered her.

Tressa was suffering in equal measure from lack of air and from vomit rising to the back of her throat. Not only could she not breathe, but the vomit was stuck in her throat as her face was pushed deep into the pillow. She was gagging on her own sick and the assault on her body was nothing compared to the feeling of choking to death.

Finally, when he'd finished, she managed to get her arm free of the dress, and as he slumped on top of her, his head close to her hand, she dug her manicured nails deep into his face, tearing at his pitted skin. The room was still dark when he jumped up and fled. She knew it was him; she hated him anyway. He was always ogling her. How the others never noticed was beyond her. Little did she know,

72

though, the worst was yet to come – this time in the form of rejection from her mother.

Tressa remembered her mother's expression of pure hatred that night. There were just the two of them in the kitchen, and for a second she mistook the venom on her mother's face for hatred towards her own son. But when Violet's hand lifted and slapped her so hard in the face that she fell off the chair, she knew then her mother would never believe her. The boys were her life; the girls were just an accessory and in many ways an inconvenience.

The words were so cruel and heartless that Tressa, for the first time, saw her mother as a monster, devoid of a conscience. She noticed the black beady devil-like eyes and was afraid – it was not fear out of respect but from terror that her own mother would actually hang her out to dry at the drop of a hat.

"You are one evil cunt," she mocked. "You strut around in tight, skimpy rigouts, thinking that every fucking fella wants a piece of you, but you're nothing but a slag. And as for even suggesting my Jim would do that … that makes you one horrible bitch and a fucking dangerous menace to our family. I am gonna make sure you never make a sick accusation like that ever again. As for being part of the family business, well, you can kiss that goodbye!"

Violet got to her feet, grabbed Tressa by the throat, and punched her smack bang on the nose, and then threw her to the floor. "Now fuck off to your shit pit and stay there until I say otherwise!"

Tressa couldn't even go to the bathroom to wash away the memories of that hideous night. She lay in her brushed cotton pyjamas, hugging herself, as tears fell relentlessly, soaking her pillow, until eventually she fell asleep.

73

From then on, the dynamics of the family changed. She was kept at home as cook and cleaner, pandering to all their needs. The boys had left home years before and had gaffs of their own – plush pads, too, but they still visited their mum almost daily. Jim had stayed away for a couple of weeks after the rape, but when he did appear, Tressa noticed the faint pink lines where she had dug her claws in. She knew then, for sure, it had been him, the sick, evil, creepy pervert.

The irony of her own situation was not lost on Tressa. She was on the receiving end of the family's harsh ways, and so it made her realise that the hideous treatment doled out to the girls in the mansion, which she had been very much a part of, was a cruel and heartless act. She knew how it felt now, but she was lucky that she had not suffered from any actual physical abuse, except for the disgusting rape. On the other hand, this was not the case with Gemma, though, who had suffered from physical abuse at her own brother's hands.

Tressa remembered it well. It was the day Bobby had brought Gemma around to the house, and she'd gasped when she'd seen the cuts on her neck, arms, and legs. "Self-harmer, the nut," Bobby would say. But Tressa knew it was him who had sliced her up. That was in the early days, when Gemma was still a kid of twenty-one. She had admired Gemma's gumption. She had got back on her feet, and she'd shown the Ruthers, including herself, what she was really made of. Then, of course, Gemma had taken over from her with the running of the mansion in Surrey. If only Gemma had stayed quiet … but she had got too big for her boots and thought she could do as she liked. They'd given her too much trust and she'd abused it. Tressa's concern for Gemma changed as she'd watched her grow into a cocky woman. She'd even made demands on Tressa such as 'make the tea' or 'iron me shirt'. Gemma was the last person who she thought would have treated her like shit too. However, the woman was delusional. She still thought that despite everything – losing the baby and Bobby slicing her up – she would end up on their side. The day she had arrived at that Sunday dinner, after she had lost the baby, she became a different person. There was no more sweet, cheerful Gemma; instead, she became cold-faced and hard and one of them – that was until she took a step too far.

She looked down into the coffee and wondered if her own life would ever change. Maybe, one day, when her mother was six foot under, or if they all got caught for … She shuddered at the thought of prison.

CHAPTER FOUR

None of the Vincents slept that night. The events of the day before were so shocking it had left them lost and bewildered. Francesca didn't have time to grieve for Cassie or to deal with her brother's pain; she had too much to do. That small piece of paper held a clue, and she wasn't going to stand by and let the police bungle things. She recalled the conversation; it was so flippant that she got the impression finding Cassie's killer wasn't high on their agenda. There was no way Cassie's murder was top priority.

As soon as it was morning, the family rose from their beds and gathered in the dining room. Bill and Mary had gone home the previous night but returned early to be with the rest of the family. Sam, Joe, and Fred had stayed in the guest rooms, and Francesca had slept in the room prepared for her by Maria for when the baby arrived. One by one, they descended the stairs and joined each other at the table. There was enough food to feed the neighbourhood; it was all Maria could do to help. She carried two large pots of coffee and placed them in the centre of the table, but trying to maintain her dignity by holding back the tears was hard. Cassie's death had hit such a raw nerve, as it had, of course, for the whole family.

As Joe looked up, he saw her red eyes like slits; she had cried all night. It then hit him that Maria had been like a mother to Cassie. After all, Maria was around sixty-five years old and probably the right age to be Cassie's parent. She might be their housekeeper, but she was much more than that. She was such a sweet and kind person that there must have been a bond between them. He pushed himself away from the table and placed a meaty arm around her shoulder. "Come on, Maria, join us for breakfast. Ya gotta keep ya strength up. Our new baby will need his Aunty Maria with a smile on her face and a warm cuddle for him." He rubbed her shoulder and then pulled out a chair for her to take a seat. More tears flowed: for Cassie, for Dan, and for the baby.

"Ahh, Joe, I must keep myself busy," sobbed Maria. She felt awkward sitting there among the family.

"No, you take a breather and sit with us. We have plans to make and they include you," he replied.

As she looked up, she saw all the Vincents nodding in agreement. Dan looked as if he had been in the boxing ring; all the sobbing had left his face battered. Mary's heart ached for her son, and although she had to be strong for him, it was killing her inside.

Taking the lead, Francesca stood up and poured the coffee. More now than ever, her family needed her to be the one in control. She was on a mission to find out who had done this, but it was far too soon yet to share that information.

Ruby and Jack arrived, shortly followed by Alfie and Sophie, and the nieces and nephews each gave Dan an affectionate gesture, before they took their place at the table. The only other time they were all together was on Christmas Day; it was a day when, come what may, they would drop everything and be a complete pack. Mary and Bill would have been in their element to have all their children in one room celebrating over a huge feast – but this was different, so devoid of joy. Mary struggled to get to her feet; her arthritis felt as though it was crippling her most days. A woman now in her seventies, she was still attractive; her hourglass figure was a little more rounded, but her soft, dewy complexion and bright eyes radiated beauty.

"I would just like to say … " she paused, fighting back the lump in her throat " … we have all been through a lot in our lives, but we have all managed to pull through it because we have each other, and we will get through this as well." She looked at her eldest son and wished she could swap places, to take his pain away. "We're all gonna be there for ya, son, and for our new baby, our little miracle."

In a trance-like state, Dan stared at his mother, and then suddenly, as if a light had come on, he spoke. "Thank you, Mum. I know you will. All of you. This morning, I'm going to say goodbye to my Cassie and bring home my boy." He gazed into the steel blue eyes of the people sitting at his table. "Then, I'm going to find the person who did this, and as God is my witness, I will rip them limb from limb." His words were slow, cold, and calculated.

The boys all nodded in unison. They would have it no other way. No one would get away with this.

Francesca, sensing her brother's new-found confidence and new focus, decided now was an appropriate time to take action. "Right, I suggest that tonight the *Palaces* are opened as normal. Ruby, please make sure the doormen don't say a word. I want this kept quiet because if anyone mentions it, I want to know where it came from."

Ruby nodded. "The only people that know are Celia, Adam, and Dominic – I had to say something. They wanted to know where the boys were. I'll call them right now."

79

"Okay, you do that, and tell them to listen out for anything. If they hear a whisper, I want to know the source. Also, Jack, don't go down the gym. Stay with Kizzy and your dad. Rubes, stay with Adam. And Alf and Soph, you two stay away from the club tonight."

The men were frowning, thinking their own thoughts, when Fred spoke up. "She's right. We have no idea what's going on. Poor Cassie might just be the first. We need to keep our wits about us until we find the muvver fucker and make sure he—" Fred was cut short.

"All right, Freddie boy, we got the picture," fretted Bill. He didn't like to see his youngest son get irate – not in front of Dan.

To everyone's surprise, Maria stood up. "I can have a look through Cassie's things to see if there is any clue as to who it was she went to visit."

Francesca gave Maria a compassionate smile. "That's a very good idea. Thank you, Maria."

After Maria sipped the last dregs of her coffee, she left the table and was now on a mission. She felt like part of the family, and more importantly, it was a relief to be able to help. She wanted nothing more than to see the killer caught and tortured. She might be a quiet housekeeper, who sometimes blended into the background, but she came from a villainous background herself. She'd left Spain years before when her family were in deep trouble; England was a safe place for her, as she could work inside a manor, so no one would even know she was there. The Vincents had always treated her very well and much better than she could have asked for, so she was more than happy to help them in any way she could.

Dan had first employed her ten years earlier, when he'd lived in a smaller house that he never had time to keep clean and tidy. Maria had her own room – just a small box room really, but she loved it.

He was hardly there; and yet he could guarantee, when he did turn up, the house would be spotless, his shirts ironed to perfection, the cupboards full, and the coffee hot. He grew to trust Maria with his life. Quite literally, he came home so drunk one night that he fell over the bed and bashed his head, and then he almost choked on his own vomit. Maria had rushed to his side. She'd cleaned him up, dressed the gash, and had him almost sober within the hour. What she did, he would never know, but the one thing he could be sure of was she'd probably saved his life. From that day on, Dan had a soft spot for her. He would buy her surprise gifts, never forgetting her birthday. She loved the theatre, and when he had the time, he would take her to see a show. It was his way of saying thank you. At Christmas, she was regarded as very much a part of the family and was invited to Francesca's table to eat, drink, and enjoy the festivities, and not to serve or cook.

Mary made plans to go with Dan to the hospital. She assumed that once Dan had said his goodbyes, and held his baby, his grief would ease. Having his new son to think about would be a welcome distraction from his loss. Unable to bear seeing her eldest son suffering, she wanted it to end. However, in the cold light of day, she knew it had only just begun.

Before anyone questioned her, Francesca made her excuses to leave and slipped away.

The warm air outside hit her, and she stopped for a second to take a deep breath. Her car was parked next to the line-up of her brothers' flash Jags. She slipped into her bulletproof car, feeling protected; after all, she could also be a target. That thought alone hastily spurred her on to find out who the nutter was who had killed Cassie before anyone else in her family was hurt or worse.

Determined to get into the prison and meet with this Gemma Ruthers, she drove straight to Jamie, her minder's son. Jamie was now doing very well for himself. His law firm was in central London and his client list was ever-growing. He was a far cry from the little boy she'd taken to the States, and who had been so poorly, and days away from death. He'd had a tumour on the brain that was inoperable in the UK, but she'd managed to find a surgeon in New York who could do the job. She'd used Jamie as collateral to ensure Adam, his father, did as she'd demanded.

Adam had been working for the Enrights at the time. They were a family who were highly admired and respected within legal circles, and Adam was Charles Enright senior's driver-cum-bodyguard. Charles senior was Francesca's first husband's uncle. They referred to him as Charlie and not to be confused with Charles junior, who they called Charles. The Enrights were a cruel family with no morals and a huge influence within the legal system. After they had left her for dead, she had to take revenge, and she'd needed Adam to be on her side. Kidnapping his son had ensured that.

As she drove up to Jamie's offices and reflected on those former times, she felt sad that she'd had to act in such a cruel fashion, but she had been ruthless back then; therefore, with only family, love, and revenge on her mind, she'd used every trick in the book to make sure her plan was faultless. Once she had kept her promise and had Adam on her side, the plan was executed and the outcome was good. Adam knew the Enrights were evil men. After Francesca had proved she was a woman of her word, he'd been glad to help her. After all, the Enrights had never offered to help his son. She might have done it for her own ends, but she'd still saved Jamie's life and he would be forever indebted to her. Their relationship had grown over the years and Adam and Jamie had become a part of the family.

She stopped at the foot of the building and looked up admiringly at the facade; it was a modern grand block, housing various high-end businesses. Inside, she gazed around at the marble entrance and glass elevator and smiled to herself. Here visitors, entering these premises, gained an insight into Jamie's personality: fresh, young, sleek, and functional. The air conditioning was a bonus and instantly cooled her down. Two other people entered the lift with her. One of them, quite a handsome young man, perhaps in his late twenties, eyed her up and down. She grinned to herself. Once they reached the third floor, she stepped out and directly in front of her was a chrome-edged glass door with a mounted plaque, which read 'Jamie Adam Walker, Solicitor'. She beamed with pride as she entered.

The pretty young woman, sitting behind the desk, instantly sat up straight.

"Hello, may I help you?" she inquired, as she admired the sophisticated woman standing before her. Francesca was dressed just in a plain cream dress, but she looked the epitome of the modern businesswoman with perfect skin and eyes that shone like crystals, which further emphasised her stunning appearance. The way she'd walked in, with such grace and poise, gave Poppy, the receptionist, the impression she was a woman of importance and definitely money. The designer bag alone must have been worth a mint.

"Yes, hello, could you let Jamie know that Francesca is here to see him." The woman's voice was calm and her smile genuine.

Poppy hadn't realised she'd said 'Francesca', as she was so focused on admiring the woman's clothes and handbag.

"Oh, err, do you have an appointment, madam? There's nothing in the diary."

A soft smile radiated across Francesca's face; the new receptionist didn't know who she was, but that wasn't her fault. "No, I don't, but if you let him know I'm here, I'm sure he'll see me."

Poppy had strict instructions not to let anyone in unless they had an appointment; Jamie was too busy these days to see clients without one. Today was particularly hectic, and he'd made it clear earlier that morning he was not to be disturbed.

"I can make an appointment—" Poppy looked on the computer screen to see where there was a free slot. "—Thursday at three p.m." She looked up to see Francesca still smiling and it unnerved her.

"Does he have a client with him now?"

"I ... err, well, he's not to be disturbed, he's otherwise engaged, but if you like, I can take your number and ask him to call you."

The young woman was only doing her job, so Francesca didn't push her; instead, she pulled out her mobile phone and dialled him direct. They both heard the ring tone next door and laughed out loud as it played 'You are my Angel'.

"Hello, Jamie. I'm outside," she said, still giggling.

To Poppy's surprise, the door suddenly opened and there was Jamie with a huge grin spread across his face.

His deep green eyes were alight, and she then realised that the woman was someone very close to him. Francesca held out her arms and the tall strapping man embraced her.

"Oh my God, what a lovely surprise." He turned to Poppy. "This is my Aunty Sisco," he said, beaming with pride. Francesca laughed. Sisco was her nickname. It stemmed from when Jack and Ruby, her nephew and niece, were only toddlers and couldn't say Francesca.

84

Instead, they called her Francisco, which was eventually shortened to Sisco. Francesca had many names: Dolly as a child, Launa as a teenager for her own safety, Bella by her husband, and Sis by her brothers. Secretly, though, she loved to be called Dolly. It was the name her father had given her, and she cherished every moment she heard it.

Poppy then knew who she was. Jamie had made it very clear that if it wasn't for her, he wouldn't be here today, and he wouldn't be a solicitor or have the offices. Francesca had been entirely responsible for helping him to be in the position he found himself. She had encouraged him and helped to finance him through university and law exams, and she had provided the finance to set him up with suitable premises with the fashionable London office address. What he didn't know, however, was that she herself had been a fortunate beneficiary when she was around his age. Thomasine, her late best friend's father, Lord Alfred William Horsham, had bequeathed a large sum of money in his will to Launa, as she was then known, which had enabled her to fund herself through university and law school.

Jamie had vowed never to let her down and to prove he could do something good with his life.

As if the queen had just walked into the room, Poppy jumped to her feet and almost curtseyed.

"I'm so sorry, I didn't know. It's just that Jamie refers to you as Sisco."

"No, it's fine. I'm impressed that you do your job so well," laughed Francesca.

She saw Poppy blush as she looked Jamie's way and sensed a little crush. This was hardly surprising as Jamie was a good catch, being tall, handsome, and successful.

As he ushered Francesca inside his new office, Poppy quickly offered refreshments.

Instantly, Francesca summed up that Jamie was a well organised lawyer: the files were neatly lined up along the bookshelves, the long glass table was spotless, containing only the bare essentials, and there was also a photo of her and his father, standing either side of him at his graduation. The window offered a panoramic view right across London.

"This is wonderful, Jamie, and the view … well, it's perfect, just perfect."

Jamie still had the grin on his face. He loved Francesca, and he regarded her as the nearest thing to the mother he'd never had. She had been very honest with him, when he was old enough to know the truth about how she'd saved him, as he hadn't known what was going on at the time. All he remembered was being on a plane, then in hospital, then being spoiled rotten with trips to Disneyland, spending weeks in a beautiful log cabin by a lake with his dad, and with Francesca always around, hugging and kissing him. He'd never had that before, not from a woman, only from his dad. She made him better, and he knew she loved him. And it hadn't stopped there: she'd made sure he had the best of everything, and so to him, she was his mother – and he was immensely proud of her.

"I have a list of clients so long I might need to take on more staff," he said, eager to show how well he was doing.

"I'm very proud of you, Jamie, but do you have time for yourself? I mean, that receptionist seems very nice and I think she has a crush."

"Poppy? Well, yes, we uhm … have been out for a few dinners, but maybe it's not a good idea. I mean she works here, I don't know … " laughed Jamie with embarrassment.

Francesca cupped his face and kissed his forehead. "If you like her, don't let that put you off. You need people around you who you can trust, and a husband and wife make a good team."

"I don't know about that just yet. It's early days. I'm so busy building the business, I probably couldn't give her the attention she deserves," he replied coyly.

"Perhaps you could build the business together. It's tough at times doing things alone. Don't rule it out. She seems very nice."

"So, what brings you here? Not that I'm complaining. It's lovely to see you." He sat on the large leather chair, facing her.

Her expression changed and she now looked serious and sad.

"What's the matter, Sisco?"

"I have some terrible news and I need your help."

Jamie leaned forward on his chair. "Tell me."

"Cassie was shot dead yesterday." She paused, waiting for Jamie to take it in. He had never been close to Cassie, as he had probably only met her a handful of times, but he was close to the family.

"Jesus ... and the baby?" He was shocked, wide-eyed, trying to take it all in.

"They managed to save him."

Jamie nodded. "Thank God." He waited for Francesca to continue; she obviously needed his help, and he would do everything in his power.

"She'd been to visit a woman in prison and was shot a few streets away. We have no idea who would have wanted to do this or even why they would contemplate such a thing, but I need to get into that prison and meet with a Gemma Ruthers."

Jamie almost jolted in his seat. "Hey, wait a minute. I had a phone call yesterday from the prison. A Gemma Ruthers called to ask for a legal visit. She said she'd been given my name by her sister. I could barely hear her before the phone died, but she mentioned your name."

Francesca chewed the inside of her mouth. "Right. Can you get on the phone and arrange it for today? I can be there in an hour. Are you free to come along? As her lawyer, you'll have to engage me as her barrister."

"Of course."

His other clients would have to be put off; this was far more important. If Francesca asked anything of him, he would always be there. He knew not to ask any questions, as she was always the one in control.

With a tray of tea and biscuits, along with a smile, Poppy entered the office. Francesca stood and took the tray from her, which was a gesture of respect. "Thank you, Poppy."

Whilst Jamie was on the phone, Francesca noticed just how sophisticated and firm he was. She admired his ability to go from sweet, laid-back, and childlike, to a man who wouldn't take any shit. He was tall and stocky, like his father, but his face had a softer countenance. Whilst Adam was rugged, Jamie was smooth, clean-shaven, and glowing.

He replaced the receiver and smiled. "Two fifteen today. How's that?"

"Great, that gives us more time to look into her background and track down her files."

Jamie had a smug grin on his face. "I have a database that can pull up the information in a flash."

Francesca raised her eyebrows and was clearly impressed.

The humidity was reaching its peak, and as they stepped outside, away from the cool air conditioning, the bellow of thunder was almost a relief. The sky blackened as they eagerly trotted to Francesca's car. Jamie placed the folders in the boot and hopped into the front seat.

"Nice motor, Sisco," he said, as he leaned back and wrapped the seat belt around him.

"You know Sergio, he insists on the cars being the best when it comes to safety. And, of course, it's bulletproof. He makes me laugh. I'm sure he thinks that someone will shoot me one day."

"No, it's not that, Sisco. Sergio just wants to make sure you're safe when he's not here to look after you. I must make a trip over ... maybe in September. I miss the ol' bugger." He laughed.

"Hey, less of the old bugger! He's younger than me."

"I can call him that because when we go out people think he's the same age as me, and he teases me." His jovial tone changed and he said, "How's Dan? Did he take it very badly?"

"Yes, he did, and far worse than I could have imagined. The whole family is in shock. Christ, who murders a pregnant woman, for fuck's sake?" Her voice was cold as she stared at the stationary traffic ahead.

Jamie was quiet, thinking about the Vincents. They had all been good to him. He was treated as one of them, and as far as he was concerned they were family; he would do whatever it took to help find the killer and have them behind bars. Unbeknownst to him, though, the family had other plans – and those centred on revenge.

For the rest of the journey, Francesca remained quiet. She needed to get her head together and make sure she walked away with answers before the police started looking more deeply into the case. Surely they would look at the CCTV footage from the prison? They could easily check the visitors' records too. Although one thing she did notice about the VO was that it was in Cassie's maiden name, not her married name. *That was interesting*, she thought.

As they walked past the visitors, queuing along the road and up to the gates, one of the officers could see instantly they were there for a legal visit. Jamie was in a suit with folders under his arm, and Francesca looked far too sophisticated and assured to be a visitor. He ushered them through and into the legal visit waiting room.

Francesca hated the smell of prisons. She should have been used to it, but it still reminded her of the day she'd visited her father and had to say goodbye for fifteen years. She shuddered every time she thought of it. She would never get that vision out of her head. His eyes had been so sunken and drenched in grief as he'd said those heart-wrenching words, "You have to go away, Dolly, it's the only way I can protect you."

Little did they all know that the man her father protected her from, Mad Mick, was not the man who would leave her for dead. The man who'd done that was supposed to love her – her former husband, Charles Enright junior.

Jamie spoke with the officer behind the desk. He showed her the various documents and signed the register. All the while, the officer glared over at Francesca.

"Err … Ruthers has been sick this morning, so I'm not sure she's up to a legal visit," she said. Francesca sensed there was something not quite right. Linda, the officer, was on edge. She had no idea that Gemma was expecting a visit, especially a legal one. Sandra would be spitting feathers. How the hell it had got past them was beyond her. Gemma must have got to the phone. Sensing doom, she had to get word to Sandra somehow to stop the visit, but the woman standing in front of her made her uneasy. There was something about her expression, which didn't quite add up.

Francesca stepped forward. "Whether she is or not, I want her in the visiting room to tell me herself. We've just spoken to your governor, and she seemed to think Gemma was well enough for a visit. I'm sure the governor wouldn't have let us come all this way if Gemma were sick."

Linda had been shuffling from one foot to the other, but her nerves kicked in and suddenly she was frozen to the spot. Sandra had made it clear that Gemma was never to have another visit, especially not a legal one. They were paid well for their little interventions. And yet, standing before her, were a brief and a barrister. Usually, if a brief was turned away because a prisoner was sick, they would take it with a pinch of salt; it was more money in their pockets, as they were paid by the hour. However, by the body language of this man and woman, they looked and sounded very determined, giving her some cause for concern. She glanced at Jamie and then back at Francesca, who just stared straight back at her with a deep warning look in her eyes.

"I'll call the wing and ask if she's up to it," replied Linda, trying to act cool.

"Well, officer …" Francesca leaned forward to take a closer look at her badge. " … Blair. If you have to call the wing, then clearly she's not in the medical unit. I can only assume that means she's not too damn sick to speak to me in person, is she?"

Linda swallowed hard; it was clear there was no messing with this woman.

"I'll call for her," she said, as she left the room almost at a trot.

Francesca peered over the desk and saw the phone. Suddenly, she spun around to face Jamie who was reading some notes. "There's something odd going on. Why would she leave the room to phone the wing? There's a phone on the desk. I get the feeling there's more to Gemma Ruthers than meets the eye."

Looking up, Jamie frowned; this was all new to him. As far as he was concerned, they were in there to question the woman. He determined that maybe that was why Francesca was so good at her job. She liked to play Sherlock Holmes.

Left alone in the waiting room for over twenty minutes really irritated Francesca. All she wanted to do was to find out why Cassie had visited Gemma Ruthers and if the woman had any idea who'd shot her. Her irritability level was rising by the minute.

Eventually, the door flew open and revealed a chunky, thickset woman with short dark hair who wore a spiteful expression. Over her shoulder was Blair, the other officer she'd met at reception. "Follow me. We can occupy the end room," said Sandra, trying to take control. Francesca took an instant dislike and glared back at the woman. She noticed the way the officer used the word 'we' and decided then she would make sure that no one would be in the room apart from her, Jamie, and Gemma. She was beginning to get seriously pissed off with these officers.

Sandra unlocked the door and held it open for the others to walk in. The room was small but bright, with bars up at the window, and there was a table with four chairs. Gemma was already seated. As soon as Francesca clapped eyes on Gemma, she winced. The frail and poor excuse for a woman sat with her head down but clearly visible were the bruises and scars on her neck and arms. For a second, Francesca sensed a cold shiver-like sensation. The woman put her in mind of Jessie Right, her dead sister-in-law; the evil bitch had cruelly treated her niece Ruby and nephew Jack. She pushed that thought to the side and tried to see Gemma in a different light. After all, she didn't know Gemma, and her downtrodden look may not be of her own doing, which would be the complete opposite to Jesse. Jesse had been a drug-taking nasty piece of work.

Slowly, Gemma looked up. She was surprised to see that Francesca looked more like a model than a barrister; she'd expected her to look very different now and much older in fact. She watched as she walked assertively to the chair, carefully pull it away from the table, and sit down. Jamie hardly looked at the woman; he was too busy fussing over some paperwork.

Nervously, Gemma peered over her shoulder at Sandra and again lowered her eyes. This didn't go unnoticed.

Francesca held out her hand. "Hello, Gemma, I'm Francesca, your barrister, and this gentleman is Jamie, your solicitor, whom you have instructed."

Gemma took her hand and lightly shook it, and then she looked over at Jamie and gave him a weary smile. "Thank you for coming.

Cassie said you would. She said you were really nice and everything." Her voice was a mere whisper but was filled with hope.

"Okay, Gemma, I'd like to take some notes, if I may. I also have a Dictaphone. Let's start with some basic questions." Francesca searched inside her bag for a small pocket book and a pen. She could feel Sandra behind her but not close enough to see what she was writing. Quickly, she scribbled *Do you want the officer to leave?* She turned the notebook around. "Is your name Gemma with a G?"

Gemma smiled and nodded as she looked over Francesca's shoulder.

Suddenly, Francesca stood up and turned to face Sandra. "I wish to interview my client in private."

Sandra had to think quickly; she couldn't leave the room without knowing full details of what Gemma was up to. "Sorry, love, but for your own protection, I have to stay." The barrister took a step forward, her face expressionless; a cold shiver ran through Sandra.

"I am assured that my client has no history of violence towards visitors. I am also sure that I have a right to question my client alone, if I so wish. Now, if that is an issue for you, then we'll have this debate with your governor. Do I make myself clear? Or is there another language you speak?" she said, with a cold chill to her voice.

Sandra was taken aback by the woman's confidence and determination. She wondered if the barrister knew she was somehow linked to the pregnant woman's murder.

Without a word, she left the room and locked the door behind her. Gemma was wide-eyed and wanted to laugh; it was the first time she had seen Sandra spoken down to.

Francesca contemplated telling the woman that Cassie had been murdered, but she thought better of it for now. Besides, if Gemma was a close friend, then she might be too upset to continue with the interview and Francesca would be none the wiser.

"I am truly grateful that you are here. Cassie said if anyone could help me get out, you could."

Unsure whether she was genuine, Francesca studied the storm in Gemma's eyes. There was an odd sensation that plagued her, but then again, she was in a strange situation. She was there for her own agenda and it was obvious Gemma was oblivious to yesterday's incident. She resolved to listen carefully to her client before prejudging her.

Jamie looked up from the file. "So, Gemma, I am assuming you have requested my services to

pursue an appeal?"

"Yes," she replied shyly.

"Okay, before we can go ahead we need to find grounds on which to base an appeal. I'll start by reading these transcripts from your court case. Please correct any information."

Gemma nodded and bit her nail. Her eyes were dull and lifeless as if she was suddenly back in court. Francesca then observed her whole demeanour change.

"On the night of Monday, 5 January 2015, almost eighteen months ago, you were found by your husband, Robert Ruthers, attempting to hang yourself. After a struggle, he managed to free you from the rope, and in doing so, you took a kitchen knife and stabbed him twice in the chest. You then fled the house and called the police."

As Jamie looked up from the file, he was met with a cold, distant look in Gemma's eyes. She was staring, but her mind was elsewhere.

He leaned forward and said in a firm voice, "Gemma, please tell us what happened from the beginning." Francesca placed the tape recorder on the table and gave Gemma an encouraging smile to continue.

CHAPTER FIVE

Jamie leaned forward towards the tape recorder. "Interview One: Gemma Ruthers."

Gemma remembered the night like it was yesterday. She was still playing the dutiful daughter-in-law and went along to Bobby's house to celebrate Violet's seventieth birthday. This was a change from Violet's house but everyone wanted the bash at Bobby's. They were all there and although she wasn't with Bobby as such, since their marriage was estranged, she was still part of their family. Perhaps it was strange, but it's just how it had to be until her plan for the future was in place. They turned a blind eye to her seeing Alex, although she never rubbed their noses in it, and they were too shit-scared to say anything. It was the next day before she realised she'd left her phone at Bobby's, as the party continued into the early hours. He had got in touch with her, and they had arranged for her to go and collect the phone later on. What she found wasn't what she was expecting. She couldn't get the vision out of her head. She remembered her husband all cocained up to the eyeballs, trying to have a fondle, but he was a bumbling idiot, and she pushed him aside. It was then that the rope appeared from nowhere, and the realisation hit her — he was going to attempt to hang her! If it had happened years ago, she would have been terrified, but no, now she saw him as a pathetic prat. He pulled her to the floor and wrapped the rope round her neck, but it was a bit too long and unwieldy, and he was struggling with it. This gave her the opening she needed. She managed to push him off and with great relish she kneed him hard in the balls. She was going to run, but then she saw the knife on the kitchen side. In a flash, she grabbed it, and as she turned, he was behind her, but she was too quick and plunged the knife into his chest. He didn't fall right away, though, being too high on drugs to feel the pain. Then she stabbed him again and laughed, "Rot in hell, Bobby!" she spat, as his body slumped to the floor.

She had made a stupid cock-up and hadn't thought it through. She had responded in the heat of the moment. She should have just run and not tried to kill Bobby. She had ample opportunity to do that and bide her time on any day of her choosing and would now pay, unless, of course, she was free to finish what she'd started. But next time, she would be more cunning. Of course, she couldn't tell the lawyers any of this.

She cleared her throat, took a deep breath, and then began with the story.

It shouldn't have been a surprise; their marriage of twenty-one years had been a joke. However, at the beginning of the relationship, she'd thought she had loved him. Now, looking back to that time, she realised she hadn't loved him at all. Maybe, needing to escape from that immoral and oppressive foster home, she'd looked at their relationship through rose-coloured spectacles and believed she'd fallen for the first man she'd met who had his own gaff and a twinkle in his eye.

There was the added benefit that Bobby, short for Robert, was good-looking, had money, and was exciting. She liked a bad boy; although little did she know back then he was bad in the true meaning of the word. She'd never been short of boyfriends; her lively and sociable personality, along with her fashionable looks, had many a fella asking for a date. Bobby was different, but he was also deadly.

It was the summer of 1992, and Gemma was standing with her friends outside the ice rink when Bobby pulled up on his motorbike. He had his helmet on, so she couldn't see who he was. Two other lads she was talking to, however, knew straight away. "Hey, it's Bobby!" said one of the boys. He seemed quite excited.

The girls stopped nattering and smiled in his direction. Their faces lit up; it was obvious they knew who he was. Gemma was intrigued and when he removed his crash helmet her interest grew. His fair, wavy hair shone in the light and then when he smiled his whole face beamed. He had perfect white teeth and grey eyes. They were eyes that sparkled and lashes that should have belonged to a woman.

Gemma looked down at herself; she was pleased she was wearing her pink combat trousers and a small crop top, showing off her neat, tight tanned stomach. Her hair was thick back then with her blonde waves bouncing off her shoulders. He looked in her direction and winked. For a second, there were just the two of them, eyeing each other up.

"'Ere, Bobby, got any puff?" asked Mikey, one of Gemma's friends. He was a wild boy himself, being cocky, but harmless enough.

"'Ere, mate, take this, it's good shit. Want any more, let me know," replied Bobby, as he threw a packet in Mikey's direction.

Gemma was captivated; he was so cool, and his face was alive.

No sooner had he arrived than he was gone, bombing down Streatham High Road. The girls were full of excitement.

"Oh my God, that was Bobby Ruthers. Cor, I'd fuck him all night long," said Tracy Smith, a school friend of Gemma's.

Gemma giggled.

"Yeah, me too, but I think he was eyeing over Gems," replied Bethany, nodding in Gemma's direction.

"Fuck off, Beth, he likes a real woman, Gems is only a kid ... no offence, mate, but he dates birds his own age."

"How old is he?" asked Gemma.

Tracy laughed. "Oh, fancy him, do ya? I think he's twenty-one."

The boys had left with their puff and the girls sat on the wall. Gemma wanted to know everything about Bobby. She hoped she was in his league.

"Gems, take that smirk off your face. He won't look at you in that way. You're only sixteen, for fuck's sake. You're probably still a virgin." Tracy laughed and pushed Gemma off the wall.

Gemma climbed back up, looked at her friend, and concluded she was jealous. After all, Bobby definitely wouldn't look at Tracy. She was a slag and shagged anything if it had a cock. And being severely overweight, she stank to high heaven – even on a cold day. Gemma liked her though; in fact, Gemma had many friends. She didn't care what colour, size, or age they were. As long as they were kind to her, then she would always return the favour.

Bethany took a deep drag on her fag. "I wouldn't get mixed up with him. Eye candy he might be, but the Ruthers are a dangerous family. Nah. I would keep well away."

Gemma was streetwise for her age and wasn't oblivious to rackets going on. Living in a foster home, and one that she hated, meant she spent most of her time on the streets, knocking about with her mates, listening to the stories, the odd bit of shoplifting, dragging

100

on a few spliffs, and rucking. She could handle herself, small as she was; she could also throw a punch and was quick too.

A week later, Gemma was hanging around the ice rink again when suddenly the heavens opened. The gang she was knocking about with all dispersed in different directions – they had decent, loving homes to go to. They might be poor, one parent, or messy homes, but they all had family. They could go home, jump in a hot bath, and have a cup of cocoa, all in the safety of their surroundings.

Gemma pulled up the collar of her fake Burberry jacket and stood alone under the overhanging sign. The wind changed direction, leaving her exposed to the rain. She decided to walk home. The water seeped through her jacket and into her T-shirt but feeling cold and damp wasn't as bad as the thought of those ogling eyes, awaiting her at the house. She hoped Cassie was home: they were safer as a pair. He didn't make his perverted glares too obvious when the girls were together. It was a case of safety in numbers.

Out of the corner of her eye, she noticed a man on a motorbike slow down alongside her. The rain was fierce and she blinked quickly; her mascara had run and was stinging her eyes.

"Hey, Blondie!" shouted the man on the bike.

Gemma turned to find Bobby Ruthers perched on his mean machine, holding out a crash helmet. She frowned. Was he offering her a ride? She hurried over to him.

"Wanna ride?"

Her heart was in her mouth; so much ran through her mind. On the one hand, she was soaked and looked a wreck, but on the other, he was gorgeous and offering her a lift. Impulsively, she grabbed the helmet, plonked it on her head, and jumped on the back of his bike.

She clung to him for dear life. Her heart raced at the thought that she had her arms wrapped around gorgeous Bobby Ruthers as they sped along the main drag. It was the thrill of a lifetime. She had no idea where he was taking her and to be honest she really didn't care.

He swerved in and out of the traffic, and as he did so she tightened her grip and savoured the smell of new leather with a hint of sweet aftershave. The rain didn't let up, and when he finally came to a stop, she was shivering and soaked to the skin. Her limbs were stiff from the cold when he helped her down.

She looked up to see where they were and saw that they had parked in a parking bay allotted to some flats. It was a new build just off the estate.

Slowly, she pulled off her helmet and looked coyly at the ground.

"It's okay, I don't bite. I just thought you might want to dry off. I got a tumble dryer."

Gemma realised that this was his flat and she was alone. She should have been afraid, and she should have just gone home, but she was cold and wet and he was so handsome. He took her helmet and flicked his head for her to follow him.

The heavy white door was the main entrance to six flats. The smell of fresh paint still lingered because the flats were recently built and Bobby had snapped one up. It wasn't too far from his mother's and yet it gave him freedom and his own space. His mother's house was cramped at the best of times. It had been all right when he was a kid because he knew no different but as an adult it was restricting.

Gemma walked up the flight of stairs, above two ground floor flats, admiring the sleek finish. The door on the left was his. There was a door opposite and another flight of stairs to two more flats.

Everything was evenly spaced. He pushed open his front door, and like a true gentleman, he stepped aside for her to walk on in.

The small hallway had two rooms leading off from the right and one on the left. Ahead was the lounge and an open-plan kitchen. Floor-to-ceiling windows stretched across the far wall and she could see for miles. The kitchen was small but it had everything, including the tumble dryer. She smiled, wishing she could have a flat just like this one. It was perfect: all modern and minimalist. The corner sofa was red leather, matching the red glass doors of the kitchen cupboards.

On the opposite wall to the sofa was a huge TV and music centre. By the side were cardboard boxes placed somewhat carelessly. And these were all overflowing with clothes still in cellophane packets. Bobby watched her face and could tell she was impressed.

"You need to get outta those wet clothes."

She shivered as suddenly reality hit her. She was alone with a stranger; yeah, her mates might know him, but she didn't. She was a virgin and now he was suggesting she stripped off. Her eyes darted from his face to the door. Should she run or just ask to leave?

"See those boxes? Sift through, babe, and find yaself a tracksuit. There must be one your size."

Suddenly, her fear subsided. She laughed. "Ya sure?"

"Yeah, course, babe, I got loads. Good quality, too. Nice pink Nike ones." He moved towards her and grabbed her arm. "Fucking 'ell, you're soaked. Go on, have a look. I'm gonna roll a joint. The bathroom's back there. Shower's hot, so be careful."

Gemma hadn't said a word; she was still taking it all in. Gingerly, she stepped forward and peered into the boxes. Sure enough, the top packet was a size small; she lifted it out and held it up. She would have sifted through the lot to see what others he had, but she thought maybe that was rude. Without a word, she tiptoed back to the hallway and found the bathroom. Once she'd locked the door behind her, she breathed more easily.

She looked in the mirror; her face looked a right mess. The mascara made her look like she had two black eyes and her hair was flat and stuck to her head. What a sight. She ran the hot water and stripped off. The hot champagne spray invigorated her, livening up her frozen bones. With an enormous fresh white towel, she rubbed her arms and legs dry; she didn't wipe her face just in case she hadn't washed off all her make-up — she didn't want to leave an ugly stain. She searched her pockets for the small items of make-up she always carried with her and applied more mascara, a touch of blusher, and some lip gloss. She fluffed up her hair and then she opened the packet containing the tracksuit. It was, as he'd said, a good quality copy and it fitted her perfectly.

"'Ere you go, babe, get ya laughing gear around that," he grinned, as she entered the living room.

He was leaning across the worktop that separated the kitchen from the living area. She giggled and took the large mug of creamy hot chocolate.

"Thank you, Bobby. This is all really good of ya. I was near-on froze to death. Nice pad ya got yaself."

Then he winked and unexpectedly she felt butterflies in her stomach. It was a new sensation and one she had never experienced before.

"When that poxy rain stops, I can run you home," he said and smiled.

Suddenly, she didn't want to go home. She liked him and his flat. She was feeling more confident. "So, Bobby, what made ya stop and pick me up, then?"

"I dunno. I guess ya looked kinda lost. I drove past ya, first. I saw ya standing under that sign. Then, when I turned around, you'd gone. I was about to ride home, then there you was dawdling up the street in the rain. So I thought maybe you had nowhere to go."

Gemma thought he was a sensitive man. She had, however, hoped he would say he fancied her or something along those lines.

"Yeah, well, you're right, I don't have a home. I live with me foster parents and he's an old perv. I hate it really. Funny, 'cos I didn't want to go home. I know that Cassie, me foster sister, is probably at school, and he'll be there on his own. Fanks for stopping."

As he listened intently to this pretty young thing, Bobby had his head cocked to the side and raised a well-defined eyebrow. "Old perv, ya say?"

Gemma took a sip of her chocolate and nodded. "Don't get me wrong. He ain't touched me or nuffin', but he's a right creep."

Bobby laughed. "I didn't pick you up just 'cos you was wet. I wanted to get to know ya. Last week, when you was with those fucking idiots, I thought you looked out of place, a pretty girl like you, hanging with Mikey and that fat shit, Tracy."

"They're all right really." She giggled again.

He edged his way from around the bar and took the cup from out of her hands. She took a deep breath and averted her eyes. He ran his hands over her wet hair and tilted her chin to meet his gaze.

"Nah, babes, ya too good for them. What's your name?" He was now staring into her eyes.

"Gemma," she replied. He placed his lips on hers and kissed her very gently. She could feel her heart beating and hoped he couldn't tell she was nervous.

"A pretty name for a pretty girl."

They spent the afternoon and early evening talking and laughing. They shared a few kisses, and when it was time to leave, he promised her that if ever the old pervert laid his hands on her, he would go in and beat the crap out of him. "No one hurts my Gemma," he said.

He gave her a ride home, kissed her goodnight, and arranged to take her out for dinner the next evening. Gemma was thrilled; he was taking her on a grown-up date out to a restaurant. She was so excited that when he rode off into the distance, she ran up the garden path and almost bumped into her foster father, Gareth. He'd been watching through the window and almost ripped the door off its hinges. She stared up at his sadistic expression and winced at his dark angry eyes.

"What the fucking hell do you think you're playing at, young lady?" he spat.

Gemma cringed; he'd been on the booze again. She hated him with a passion but couldn't tell social services as they wouldn't believe her. Gareth and Judy were both in their forties with good professional jobs. He was a banker and she was a lawyer, but they had debts, due to his serious gambling habit, so they took up fostering. He had let that slip a couple of years back.

"Nothing."

"Nothing? Don't tell me nothing, you little tramp. I saw you kissing that man."

Gemma froze; he was more drunk than she had seen him before. He looked scruffy even in his suit. He had possibly been a smart and handsome man a few years ago. She assumed his ego had taken a knock when his wife began climbing the ladder at a speed of knots. She paid him no attention, tutting and snarling at his slovenly appearance. He did look a mess. His thinning hair was unwashed, and he was nearly always unshaven and red-eyed through whisky. He was a man on a downward spiral, turning to booze.

Suddenly, he grabbed her by her arm and dragged her inside, tugging her towards the kitchen. His fat hands clenched her arm so tightly she screamed for him to let go, hoping that either Cassie or Judy would hear, but there was no sign of them.

He pushed her into the fridge and pinned her there by her shoulders. "So, my girl, grown-up enough now for a real man, are you?"

The horror of what he might do filled her with dread. She could smell the stale whisky on his breath but it was the deranged expression that shook her to the core.

His voice lowered to a creepy pitch. "I'll fucking show you what a real man feels like," he boasted.

In a panic, Gemma looked around for some way to escape, but he was stronger than her, and she was held up against that cold fridge door with so much force.

Coarsely, he grabbed her by the throat and slid his other hand inside her tracksuit bottoms, and then he started fumbling around. Gemma tried to scream, but he clenched her throat tighter. Try as she might, she couldn't remove his hand from around her throat, and she thought she was going to die. He picked her up like a rag doll and threw her onto the table, knocking the breath out of her. Desperate to get away from his vile clutches, she fought back. Kicking and screaming, she went into a frenzy. Luckily, she managed to roll off the table and land with her two feet on the floor. He was strong, but in his drunken state he was slower. Just as she ran to the front door, Judy appeared, carrying bags of shopping, followed by Cassie.

"Gemma, fetch the rest from the car, will you, dear?" Her voice was high-pitched and haughty. She must have been in her own little world not to have noticed the fright on Gemma's face. Cassie noticed, though.

"Gems, what's happened?" she whispered.

"Hurry up, girls, the food won't put itself away."

Cassie rolled her eyes.

"I'll tell you upstairs," whispered Gemma; she was struggling to breathe through fear and adrenaline.

Gareth was in the garden, smoking, when Gemma returned to the kitchen. Judy was fussing over bruised apples and hadn't noticed the marks around Gemma's neck – or, at least, she hadn't mentioned them. She must have known her husband was a pervert, but she lived behind a veil, pretending to the outside world that her life was perfect. She clearly thought she was attractive, as she strutted around with her neat bobbed hair, although her thin lips, covered in orange lipstick and set in a permanent smirk, did little to enhance her looks.

She was always disgusted with one thing or another; that was how she made herself feel better about her own dismal life. She was born middle class and into inherited money. Gareth wasn't; he had money but not the position in society his wife had. It was all pretence with Judith. She didn't know how to survive any other way, so she turned a blind eye to what was really going on and stepped outside the front door dressed in a suit and shrouded in arrogance.

Once the food had been put away, both girls dashed upstairs and into Cassie's bedroom. Cassie was only fourteen then. She was taller than Gemma and probably more intelligent, which possibly explained why she hadn't got into so much trouble with the authorities. But, although very different personalities, they would look out for each other, living in the house of tension.

"He fucking grabbed me, Cass. He dragged me into the kitchen and shoved his dirty hand down me drawers. I swear on me life, he was gonna rape me. Oh my God, if you two hadn't come home when you did, I think he would have, honestly I do, the fucking ol' pervy cunt."

Cassie sat on the edge of her bed, her mouth wide open.

"I gotta go, Cass, I can't live like this. I swear, it's gotta be safer on the fucking streets than in this scary dump."

Cassie looked at the floor. "I'll come wiv ya, 'cos if you ain't 'ere, he'll come after me."

Gemma shook her head. "Nah, you won't be able to hack it. I did it before, remember. I was younger then. It's hard." She looked around Cassie's room and at her childhood dolls and grubby teddy bear.

"Look, I'll stay for a while, but we stay together, right? I can't be left alone with that creep."

Relieved, Cassie clung to Gemma. They lay on the bed together, not speaking, listening to Gareth and Judy arguing. Both girls had a lot to think about.

The following evening, Gemma put her glad rags on. It was an outfit she'd stolen from a boutique in Clapham – easy pickings, being as there were no cameras. She'd been thrilled when she'd got home and noticed the price tag: two hundred pounds. With her hair curled and an extra layer of mascara on her lashes, she was ready to skip down the path and into the flash car waiting outside. Gareth was working late and Judy was slumped in the armchair. She must have taken sleeping pills again.

Bobby was dressed in jeans and a white shirt. He opened the door for her, complimenting her on her dress as she slipped onto the front seat. She was trying to act older; she needed now to look more sophisticated. She remembered Tracy had said he dated women his own age. He must have known she was younger, but she decided if he asked she would tell him she was eighteen. But he never did ask.

The first date was impressive as he pulled out all the stops. They arrived at a plush restaurant and were greeted by two waiters; it was obvious they knew him by the fuss they made. The small cosy booth was classy with high-backed white leather seats and a crisp white tablecloth. The champagne was brought over in an ice bucket and served in tall champagne glasses. She remembered the meal like it was yesterday. She ordered the same as him, not understanding the French menu, and the food was certainly stunning and presented like a piece of artwork. Gemma was aware that there were a few people craning their necks to see her. She sussed out early on that the customers were loaded but not posh. She didn't realise, though, that they were gangsters and they only treated Bobby with respect because of who his brothers were.

They finished their meal. Gemma was a little tipsy from the champagne when they went on to the nightclub. The *Cat's Whiskers* was a club in Streatham, nothing too glamorous by any twenty-year-old's standards, but Gemma, being a lot younger, had only ever dreamt of being old enough to dance in a club and drink champagne. The flashing lights, the long bar, the pretty girls, and the attention Bobby got, were thrilling. To top it all, he only had eyes for her. Other girls tried to flirt, almost dismissing her, but he turned his back on them and kissed Gemma, showing everyone she was his girl.

The weeks that followed were spent in each other's company. She loved the attention and he loved showing her off. The gifts and meals were all a lead-up to getting her in the sack, but she was just as ready for it as he was. She was taken to parties and nightclubs and no one batted an eyelid. Her new outfits and tamed curls gave her a more mature appearance. She even learned to walk with more grace. She was living the dream and excited to be caught up in this whirlwind romance.

Meanwhile, back at home, Gareth's advances and sick comments increased; she couldn't pass him in the hallway without his hands skimming over her body. The kitchen was a fearful place, and Gemma would only ever go there if she was with Judy or Cassie.

One evening, after a night out with Bobby, Gemma was asleep in her bed when something stirred her. She thought it was a fox and tried to drift back off to sleep, but having drunk half a bottle of champagne, her mouth was dry. She gingerly opened her door and tiptoed downstairs, careful not to wake anyone, especially him.

Downstairs was in total darkness as she crept lightly into the kitchen. The moon was full and the kitchen window allowed some light to fall on the table. She shuddered. There was a glass on the draining board and quickly she snatched it and ran the cold water. Her thirst was so great she gulped down the icy water, unaware he was lurking in the shadows. Suddenly, she heard him breathing. Too afraid to move, she froze to the spot. She was standing there in nothing but a T-shirt and knickers, almost totally exposed. He never spoke, but she could sense him there somewhere behind her. For a second, she hoped it was a burglar, which would have been less frightening. In an instant, he lunged towards her, gripping her mouth, and showing her the knife he held in his other hand; she didn't have the chance to turn around. Her muffled squeals amounted to nothing. She dropped the glass, but as it fell into the sink which was full of water, there was only silence as she struggled. He never said a word but that cold sharp knife against her throat spoke volumes. She couldn't move; she was paralyzed with fear she was going to die. He thrust her face down onto the kitchen table.

"Scream and you're dead." His voice was a terrorising whisper.

She didn't scream or move as she was too afraid of dying. He was rough and angry and it hurt, but she still wouldn't make a sound. When he'd finished, he whispered, "There's plenty more where that came from," and then he was gone. He was clever; she couldn't scream rape, there was no proof – he'd worn protection – and she had no evidence. Besides, who would believe the girl with the scars up her arm and the girl who had accused the warden at the children's home of trying to touch her up? He had, though, even though no one believed her. "A self-harmer with psychological issues," they'd said.

112

She returned to her room and packed her things. In the morning, once everyone was out of the house, she called Bobby from the new mobile phone he'd given her.

"Can you come and get me, Bobby?" Her voice was flat and resigned.

"What? I've just woken up. Gemma, can I see ya tonight? I got work to do, but I'll pick you up at seven. We can try out the new Italian on the High Road." He had no idea.

"No, don't pick me up here. Meet me by the ice rink," she replied.

"Yeah, see ya later." Too tired to think about the low tone of her voice or ask what was going on, he turned over and went back to sleep. Gemma looked at the large suitcase and sighed; she would have to take the bare essentials.

She crept into Cassie's room and gazed around at the teddies and dolls; she was so neat and tidy. She would miss Cassie, her little foster sister. They had been through such a lot together. The first foster home was a nightmare; the woman was a slave driver. They were put together again in the next one but that didn't work out and so Gemma ran away. But it was only a few months later before she was picked up and put back into a children's home. Finally, they both ended up with the Williams, Gareth and Judy. A tear trickled down her face; she hated leaving Cassie behind, but she had no choice. He'd raped her and she knew he would do so again with every chance he got. The thought of leaving her a note was too unbearable; instead, she sneaked out of the house with just a holdall and headed for Streatham High Road.

She could have stayed in the house – no one was there – but the mere possibility that Gareth might return put the fear of Christ in her. She never wanted to see his face again.

October weather was so unpredictable; the wind whirled around the buildings and whistled through her thin cardigan. She wandered down to the café, contemplating how she would ask Bobby if she could move in. His shower of affection lately had been enough for her to assume he would agree. The hours ticked by slowly. No one was around to pass the time with. Her phone didn't ring, and she guessed that she would just have to be patient and wait until seven o'clock. After her fourth coffee, she left the café. She sat on the wall where they planned to meet, feeling cold; her bum was numb. Waves of tiredness crept over her, for she hadn't slept the previous night.

Bobby was late and her heart hammered in her chest as her mind ran away with her: something must have happened as he was always on time. Then, suddenly, she saw his car in the distance. He swerved alongside the kerb with a beaming smile. She loved his radiant face, the sleek cheekbones, and the gentle blond waves, which gave him a look not too dissimilar from a younger David Beckham. He always looked bubbly and fresh. She often wondered what it was that gave him such a completely untroubled expression. Throwing her holdall over her shoulder, she jumped off the wall and skipped down to the car.

His face lit up when she fell into his arms. "It's so good to see ya, Bobby."

Bobby was taken aback. "Yeah, all right, girl. I only saw ya yesterday. What's the matter with you, ya divvy?" He laughed affectionately.

"Bobby, can I stay with you?"

114

"Yeah, of course. Got ya overnight bag, I see."

Gemma misunderstood; she took his answer as *yes, forever*, but he meant just for one night. He drove them home and they decided to stay in, order a takeaway, and then watch a movie. Gemma was in her element; she stood in the kitchen and washed up the plates like she already lived there. Bobby took no notice. He was enjoying his bottle of brandy and a spliff. They spent the rest of the evening in bed, both too tired to have sex – much to the relief of Gemma, who was still feeling sick at the thought of what had happened from Gareth's evil hands. By the time morning arrived, they had both slept like babies and were wide awake by eight o'clock.

Gemma held on to Bobby, absorbing the warmth that radiated from his tight, muscular body. This was the life: no more looking over her shoulder, no more high-pitched moans from Judy, and no more misery. She could be a wife, and perhaps, in a few years, even a mother. Her Bobby was a good man, he treated her like a princess, and his flat was a dream home … what could be more perfect?

"Come on then, Gem, get yaself up. I've got work to do. I'll drop you off at your home on the way."

She froze: *what does he mean, drop me off at my home? This is my home.* She wanted to cry and then the realisation hit her; he'd meant stay over for the night, not for good.

"Bobby, do you like me here with you?" She tickled his back.

"What do ya mean, Gems?" He turned around to face her.

"Can I move in?" She'd said it now; her heart pounded, hoping he would say yes.

He laughed. "Gems, we've only been seeing each other for a few weeks. I ain't into settling down, babe. Besides, you're too young …" His voice trailed off.

Her world then just fell apart. She had misread all the signs. Fucking hell, she was just a temporary girlfriend – nothing more than that.

"Gems, don't look so disappointed. I never promised anything. I like me own space."

She was nodding, but inside her heart was dying. She braved a fake smile.

"Look, I like taking you out, ya make me laugh, you're a good kid. I'm quite proud, having you on me arm. I know you're young, but you ain't a silly tart. I like ya, Gem, but I don't have the headspace for a permanent fixture in me life. Know what I mean?"

As those words whirled around in her head, she felt heartbroken; how stupid was she? He hadn't led her up the garden path. She was just too young to know the difference. *My own stupid fault.* She kept up the fake smile, then said, "Yeah, ya right, Bobby. We would suffocate each other. Nah, it's nice what we got, and you make me laugh an' all."

"Great, right, get your arse in gear. I gotta see a man about a dog."

She knew then that her life would be on the streets. She couldn't go back; she couldn't live in fear and suffer more violent attacks from that bastard ever again.

She had been so terrified when Gareth raped her. Knowing he would do it again, believing he was going to kill her, she concluded the streets were her best bet.

The first night, Gemma stayed at King's Cross; it was safer than on the streets in Streatham. Daisy, an old tom, touting for business, saw the girl huddled in a corner. She looked too clean and fresh to be treading on her toes. She reminded Daisy of herself, thirty-five years back, escaping the children's home, and huddling against the wall, trying to stay warm, in that exact spot. She'd been around the same age, and she'd only wished that back then someone decent had come to save her. Instead, she'd been offered a couple of quid for a blow job. All these years on, there'd been a price increase for a blow job, but she was still touting for business at King's Cross station.

Gemma had her phone perched on her bag. She'd put it there, hoping Bobby would call, having had a change of heart. She wrapped herself in her fake Burberry coat and let the tears flow. She was a nobody here. The twenty quid she had in savings was dwindling away. She watched the late night city slickers make their way, half-cut, into the station to catch the last train.

Daisy kept one eye out for her last punter and one eye on the kid.

A fat man, balding, dressed in a grey mac and carrying an umbrella, approached Daisy. Gemma watched as he whispered in the woman's ear. They laughed and then they walked away to the hotel across the street.

Gemma was sitting with her head in her hands; she was almost afraid to look up. The chill was biting into her bones and she shivered, knowing it was going to be a long cold night. She was tired but sleep was not an option. Who knew what would happen if she drifted off? The idea of going home crossed her mind, but only for a second, and she dismissed it; she couldn't handle the terror.

She listened to people still wandering around. London never really slept; maybe she was safe, and there were too many people for anyone to hurt her. Weariness made her sleepy and she closed her eyes. Eventually, she drifted in and out of sleep, and so she didn't notice two men in their early thirties, right by her side, until one of them bent down to steal her phone, which was still perched on her bag. As soon as the man snatched the new mobile, Gemma sprang from the ground and grabbed his arm. She wrestled with him, but he laughed and threw the phone to his mate. Not content with doing this, however, he then punched her in the side of her head.

"Fuck off, ya dirty whore!" he spat.

"Give us back me phone, ya cunt, or I'll call the Ol' Bill!" she screamed.

"Ha ha, fuck off, tramp, it's my phone now. Go and suck a few more cocks and get ya own one!"

They ran off down the street, laughing. She turned around to grab her bag and found that someone had stolen that too. In no time at all, the street was empty, as if she had entered a different world. Stripped of everything, her belongings, her dignity, and now her lifeline to Bobby, and too tired to walk all the way back to Streatham, she curled in a ball and huddled herself in the corner. Too numb now to cry and too cold to sleep, she waited for the morning to arrive.

The shivering was relentless and her teeth were chattering non-stop when Daisy appeared. At least Gemma guessed it was the same woman, but this time she had on a tracksuit.

"What you doing, my love?" She bent down and gently tugged Gemma's arm. "Come on, girl, let's get you warmed up with a nice hot cup of cocoa."

Gemma was frozen to the bone and shattered. Slowly, she got to her feet and allowed the woman to guide her across the road and into the warmth of the hotel. It certainly wasn't five star; it was probably only one and a bit. She didn't care, though; she just wanted to get warm. They walked up three flights of stairs, turned the corner, walked again along a corridor, and then stopped at a red door. Daisy turned the key and kicked the door open. "Come in, lassie, let's get ya sorted."

Gemma liked the woman's accent; she was a northerner, with a croaky fag voice, but it was soothing just the same.

"Do ya live here? Um—"

"Daisy, that's me name, and yeah, it's not much, but it's homely. It's just how I like it."

Gemma gazed around the large room. It was odd. Despite it being a hotel, the room was more like an apartment. It was basic and old-fashioned but also warm and cosy. A double bed was pushed up against one wall, and on the other wall was a fireplace with a long settee covered in crocheted blankets. Gemma could just make out the small room next to it, a tiny kitchen, and a door into the bathroom. The carpet was faded, but clean, and a golden glow emanated from a lamp.

"Right, then, let's get warmed up with a cup of cocoa. You sit yerself in front of that fire and warm ya bones."

Daisy flicked on the side switch and the electric bar instantly glowed red. Gemma almost wanted to climb on top of it, she was so

119

cold. Daisy was humming some old-fashioned tune and got busy making a hot drink. It wasn't long before she returned with two large steaming mugs.

"There you go, my lovey. You drink that, and you'll be warm in no time."

Daisy sat on the armchair and wiggled her toes next to the fire. Gemma wanted to laugh. There she was, in a stranger's flat, drinking hot chocolate, and yet for the first time in her life she felt at home. She curled her feet around herself and smiled at Daisy. "So, is this your gaff, then? 'Cos it don't look like a hotel room."

"Yeah, I got lucky. Stanley, the maintenance man, he's been 'ere for years. He condemned this room and let me have it. I done it up meself and made it into a bit of a home." She laughed. "He's good is old Stanley. He reckons when we're old we can run away together. I don't have family and neither does he. We always spend Christmas together. Yeah, every year we do that." She smiled, looking into space.

Gemma was warming to the old girl and bemused that she was so matter-of-fact.

"So, what's yer name, kid?"

Gemma was wide-eyed and suddenly full of dread. The woman could call the police, and for sure, she would be returned to Gareth and Judy.

Daisy laughed again. "It's all right, lovey, we all have a good reason why we're running away. I did, years ago, so I ain't going to ask questions. I'll just call you Autumn. There now, that's quite a nice name."

Gemma giggled; she was right, as it was quite sweet.

"Right, lovey, you get yerself into that bed over there. You look dead beat. Get some shuteye. No one will disturb you. I'm shattered meself."

The double bed looked inviting, but Gemma was hesitant. "Where you gonna sleep? I mean, I don't wanna take your bed."

Daisy smiled. "I don't sleep in it anyway. I got a bad back. This sofa serves me well enough."

Gemma looked at the bed and without thinking she said, "Is this for ya punters?"

"Cor, Autumn, you ain't slow in coming forward." Daisy looked at the young girl and laughed but not at her. "No, lovey, this is me own home. I don't do business from home. They pay for a hotel room, usually downstairs. Anyway, I don't want you thinking I'm an old brass. I'm a high-class call girl."

Gemma wanted to laugh out loud. She remembered how Daisy had looked, standing out there in a skimpy black miniskirt, showing her mottled legs, and a fur coat that really should have been binned. Her hair was dyed red but the colour had faded, and her red lipstick had bled into the lines around her mouth.

"Me name's Gemma, and I really appreciate this. I don't have any money, though, to pay ya."

Daisy got up from her seat and pulled back the covers. "'Ere, lovey, get in there, and I didn't ask for money. I just wished someone would have helped me when I first arrived in the Big Smoke. I remember being out all night alone and fecking freezing. So you just get your head down and sleep."

121

As Gemma clambered in, she let Daisy tuck the blankets under her, as if she were five years old. Not that she ever remembered being tucked in. The relief of lying in a warm bed and being off the streets was enormous, and with peace of mind, she soon drifted off to sleep.

With a heavy sigh, Daisy pulled out her bottle of vodka and gulped back a large mouthful. She sat staring at the young girl and then contemplated calling a contact of hers. This would make her a stack of money; Jimmy Ruthers wanted a young tearaway for himself. He pimped his girls, gave them digs, but worked them hard. Most were on crack and couldn't run from his clutches. He was raking it in; he had them on the game as young as thirteen.

Gemma was snoring softly, and as she turned over, her arm flopped down the side of the bed. Daisy noticed the scars: the kid was a self-harmer, like herself. She screwed the number up and threw it in the bin. She hadn't done much good in her life but that was about to change. The kid was like her when she was younger: she was a runaway, a self-harmer, probably with no family, and so she wouldn't see her end up on the streets. Daisy wanted to kick herself for even thinking about calling any of the Ruthers.

The sun shone in through the blinds and Gemma stirred. She was in such a deep sleep, she hardly knew where she was. But then she saw the settee, and the crocheted blankets, and remembered. After tiptoeing into the kitchen, she put the kettle on and then turned to face Daisy, who was still crashed out on the sofa, clutching an empty vodka bottle. Gemma went to the bathroom to freshen up. She was in the kitchen when she heard Daisy say, "'Ere, don't you go robbing all me best china."

Gemma giggled. "Do ya take sugar in ya tea?"

"Yeah, three, please," she replied, trying to sit upright. "Cor, that's a first, having a brew in bed and me not having to make it."

Gemma handed her the tea and sat in the chair. "Thanks for last night, Daisy, really kind o' ya."

"Yeah, well, I might be going soft in me old age. But, besides that, there's talk of a serial killer around these parts. Slicing the girls up, he is. He's a right butcher from what I hear. I didn't want you to be his next victim. I couldn't live wiv meself."

The thought made Gemma shudder.

"Ain't you scared? What if he nabs you?" she asked, still shocked.

"Naw, not really. I've had me day. Don't s'pose he would want to wreck my face. I did that on me own, just growing old, walking them there streets, getting weather-beaten. I should have used more moisturiser ... still, there's a lesson learned. Don't you forget to slap that cream on every night."

Gemma looked closer at Daisy's face; she *was* wrinkled. Then she stared down at her feet; they had walked the streets all right. She noticed the hard skin with cracks as wide as a five pence piece and grimaced.

"Right then, lovey, I have to go out, get a bit of shopping. I guess you're gonna stay a while ... well, until ya get yerself sorted, like?"

Gemma's cheeks flushed. "Are you sure? I mean, can I stay for a while? I won't be here long. It's just that I can't go home. Once my Bobby finds out, I'm sure he'll sort me out."

Not wanting to pry, Daisy nodded and smiled. If Gemma needed to talk, then she would do so in her own time.

"'Ere, why don't I go shopping? You can stay in here, enjoy your tea, and I'll be back in a jiffy."

Daisy looked her up and down. "Yeah, go on, then. I guess I can trust ya with me hard-earned cash. Pass us me purse." She pointed to a cracked leather bag, which had been out of fashion since 1967. Gemma noticed then just how worn-out Daisy's things were. From the tea cups to the curtains, nearly everything in the room consisted of old-fashioned colours and designs – red and orange circles and diamonds. It was like stepping back in time and yet it was also very comforting.

After handing Gemma fifty pounds, she reeled off a shopping list. "Now, then, make sure the butter ain't that fake shit, proper butter, mind. And none of that sliced bread. I wanna real loaf."

Gemma was nodding, taking it all in. She slipped her shoes on and wrapped the Burberry coat around her shoulders, as she was eager to do Daisy a favour in return for saving her. Well, that's how she saw it; Daisy had rescued her from probably being sliced up by the serial killer.

Outside, the picture was different: workmen, tourists, and business suits, marched in all directions. She felt safe and was now on a mission. The one thing she was good at was thieving. She'd learned from a young age, as young as nine, she could pinch from under a shopkeeper's nose. The older kids in the home showed her how to steal all sorts of stuff, and if she had a twenty pound note she could con with illusion by numbers and gain a tenner. Not many people knew how or could grasp the art, but she did, and she could do it well. Her schooling was of no interest to her, except for maths; she could have passed a degree if she'd taken the time and hadn't messed about so much. Gripping the two twenties and the tenner, she went straight to the nearest newsagents. However, she immediately spun on her heels when she noticed it was run by an Asian. The con never worked on them; they always had a keen eye when it came to money going in and out of their hands. Then she spotted a bakery where two young girls were working behind the counter. *Easy pickings*, she thought to herself and it was. She walked out with an uncut loaf and an extra tenner. Within an hour, she had all the shopping and still the fifty pounds shoved in her pockets. Then she went to a clothes shop; it was busy because of the fifty per cent off sign in the window. She grabbed two sweatshirts, placed one over the other, when no one was looking, and went off into the changing rooms. The shop was buzzing with people and the assistants were rushed off their feet. She tried on the sweatshirt, removed the tags, put her coat over the top, and handed back the other sweatshirt still on the hanger. Just as she went to leave the shop, she noticed some rather pretty pink and fluffy slippers, just begging to be taken, sitting in a basket. With a furtive look behind her, she very quickly grabbed a pair and slid them inside her jacket.

Flushed and out of breath, she hurried back to the flat.

"Cor blimey, lovey, I thought you'd run off wiv me retirement fund." Daisy laughed.

Gemma hurried inside and placed all the shopping in the kitchen, including an extra bottle of vodka, and then she handed Daisy the fifty pounds back, plus the pink fluffy slippers. "'Ere, these are a present, ya know, just to say thanks for last night."

Daisy looked at all the money in her hand and then gazed at the slippers. "What's all this?"

"For you." She smiled, pleased with herself.

"But I thought you had no money?" She had her head cocked to the side.

"You give me all that money. I'm good at a con, so I know how to make more than I was given. I'm not good at much, but I have a head for sums and I can chore." She felt safe telling Daisy.

"Aw, lovey, yer didn't have to do that, but these are beautiful, just my sort of thing. Oh, and they are so comfortable," she said, as she slipped her sore feet into the expensive fur-lined slippers.

Daisy shuffled into the kitchen and began making bacon and eggs; that bottle of vodka might have knocked her out but it had left her slightly heady and ravenous.

Gemma looked at the pictures on the wall. One was a faded print of a tiger, walking into a lake, and the other was a copy of Constable's *The Hay Wain*.

On the melamine sideboard sat a few balls of wool, knitting needles, crochet hooks, and knitting patterns. Gemma's heart went out to Daisy. She was working the streets to survive, and yet underneath the tarty clothes and red lipstick was an old lady just wanting to relax and knit like grandmothers used to do.

"'Ere yer go, Gemma, a nice bit of egg and bacon. That should hit the spot." They sat in front of the fire and devoured the fry-up. Gemma was right at home and wished she had a mother like Daisy; even if she was selling her arse, she still would have been a good mum.

"So, lovey, did you wanna tell me what brings you to this part of London?"

Before she knew it, Gemma was telling Daisy everything. She was more like Daisy than she realised. The old girl had once been in her exact shoes but it was her stepfather who had molested her. He had done so for years apparently until Daisy was old enough to make a run for it.

"So what about this fella, Bobby?" she asked, showing a keen interest.

"Oh, yeah, he's lovely. I do love him. His name's Bobby Ruthers, and he's got his own place, but he says it's too soon for us to live together—" Gemma stopped in mid flow and frowned. "What's up? You look like ya seen a ghost."

"Did you say Ruthers?"

Gemma nodded with a beaming smile.

"Does he have brothers – Charlie, George and Jim – and a mother called Violet, by any chance?"

Gemma's face changed. *Why is Daisy looking so concerned?* "Yeah … well, I know he has a brother called George and another called Charlie. I ain't met them, though. Apparently, they're inside. I'm not sure why, but Bobby says they'll be home in a few years. Do you know them, then?"

Daisy knew them all right. All the toms at King's Cross knew them. And they paid well for rounding up teenage runaways to lock up in their flats. Daisy had had that phone number for years and never called it, although she had been very tempted to do so last night. Her punters were few and far between nowadays. What man wants a session with an old has-been when there's young flesh on offer? She couldn't charge the money the other girls did. It was really the old guys or those who wanted a taste of an old bird. It was hard going, spending hours on her feet, just waiting for a punter to pay her a quick score and hoping it didn't come with a black eye.

"Well, I know of 'em. Far be it from me to stick me oar in, but are you sure ya wanna be mixing with the Ruthers? Only they're dangerous men without scruples. I don't know about this Bobby fella, personally, but the old woman, Violet, is a nasty piece of work. As for her other sons, well, yer best off keeping away." Daisy paused, took a deep breath, and sighed. "Ya might as well know, the Ruthers 'ave their dirty fingers in many pies, including running whorehouses." There, she had said it; now it was up to Gemma to decide what her future would be.

Gemma chewed the inside of her mouth. Bobby hadn't mentioned his mother; he hadn't mentioned much about his family at all. When she came to think of it, she didn't really know much about Bobby. They had only very recently started dating each other. They went out, ate, drank, and partied. She didn't even know what exactly he did for a living. There was never any mention of whorehouses; he just didn't look the type, whatever that was. However, she still loved him. Her mind wandered and she wanted to cry. He wouldn't date her now, not with her being homeless, with no clothes and nowhere to get changed into her once beautiful outfits so he could show her off.

"Yer miss this Bobby of yours?"

Gemma nodded. "Don't know what I'm gonna do, Daisy. It's a bit of a fucking mess all round, really."

"Listen to me, lovey, you're a good girl. You may have had it rough, but don't go down the slippery road to self-destruction. I had no choice at your age. I knew no different, and for me to survive … well, I had to sell meself. You, though, you can stay here, get yerself a job, and find a good man, not a bad one."

Gemma looked sad and she asked the ultimate question. "Please be honest with me. What are the Ruthers all about?"

The tape recorder suddenly stopped and the clicking sound caused Gemma to look up and face Francesca.

So far, so good. This part of the story she didn't have to act or put on a sad expression, as it was true, and her emotions were real. Francesca was buying it. Well, who wouldn't? she thought.

CHAPTER SIX

Francesca stared at Gemma. Her face had crumpled, her pain clear to see, and she assumed then that there was much more to the story than had been told in court.

"So, Gemma, was that true? Did you try to hang yourself and did you try to kill your husband?" Her tone was soft and caring.

Gemma snapped out of her daze and shook her head. "No, I didn't try to kill myself. It was the last thing I wanted to do. It's true, I swear. Bobby was trying to kill me. He put the rope round me neck. He wanted it to look like I had just committed suicide all because he knew I was going to expose his family's secret."

Jamie interrupted; his face was expressionless and his tone stern. "So how did you manage to stab him if he was, as you say, trying to hang you?"

Gemma looked from Francesca back to Jamie. She so wanted them to believe her. They were her last hope of getting out. She looked over Francesca's shoulder. In a flash, Francesca spun round to find Sandra glaring through the glass in the door.

Francesca jumped to her feet and almost ripped the door open. "What do you think you're doing? I'm interviewing my client and this is a confidential visit. Your behaviour is causing me some concern. I'll have this matter recorded with the governor. Now, I suggest you get away from the door. In fact, you can fetch us some refreshments."

Sandra was almost knocked sideways. No lawyer had ever spoken to her in such a way. There was something about this one. She unnerved her; she sent shivers up her spine and put an uneasy feeling in the pit of her stomach.

Francesca returned and sat down. Composing herself, she asked, "Now then, where were we? Oh yes, you were about to tell us about how you attacked your husband."

Gemma's eyes filled up. "I didn't attack him. It wasn't like that at all."

"Well, Gemma, in your own words, tell us how it was." Her voice was reassuring and Jamie noticed that Gemma responded better to Francesca than to him, and so he sat back and let her continue.

"He pinned me down and slipped the nylon rope round me neck and pulled it so tight I could hardly breathe. Then he pulled me up the stairs like a dog on a lead. That rope was tearing into me throat. I thought I was gonna die. I was in shock. He wrapped the other end around the bannister and tried to push me over. It was terrifying. The man I had loved was going to kill me. He was really going to hang me." Tears rolled down her cheeks and she stared into space.

Francesca listened to Gemma's words and for a second she was in her shoes – her own husband had done the same to her. He'd tried to kill her. At that point, she assumed that Gemma was telling the truth. "Go on, Gemma," she said, and patted her hand.

Jamie was scribbling notes when the door opened. Without knocking, or waiting to be asked in, Sandra stomped over to the table and plonked the tray of tea down.

Francesca looked up and smirked. "Thank you. That will be all."

Gemma continued. "Eventually, I was too weak to fight, and he was strong. That's when he threw me over the bannister. But, luckily for me, the rope was too long, and I managed to land on me feet. I don't know how I managed to pull that rope off over me head before he tugged it tight again. But once I was free, I ran to the kitchen to escape through the back door. By then, he'd jumped down the stairs and he'd grabbed me hair. It was then I saw the carving knife, and as he threw me to the floor, I had the knife in me hand. He didn't see it, but as he jumped on top of me, that knife went straight through the side of his chest. He couldn't have felt it at first because he still managed to punch me in the face. Then he dragged me up by me hair. It was then that I stabbed him. He fell back against the table, clutching the knife. It was embedded in his side. I ran as fast as I could to the phone box and called the police. I thought they would believe me but they didn't. Instead, they arrested me, like I was some kinda murderer, just because Bobby was worse off than me. They even dismissed the marks around me neck. He was stretchered off in an ambulance and I was carted off in a meat wagon. Then, I ended up here on an attempted murder charge with GBH. No one would believe me, though. No one."

Francesca remained serene. "Gemma, I think we need to hear the full story. I'm going to continue to record this. Do you mind?"

Gemma shook her head.

"Okay, now I want to hear about when you met back up with Bobby because you obviously married him."

It was so hard to talk about Bobby now. She wanted to talk about the good times, about how loving and kind he was then, but all she saw when she thought of him was a monster — a cruel, heartless devil. She lowered her head and continued her story with the sense that it was all going to plan.

Gemma had listened and hung on to every word Daisy had said that day. As the weeks rolled on, she felt healthier and comfortable living with Daisy. However, she missed Bobby so much she was pining for him. Even though Daisy was good to her, and she felt at home there, the excitement and attention she got from Bobby was like a drug; she craved it. Eventually, she convinced herself that Bobby was not like his brothers and that's probably why he never spoke about his family. One day, when Daisy was visiting a friend, Gemma got up and dressed, fussing over her make-up and hair, and left the flat. She didn't intend to stay away; she was just going to pop over to Bobby's and explain her situation. She had a gut feeling that he had probably moved on with another woman, but she felt she had nothing to lose. She had some money of her own now, having chored a few bits that she'd sold to Daisy's mates.

She caught the bus and headed back to Streatham. The new estate looked gloomy. It had been late autumn the last time she was there and now it was winter and a cold one too. She pulled her new winter coat tighter round her waist and looped the scarf one more time round her neck. The stop was a few minutes' walk away from his flat. She jumped off the bus and searched her bag for a fag; nerves were making her feel nauseous. *What if he has a woman with him there in the flat; what if he shuts the door in my face?* It was no use: she had to find out if there was a life with Bobby. So she carried on walking. The cold wind made her eyes water and she swore out loud. The air in her lungs was burning from the icy chill. Suddenly, she saw his car parked in the reserved parking space and her heart leapt into her mouth. She looked around the corner of the building and there was his bike too; he must be in.

Stubbing the fag out, she popped a piece of chewing gum in her mouth and nervously climbed the stairs. She hesitated before she knocked. There was no answer, so she knocked again. This time she heard a groan coming from inside and then his voice calling, "Who is it?"

Not wanting to shout through the letter box, she knocked again.

"Unless you got money for me, ya can fuck off." With that the door opened and there was Bobby, standing in his boxer shorts with his hair flopping forward. He was half-asleep and rubbing his eyes. Gemma wanted to run into his arms but she remained calm and smiled nervously. He didn't smile back. It was awkward. He just stared; there was no invite in, no falling into each other's arms, and no tears of joy.

"Can I come in, Bobby?" She smiled sweetly but underneath she was crying.

He lifted his chin and looked over her shoulder. "Yeah, s'pose so, just for a minute. I gotta get to work."

She shyly crept inside and almost jumped when he slammed the door behind her.

"I missed ya, Bobby."

"Ya could 'ave fucking fooled me." He spun around and glared at her. "You caused me no end of trouble. I had the fucking filth crawling all over me pad, following me day and night, all because you went and did the off. That sister of yours, Cassie, told the Ol' Bill I was your fella and they fucking wouldn't let up."

Gemma was shocked; she had no idea. He could see the look of surprise on her face.

"So, where d'ya go, then?" His voice was cold.

She looked at the floor. "I'm sorry, Bobby. I had no choice. I had to go. That pervert raped me. I couldn't go back." She started to cry. Once the tears started rolling down her face, he softened.

"Babe, why didn't you tell me? I would have bashed the cunt!"

"I wanted to tell you, but I didn't want any agg. That's why I asked to move in with you. But ya said no. I couldn't go back, so I run away—" She was trying to catch her breath. "Then some bloke nicked me phone, and I couldn't even call you to say where I was."

He grabbed her arms and pulled her close to him. "Ahh, babe, that must have been terrible. You should have just called a taxi and come back to mine. I could have sorted you out and got ya somewhere to stay. Me brother has flats all over. Ya could have had one of them."

Gemma stiffened. He still hadn't offered to take her in. Maybe he hadn't missed her; maybe she'd been nothing but a few dates – no more serious than that. After what Daisy had told her about his brothers, there was no way she would be beholden to them. And those flats held nasty secrets – young prostitutes hooked on drugs.

"It's all right. I got meself a place in London."

Bobby smiled. "Well, if you're sorted, great. Anyway, look, I've gotta go to work. You can wait here for me to get back or—" He stopped suddenly and looked quizzically at her.

This was awkward. She wiped her tears away and suddenly felt a great distance between them. She was going to have to ask him

136

directly. This time there would be no fannying around. "Bobby, do ya love me or was I just a bit of fun?"

He looked at the floor and then back at her. "I dunno, babe. I thought I did. I was worried sick when no one had seen you. Then the Ol' Bill started questioning me. They backed off when they discovered your suitcase was packed at your foster home, and by all accounts, they reckoned you have been a runner in the past. They said you have psychological issues, cut yaself, and shit like that. I guess I thought that I wasn't important enough to you because you would have come to me. So I moved on."

Gemma was gutted and it showed. The tears streamed but she didn't care. She loved him and wanted him. The idea he had met someone else was ripping her in half. "Is she nice, then?" was all she could say.

Bobby frowned. "What? Who ya on about?"

"Ya said you've moved on," she cried.

Bobby laughed. "Nah, I mean I got meself stuck into a few projects, shall we say, taking over me brothers' business for a bit and learning the ropes."

Suddenly, her spirits lifted; if he wasn't seeing anyone else, then she stood a chance.

"Did you miss me, though, Bobby?"

He looked at her soft skin and wide childlike eyes and smiled. "Yeah, I s'pose I did." A generous smile lit up his face and all the tightness left. He was her Bobby again. That sexy look he always gave her. He ran the back of his hand down her cheek. "Yeah, I missed ya. That's why I was so annoyed. I didn't want to miss ya. I didn't want to feel like that. No one's ever bothered me before. I guess I let me feelings run me head." He pulled her close and kissed her with so much passion her limbs felt weak, and she vowed never to walk away again.

"Shall I come by tomorrow, or have you got work?"

He laughed. "Babe, I got work every day and some nights. As I said, I have to look after me brothers' business while they're away, but I'll always have some time for you. Why don't you wait here until I get back and then we can go out for a nice meal or a few drinks … wha'd'ya say?"

Gemma was nodding. She would have stuck her head in the oven if he'd asked her to. Right now, she was so excited he hadn't given up on her, she would do anything to keep him.

She followed him into the bedroom and watched as he got dressed, admiring his tight muscles under his white T-shirt. He moved with so much composure and control. She was in love; there could be no one else. The sideways glances and winks gave her butterflies. He was such a good man that Daisy must have got it wrong about the Ruthers. If they were so wicked, then Bobby was an outcast because in her eyes he was a soft, gentle-natured man, with eyes that sparkled and melted her heart. He treated her with respect too. Unbelievably, for a man of Bobby's reputation, he had yet to take her to bed. Okay, they had had a few quick fumbles but nothing full on. But she didn't mind. She truly believed she was literally 'Bobby's Girl', to quote the song, and for her that was all she needed right now.

She knew he was not legitimate, as he always had a bag of gear to flog. In the clubs, he made sure she had a seat and a drink, and if he was doing business he would look over and wink every now and then, making sure she was all right. He could dance too and always pulled her on to the dance floor and finished off the evening with a slow one. She was impressed and proud; wherever they went, he knew people. No one stopped them going into the clubs or questioned her age. She was surprised how he could jump to the front of any queue and walk straight in. The bouncer would smile and pat him on the back. To her it was thrilling, and she was part of it, as she was always by his side with his arm around her shoulder.

"Right, my Gems, I won't be long. Make yaself comfortable and I'll be back in a few hours." He kissed her passionately again and left.

The hours ticked past, so Gemma cleaned the flat and sat watching the TV, when suddenly there was a key in the door. She jumped to her feet, ready to greet her man, but was shocked to find two big women and a skinny man bowling through the door. The older of the two women looked particularly scary as she focused her dark beady eyes on the young girl before her.

"Oh, for fuck's sake," she said, "he's had one of the girls in the flat. Right, girl, has he paid ya? 'Cos ya need to fuck off now."

Gemma frowned. "What, sorry, who are you?"

"Lenny, get her out. We've only got a few minutes," the woman shouted.

Gemma took a step back. "Who are ya and what ya doing in me fella's flat?"

The younger woman, who looked identical to the older woman, laughed. "It looks like our Bobby's got himself a bird. Hop it, love."

"Bobby told me to wait here for him. Who are you?"

The older woman stepped forward and her beady eyes bored into Gemma's soul. "You best do one," she spat coldly.

Lenny stepped forward. "Are you that Gemma bird?"

She nodded.

"Well, Bobby's been nicked, so no point in you hanging around." His words were as cold as the big woman's. Gemma was full of mixed emotions: she was particularly angry that these three were talking to her like that but also afraid they were telling the truth.

"Oh, shit! What's he been nicked for?"

The older woman cocked her head to one side. "None of your fucking business. Now fuck off!"

Gemma put her hands on her hips and defiantly demanded to know who they were.

"I'm his fucking mother. Now, unless you want a right good clout, I suggest you get your skinny arse out of 'ere!" She was talking through gritted teeth. Gemma could not see any resemblance. This woman was fat and butt ugly, whilst Bobby was the complete opposite.

"Well, Bobby told me to wait for him here, so I'm not going anywhere." She flicked her hair and stared. As sweet as she was, Gemma could still stand her ground. Growing up in a children's home had taught her that much. She didn't take too kindly to bullies.

In a flash, the younger woman jumped forward, grabbed Gemma by the hair, and tried dragging her across the living room towards the door.

"Let go of me, you fucking bitch!" screamed Gemma, as she tried to battle with the woman.

"Let her go," said the man, "she's Bobby's bird. He won't be too impressed at you giving her a good hiding."

Suddenly, the woman let go and sneered at Gemma.

"All right, if you're Bobby's bird, then you'll know where he's hidden the gear," said his mother.

Gemma shrugged her shoulders.

"Now, you fucking listen to me, ya cocky cunt. The Ol' Bill are gonna swarm this place in a few minutes, and I need to clean it, or ya boyfriend's gonna serve a hefty lump inside."

It suddenly hit Gemma why they were there. She nodded and ran into the bedroom. She knew he kept a holdall under the bed. She never asked questions, but he was always going in it and taking stuff out. Violet, his mother, followed her in and watched as she dived to the floor and dragged the bag out. She unzipped it and almost gasped; inside were hundreds of packets of cocaine.

She slid the bag over to his mother. "There! Is that what ya looking for?"

Violet snatched the bag and leaned into Gemma's face. "Bad move, girl, I could have been the fucking Ol' Bill. Ain't Bobby taught you anything?"

Gemma smirked and decided to make an educated guess. "I knew ya were his ol' lady. You fit the description." She stood up and glared back at those cold, lifeless eyes. Violet was just how Daisy had described her: harsh, cold, and ugly. She should have been scared after the stories Daisy had told her but for some reason she wasn't.

She just saw a mouthy old fat woman. Little did Gemma know that this mouthy old fat woman was at the epicentre of one of the vilest criminal families in London.

"You'd better check the wardrobe. Make sure this is all of it, 'cos, girl, if the filth find anymore, then he's serving a long time." Gemma nodded; they had, as she thought now, an understanding. She almost ripped the doors off their hinges, searching for any bags or boxes. Meanwhile, Lenny ran out of the flat with the holdall, leaving the three women hunting through every cupboard and tin box. His sister was pulling the side off the bath, lifting rugs, and even searching through the cereal boxes.

"Right, come on, we gotta get out of here. The Ol' Bill will have his name by now," demanded Violet.

They hurried down the hallway and out the door. "Oi, you're coming with me," ordered Bobby's mother.

Gemma was caught up in a situation she really knew nothing about but thought it best to do as she was told.

"Wait! His car—" But they'd gone. She grabbed the car keys off the side and ran after his mother, slamming the door shut behind her.

Lenny was waiting in the car with his sister. Gemma followed Violet.

"'Ere, ya better check the car," she said and threw Violet the keys.

"Rita, get out. You're driving Bobby's car. Take it down to the garages. We ain't got time to search it. You!" She rudely pointed to Gemma. "Get in with Rita."

142

Gemma jumped in the front of the car and away they went, followed by Lenny and Violet.

Rita didn't speak to Gemma; instead, she was staring at the road ahead.

"So, what they nicked him for?" asked Gemma.

"A bit fucking nosy, ain't ya?"

"Well, he is my boyfriend," she replied, curtly.

"Yeah, that's what they all say. Look, love, just 'cos he's been giving you one don't make you privy to our business," she spat, her tone all vinegar and piss.

Gemma looked at the spiteful expression on Rita's face out of the corner of her eye. She digested those words, *our business*.

It was time she made a choice. After what Daisy had told her about their business, and it was now obvious Bobby was part of it, should she stay or go away and get on with her life without him? Dealing a bit of Charlie was okay, but she had morals and running a whorehouse was way off her moral compass. That was a world miles apart from her own. Sure, she might live with an old tom but that was different. Daisy was always steering her in the right direction, encouraging her to get a good job and even go to college. Daisy was kind and caring; she was a bit of a mother figure. Odd, really, that anyone would look up to a prostitute, but Daisy *was* someone to look up to; she never hurt anyone. In fact, the other girls on the street often popped in for advice or a favour. She was like a mother hen. She rocked them when they cried, she bathed their bruises when they'd had a rough punter, and she lent them money if their pimp was after them. All in all, she was a good person with a big heart. She thought about what Daisy would say if she knew she was in a car with Bobby's fat sister and off to stash away a load of drugs.

"It ain't like that. I ain't any old slapper, ya know. Bobby and I . . . well, we . . . ."

Rita laughed. "For fuck's sake, you're nothing but a kid, running after me brother, just 'cos he's a looker and got a few bob. Take my advice. Mix with kids ya own age. This is grown-ups' business."

Gemma was silent for the rest of the journey; she had a lot to think about. Maybe Rita was right. This was a whole different ball game and perhaps she should go back to being just a seventeen-year-old kid. Then her thoughts turned to Bobby; she loved him so much. Rita didn't know what they had but it was special.

They parked up behind the garages not far from Streatham High Road, and Rita pushed open the door, shuffling herself off the low bucket seat, mumbling under her breath. Gemma got out, too, not really sure what to do.

"Don't stand there like a long streak of piss. Get looking under the seat for anything." Rita was lighting up a fag and staring up the road. Gemma didn't argue. She searched around and found nothing but a box of Durex. Her heart was in her mouth. What was *that* doing in his car? Rita lifted the boot and peered in. She then ripped the tyre cover off and smiled.

She slammed the boot down and locked the doors.

"Right, now, where's that fucking drippy brother of mine?" Her voice was deep and harsh and just like her mother's. Gemma kept looking at her out of the corner of her eye; she was nothing like her Bobby. Lenny's car spun around the corner and pulled up alongside Bobby's car.

144

Violet lowered the window. "Well, get in, then."

Rita almost ripped the door off its hinges, she was so heavy-handed. Gemma stood, not knowing if she was meant to jump in too.

"What you waiting for? Get in, girl!" hollered Violet.

This was awkward and she felt uneasy. A few minutes ago, she'd been in Bobby's flat, watching TV; next, she was in a car with half his family, hiding his stash of cocaine.

They arrived at Violet's house and casually got out of the car as if all this was normal. Still unsure why she was with them, Gemma followed them up the garden path.

Once inside, Rita nodded for Gemma to go through into the kitchen.

"Get that fucking kettle on, Len, I'm parched," shouted Violet, who was shoving the holdall under the sink. "When ya made the tea, get rid of that fucking gear. Take it around Charlie's." She didn't speak with a feminine tone; it was loud, harsh, and hostile.

"All right, Mum," said Lenny. He seemed to obey his mother automatically, just like a robot.

Violet turned to face Gemma, who was standing in the middle of the kitchen looking totally lost and bewildered.

"You, girl, sit ya arse there. We have things to discuss."

Gemma pulled out the heavy wooden chair and sat down. Rita was already at the table. She had pulled out a make-up bag and was reapplying another layer of thick purple lipstick and fluffing up her mass of black hair. Even with fake tan and a ton of slap on her face, she still looked like a pig. There was something very manly about

145

both of them. Lenny, meanwhile, was pouring the hot water into a huge china teapot as if it were his job in life.

"Right, now tell me everything you know," ordered Violet, leaning forward and glaring menacingly into Gemma's eyes.

"Like what?" she replied, quite innocently.

"How did you know my Bobby kept that gear under the bed for starters?"

Gemma looked from one pair of beady eyes to the other. "I've seen him go in it enough times, so I assumed he had something in there, but I didn't take much notice until you arrived. Please tell me what he's been nicked for? I ain't being nosy." She looked at Rita. "I do care about him."

For a second, she thought she saw Violet soften. Instead, she grunted.

"Well, it's my guess that the coppers will be sniffing around you, and I would hate you to say the wrong thing and fuck him up. It's best you stay here until we sort this shit out."

Gemma shuffled nervously on her seat; she didn't want to even be in Violet's company, let alone stay in her house.

"I gotta get home. Don't worry about me. The Ol' Bill don't know where I live, and like I said, I don't know any more than I've told you." She got up to leave.

"Me Mum said—" Rita was gritting her teeth.

Violet quickly jumped in. "Gemma, I'd like ya to stay. If you're our Bobby's girl, then it would be nice to get to know ya. We can have a bit of dinner and you can stay in the spare room. Wha'd'ya say, babe?" Her voice had slackened so much that she sounded like a different person.

Gemma smiled and the tenseness on her face lifted; perhaps all the panic had put her nerves on edge and Violet really was a nice woman.

"Lenny, pour our Gemma a nice cuppa. She must be dried out. A bit of a shock seeing us burst in like that and banging around orders. Now then, babe, I should explain. You see, I got a call from one of Bobby's friends. They said they saw him getting pulled over by the police this morning, up Streatham High Road. Now, the thing is, I know me boy is a little bit naughty and likes to earn himself a little extra by selling some gear now and then. So if they found any on him, then they'll be in his flat like flies around shit. I appreciate you helping us, 'cos, ya see, if they found that stash, then he'd be looking at a long prison sentence, and you don't want that any more than us, eh?"

Gemma was nodding. "Of course not. I love Bobby. I couldn't bear it if he got locked up. He is all I got, really."

Violet smiled; the kid was so naïve and that's how it must stay. She knew only too well that if this girl had any idea of what was really going on, then one silly argument with Bobby and she could go singing like a canary to the Ol' Bill and they would all be fucked.

"So, wha'd'ya say?"

Acting impulsively, Gemma agreed to stay, but her mind was all over the place. She genuinely was worried about Bobby and nervous being in his family's company. She could tell that Violet was trying hard to be nice but it just wasn't her real character. She was a bit over the top.

Whilst she was sipping her milky tea, the back door opened and in walked two young black guys laden with what looked like huge long army bags.

"'Ere, Vi, where do you want these?" asked the tall one with the gold teeth and red Nike tracksuit. "Kappa, get the rest out of the car," he said to the shorter guy.

Violet pointed to the table. "Throw 'em on there. I wanna check this lot over. The last lot were fucking crap," she said, standing with her hands on her hips and a nasty smirk on her face. "I'll tell ya now, Kane, if I can't shift this lot, 'cos me reputation has gone to shit, then you owe me."

Kane looked at the floor; if ever a black man could go white, he did.

"I had no idea, Vi, I swear. You should have said. I would have taken 'em back meself and given me man a clump."

"I trusted you enough not to check. Me girls took the lot and flogged them, but in me name. Now I'll be after you if me customers have gone elsewhere. Got it, boy?" Her voice was scary and Gemma was stunned by the way the big, beefy black guy looked like he was shitting hot bricks.

Violet stared at Kane.

He nodded. "Got it," he said and then he left.

Gemma was intrigued to know what was in those bags.

Kappa hurried in, but he tripped over the doorstep, and the bag he'd been carrying came flying through the kitchen and hit the chunky dining table. He jumped to his feet to grab the bag before all the

148

contents fell out. It was too late. Rolled bundles of twenty pound notes spewed out of the opening.

"Get out, ya fucking clumsy cunt!" spat Violet. He instantly turned and left. Rita was annoyed that he had jolted the table and her nail varnish had been knocked over.

"For fuck's sake!" she hollered.

Lenny grabbed the bags and carried them out of the kitchen, leaving one of the bundles by Gemma's feet. She saw it out of the corner of her eye, swooped down, and picked it up. Sounding more confident than she felt, she called out, "Lenny, 'ere, you left one."

Violet was watching and waiting for Gemma to ask nosy questions but was pleased that she didn't. There was no surprise or excitement on Gemma's face; she returned to her cup of tea as if this situation might be a normal occurrence. Of course, Gemma was playing a game. She was shocked but played it cool, as if she had seen it all before.

"So, Gemma, where do you come from, then?" asked Violet. She was intrigued to know if she came from a known family.

"Nowhere, really. Children's home, foster care, all that shit. I ain't got a family, only Bobby."

Violet watched her expression and concluded she was just a kid who had seen a lot. She could see why Bobby liked the girl; she had a pretty face and a neat body with a personality that was far from dull. Secretly, she liked the way the girl stuck up for herself. There was an innocence, though, probably because she was still a teenager.

"So our Bobby must like ya, then? He kept you a secret." She grinned.

Gemma nodded. "He said he did. We've been dating for a while. He's a good man and we never argue."

Violet was intrigued by Gemma. She was so full of life. Her face lit up when she spoke about her Bobby, and as she did so, she flicked her long waves and her big round eyes came alive. She listened to Gemma chatting about the laughs they had and the places he took her to and concluded that Gemma was too attached to allow her to stop the relationship. There would be repercussions.

A few hours later, after more tea and random chitchat, the back door opened. To everyone's surprise, it was Bobby.

Gemma jumped from her seat and flung her arms around his neck. "Gawd, I was worried to death."

Bobby was surprised to see her there and glared at his mother. Judging by her flared nostrils, she was clearly in an agitated state.

"So, boy, what happened?"

He kissed Gemma on the cheek and sat down. He felt very uneasy and could have done without this added hassle. He had no idea how Gemma had got there or what his mother would think.

"Nuffin', really, I just got pulled over for speeding and then they started to search the motorbike. They found a bit of personal and took me down the cop shop."

Violet was frowning, "But Jimbo said—" She stopped. All Jimbo had said was that Bobby had been stopped on his bike and taken away by the Ol' Bill. "Never mind," she said. "So what happened?"

"They gave me a ticket for speeding and confiscated me puff."

150

Violet was uneasy; she knew that was odd. The police would love to nick any of her sons.

Bobby turned to Gemma. "So, what ya doing here, Gems?" His tone was friendly.

"She showed me where ya stash was and helped us clear it out in case the filth wanted to raid ya place. Helpful girl, your Gemma," said Violet, before Gemma had a chance to speak.

Bobby smiled nervously. The last thing he wanted was for his mother to get her hands on Gemma. He liked Gemma. She was sweet and innocent, and he didn't want his mother controlling her too. She was a free spirit. She'd been through enough in her short life, what with the cuts up her arms and the abuse from the man who was supposed to protect her. Now, here she was in the heart of his mother's house and ready for the chains to go on.

"Right, Mum, we're off. I got stuff to do." He grabbed Gemma's hand and made to leave.

"Wait a minute, boy, I wanna word with ya in the living room." Violet gave him a fake smile that turned his stomach. Both she and Rita stood up, and the younger woman couldn't resist sneering in Gemma's direction.

She didn't like the pretty young girl; jealousy was a big part of her personality – a very dangerous trait.

Bobby's shoulders slumped, but he did as he was told, leaving Gemma alone in the kitchen.

The door was slammed shut, but their voices were so loud, Gemma could hear them.

"Are you fucking stupid or what? You know the fucking rules! No birds, no strings, and no fucker is s'posed to know where ya live. So, boy, you've just broken all three. There I was, thinking you were up to the job. I promised George you could handle it, but nah, ya fucked up. If you fancied a young bit of arse, then Charlie's got plenty on his books; ya could take ya pick. And, my boy, how do you know she ain't a plant?"

Gemma listened, hanging on to every word.

"'Cos she didn't go after me, I went after her. She's just a kid. She ain't got a clue what my business is. She might think I deal a bit, but that's all, I swear to ya."

"Well, my boy, you made ya bed, now you best lie in it. If she's what ya want, then ya best wed the girl and make sure she keeps her mouth shut, or ya'll have us all nicked. I mean it, son; you keep her in your sight at all times, and don't ya dare tell her anything. If she thinks ya just a small-time coke pusher, then make sure it stays that way. I dunno, you got a lot to learn. From now on, you keep ya head low, no more flash cars, bikes, or anything else. You know how it works. Selling ya hooky clobber is small-time, and that's what you need to look like: small-time. Got it?"

There was silence again. Gemma wondered whether to sneak out of the back door. What she'd heard made her shudder. Then, it was too late; the door opened and they all returned to the table. Rita was glaring at her with a peculiar sneer.

"Sorry about that, sweetheart. I was just giving me boy a few choice words." Violet smiled.

Gemma nodded; she wanted to get out of the house and away from Bobby's mother and fat sister as soon as she could.

152

Bobby grabbed her hand again and said, "Come on, Gems, let's go." He looked at his mother and choked down his fear as she smiled at them both with a knowing and eerie grin.

"'Ere. Ya forgot ya keys." Rita threw him the bunch and laughed. "It's parked behind the garages."

Bobby gripped Gemma's hand and walked her out through the back door and along the garden path. Suddenly, the back gate opened and there stood a tall, slim, and very attractive woman, dressed in a classy but tight-fitting dress. Her thick fair waves bounced off her shoulders as she walked with a confident stride and a smile on her face. Gemma guessed she was a relation of Bobby's because she had his big round eyes.

"All right Tress?"

The woman nodded. "Nice bit o' skirt, Bobby, you have on your arm." She winked and continued on.

That was the first time she had laid eyes on Tressa, the younger sister.

The drive back to the flat passed in silence. Gemma was going over in her mind the words his mother had said. Suddenly, as they reached the flat, his voice made her jump. "I'm fucking starving. Fancy an Indian takeaway?"

Gemma snapped out of her thoughts and nodded. "Yeah, then I gotta get off home."

"Oh, babe, I thought ya might like to stay the night. Ya know, watch a movie, early night ..." he winked.

She wanted to run back to Daisy and think things over, but that sexy smile of his lured her thoughts away and sucked her in. He was kind and sweet. They were good together, she thought, so maybe marriage wasn't such a bad thing. After all, she wouldn't be marrying his mother, and she could talk him into perhaps moving away, getting a good job, and playing happy families.

He held her hand as they entered the flat. "I'm gonna take a shower and wash the fucking stench of the Ol' Bill off me. Why don't you wash me back?" he whispered in her ear and then kissed her neck.

She could never resist his advances. He knew how to handle a woman.

Although she'd been nervous their first time when they'd caressed each other in the dark, which had amounted to nothing much, she quickly relaxed when he gently touched her skin. His kisses were slow and his hands were tender. Her previous experience of sex had been either at the hands of the warden in the children's home or a messy fumble with one of the local lads, but she had never gone past second base before, apart from when she was cruelly raped by Gareth. So when Bobby kissed every inch of her body, in-between loving words, she was ready for him. Her legs shook and she felt a warm burning sensation that ached for him to be inside her. That first time she climaxed was like nothing on earth. She was addicted and wanted it more.

She knew she had to please him. Her friends had told her he was used to older women. So one night, after they had been out for a meal and consumed quite a few glasses of champagne, she dived on him. Ripping her clothes off and unzipping his flies, she knelt on the floor and held his cock in her hand, ready to give him a blow job. He sat up, a half-smile on his face, and said, "What ya doing, Gem? No, stop it. Babe, if I want a freak in the bed, I'll pay for it. Don't do this. It ain't you."

Gem was dumbfounded; she assumed all men liked a rough, wild woman bouncing on top of them, sucking the life out of their dicks. At least, that's what she had heard. "Don't you like me, Bobby?"

"Yeah, babe, but you're my girl, not some ol' tart. You're clean and sweet, just how I like my girl to be. Acting like that makes me think you're used to it and you've jumped on other blokes' bones."

Gemma was embarrassed. "Nah, I ain't, I just thought—"

She was prevented from saying more as Bobby placed his fingers over her soft and warm lips. He pulled her off the floor and held her close. "Ya just acting like an old tom, Gem. I need you to be just you, so don't try to be different."

"I thought all men liked that sort of thing. Sorry, Bobby, I was just trying to please you."

He stroked her hair and gazed into her eyes. "I ain't all men, babe, and I like it as it is. You ain't no cowgirl. I get my pleasure from you, not from some fucking nutty sex act."

They stepped into the shower together and she looked at his well-defined body, which had not an ounce of fat on it. She loved his hair when it was wet and the dripping curls just added to his sex appeal. His eyelashes looked even longer and she melted as he kissed her neck. She always did; it was like an injection of a drug. Even as he held her up against the cold tiles, he was still gentle. She could never have imagined him any other way.

A week later, Bobby had a call and was off to his mother's. Gemma hadn't been back to Daisy's and was fed up with washing out the same pair of knickers. She needed to go and get her belongings and face the music. As soon as he was out of the door, she got dressed and headed back to King's Cross.

155

As she entered the hotel, she felt comforted. Shirley, one of the regulars, smiled and ruffled Gemma's hair. She'd just left a punter and had a huge grin on her face. She waved a few twenties under Gemma's nose. "Touch," she said and laughed.

Instantly, Gemma felt at home. The hotel might be old and tatty but the feeling was comforting.

She knocked on the door gingerly and shuffled her feet, knowing it was awkward. Daisy answered, looking haggard.

"Gawd, girl, I've been worried sick about ya. Get inside."

Gemma smiled; she liked Daisy fussing over her.

"Where yer been, lovey? That evil face slasher has had another one of the girls and I had visions of you lying dead in a ditch."

"I'm sorry, Daisy, I didn't realise. I didn't expect ya to worry about me." Gemma was genuinely surprised.

"Sit down. I need to talk to you. I can guess where ya been. But forget that, I need you to listen to me. Those Ruthers are bad news. I thought you would stay away after that conversation. My guess is, he's drawn you back in. I know you think you love him, but trust me when I tell you, they are more dangerous than you could ever imagine."

"But—"

"No, let me finish, babe. I can't give you anything but my experience and advice. Yesterday, a kiddie, a young girl called Lindsey James, was found dead in some flat. They found her decomposed body. She'd died, choking on her own vomit after a drugs overdose. Now, I know the Ruthers ... well, Jimmy Ruthers, to be precise, was responsible. That kid came from a good home. Her ol' man was a copper. She weren't a runaway, she was a bit like you – liked the excitement of the fast life. She got caught up with those scumbags and ended up on heroin. Evil powder, that is. From what I've been told, that ugly bastard, Jim, was after her for himself, and the only half-decent woman that would touch him with a bargepole was one high on drugs or desperate for a score. Now then, that Jim was supplying the pretty kid, and she's now dead. Imagine that, Gemma, alone in a derelict flat, fucked out of ya head, and choking to death on ya own vomit. Imagine, Gem, her poor father's face, when he had to identify the body. Now do ya see why I want ya to stay well away?"

Gemma was wide-eyed and pale. "Jesus! That's fucking terrible."

Daisy eased herself off the chair and went to the kitchen. "I'll make us some tea, while you think on."

Gemma watched Daisy swan off in her 1970s negligée and the fluffy slippers she'd bought for her. She wanted to laugh; it was surreal. There she was sitting in an old tom's flat, unchanged since before she was born, hearing horrific news about her boyfriend's family, and she was still almost unmoved.

"'Ere ya go, girl, drink that tea, and think seriously about that, 'cos, mark my words, Gemma, you'll be next, if ya get involved."

"Bobby's different, though. Honestly, he's kind and sweet, and I know he would never hurt me. If he offered me drugs, I promise you, I would say no."

Daisy put down her cup and stared at Gemma. "I'm not yer mother. I can't tell you what to do. You owe me nothing. What you do is your business, but I couldn't live with meself if I didn't tell ya what those Ruthers are all about."

Just as they were ready to tuck into some of Daisy's homemade ginger cake, Gemma's favourite, there was a loud bang at the door. "Daisy, quick, I need ya help!" called a desperate voice.

Daisy jumped to her feet and pulled open the door. There stood Shirley, trying to hold up a woman who was foaming at the mouth.

She grabbed the girl's other arm and between the two of them they carried her in and laid her on the bed. Gemma was shocked to see the girl in that sorry state.

"Turn her on her side. Get that vomit out," hollered Daisy. Shirley knelt on the bed and tipped the girl over whilst Daisy bashed the girl's back.

"It's no use. It's not going to work. We need to get her on her feet and get her adrenaline pumping around her body. If she don't come around soon, fully conscious, then we need to call an ambulance."

They struggled to get the lifeless girl to her feet, but it was no use. Her limbs were limp and her head drooped. Gemma was frozen to the spot, gawping at the girl, horrified to see her sunken eyes and bruised body. She had been beaten badly and horrendous bite marks were clearly visible. She shuddered and felt vomit rise up in the back of her throat. She was witnessing a girl on the brink of death. The colour was disappearing from her face and there was nothing they could do to help. Gently, they laid her lifeless body back on the bed.

Daisy was kneeling beside her and Shirley brushed red curls away from the girl's face. It was then that she took her last breath. They all stared in silence.

Gemma spoke first. "Is she dead?" She couldn't accept she'd seen someone die.

Shirley turned to her. "Yep, we couldn't save her. That brute did this. I hate him. If I had the guts, I would run a knife right through his chest."

"Where did ya find her, Shirl?" Her voice was a mere whisper. Daisy leaned over the girl to get a closer look.

"She was in the safe flat. I went there to grab some sheets and I found her slumped on the floor, the poor little prat. Another one … she was only sixteen. My God, that family have a lot to answer for."

Gemma's hands flew to her mouth. That girl was younger than her and yet she looked at least thirty. Her hair was beautiful, long, and curly, but her body was ruined. The skimpy red dress only just covered her arse and tits. The black and blue marks, the scabby lips, and those dark circles around her eyes, made her a sad sight to see. Gemma's eyes teared-up.

"Who do ya reckon did this to her?" asked Gemma.

Daisy threw her a harsh look and Shirley mumbled under her breath, "That cunt Jim Ruthers. Cor, I hope he gets his comeuppance one day soon."

Gemma gasped. Those things Daisy had told her weren't exaggerations; she believed her now.

"Right, Daise, we best call Stanley. He can take her outside and call the Ol' Bill. I can't do it, me name's mud down the station already. Come 'ere, Gem, give us a hand. We need to get her outside, love her heart."

Gemma was almost heaving from shock and disgust. "Me? But I've never even seen a dead body before, let alone touched one!"

"Gawd, gal, get over here. She's still warm. It's just like she's asleep. Help us get her outside."

Gemma was shaking. This was madness. The poor girl had died right there in front of her eyes and now they wanted to move her body out of the room. She suddenly jumped into action. With all her strength, she lifted one half of the body, whilst Shirley held the other, and Daisy peered outside the door.

"All right, girls, no one's about." Daisy took the girl's shoulders and the three of them shuffled along the hallway to the end flat. Daisy kicked the door and it flew open. Hastily, they carried her body inside, laid the girl on the bed, and left, hurrying back to Daisy's flat.

"Whose room is that, then?" Gemma asked.

"That's our safe flat," said Shirley. "We use it if we get in trouble. It's strictly out of bounds to the punters. We all chip in once a month and any one of us girls can run there and hide. Sometimes, they lay low if their pimp's after money or if a punter's acting weird. Poor little cow must have dragged herself there before that heroin kicked in. I dunno, it's all fucked up. Maybe I should hang up me silk drawers and turn it in."

"Not just yet, eh, Shirl. Yer might have to flash them in front of our Stanley when I ask him to deal with that poor girl's body."

Whilst Shirley sat gently on the sofa and took a deep breath, Daisy phoned for Stan to come up and help them. Gemma looked at the younger woman and in some respects she admired her. She was good-looking with long legs and clear skin. Her face, although heavily made-up, was attractive, and compared to the others, she didn't really look like a hooker, except for the tiny skirt and tight buttoned-down vest. She liked Shirley and often sold her the best bits she chored – after Daisy had had first pickings, of course.

160

"Yeah, I don't mind. He ain't like the others. He's a kind man. He's always looking out for us, bless him."

There was a gentle tap at the door and Daisy jumped to her feet. "That'll be him," she said.

Stanley was seen by the prostitutes as caring and trustworthy and he was surprisingly eye-catching for a man of fifty-five. The endless heavy maintenance work of the old crumbling hotel kept him fit. He put Gemma in mind of an older version of Richard Gere with his grey neatly layered hair and soft eyes. He loved his job and had worked for the hotel for many years. He lived on the top floor and rarely ventured outside King's Cross; his work kept him busy and the girls kept him amused. He wasn't there for the freebies but a little play now and then suited him since he wasn't married. The girls loved him and flirted all the time; he was a bit of a father figure in some respects, watching out for them as much as he could.

He stepped inside and peered over at Gemma and Shirley, shaking his head.

"Are you sure the girl's dead?" he asked with a sad expression.

"Oh, yes. She stopped breathing and there was no pulse. We bashed her back and tried to get her to her feet, but there was nothing—" Shirley's voice cracked, unable to speak. "That poor kid. Only fucking sixteen she was. My God, what a fucking way to go, eh?"

Stanley sat on the sofa next to Shirley and placed a meaty arm around her shoulder. "Listen, love, you did all you could. Sometimes heaven is the best place."

Shirley blew her nose and nodded. "I know, Stan, being in the clutches of those Ruthers must be like living in hell, especially Jimmy, evil cunt that he is."

Daisy was watching Gemma's reaction, hoping that some of this was sinking in enough to keep her well away from the Ruthers.

To her surprise, Gemma spoke up and in her innocence asked, "So why don't the police arrest him? Why don't anyone report what he's doing?"

Stanley smiled. "Ahh, Gemma, if only it were that simple. Those monsters have too many people on their side. Take their lawyer, for instance. He ain't just a lawyer, he's a judge, hooked on cocaine." He laughed. "Imagine that, eh? The pinnacle of high society, snorting his face off. Anyway, along with the legal system, they have heavies – nasty bastards they are. One word to the Ol' Bill and then next minute you get carted away, locked in a room, and jacked up with shit, followed a week later by an overdose and left in the streets to rot. Nah, they're getting away with it, and there's fuck all we can do. And it wouldn't surprise me if that serial killer, the face slasher, ain't Jimmy, the dirty bastard."

That should have been enough to have stopped Gemma from going near the Ruthers ever again. Gemma had planned what she was going to say on the journey there, and not without a deep ache in her heart, as she was trying to use her head for once. It was a case of heart versus brain, and the latter, for the moment, was winning the day. She carried that lump of regret for her lover in her throat and sadness in her belly, but what she had seen and heard that day would never be forgotten. She honestly believed she would end up the same way. It would be hard, but she would eventually get over Bobby.

So she left that evening with the firm intention of telling Bobby that it was over. It didn't work out that way though. As soon as she knocked on his door, he was there, dressed in a suit, and with a huge smile on his face. He was excited and hurried her into the flat. "Come and see, my angel, what I got for ya."

"Look, babe, I know you ain't got any clothes, so I bought ya a new wardrobe." He was skipping around the bed, pointing to all the outfits laid out there. Sparkly dresses, designer jeans and tops, Jimmy Choo shoes, and a Prada handbag. Her eyes widened. He did love her and he cared. She gazed in wonder at the boxes and gifts; it was unbelievable and everything she could possibly need was there and so much more.

"Gem, you don't have to run anymore. Your home and life is here with me, and I'm gonna make you happy: you watch. You're gonna be by my side like my little princess."

Suddenly, he got down on one knee and presented her with a small, dainty white box. She opened it and her hands went to her face in astonishment. The diamond on the ring, which was inside, certainly wasn't small and dainty. She was definitely no expert on the value of any jewellery, let alone a ring, but this little gem must have set Bobby back thousands. "I was gonna wait until we reached the restaurant, but I can't. Please marry me, Gemma?"

She was still in shock and wonderment. His eyes gazed up at her, twinkling like the diamond. She nodded. "Yes, of course I will."

So the heart won after all.

CHAPTER SEVEN

Immediately, Francesca stopped the tape and got up from the chair to walk around the table. There was silence as she paced the floor. Jamie watched and felt concerned; she suddenly looked pale and almost vulnerable.

Gemma looked down at her lap; it was hard reliving the past. The tears trickled relentlessly down her face because she had sat there describing the good part, the part where she really and truly had loved Bobby, but she was young back then and so naïve. She was to find out for herself what they were really like though.

Francesca took a couple of deep breaths and looked up at the clock. Time was running out. The interview would be over in a few minutes and there were so many questions she had to ask. There were too many coincidences, too many paths crossed, and too many personal emotions being stirred up. Nevertheless, she had to remain calm and continue.

Slowly, taking a seat, she took Gemma's hand and with sadness in her eyes she said, "I know this has been painful for you, but can you give me Daisy's second name? And do you remember the name of the lawyer – the one working for the Ruthers?"

"It's Daisy Burrows," Gemma replied, with no emotion.

Francesca's eyes widened. "And the lawyer?" Her heart was hammering in anticipation.

"What, the cokehead?"

Francesca nodded. Gemma appeared to be in deep thought. "I'm sorry, I don't ... hang on, it was Charles. I remember now, 'cos my Bobby used to have him on speed dial under 'Charlie boy'."

Francesca froze, and she felt the hairs on the back of her neck stand up. *It couldn't be, could it? But it must be: it was too much of a coincidence. All these years later and the bloody Enright family name keeps reappearing.* The thought that Charlie, her dead husband's uncle, was linked to the Ruthers – and Daisy Burrows had been a key witness in the court case against a young Italian man called Mauricio Luciani – was definitely too much of a coincidence. He'd stood accused of being the serial killer Gemma had been talking about. Francesca had won the case and got the man off, but she'd paid a terribly high price for achieving this, having been left horribly disfigured and requiring lengthy and costly plastic surgery, which had dramatically altered her appearance. And at the time of the trial, there had been no indication at all that Daisy was in some way connected to the Enrights through the Ruthers.

"Was it Charles Enright senior otherwise known as Charlie Enright?" She needed an answer.

Gemma raised her eyebrow. "Yeah, how do you know?" But Gemma was well aware of how Francesca knew Charlie Enright. Even so, she still had to play the innocent at this stage of the plan.

Jamie sat upright in his seat and looked on in horror at Francesca; he knew only too well how the Enrights had tried to destroy her. "Oh

166

my God, Sisco, is this a revenge kill—" He stopped suddenly, realising he had nearly let the cat out of the bag about Cassie's murder.

"What is it? What's going on?" Gemma could see there was something other than her predicament on their minds. *She now had Francesca's full attention, just as she had wanted*, she thought.

Francesca had turned white and she looked like she was about to collapse. "Listen, sweetheart, we have some terrible news." She edged forward on her seat and stroked Gemma's hand. "Cassie was shot dead yesterday after visiting you."

The tears, which had been trickling down Gemma's cheeks, were nothing compared to the sobs that followed the news, as the floodgates opened. She could hardly breathe for the heartache and pain. "No! No! No! Not Cassie. Please, God, don't let it be true, not her!" Her sobs were loud and heart-rending. Some of these tears were actually genuine, as Cassie had been a true friend in every way possible, and this shouldn't have happened. And given normal circumstances, her mind and emotions would have been far more sincere. But she, Gemma, had got herself into all kinds of high-end shit. She needed to play the game. *She should have auditioned at drama school with this kind of performance*, she thought.

They waited until the shock had passed and Gemma was able to look up. She saw the resigned despair on Francesca's face.

"Dear God, she was having a baby. She was only trying to help me get out of here to tell my story. Why did they have to kill her? I wish I had died now. I wish that rope had not been too long."

Francesca got up from her chair again and knelt down beside Gemma. She put her arms around her and rocked her like a child. "Listen, we need your help to find who did this and to get you out of here. Our new baby boy will want to know, when he's older, who killed his mummy."

Suddenly, Gemma stopped crying and sat up straight. "What? Her baby survived?"

Francesca smiled compassionately. "Yes, bless Cassie, she hung on to life just long enough for her son to come into the world. He's beautiful, and he'll want to have his Auntie Gemma in his life. So listen to me. You have to be strong and help me."

Gemma nodded furiously. Even with her face red and tear-stained, she showed determination. "I promise you, I'll do whatever you want, as long as I don't die in here first."

Jamie's face turned sour. "What do you mean?" he said. He was drawn in by the woman's story and felt for her. The sneers and sideways glances from the prison officer, Sandra, hadn't gone unnoticed, by him or Francesca.

Gemma was growing in confidence that the lawyers were on her side and for the first time she felt hope. "I don't know, but I get the feeling the screws and some of the inmates have it in for me. I've already been told by a few of them, the really nasty ones, that I'd be better off topping meself."

"Okay, listen, we're going to arrange another visit, so you just stay strong and try to remember as much as you can, anything at all. Even something that may seem trivial to you might not be to us. Oh, and one more thing. If the police come asking questions, you just say Cassie came to see you to tell you about the baby. Don't tell them about us."

Gemma was nodding. She would agree to do anything for this woman if it meant she could get out of this shithole. "My God, will they stop at nothing?" she cried out.

"Who?" Jamie was quick to jump in.

Gemma looked up and shook her head. "Bobby Ruthers, or, if not him, one of those other evil bastards."

"Do you honestly believe they killed her? But why would they?" asked Jamie.

She lowered her head. "Behind every bad thing in my life is a Ruthers' hand."

As soon as five fifteen arrived, Sandra was through the door and even more bolshie than ever. Francesca witnessed the sudden crumbling of Gemma's face. She really looked terrified.

"I want a word with you, in private," snapped Francesca.

Sandra glanced at Gemma and back at the lawyer and her throat tightened. "What about?" she asked.

Francesca raised her eyebrows. "It's of a professional nature." Another officer led Gemma away and Francesca closed the door behind them. Left alone with the lawyers, Sandra was nervous. She was used to having one up as a screw, but the female lawyer, in particular, was sharp, and right now she had no idea what to expect.

"I'm concerned for Gemma's safety. I recorded the conversation I had with her, and I'm going to record ours, too. Are you happy to continue on that basis?"

Sandra was worried; the lawyer was acting like a detective. She decided to brazen it out.

"Yeah, sure," she said. "What's the problem?"

It was obvious from her body language she was on edge. Francesca knew then that there was more to Sandra than just an officer doing her job. She had to be clever. She nodded to the chair and Sandra sat down. Jamie was admiring Francesca's confident tone and was glad they were on the same side.

"I've had a very interesting conversation with Gemma and I'm tempted to take the tape to the police." She paused and stared, watching the colour leave Sandra's cheeks. "So, between now and tomorrow morning, when I return to continue the interview with my client, I'm requesting that you personally ensure Gemma's safety and well-being. If I return to find that my client has come to harm in any shape or form, then of course your position and involvement will come into question. Do I make myself clear?"

Sandra was trying to pick out the meaning in the woman's words; had she actually said she had something on her? She wasn't going to take any chances. The blood was running wildly through her veins and she could barely speak. She nodded pathetically and got up to leave.

"I'm sorry, Officer McFee, I didn't hear your reply."

"Yes, of course, it's my job to ensure the safety of the inmates." Sandra tried to put on an educated, authoritative voice, but it sounded woeful compared to Francesca's ice cool professional tone.

Francesca smiled. "I'm glad you've taken this situation extremely seriously."

Jamie was laughing inside, but he kept his poker face well and truly on.

They booked the visit for the next morning and left.

The early evening brought some relief from the hot sticky weather but not from the turmoil of confusion spinning around in Francesca's head.

"Are you all right, Sisco?" asked Jamie, as they sat in the comfort of the car. She paused before she started the engine. "I guess ... but I thought the Enrights were dead and buried."

"They are dead and buried. At least we know two of them are here and one in the States. I think this is just a coincidence. Gemma was married to a man whose lawyer was Charlie Enright, who happened to be your former husband's uncle. Cassie's murder isn't linked. The only Enright left is William and he must be in his dotage by now, so they can't get to you. As I see it, those Ruthers are evil, and evil attracts evil. He probably had a comfortable set-up. They supplied him with cocaine and he kept them out of the nick. Nothing more to it than that," replied Jamie.

Francesca was in a trance. The whole story was too close to home. The serial killer they called the face slasher had been her former husband – it had to be. Surely? Once he was out of the picture, the killings had stopped. Yet, oddly, of all the prostitutes, Daisy Burrows had been the one to stand up in court and identify an innocent man, namely, Mauricio Luciani, as the one responsible for the killings. The Enrights had tried everything to get that Italian family behind bars. She shuddered. They were cruel and Jamie was right; they were evil. But Charles her first husband and Charlie Enright were dead. She did not believe that William would be keen to get back into this area of crime, but she couldn't rule it out. So was he involved in some way, and why would he or anyone else want to murder Cassie?

She noticed her phone, sitting on the dashboard of the car, and then saw all the missed calls. Her family were worried; she'd been out all day with no word as to where she had gone. After Cassie's murder, they would be worried sick. She dialled Dan's house number and in a second her mother answered.

"It's me, Mum. I'm sorry. I had business to attend to. I should have let you know, but it's taken longer than I thought." Her heart was in her mouth; the last thing she would ever want to do was cause any stress to her family.

"It's all right, love. Fred called Jamie and was told you went out together."

Francesca's heart melted. Her mother was so kind. Anyone else would have gone mad and screamed down the phone but not her mother. Francesca could hear crying in the background and a lump rose in her throat. *That must be the baby*, she thought. She had a sudden feeling of guilt; she should have been there for Dan. He'd been going to say goodbye to Cassie and pick the baby up at the same time. He was probably in a right state. She hurried back to the office, eager to get back to Dan.

"Are you coming in, Sisco?" asked Jamie.

"No, I have to be off, but Jamie, if you don't have plans for tonight, could you interrogate that database of yours and dig up anything and everything on the Ruthers and any Enright cases that have anything to do with them?"

"I was going to do that anyway. I'll see you tomorrow." He kissed her on the cheek and left.

As she pulled up at Dan's house, she noticed all the cars were still there. She was so lucky to have been born to a kind and loving family who stuck together through thick and thin.

No sooner was she through the door when Ruby jumped up to greet her. "Sisco, come and see our new baby. He's so cute, but he can't 'alf 'oller."

She entered the living room to find her mum bouncing the screaming baby. "I dunno what's up with the little mite. I just can't seem to settle him. We've all had a go," she said, with a half-smile on her face.

Francesca looked at Dan. "Are you all right? Did you go to …?" Her voice trailed off.

Dan smiled and nodded. "Yeah, she looked so peaceful." He got up and hugged his sister, whispering in her ear, "We will find who did this, sis, and I will kill them."

She hugged him tighter. "Yeah, Dan, I know, and we'll all be behind you. I promise you that."

"'Ere, Dolly, you have a go," said her mother. Francesca smiled. Even though she was a grown woman, they still often called her Dolly. In the family's eyes, she was still that precious china doll who had to go and live with her aunt all those years ago.

She took the screaming, wriggling bundle and walked over to the window. She had her back to her family so was completely unaware that they were gazing on with mixed emotions, Mary especially so. *Francesca would have made a wonderful mother if it hadn't been for that cruel bastard, Charles Enright.*

"There, there, little one," she said. Then she sang: "Hush little baby, don't say a word, Daddy's gonna buy you a mockingbird …" As she sang the song and rocked the baby, he slowly drifted back off to sleep. Bill was standing by the mantelpiece and a tear rolled down his cheek; he quickly wiped it away. Mary looked at her sons and they were all teary-eyed. She knew why. After all these years, it was still painful for them to recollect the terrifying ordeal Francesca had suffered under Charles Enright's evil influence.

Francesca kissed the baby's mop of black hair and gently placed him in the crib. "There, little boy, you were tired, that's all." She turned to Dan. "So, have you decided to call him Billy, then?"

"Well, as you know, Cassie wanted to name him after Dad. She had said that it would be right to call him Billy."

Bill wiped away another tear. "That was because she was still with us. But now she's up there somewhere with the angels, I think he should take his mother's name."

Suddenly, Joe spoke up. "What, Cassandra?"

It was the first time they'd all laughed for what seemed ages and it released some of the tension among them.

"Gawd help us, Joe. No, ya dope," said Bill. "Cass. I think that's a good idea. What do you think, Dan? It's got a nice ring to it, Cass Vincent."

Dan got up and peered into the crib. "Yeah, Cass Vincent. It's kinda special."

As the evening approached, they all sat together and ate dinner, carefully prepared by Maria. While there were bursts of small talk, no one broached the subject of what to do next. Even so, each brother glanced in turn at Francesca, knowing she had a plan. By nine o'clock, Bill and Mary had left to go home. They promised to be back first thing in the morning to look after Cass. He was the only thing holding Dan together now and he was a blessing that helped ease the pain. Joe called Belinda to take Sophie and Alfie home; from now on he wanted them with someone at all times. Jack, Ruby, and Kizzy left together in the same car. The Vincent family had the resolve to protect their own, by any means necessary, and they would exact retribution on those responsible.

The house was quiet. The brothers gathered around the table, placing a bottle of brandy and five glasses in the centre. Francesca took her seat at the head of the table and from her bag pulled out the tape recorder. She sighed. This device had been given to her as a present from her Aunt all those years ago, when she had started at the Enright's law firm. For some reason, she had an uneasy premonition about using it. But she wouldn't part with it, even though these days a modern digital recorder was the device of choice for busy lawyers.

"Dan, I'm sorry I didn't tell you yesterday, but I found a visiting order in Cassie's bag. She'd been to the prison that day."

He frowned. "What? Who the fuck did she know in prison?" It was as if he'd suddenly woken up from his grief. His sluggish movements and the glazed expression in his eyes were gone. Now he sat upright and his face was alive.

"A girl called Gemma Ruthers. I didn't want to say anything until I'd got all the facts. I recorded the conversation, so please just listen to it. I need your reassurance that I'm not going out of my mind and that everything you are about to hear isn't just a coincidence. If it's not, the reason Cassie was killed is the past coming back to haunt me."

The brothers all leaned forward. They guessed right away that Francesca's disappearance was to do with finding out who killed Cassie because nothing would be more important to her. It's just how she was. They hung on to her every word and now they would listen to the device.

The muggy, stifling weather over the last few days had come to an end. The thunder and lightning was relentless. Cass screamed, but he was easily settled in Francesca's arms. She gently rocked him, pacing the floor, whilst the men listened to the recording. Maria came in with a bottle and took Cass upstairs. She knew they had business and a screaming baby wouldn't help matters. He nuzzled under her chin and she breathed in the soft, sweet smell of innocence. As soon as she was in the rocking chair and the bottle was under his nose, he settled completely. A tear dropped onto his cheek as she gazed down at his tiny perfect face. It was unthinkable that anyone would be so wicked as to kill a pregnant woman. She could hear the faint sound from the recorder and hoped to God it held the key to whoever had committed this unimaginable crime. She, herself, would take a gun and shoot the cowardly bastard. However, she'd heard whispers about how Francesca was the ruthless one, and it wouldn't surprise her if the culprit soon came to an unsavoury end. She smiled.

Just after ten o'clock, the tape recorder stopped. Dan leaned back in his chair and took another gulp of brandy. Fred ran his hands through his hair and Sam was staring out of the window. It was Joe who spoke first. "D'ya think we should call the Ol' Bill?"

He no sooner had the words out of his mouth than Dan almost flew at him across the table. "You what? I'm gonna kill the cunt with me bare hands. Fucking call the Ol' Bill? What's the fucking matter with you!"

Francesca jumped in. "Hey, this ain't us. We don't fight each other, remember!"

"Sorry, bruv, I didn't mean to—" Dan stopped suddenly and sighed.

Joe's eyes glazed over. "I just can't handle the thought of anyone else in this family getting hurt, that's all. Our Cassie's gone, and we ain't getting any younger. But all that said, I'm with ya, always have been, always will be," he replied with a gentle grin.

Dan gave him a compassionate smile. "Sorry, Joe, I'm just so angry, so ..."

"We know," said Francesca. She turned to look at Sam, who was still staring into space. The others followed her eye line. "What's up, Sam?"

He snapped out of his deep thought. "Remember DI James? That girl she mentioned, Lindsey James, left dead in the flat. It was his daughter, and he thought all those years ago it was Charlie McManners. Maybe I should give him a call. He needs to know what's on that tape."

"Cor, he's gonna go fucking ballistic! I reckon we need to pay these Ruthers a visit," said Fred, fired up as usual.

"No, wait. I need to get to the bottom of all this. Tomorrow, I have another interview with Gemma. I couldn't push her for answers today. She was telling her story, but to be quite honest, I want to hear the full story – every fucking last gory detail. I want to know who they are and what they do, and why they hurt our Cassie, if it was them. I want to make sure we have the right person because if it wasn't the Ruthers, then who the fuck was it?"

All eyes were on Francesca. Her polite words had gone and she spoke with venom.

"Give DI James a call, Sam. Don't give too much away, but just test the water. Fred, find out as much as you can about the Ruthers, discreetly though, and you, Joe, make sure all the kids are looked out for. Tomorrow, I'll have answers, I hope, and we can make plans then. But for now, say nothing. From what Gemma's said, those Ruthers are a pretty reckless bunch. I don't want any of us walking in blind. Remember what I've always said when others confront us: knowledge is power."

They nodded. She knew best; she would devise a good plan – if anyone could, she could.

Francesca could hear the baby crying and she left the room to make sure he was all right. Maria was rocking him but he was wide awake and hollering.

"Must need another bottle," said Maria.

"Shall I go and get it? Is it in the kitchen?" asked Francesca, eager to help.

Maria smiled. "No, here, you have a cuddle and I'll fetch it." As soon as Cass was in Francesca's arms, he stopped crying. Maria looked over her shoulder. "You've certainly got the knack."

Francesca peered down at his round blue eyes; he was the sweetest baby she had ever seen. She yearned for a baby of her own but it was never meant to be. She was grateful that Sergio, her husband, was content with nieces and nephews to spoil. Cass was different; she felt a bond, somehow. Maybe it was because he was a new-born, and she loved him anyway because he was the new Vincent addition.

Sam decided to call Terry James straight away; it was late, but it had to be done. The phone rang with an overseas dialling tone.

Terry James was sitting on the plush couch in his luxury villa, courtesy of the Vincents, and was surprised when the phone rang. It never rang. He answered it instantly. "Hello?"

"Terry, it's Sam Vincent. Are you all right, mate?"

"Hey, Sam, yeah, I'm good, mate, and how are you?" He was not too upbeat, having sensed there was something wrong. There was a pause.

"Tel, we might need your help, mate."

Terry jumped up. The truth was he had longed to retire to Spain and had grabbed the opportunity with both hands when Sam had offered it to him. It had been a dream at first, lying by the pool, drinking wine, and relaxing, but he was perhaps too young to have retired from the force – he was bored. The endless books he read and the walks along the beach he took just didn't occupy his active mind.

"Anything, Sam, what's up?"

"Dan's wife, Cassie, was shot yesterday, shot dead in the fucking street, pregnant an' all. We need to find who did it, but there's more to this, and I hate to say it, mate, but your girl may have died at the hands of the same fucking killer." He took a deep breath, knowing this news would stir up feelings that Terry might have fought to bury.

"If you know who killed my Lindsey, then I'll do whatever I can to help. I've fucking wanted nothing more since the day she died than to get my hands on the cunt who did that to her. To be honest, I thought it was Charlie McManners, but if you think it's someone else, then mark my words, I'll do everything in my power to make sure

179

they never do it to another soul. Jesus Christ, is Dan all right? My God, how terrible, to lose a wife and baby. He must be devastated."

Sam was surprised by how in control Terry was. The last time he'd seen him was when he'd handed him the keys to his villa and said goodbye. He'd looked tired then and a little out of breath. "He's in bits. They managed to save the baby, thank God, but not poor Cassie."

Terry James was standing in front of the mirror. He looked different now. He was fit and ready to take on the world. The one family he would always be there for was the Vincents. He hadn't been involved with them as such, but he'd looked out for them, making sure Sam's wife served time, their clubs were signed off, and the case of the McManners' disappearance was closed. He knew they'd murdered them and the O'Connells. He would have killed those families himself if he hadn't been a detective inspector.

"Sam, I'm on my way. I'll go to the airport and be on the next flight."

"Call me when you get here. I'll pick you up. You can stay at mine or me sister's place in Kent."

Terry thought about their sister; he had never spoken to her, but he'd watched from a distance. He knew she was the one who led their pack as she had a confident persona and plus there was an edge to her he had never seen before in another living soul.

Sam had expected Terry to be emotional, and yet he concluded he was driven by finding his daughter's killer and was content that he would come over and help in any way he could.

Francesca said goodnight and crawled into the bed next to the cot. She lay there, staring through the bars at her nephew. He slept, content, but she couldn't. Gemma's story rolled around in her mind. Regrettably, it left her conjuring visions of her former husband again —visions, which over the years, she'd tried so hard to keep at bay. She would never be able to blank them from her mind entirely. It wasn't just the injuries she'd sustained but also that terrifying ordeal of having been left in that icy cold salt water, which had stung the injuries to her face and crotch, as she'd been dragged beneath those waves. How she'd been able to reach the surface and float for what had seemed like an eternity was beyond her capabilities to rationalise those frightening events. She'd been incredibly fortunate to have survived, she knew that. That fucking bastard had butchered her, thrown her over the cliff, and thought she would end up as fish food. Charles Enright, his uncle Charlie, along with William Enright, her father-in-law, had made her life a living hell, all because she'd won a court case she was supposed to lose. Her mind drifted to Sergio and his cousin Mauricio. If she hadn't got Mauricio off the murder charge, if he'd been found guilty of being the slasher serial killer, then her life would have been so different. She would also have lived a life of hell with Charles and his family. Who could she have turned to? They were the legal system – judges, barristers, and with enough police in their back pockets to run amok.

The fact that Charlie Enright was wrapped up with the Ruthers disturbed her. She tossed and turned, trying so hard to sleep. She needed to be on the ball when she questioned Gemma. Poor Gemma; she must be suffering too. Eventually, she drifted off, only to be woken by Cass whimpering. She jumped up and scooped him out of the cot, holding him close, and kissing his head. The bottle was placed by the cot. Maria had made one ready for the nightshift. Francesca was tired but caring for the baby was not a chore; it was a precious gift. She gazed at his tiny face while he sucked away at his bottle.

Eventually, they both drifted back off to sleep. By six o'clock in the morning, Maria had crept quietly into the room and for a second she stood admiring the perfect picture of Francesca cradling Cass in her arms as they both slept. Carefully, she removed the baby before he woke up Francesca. She knew they had business to attend to and wanted to help in any way she could.

By eight o'clock, they were all up, ready to face the day. Dan was sipping coffee when Francesca came down the stairs. She looked immaculate with not a hair out of place. His eyes were still pillowed from the endless tears he'd shed. "Sis, I appreciate what you're doing," he said.

She cocked her head to the side. "I'm only doing what we would all do. It's just the way it is. But I promise you this. I will find who did it, Dan, if it kills me."

As she looked at her brother's tired face, it dawned on her that he hadn't yet held his own baby; in fact, he wasn't showing much interest in him at all. She concluded he was just too preoccupied; after all, Cassie wasn't even buried.

CHAPTER EIGHT

Rita came into the kitchen, stretching and yawning. "Make us a brew," she said to Tressa, who was reading a copy of *Heat* magazine. She was gazing at a picture of Cheryl Cole, wondering if she could make her own face up to look the same, or if it was airbrushing which gave her that perfect look. As soon as she faced her sister, she wanted to laugh. Rita looked like something out of the horror movie *The Hills Have Eyes*.

"What ya gawping at, bitch?" spat Rita.

Tressa smiled. "Nothing," she choked, as she got up to put the kettle on. Christ, her sister was one ugly cunt. She favoured a hog. Without make-up, her narrow eyes almost disappeared, and her skin was mottled and pitted. The hairpiece, a long shiny black ponytail, was the only thing that made her look feminine. Without it, she was a fucking moose and could easily be mistaken for a man – and not a good-looking one either. Just as she placed the cup under Rita's nose, they heard a heavy thumping sound. Violet was up. *Another ugly pig,* thought Tressa. She secretly despised the pair of them; in fact, she hated all of them. They'd treated her like a slave ever since the Jimmy incident. She'd planned, many a time, to run away, but she knew they would hunt her down and kill her. They had no scruples, not any of them. She'd always thought Bobby was different and that he was like her. Bobby, Lenny, and her, all had the same father, whoever the fuck he was, which was why they were slimmer and had rounder eyes, unlike the other gross, repulsive bastards. She was wrong about

Bobby and Lenny, though; Bobby was just like them, and Lenny, the little shit, was getting too big for his boots, living in Bobby's shadow. The pair of them were flash, cocksure, and arrogant.

Violet sat down heavily. She was farting and grunting and stinking the kitchen out. Tressa handed her a cup of tea and smiled. Inside, she was laughing at the state of them. No sooner had she placed the box of biscuits on the table, than they dived in. The dipping and slurping was relentless. She wondered how Rita had time to breathe in-between mouthfuls. Her stomach churned; no wonder she was so skinny. The sight of them eating would put any sane person off their food for life. Eventually, they stopped and each lit up a fag. Identical, they were. Tressa concluded that Rita was the image of Violet's younger self.

Violet had raised them, all on her own, but she hadn't been a mother figure – more like a father figure. Tressa looked back over her younger years and it wasn't pleasant. She'd never wanted for anything, but on the other hand, she had missed the loving affection, which she had seen her school friends receive from their mums. She'd watched her mother fight her way through life. If Violet was angry, you got a bashing: man, woman, or child. She recalled the time about thirty-five years ago when she'd come home from school sick. She'd contracted hepatitis A. The vomiting was relentless and she'd crawled through the back door, hoping her mother would help her.

"Mum, I feel ill. I can't stop being sick and I ache all over," she'd managed to say. She was completely exhausted.

Violet was at the kitchen table with two men, talking business as usual.

"Yeah, well, what d'ya fucking want me to do? Go grab a bucket and get to bed." She'd returned to the conversation with the two men and ignored Tressa's pleas for help.

That night, Tressa collapsed going to the bathroom and came around to find her mother, dragging her back to her bedroom. There were no words of comfort. Instead, with just grunts and a heavy-handed grip, she was thrown back into bed.

Next morning, she was awakened by her sister, banging on her mother's bedroom door and shouting, "Muvver, ya better look at Tressa. She's a funny colour. That better not be catching. I don't wanna look like a fucking banana."

Violet's bedroom door was always locked and she didn't see the need to open it now. "Cor, fucking 'ell, stop being a couple of drama queens. Ya don't hear me boys prattling on like you two. Shut up. I'm trying to sleep."

Rita was more cocky than Tressa and would have a go back sometimes. "Muvver, she's chucked up all over the floor, the dirty bitch. I can't sleep in 'ere wiv her. It stinks!" she'd hollered.

There was the rattle of a lock and key, and suddenly there, in the doorway, stood Violet, wearing a huge pink dressing gown and looking bigger than ever. Tressa was delirious and couldn't see clearly but she could hear well enough.

"Aw, for fuck's sake, look at the state of the floor. Wake up, Tressa, ya dirty tramp. Look what ya done!"

Tressa could barely focus through her puffy eyes. The pain in her stomach was unbearable and she was burning up.

"Rita, go and wake George. She's gonna have to go to the quack."

There were no soft arms around her comforting her and there were no gentle words of reassurance either. That was all she remembered until she woke up in a hospital bed.

Sad, really, that during those three weeks she lay there, her own mother had visited her just the once. She knew then that it was sink or swim and she would have to be like them to fit in. They were tough and heartless and she would be too. The world as she saw it now was dog-eat-dog.

Major, their Staffordshire bull terrier, was whining at the door. Tressa opened a huge can of dog food and mashed it in his bowl along with some biscuits and crept outside. She sat on the back doorstep and watched the poor mutt lick the dish clean. He was a lovely dog, really, but vicious. When he'd arrived as a pup, she'd been over the moon, playing with him and cuddling him. That was until Jim stepped in, shouting at her not to fuss over him. He was a guard dog, he would say, so he had to be kept on high alert. A kick or a punch made the dog angry. Jim trained him to attack and the beast was top class at acting on command. He still had a soft spot for Tressa, though. She was the one who fed him and made sure his kennel was clean and warm. The dog would otherwise have been half-starved and freezing.

"Don't you go overfeeding that mutt. I don't want him shitting all over the garden, d'ya hear me, girl?" spat Violet. Tressa ignored her. She was the one who picked the shit up anyhow because the others were too lazy to give a toss. She looked down the garden at the expensive knocked-off garden furniture and grand marble statues, which were sitting among the overgrown weeds and long grass. It was typical of her mother; she liked a bit of class, but at the end of the day you really can't polish a turd.

The dog stopped, looked up, and faced the gate. You couldn't see who was outside the garden because Violet had put an eight foot fence around to stop any nosy bastards gawping in.

The gate opened and in walked Igor with two of his men. Tressa should have let Rita know because she surely wouldn't want Igor to see her first thing in the morning; it would be enough to put any man off his Fruit 'n Fibre. She grinned again and stepped aside. She had her little ways of getting her own back but nothing too obvious, though.

Igor gave Tressa a compassionate smile. He had known Tressa from the outset of opening the first villa nineteen or so years ago. She had been the go-between for the men from Russia and her family in England. George and Charlie had used Tressa initially probably because she had more brains than her sister. And she was certainly far better looking. He had liked the fact she had been sweeter and kinder to the girls compared to the years that followed when Gemma had been in charge, whom he'd disliked. She had been underhand and hardly had any emotion except for the love for one of the punters and of course her strange affair with Alex. Then, when she was temporarily locked up, the Ruthers had let the evil weirdo Rita take charge. At the time, he hadn't known who was worse: Gemma or Rita.

The door was left ajar and Tressa listened and imagined Rita squirming in her seat.

"Two of da girls are sick," Igor said, his Russian accent deep and harsh.

"Well, what's wrong with them?" asked Violet.

187

One of the other men, an Eastern European, spoke up. "Poison. I have seen dis in my own country. They have funny grey colour and shakes. It is not heroin, dis is something else."

"Well, if the silly little slappers want to kill 'emselves, let 'em. I don't know. I give them a bed and food, so what more do they want? Dirty little slappers. I bet they don't get fed in your country, do they? That's why the fucking whores wanna live here. Well, living 'ere ain't free."

Igor cringed. He was a hardened man, but he didn't much appreciate Violet slating his country. He was on a good earner, far more than he'd get laying bricks with his shovel hands, but he'd had no choice, doing what he did.

"You got shit loads of brown gear. Jack 'em up and sling 'em out. For fuck's sake, you have enough money outta me to take care of it. What ya waiting for?" snapped Violet.

The smallest of the three men, a young guy called Victor, stepped forward. "We have problem. Da girls are too young to leave on da street. Der will be questions." His English was broken which made him sound harsh.

"Gawd help us. Sit down, boys, we need to talk. And where are you off to, Rita? We need to sort this shit out," growled Violet.

"I'm just gonna get some clothes on. Give me two minutes." She tried to sound sweet.

Tressa listened intently; she wanted to know how old the girls were. When she was on the job, they were sixteen and classed as women.

Rita hurried up the stairs and into her bedroom – well, the bedroom she used when she was staying over, which was more often than not these days. She had a luxury apartment in Crystal Palace, which overlooked the green. It was all plush and new, and yet she was alone and bored there.

Pulling her handbag from under the bed, Rita removed a plastic pop bottle and then she went into the bathroom and poured the contents down the sink. Back in her room, she looked in the mirror and saw what Igor saw. In a mad rush, she slapped on her make-up and then had to clip her pony tail in before she pulled on her body-hugging dress. Unfortunately, to anyone else, this did her no favours whatsoever, but she was oblivious to this. She grabbed the bottle of perfume and sprayed herself all over. Even she could smell her own body odour and it wasn't nice.

The three men were sitting around the table, waiting for Rita. When she appeared, Igor almost laughed. The thick make-up, plastered on her face, still didn't change the fact that she was a spiteful fat cunt. He hated her. Selling the girls was one thing, but there was no need for the added cruelty from her. It was as if she got pleasure from humiliating the girls, leaving them tied up, naked, and horribly exposed. He would wait until she left to untie their legs and cover them over. The shit she gave them to eat was worse than he fed his dogs: tinned curry and tinned stew. It smelt like Chum. She laughed when she washed them, using the power hose. But he couldn't do anything about it. The money was too good – much better pay than in his homeland – and his boss back in Russia had taken his family as collateral so he was forced to do what he was told.

"Right, it seems to me that you can't think for yourself, so here's what ya do. Dose them up and take them to Liverpool, Birmingham, Tim-buck-fucking-too. Just get them away from London. They don't know where they are now, do they?"

189

Igor shook his head. "I am not stupid. They come to me in van with no windows."

"Well, then, it's simple. Jesus, ain't George taught you anything?" spat Violet.

"George does not know yet, and also the girls could not kill themselves. They only have what we give them."

Violet waved her hand, showing her lack of interest.

"Dey are only thirteen years old," said Victor.

Violet cocked her head to the side. "Do you have a fucking problem with that? Only, if they're good enough to start work at twelve over there in your country, then, by Christ, they're good enough to sell their arses over here at thirteen. You cheeky cunt!"

Victor flared his nostrils. He was a quick-tempered man and was on the run for two stabbings in Russia. He'd done these for less lip than Violet gave him.

"Dey work in factories or fields, not from da bed."

Igor grabbed him around the throat and squeezed. "Shut it, Victor, have respect."

Victor was scared of Igor. He had a serious reputation in Russia. Not many men fucked with him and lived to tell the tale. He relinquished his grasp and Victor curled his lip.

The other man, Yakiv, watched in silence, taking it all in. His brother Alex, a wealthy villain without a shred of conscience, was the main man in Russia. Igor and Victor worked for him. Alex, however, worked in partnership with George, so the three of them had to go along with Violet's wishes, regardless. Any fuck-up and Alex would have their families shot. Yakiv, or Yak, for short, worked tirelessly for his brother and hoped that one day he too would be sitting in a huge marble mansion surrounded by guards; but for now he had to prove himself. Alex trusted no one, and family or not, he would shoot you without hesitation. Known as the man who never blinks, Alex's eyes were enough to send shivers up your spine. The scars all over his head spoke volumes and his confident stance evoked fear in most men.

Yak looked around the kitchen, focusing first on Violet and then on Rita. This was a strange set-up. The family were so wealthy, and yet they lived here in a little house in a street. Violet could be in a guarded mansion with fifty bedrooms. Why would she choose to live in this dump? He put it down to being a British thing.

"Where is Bobby? He was supposed to pay out last night. He did not show up," said Igor, eager to get his money.

It was obvious that George hadn't told the Russians about the shooting.

"Rita will bring it over tonight, won't ya, girl," answered Violet for her daughter.

Rita was smiling coyly in front of Igor. He looked away. Violet noticed the lack of interest from Igor and decided to find out what was going on.

"So, you two love birds off out tonight, are you?" smirked Violet.

Igor almost snarled, "No, I keep business separate."

Rita was glowing red now. Victor was amazed by how unperturbed they were about the two kids who were dying. It was

191

nothing to them. They were just going to throw away the bodies. He was nervous and hoped they didn't ask him to drive them up north.

"The takings are down lately. We have a list of brokers, bankers, and legal nobs, and yet the interest seems to be dying a fucking death. I don't know. There's no excitement. Are you sure those girls are up to scratch? You haven't got a load of ugly bastards down there, have you?"

Igor curled his lip and snarled, "The girls are pretty, every one of them. I hand-picked them myself." The words that left his mouth made him cringe inside. They were true and it sickened him. He was well aware that he was bad. And back home in Russia, he had done terrible things, but this work in England was on a totally different level of immorality and it repulsed him. He had no choice, though; Alex had his family and wouldn't think twice about putting a bullet through their heads, or worse. He was paid well and they were safe as long as he did as he was bid, so that was that. He tried to close his mind to the cruelty and carried on with the job in hand. However, the last chase with the youngest girl, dear little Anya, had particularly sickened him. He recalled her sweet innocent face, when he'd told her to run, and she'd looked back at him with such hope in her eyes; she really thought she'd had a chance. She hadn't, though, and worse, she looked so much like his own daughter.

Rita was seething. How dare Igor call those slappers pretty and say they were hand-picked by him? Her heart beat fast, but she bit her lip; she mustn't be too sharp-tongued, not with Igor. She hated the girls with a deadly passion because in her heart she knew they were beautiful and was aware that Igor looked at them with sympathetic eyes and then at her with contempt.

"The men you send are fat and old and too past it to be chasing the girls on a hunt. It is the younger men who like to do that, and we do not have any."

Violet glared at the tall, thickset Russian. She could see what Rita saw in him. He wasn't handsome but he was fit and had a serious hard look about him.

"More like you and your fucking men are too lazy to go on the hunt with the old codgers, making sure the girls don't get away. I thought you Russians, or whatever ya call yaselves, had more fucking stamina. A bunch of poxy pussies, if ya ask me. Anyway, mate, you had better start thinking of a new game – something else – because there'll be no point in having a mansion just for plain old nooky. The old fuckers can go anywhere for fanny. We had something special. Now, if the takings keep going down, then Alex will wanna know why, so best you come up with some other game. Got it?"

Igor wanted to punch the old woman; he detested her with a passion. "No. Your customers prefer to use a whip or tools, not run around the fields hunting them down. Times have changed. They find it too risky and those weapons ..." he paused and swallowed hard, "they can leave a mess."

Violet glared at Igor; maybe he was right. The hunters were wealthy younger men. It was a good earner, as much as ten grand for a chase, but after the Enrights disappeared that little moneymaker seemed to be dying a death. Charles Enright had been her best customer; he'd loved the chase. He had been good, too. Never had the older men had to catch the girls themselves – he'd always done this and very quickly. What had made him so different from all the others though was he had tied them up and taken them away. Some he'd returned and others he hadn't. But it didn't matter because he'd paid a fortune.

193

"Well, it ain't my job to keep them interested, now, is it? I do my bit and you get paid a shitload to keep up your end of the deal." Smirking and daring him to look at her directly, she stood with her hands on her wide hips. It was a look that would make you want to slap her across the face.

"Right then, boys, d'ya know what ya doing?" She raised a drawn on eyebrow.

Igor stood to leave and he was followed by the others.

"See ya later, Igor." Rita smiled, just for him.

Igor almost snarled back, "Yes."

They marched down the garden path, dismissing Tressa as she stepped back into the kitchen.

"More tea, Mum?" she offered and smiled sweetly.

Violet grunted, "Yes," then turned to her other daughter. "So, Rita, Igor seemed a bit pissed off. I thought you said you and him were an item now," she sneered, shoving another chocolate Hobnob in her mouth.

"Yeah, well, it's supposed to be a fucking secret."

Violet nearly choked on her biscuit. "Yeah, girl, such a secret not even he knows about it yet."

Rita jumped up and stormed off out of the room.

Tressa was enjoying the torment. "I thought Igor and Rita were getting it on? I thought I might need to buy a hat."

Violet gave Tressa a sideways glance. "You wanna shut your fucking mouth. It ain't none of your business what she does. As for you, you'll be lucky to find a fella that would want your skin and bone arse. You're the last one to talk."

Tressa should have felt hurt, but inside she was smiling; that comment had got up Violet's nose, no question. No sooner had she plonked another cup of tea under her mother's face, than in walked her two older brothers, George and Charlie. They looked worried. Charlie had his tie loosened and George was sweating.

"Hello, boys, nice surprise," welcomed Violet. It was the only time Tressa saw her mother smile.

"Ma, we gotta ourselves a problem. That fucking bird he shot is only a Vincent," exclaimed George, as he plonked his heavy weight on the chair. Charlie rolled his eyes and sat more easily.

"Is that supposed to mean something to me?"

George looked at Charlie to say something.

"Well, Muvver, put it this way, the Vincents ain't the type to roll over and let it go. I'm telling you, if they get one word that it's anything to do with us, there'll be bloodshed. They'll be coming for us. Oh, and by the way, they might own a string of nightclubs, but word is they're a dangerous lot," added Charlie, as he wiped the sweat dripping down his nose.

"How the fuck did you find that out?" asked Violet, as her face took on a serious expression.

"Well, by chance, really. I was having a drink in the Bell with Micky Margant. He used to work for Mick McManners years ago—" Before he could finish, Violet interrupted.

"Yeah, I knew Mad Mick, the ugly cunt. He married a mate of mine. Lived over the East End."

Charlie and George were both nodding, "Yeah, well, he was talking to his mate that works on the door at *Dan's Palace*. He was told to keep it quiet, but the word is that it was Dan Vincent's wife, no less, that was shot nearby the prison."

Violet stared in silence.

"Well, Muvver, what the fuck do we do now?" snapped George.

"Nothing. They don't know anything. How could they?" she said in a less harsh tone. The news should have given her cause for concern.

"Oh, yeah, and to top it all, their sister is a top lawyer. She's supposed to be a fucking dangerous woman. Who do you think was responsible for the complete wipe-out of the McManners?"

"Don't get dramatic, George. The McManners had loads of enemies. It could have been anyone. Besides, if they were a face, I would have known of 'em."

"Muvver, you won't have heard of them because they aren't the type to go throwing their weight around. They are shrewd business people. They have their own security. They're wealthy cunts with clout. They don't have to get their hands dirty. Anyway, I'm just saying because trust me, once they find out, they'll be coming. That I can promise."

Violet snatched the packet of fags and lit one up. "Well, ya best make sure they don't find out, then."

George and Charlie looked at each other as if their mother were mad.

"Anyway, boys, we have another problem. That Igor was here this morning. Two of your girls are sick and he reckons they've taken

196

poison. I've told Igor and his men to take them up north and dump them."

George's heavy lip drooped until it almost touched his chin. "What? How could they do that? There ain't anything in their rooms, and our Rita takes care of the food." He stopped suddenly and glared at Charlie who flared his nostrils and shook his head.

"Well, maybe the daft cunt got it wrong about the poison, but they are sick. To be honest, if they're as bad as he said, then ya better off losing them. What punter's gonna pay for a kid chucking up and looking like a corpse?" stated Violet, completely oblivious to the connection between Rita and the sick girls. George nodded. He followed her logic but his mind was still preoccupied with Rita and also with Bobby's cock-up. Charlie was equally stressed to the eyeballs, but unlike George he pushed the thought of his sister and the poison to the back of his mind. He could only deal with one matter at a time, and right now, the Vincents were a serious worry.

CHAPTER NINE

By the time Francesca had reached Jamie's office, he had pulled well over a hundred files from his database, linking the Enrights with the Ruthers. Poppy almost stood to attention when Francesca walked in. "Shall I make some tea, or would you prefer coffee, Mrs Luciani?"

"Tea would be wonderful, and please, call me Francesca." She smiled and walked into Jamie's office to find him still printing off files.

He jumped up, full of eagerness. "You won't believe the amount of crimes those Ruthers were into and all of them became unfounded by the time they went to court. Also, every time they were represented by none other than the Enrights."

Francesca nodded; she'd guessed as much.

"Also, there was another barrister called Wiers who seemed to be in the mix." Jamie handed her the files, all of which were carefully sorted into date order.

She sat with perfect poise and opened the top file. It wasn't just the Enrights; it was also the judges presiding over the cases who were the same. She flicked through each one and found that if Wiers was the barrister in the case, then William Enright was the judge, and if

Charlie or Charles was defending their client, then Johnson or Foster was judging their case. Every trial was similar. Then George and Charlie Ruthers were found guilty of intent to supply cocaine and counterfeit money all because Foster was taken sick at the last minute and a different judge presided over the case. They had each received four years between 1992 and 1996.

Francesca's cool exterior masked her troubled mind. She knew all of the legal names in the files and despised each and every one.

She had been over the moon to be taken on by William Enright as a junior barrister. She remembered the overwhelming sense of excitement to be offered such a respectable position, and she recalled how she'd worked hard to secure herself a good name. Even at such a young age, she'd won far more cases than she'd lost. The lawyers and other barristers had admired her and soon she was taking on more serious crime cases. Her fate was sealed when she had married Charles Enright, although, at the time, this had not been part of their scheming plan.

Unbeknownst to her then, William Enright had hand-picked Francesca because she was intelligent, and she was also young enough, he believed, for him to manipulate her. She was to be groomed to lose a murder case that would secure the Enrights ownership of a substantial amount of French land worth millions.

Roberto and Mauricio Luciani were related to the Enrights, going back a few hundred years. However, whilst the Enrights knew this, the Lucianis didn't.

Roberto Luciani was the rightful heir to an age-old title, the release of which was due in 1999. The heir had to be a son of direct lineage, a Catholic, and a law-abiding citizen.

The Enrights intended to ensure the imprisonment of either Roberto or Mauricio Luciani, which would invalidate their claim and secure the Enrights' position as the legal heirs to the title and to the land.

Mauricio Luciani had been found in a car with a dead girl's body in the boot. Her face had been slashed and a clump of his hair was in her hands. Francesca had been his defence barrister, and Charles had tried to manipulate her into believing, come what may and no matter what she heard, Mauricio was a guilty man, and he must never be allowed to roam the streets. He was a dangerous serial killer.

Francesca had been thrilled that the Enrights had let her take on the case, which turned out to be the biggest in twenty years. She had wanted to prove to the Enrights and her professional colleagues she could handle a case of this magnitude.

However, where it all went wrong for the Enrights was their arrogant belief in their own infallibility and in their mistaken perception that their young barrister was wet behind the ears, when as events turned out, she was anything but naïve.

They had never dreamt she would go in search of answers herself. They had believed it was a done deal and Mauricio would be named as the face-slashing serial killer who would serve a very long time for killing all those prostitutes.

Francesca's investigations revealed the truth: she had learned that the Enrights were corrupt; they had deliberately staged a murder and placed Mauricio Luciani at the scene. Armed with this knowledge, she had used everything she had to secure a not-guilty verdict.

The Enrights had been so confident she would lose that they went away on a fishing trip – only to return to the devastating news that Mauricio was free.

From that point on, Charles and his evil family had done their level best to banish Francesca from their lives. They had humiliated her professionally, and those friends who had some sympathy for her – and they were very few – largely distanced themselves from her. So, she became virtually a prisoner in their own London apartment until that fateful trip down to their cottage on the south coast. That was over seventeen years ago now. Luckily for her, the Lucianis had taken her in and treated her as part of their family. Along with her own family, she came back to take revenge. Three of the Enrights, though, paid with their lives.

Francesca had never thought the past would come back to haunt her. However, as she stared at the details of the trials, and saw their names in print, the brutal recollections of events in the past caught up with her again and she felt violently sick.

It might have been a very long time ago, but she would never forget their awful cruelty and the pain she had felt when Charles had thrust that sharp knife up inside her. He had killed her unborn child and left her unable to have children.

"Hey, Sisco, are you okay? You look pale."

"I'm fine. It's just that by reading these files, I am reliving all those awful events all those years ago, which makes me feel nauseous. I don't know, but it seems to me that evil really does find evil. I'm more determined than ever to get to the bottom of this, for all our sakes, not just Cassie's."

Jamie nodded. "You won't be alone."

Francesca looked up and remembered those words. Her family had said the same – that she would never be alone again. They had kept their word. The Lucianis and the Vincents were two families with the same moral code. She knew that if she ever looked over her shoulder, one of them would be there and it was usually Fred. She shuddered. Maybe this fight was one they should not be involved in. The search for the truth was going to be hard, but she was not going to let it beat her, not if it was true that the evil side of the legal system was involved with the Ruthers. Only Gemma held the answers, and Francesca was going to make sure she got all the facts before she planned any action.

The weather had cooled down as the previous night's thunderstorm had cleared the stuffy air. It was a major release for everyone – everyone except Sandra, that is, who was still hot under the collar when Francesca and Jamie arrived for their legal visit. As Francesca approached the desk to sign in, Sandra's heart raced. She searched the barrister's face for clues and for anything to determine what the woman was thinking. But all she saw was a blank hard look.

"Please sign here, err—"

"Mrs Luciani," replied Francesca, interrupting the officer.

Sandra nodded; she knew the woman's first name and last name but didn't know how to address her.

"Gemma's in room two. I'll take you there. Follow me, please."

Francesca noticed that Sandra looked tired and on edge. Her hair was lank and she had a thin film of sweaty grease covering her face. She'd either had a late one on the piss or had been tossing and turning all night with guilt. Francesca surmised the latter.

Gemma was sitting facing the door when they arrived. She looked bedraggled and red-eyed, which didn't surprise Francesca. The poor girl must have cried herself to sleep.

"I want you to change seats," she said, "so you don't face the door."

Gemma smiled and Sandra left the room, even more on edge.

"How are you today?" asked Francesca.

"I'm more clear-headed than I've ever been. I dunno, something snapped in me last night. I lay in me bed crying over Cassie, then it was as if she spoke to me. Not that I believe in all that shit, but something was telling me to be strong and fight for freedom, fight for justice, so now I'm ready."

Jamie grinned. "Great, that's what we want to hear. It's going to be a long day. We've booked the morning and the afternoon. Are you ready?"

Gemma nodded.

They turned on the tape recorder. "Where shall I start?" she asked.

Francesca leaned across and held her hand. "I want you to carry on where you left off. It'll be hard, but we can stop for a break whenever you need to."

Gemma liked Francesca. She was a hard and clever woman, but she knew that underneath the steel exterior there was a compassionate and kind-hearted person. It was odd to feel like that about her now because years ago Gemma had hated Francesca with a passion. Now, though, she needed her.

Jamie smiled and spoke clearly into the tape. "Interview Two: Gemma Ruthers. You may continue, Gemma."

"I'd just told you Bobby had proposed when we finished our interview yesterday. After that, I moved in with him." She lowered her gaze as she continued her story because it hurt to have to go over the early days. Bobby had been so different back then. But then, she needed to remind herself, so had she.

*

The wedding took place in the summer of 1995 when she was only nineteen. It was a small affair with just his brother Lenny, his sisters Rita and Tressa, his mother, and a few friends and neighbours. George and Charlie were still in prison at the time. She had no one, but it didn't matter. Daisy wouldn't go. She said she didn't ever want the Ruthers to know she was connected and that was how it stayed. How could Daisy stand there in a big hat, her fur coat, and a fake smile, pretending she was at the wedding of the century, when she hated the Ruthers and would wish it were their funeral instead?

Violet was ugly back then, in all senses of the word, although she did try hard to be civil to Gemma. Bobby was full of gifts, flowers, and promises of a good life – just the two of them. He would always say 'just the two of us' because after the wedding they seemed to spend so much time together in Violet's back pocket, although even that was fun and exciting at first.

Gemma remembered sitting around that big wooden table in the kitchen, in among the knocked-off gear and counterfeit money. The scams they'd had were endless. Violet soon had Gemma working. She made sure she could drive and gave her a van.

"There you go, girl," she said, as she proudly handed Gemma a set of keys. "I can't 'ave me daughter-in-law without a set of wheels, now can I?"

Gemma was excited and rushed outside to see the small van. It was a dream. She lived in a luxury flat with her perfect husband and now she had a set of wheels.

"Right, me gal, I got a little job for you."

Gemma was nodding; she was part of their family and wanted in on the action.

Rita grimaced; she'd made no effort to befriend Gemma and had continued dishing out the odd spiteful remark, which Gemma and the others had learned to ignore.

"Here's the address. Go and pick up ten bags and deliver one each to these addresses. Don't listen to any of their shit. Just say, 'Violet wants the money today'." She handed over a piece of paper with a grin.

Gemma did as she was told. She had the music blaring and happily drove to the first address, which was quite a nice respectable home in South East London. A young woman, with plenty of money, dripping in flash jewellery, pointed to the black bags. Gemma reversed the van up and loaded the bags into the back. She looked at the first delivery address and off she went. The man who opened the door to the shabby-looking Victorian flat in Penge snatched the bag and went to shut the door.

"'Ere, mate, where's the money?"

The scruffy-looking man eyed her up and down and glared at her. "What fucking money?" he said. He was an older man, roughly seventy, with long, thin grey hair, grey eyes, and a roll-up stuck to his lip. He put her in mind of Catweazle.

Gemma glared back, trying to intimidate him. "Violet's money."

"She'll have to wait. I ain't got it." He went to close the door.

Quickly, Gemma shoved her foot in the gap. "I ain't fucking asking, mate, I'm telling ya. She wants that money today and no fucking excuses." She stopped and stared.

The man huffed and puffed and then he mumbled under his breath, "Wait there." He returned with a packet and handed it over. He had underestimated the kid, thinking she was just a scatty teenager.

Almost every address she went to, they tried it on, not wanting to hand over the money, but she stood her ground. By the time she returned to Violet's, she had ten packets on the seat next to her in the van. She hadn't known then that it was a test.

Violet, Rita, and Lenny were sitting around the table laughing, assuming that Gemma wouldn't handle the job, but as soon as Gemma placed the ten packets on the table, their faces changed. Violet didn't say a word; she was eyeing Gemma up and down. The girl was not the soft touch she'd assumed she was.

"No agg, then?" Rita smirked.

"No, nothing I couldn't handle," Gemma replied curtly, which got up Rita's nose. She didn't like the pretty kid and despised her even more, knowing she wasn't a pushover and would soon earn her mother's respect. Violet looked down on wimps; she liked a hard man or woman. The relationship was blossoming and Rita would not have it. She wanted to be the number one girl in the family. She wasn't going to have a skinny Barbie doll take her place. Jealous of every woman with looks or power had eaten away at Rita for years and left her spiteful and treacherous.

Every job Violet gave Gemma was another test. She was pushing her to see how much bottle she really had. Bobby was happy to go along with it as he wanted nothing more than to prove his missus was as tough as them. He had to show them he'd made the right decision in marrying her. Having their respect meant more to him than anything.

The day Gemma was sent to collect from the Rastas was the ultimate test. Violet knew the Rastas were a handful, and for a reason unknown to her, they hadn't come up with the money they owed. She called to Rita and asked whether she had made the delivery; she just nodded and walked away. She failed to inform her mother she'd palmed the lesser quality gear off on them, knowing full well that Violet would send Gemma in for the readies and there would be a serious backlash. They didn't fuck about. Rita wouldn't put it past them to hurt Gemma or worse. She grinned to herself as she sneaked off upstairs.

Gemma arrived that morning bright and breezy. She was dressed in a new designer dress, leather jacket, and high boots. She looked older but still very pretty. Violet noticed how she carried herself, too; she was confident and womanly.

"Gemma, can you go to Riff's for me? Only the cunt ain't weighed out for his puff, the cheeky bastard. Thinks he's gonna knock me, he can think again. Anyway, tap him for us, will ya?"

Gemma smiled. "Yeah, no worries, how much?"

Violet was squinting at a letter. "Err, yeah, five grand." She handed Gemma the address.

It wasn't too far; it was just the other side of Streatham Vale. Gemma was in a world of her own. Bobby had suggested they take a late honeymoon to Barbados, and she was thinking of what she would pack.

The house looked dark. It was another old Victorian structure. The windows needed repainting and the concrete doorstep was crumbling. She could smell the weed through a crack in the doorframe.

She knocked and stood back, waiting for a reply. Nothing happened. She knocked again. Suddenly, the door was ripped open and there to greet her was a monster of a black man with dreads to his feet. "What?" he snarled, showing a row of gold teeth.

Gemma looked him up and down. "Violet wants her money." She had learned to play the cool collector and up until now it had worked. Giving this pretty young girl a menacing grin, he looked up and down the road. He then suddenly snatched her arm and dragged her inside.

She tried to shake him off, but he threw her into the living room where four other guys were sitting slouched on sofas, which had clearly been destined for the skip many moons ago. The room had a layer of blue smoke and the smell hit her hard. If she stayed in the room, she would end up as stoned as they were. The rhythm of reggae music was almost in sync to the beat of her rapid pulse.

"Looks like Violet sent us a present." He pushed Gemma into the centre of the room.

The man sitting next to the fireplace jumped up; he was skinny and moved fast. "My turn first." He grabbed Gemma by the arm, and as he stepped back, he pulled her with him and she fell into his lap. "Nice piece of sweet meat." The skinny guy had a sly expression. His hair was long, red, and greasy, and his high cheekbones pushed his eyes into slits. Gemma noticed black raised moles on his pale and sickly face. She shook in terror.

As she struggled to get off him, he pulled her back and gripped her throat. "No you don't, me little piece a heaven." He spoke with a Jamaican twang, but he was as white as any redhead could be.

The others laughed. "What's she look like?" asked one.

Gemma was petrified. *Oh my God,* she thought, *they're all going to rape me.* The blood coursed through her veins as she searched around, desperate to find a way of escape. She tried again to break loose, but the man's grip was tight and she was a mere doormat compared to him – in fact, compared to all of them.

"Listen, mate, this ain't a good idea. Trust me, you don't know who I am. Touch me, and you're a dead man," she spat.

The man threw her with such force she fell to the floor.

"Violet owes me for a bad deal and I'm taking what's mine. Now get ya kit off and let me have what I'm owed, or I'll take it and it won't be nice. I'll split you in half!" he hollered.

Gemma froze; this was a nightmare, but she was going to die before she let him rape her. She jumped to her feet and flew to the door, but the skinny man had hold of her in a split second. He threw her to the floor again and jumped on top of her. She wriggled and punched as much as she could, but he just grinned, totally unperturbed by her attempt to defend herself and her modesty. The others were laughing and talking in a deep Jamaican Patois she couldn't understand.

"Please, let me go, please don't do this. I ain't done nothing to you!" she cried out, as she begged for her freedom. It was no use. He pinned her down, knelt on her arms, and unzipped his baggy jeans. Gemma's eyes widened when his huge erection fell out. It was touching her mouth. She kept her lips closed tight and turned her head to the side. He pushed and shoved that rod into her face. Suddenly, she felt her knickers being ripped off, but the man with his penis in her face had his hands where she could see them. She realised another one of them was pulling her legs apart. She fought as hard as she could. She didn't scream, just kicked and struggled, but it was no use; there were too many of them. She didn't know who had a hold of her, but it must have been two more. Suddenly, she felt something between her legs. It was too late: she had nothing to fight with. The skinny guy jumped off and spun around. Then she saw them, like wild animals, all getting ready to take a turn. Two men were holding her legs open and one was having a feel. She felt her stomach churning with fear, as the size of the skinny guy's penis made her wet herself. She could feel her bowels going. Gripped by terror, she closed her eyes and prayed it would be over soon. The pain was like nothing she had ever felt before. They threw her around like a play thing, each one taking his turn. She didn't cry or speak. It was as if she'd left her body. The pain was intense – it was far, far worse than having them beat her. She could smell their vile skin, the sweat, and the spunk all over her small body. Two were particularly ruthless; they shared her. Her dignity was the least of her worries, as she now feared for her life. Eventually they stopped, and in turn, they sloped away. Two left the house and two went upstairs, leaving her with the big man with the long dreadlocks. He threw her clothes to her, but she could hardly move. They had managed to tear a ligament in her leg. With blood everywhere, she stayed where she was, curled in a ball on the floor. She was a wreck: her dignity utterly exposed, she knew she had bitten off far more than she could chew. However, at least she was still in one piece – for now.

"Get dressed and get out. Tell that dirty whore Rita if she ever thinks of passing on shit gear again, then she'd better watch her back. Take that as a warning. Next time you or any of the Ruthers knock at my door, it better be top quality gear. I ain't having my reputation fucked – got it?"

Traumatized and weak, Gemma disengaged herself from what had really happened to her. All she thought was that it was strange that he looked like a Jamaican but talked like an East Ender. He left the room and she managed to pull her clothes on. She couldn't feel down below; it was numb. She wondered if she had anything left down there or if she would ever be able to go to the toilet. Oddly, her anger wasn't with the men – it was with Rita. The penny had finally dropped: the bitch had set her up.

She managed to drive home to her own flat. Bobby was out. She climbed into the shower and washed away the blood and other mess. The hot water burned between her legs, but she didn't care. She had to remove every last memory of that horrendous ordeal.

She threw her clothes in a plastic bag, ready to take to the outside bin. After she'd pulled on a pair of cotton knickers and a bright green tracksuit, she got to work, putting on make-up and combing her hair. She had to put a sanitary towel between her legs because she was still bleeding. She closed the door behind her, and on the way to her van she tossed the bag of clothes into the outside dustbins. Her life from then on would never be the same. As she got to the end of the road, she paused; she had a sudden urge to run to Daisy and never look back. Then she thought of Bobby. What would he say? Would he side with his sister or with her? It was strange, really, because she should have known the answer to that question, but she didn't. It wasn't Bobby and her facing the world: it was Bobby, *his family* and her facing the world. Maybe she could get him to break away if she had something over him. What if she got herself pregnant by him? He would be at home more and their life could be different, away from them. She had initially liked all the excitement but with that kind of business there were consequences, and she'd paid the price.

As soon as she had walked to the back door and entered the kitchen, she noticed the look of surprise on Rita's face. She knew then that it had been that fucking evil bitch who had set her up because Rita's expression confirmed it.

No one could hurt her as much as the pain she experienced that day, and Rita's jealousy issues were nothing new. "What's up, Rita? You look like you've seen a ghost." Her tone was cocky with a touch of menace.

"What you fucking on about?" she spat back.

Violet was going over some accounts and didn't look up. "Got the cash, Gemma?"

Gemma slid her legs under the table. "Nah, he said he didn't know who I was. I tried to tell him, but he said he would hand the money over to Rita since it was her that handed over the weed." She slowly turned to face Rita and grinned sarcastically. It was then that they both knew exactly what had gone on. Rita glared venomously at Gemma, who just sat there with a Cheshire cat smile spread across her face.

Violet was still looking at the accounts – pen, paper, and calculator at hand. "Well, Rita, what ya waiting for? Get your arse over there and pick up me five grand."

"I'll run you over there, Rita. Me van's just outside," smirked Gemma.

Violet put the pen down and looked up. "What's going on?" She glanced at Rita.

"Nothing," she replied.

"Well, what ya fucking waiting for? Get over there. I want me fucking money!" hollered Violet.

"I'll go later. I want to have a bath first. I'm meeting someone later."

"Cor, fuck me girl, you were all laughs a minute ago. Now you look like ya lost your fanny."

Rita sneaked off to her room. Just as Gemma got up to leave, Bobby appeared. He gave her a kiss on the cheek and then one to his mother. "What you been up to, babe?" His voice was sweet and she noticed that when he smiled a really big smile there was half a dimple in his cheek.

"Never you mind, Bobby boy," replied Violet.

"Where have you been?" asked Gemma, in her sweetest voice.

No sooner had she got the words out of her mouth than Violet jumped in. "None of your fucking business, girl."

Gemma wasn't shocked. She could be privy to the girls' stuff but what the boys got up to was a secret. She didn't mind. Bobby would come home when he said, and he treated her with respect, which was all that mattered.

They left to go home. Bobby drove his car and she drove her van. As she turned the corner, she felt odd, as if everything was in slow motion. She managed to pull over and take a deep breath. Her heart was racing and she thought she was going to die. Her head was raging and she saw flashing lights. The heat from her feet raged up to her brow. Suddenly, the contents of her stomach came up; she opened the door and then vomited on the pavement. Her legs were shaking so badly she couldn't move them. She tried to open the bottle of water, sitting in the centre console, but her hands were trembling too much. The images of those men flashed through her head. She opened her mouth to scream but nothing came out. Racked with pain, she rocked back and forwards. Unable to remove those images of the last few hours' brutality as they flashed through her mind, the tears came and then they just continued to flow uncontrollably. But an hour later, she managed to pull herself together and head home.

Bobby was in the shower but heard her come in. "Fancy a curry?" he shouted.

She heard his words, but they just whirled around in her head. The mental pain was killing her; she needed some release. That built-up anxiety was ready to explode. She looked down at the random scars on her arms and then told herself she shouldn't, but there was no other way. She couldn't handle the feeling of suffocating in the mire of despair she had suddenly found herself in — all because her heart had ruled her head and because she was so much in love with Bobby.

Eventually, he emerged from the bathroom with just a white towel round his waist. His wet hair stood on end and his tanned chest glistened in the light. She would have jumped up and hugged him or dragged him to bed, but she couldn't. Sex was the last thing on her mind. The thought of anyone touching her made her want to puke.

"Well, babe?" he was rubbing his hair dry with another towel.

She tried to sit up on the bed and act like everything was normal. But it wasn't and it couldn't be — not by any means. She lay back down. "Sorry, Bobby, I don't feel well. I think I'm coming down with something."

He sat next to her and stroked her head. "You're hot, babe. D'ya wanna drink?"

She shook her head. "No, I think I might just have a nap."

He smiled and left her alone. She fell asleep but awoke in a sweat. Her clothes were drenched and her head was banging. Bobby was asleep in the living room with a horror movie still on the TV. She crept into the bathroom and turned on the shower. The cool bubbles instantly relieved the burning sensation, which held her head alight. The blood was still dripping from her crotch. The shakes returned, and then, suddenly, she was freezing. With a chunky towel wrapped round herself, she sat on the edge of the bath and looked down at her arms; one little nick would take all that pain away. The razors were there, on the side, just in sight. One little cut would stop the feeling in her head. She snatched the blade and sliced her arm, just above her wrist; the blood trickled into the white sink, and she watched the water dripping from the tap as it diluted it. Then the pain in her head disappeared. That feeling of desperation and anxiety, which she had experienced only a few minutes ago, subsided.

It was a week later when everything changed and her world was turned upside down. Bobby could not get her out of the flat. She hardly spoke; she just wanted to sleep. He became disgruntled. Then, one morning, he snapped, "For fuck's sake, what is the matter with you? You just lie there all day, and to be honest, ya don't look sick to me. Muvver needs some errands run, and I've got business of me own. I suggest ya get ya fucking arse outta bed and get over there!"

The problem was, though, Gemma *was* sick. Every time she went to the toilet the pain inside was excruciating and passing urine

216

was like passing hot water with blood clots. She did get up, however, and into the shower. The door slammed shut and he was gone. How could she tell her husband she'd been raped by five men? It was absurd. Gemma cried – for herself, her shitty life, which just kept getting even worse, and for her own stupidity, by ignoring the advice of her saviour. Once she was outside, the cooler air soothed her mind, and she took the bus and headed to King's Cross. The bus ride seemed to take forever and the burning between her legs was making her feel sick. Eventually, she arrived at Daisy's door and prayed she was in.

Luckily the door opened, and there she stood in a pink negligée and the same pink slippers, which were now worn out.

"Christ, girl!" She grabbed Gemma by the arm before she collapsed. "Let's get yer inside. Yer look like death warmed up. What's happened?"

Gemma slumped down on the sofa and burst into tears – uncontrollable and relentless sobs. Daisy quickly gathered her in her arms and rocked her like a baby. "Now then, girl, whatever it is, you're here now with me, safe. Come on, babe, tell me what's happened, and let's get ya sorted out."

Gemma stopped crying and looked up at Daisy. Her eyes, round and scared, were like a small child's. Daisy frowned. "What's up, girl?" she whispered.

"I was raped by five men, cruel men, who took it in turns."

Daisy's hands flew to her mouth. "Jesus help us!"

As Gemma calmed down, she told Daisy everything, including how much pain she was in and about the constant bleeding.

Daisy headed to the bathroom. "Right, my girl," she said when she returned. "I know what's wrong. It's happened to us enough fucking times, bless ya heart." She held out a tub of pills. "You need to take these antibiotics. Go on, get one down yer neck now." Gemma took the tub and Daisy brandished something else. "This tube, you have to insert in yer back passage. The dirty bastards have torn ya, so this stuff is for that. Aw, babe, I wish you'd come sooner. I'll always help ya, ya know that."

Gemma swallowed a tablet and smiled. "Thanks, Daise."

Daisy sighed. "Ahh, this is awful. Yer must have been scared to death."

"I thought they were gonna do me in. It's strange. It was like it was happening to someone else."

"I know, I've heard it all before – but from our own kind, not innocents like you."

Gemma looked to the floor. "But I am like you, Daise."

Daisy half-laughed. "Gemma, people like me and the other girls are the way we are because we had reached rock bottom. We had no choice. Drugs, booze or a fucking bad past, led us to this life, and it's a shit one, too. You, my girl, have a life … well, you would have, if you kept away from the low life Ruthers. Oh, Jesus, I could kill that 'orrible mare, Rita. Cor, she's her mother's daughter all right."

She stood up and walked back to the kitchen.

"Right, I got cranberry juice and a few of these sachets you need to add to water, and then ya need to drink it all. That'll ease the burning."

218

Gemma was so relieved she was going to finally get rid of the pain, and she did feel safe with Daisy. She was like a mother to her. Working for Violet had left no time to visit Daisy, and yet although a year had passed, it was as if she had seen her only yesterday. They still had a special bond.

It was late when Gemma finally got home. She didn't notice the cars parked outside, but she had a rude awakening when she turned her key in the lock and opened the door. Bobby grabbed her by the hair and dragged her into the living room, where she was confronted by his mother and two sisters.

Tressa, she'd only met a handful of times and had barely said two words to as she was always on her way out with no time for small talk.

They were sitting on the sofas like two hippos and a hyena. Bobby threw her to the floor. "Ya fucking dirty slut, where ya been?"

Gemma tried to sit herself up, but she must have hit the coffee table hard and her arm was void of strength. "What's going on, Bobby? I ain't been nowhere." She glanced at his mother, hoping for some kind of reassurance, but instead she was met with a spiteful raised eyebrow. Bobby grabbed something off the side and pelted it at her.

"Ya been having some fucking fella in here, in me cunting flat. I should have known ya were up to no good. Staying in bed all day, pretending ya sick."

Gemma was shocked to say the least. All of this had come out of nowhere. She looked at the floor to see what he had thrown at her. It was a man's gold watch.

"What's *this*?" She pointed. It was all surreal.

"What's that? You should fucking well know! Ya fella left it here!" Bobby was red-faced and raging.

Gemma pulled herself to her feet and frowned. "No, Bobby, I ain't seeing anyone. I've never seen that watch and I swear to God I have been sick."

Rita shuffled off the sofa to her feet and with a hard finger poked Gemma in the chest. "Fucking cheat on me brother, will ya? Well, he might not hit you, but I fucking well will!" With that, she punched Gemma in the face and knocked her to the floor. No one stopped her and no one cared. Her lip was smashed and the blood poured out of her nose. She looked at Bobby, her Bobby, the man who was always so gentle, but his eyes were now cold and heartless. How could he let his sister hurt her like that? She was still staring at his raging face when Rita kicked her hard in the ribs.

"I fucking saw ya, snogging a bloke's face off by the bus stop!" She kicked Gemma again. "I came here to talk to ya about it, and I would have given you the benefit of the doubt, until I asked Bobby who the watch belonged to. Cor, you got some front, bitch, having a bloke in my Bobby's bed. A proper liberty that is."

Gemma couldn't speak. Her mouth was swelling up and blood was still running down her face. The kick had cracked a rib and she found it hard to breathe.

Violet pulled Rita away. "That's enough, girl. Leave the dirty rat to Bobby. He has every right to give her a beating. I fucking warned ya, Bobby. She ain't nothing but a silly prat that will bring you down. Ya best do something about it, and sharpish, before my George and Charlie get out, 'cos, by Christ, when they find out ya taken on a wrong 'un, they'll go apeshit!"

Gemma was in a daze; the beating had been harsh and the words even more so. Even Tressa, the pretty one, had grabbed Gemma's face before she'd left and whispered, "That's nothing, love. Fuck up again and you're dead." She hadn't realised at the time, though, that Tressa wasn't threatening her. She was trying to warn her, but she'd had to make it look like a threat in front of Violet.

Bobby stood at the kitchen counter and rolled himself a joint. He wouldn't look her way. Maybe the sight of her smashed face had stirred guilty emotions. The bathroom was her haven. She wiped her face with a flannel and stared at the nasty gash on her lip and the black bruising around her nose. She knew then she could never beat Rita – she was just too sly. To go that far, to make up such disturbing lies, was proof enough that this family were made of cruel stuff. The razor was there on the side and she sliced another line across her arm.

The weeks that followed were hard. She packed her clothes to leave. If he believed them over her, then she would let him get on with it. But there was no opportunity for her to take control over her life. From this point forward, Gemma was now a prisoner. He locked her in the flat. She had no rights to him, yet he still saw her as his property – to be used, or abused, as he saw fit. His bedroom was his and his alone, leaving Gemma no option but to sleep on the sofa. Still she tried to get through to him, begging and pleading her innocence – that she had not in any way betrayed him. But it made no difference: he wouldn't listen to her. One Sunday, when Bobby left to go to his mother's for a planned house party to celebrate the brothers' homecoming, Gemma checked her diary. She had missed her period. She gasped. She'd put the sickness she'd suffered lately down to stress, but there was no doubt she was having a baby. All the signs were there: the sore breasts, the constant nausea, and the missed period. Sudden realisation hit her, harder than the punches thrown at her by her new family. What if she was pregnant but *not* by Bobby?

221

But how likely was that? No, she instinctively held on to the notion that the baby – if she was having one – was Bobby's. She had to believe this. Any other alternative was too scary to contemplate.

That was it; she could tell Bobby and maybe things would go back to normal – he would love a baby. She wouldn't tell him just yet, though. Maybe she would wait another month. She would be three months gone then. A smile spread across her face: *a baby, me a mum,* she thought. The excitement suddenly vanished when Bobby arrived home. He had been drinking and snorting cocaine. She didn't like him much when he'd taken gear; he was edgy and unpredictable. She emerged from the bedroom, wearing a T-shirt and pyjama bottoms. She had forgotten to cover her arms. He was grinning at her in such a peculiar way and walking towards her like a robot with his eyes transfixed. Suddenly, he lunged forward, snatching her arm, and eyeing up the two fresh cuts which had just scabbed over.

"Like fucking cutting yaself, do ya? Enjoy it, do ya? Wanna look like a freak? Me wife, the freak! Are you ever gonna show me respect? How the fuck can I have you hanging off me arm with those marks? Anyone will think ya trying to kill yaself, and who will they blame, eh? Me!" He was poking himself in the chest. "Yeah, fucking me!"

Nothing made sense, but the more he screamed the angrier he got until finally he dragged her into the bathroom and snatched the blade.

Gemma stared wide-eyed and terrified. "No, Bobby, please don't hurt me! I'll cover up, I swear, I won't disrespect you, never. Believe me—" But it was too late. He went into a mad frenzy and sliced open her arms, her chin, and her neck. She struggled to stop him, but it was as if he was enjoying it. She screamed at the top of her voice and only then did he snap out of the weird trance that had gripped him.

He looked down at the bloody mess. Gemma was sliced to pieces, and although the slashes were not deep enough to kill her, they were certainly serious enough to scar.

Bobby jumped up and glared as if he couldn't believe what he saw. Gemma curled up in a ball and sobbed. Was this going to be her life from now on — locked in a flat and abused every time her husband came home?

CHAPTER TEN

Francesca stopped the tape and took a deep breath. Gemma slowly blinked and shook her head.

"It sounds like a horror story. Unbelievable, I know, but I swear it's the truth ... and that's not the worst of it," she cried. Her visage was not faked; the sadness in her eyes was real because at this point she was reliving what had really happened. The next part of the story was hard to reminisce. It was the most poignant and darkest moment of her life. It was one that would eventually turn her into the monster she had become.

Francesca believed every word. She looked at the scars on the girl's neck and her arms. "Do you need a break? They're going to call you for dinner in a minute."

"Oh my God, I need to finish the story. You have to know what they did. You have to get me out of here!" Her voice was panicky; she glanced up at the clock.

"Hey, it's all right, we'll still be here when you get back."

"What if I don't make it back?"

Francesca frowned. "What do you mean?"

"They want me dead. They'll do anything to stop me telling me story."

Francesca knew this wasn't a mad illusion; Gemma was serious.

"Jamie, can you get special permission to extend the visit over lunch? I know they won't normally allow it, but——"

Jamie jumped in. "Yes, I can call the number one governor and suggest we continue. We have reason to believe the police need to be called, but as it's a legal visit we are at this stage not able to discuss this interview outside of these four walls."

Francesca smirked; he was a clever kid and so on the ball. He was right; there were, in fact, special circumstances and this was one of them.

He made the call away from the room and out of earshot of any other officer. Luckily, the governor was fine about the request and found no reason why Gemma's food could not be brought to her to allow the interview to continue. The truth was the governor had suspected something amiss and wanted to get to the root of it. If the lawyers were on to something, then she was happy to agree special circumstances.

Sandra arrived to take Gemma away to the canteen. The rapist had been paid heavily with a serious stash of weed and two bottles of scotch. A good thrashing and Gemma would be in sick bay and unable to carry on the interview.

"Right, Ruthers, follow me," she said, standing with her legs apart like a man.

Francesca cocked her head to the side. "Oh? Have you not been informed?"

Sandra looked uneasy. "Err, about what?"

Francesca grinned. "Gemma is having her lunch here, under special circumstances, signed off by the governor. Oh, yeah, can you fetch teas and sealed sandwiches, please?"

Sandra swallowed hard; the lawyer knew something and this was getting too dangerous. She wasn't about to argue, so instead, she spun on her heel to do exactly as requested. She had to get away to think. How was she going to tell Bobby? Maybe it was best just to ignore him and let things play out: *what will be, will be*, she thought. The money was good as were the little freebies with a young fresh piece of arse, but her liberty was worth more.

She returned with a tray of refreshments and left. The look in that lawyer's eyes was enough of a threat to make her stay out of the whole business.

They drank the tea and nibbled on the food, but no one was really hungry; the mood was sombre and the events Gemma had described were truly shocking.

"Are you all right to continue? You said that was not the worst of it," said Jamie, eager to get on and hear more.

Gemma continued, but this time she was staring into space and her face took on an empty and deep sadness.

She was pregnant and after Bobby had sliced her up she was afraid both for herself and her baby. The months went by and still she was locked in the flat. He hardly came home, staying over at his mother's most of the time. He was civil sometimes, but the coldness in his eyes was still there. She begged and pleaded with him to believe her, but he shrugged her off. Her tiny bump grew, but she managed to keep it hidden. Day after day, she searched for a way out, even trying to smash a window to get someone's attention, but it was no use. Sadly for her, the other flats were owned by an overseas buyer and remained empty, and there was no one to hear her screams. Bobby slept with the keys under his pillow, so she couldn't even sneak out in the dead of night.

After eight months, she went into labour. It was a Friday and Bobby had left that morning. The pains intensified. With no phone or internet, she was going to give birth alone. For the first time in her life, she knelt down, put her hands together, and prayed to God to help her deliver a healthy baby. She paced the floor for hours, feeling the contractions engulfing her, but she had to stay calm. A blind panic would help no one. She searched the flat for a pair of scissors but couldn't find any; there was not even a sharp knife. Bobby had removed them all. Perhaps he thought she would stab him while he slept. Maybe she would have, but she still loved him.

As she searched every cupboard, her fingers finally felt a sharp object jammed at the back of the so-called 'man's drawer'. She pulled the drawer away from the cupboard and the knife fell to the floor. She held it in her hands and shook all over. The realisation that she would have to do this alone – cut the cord, and perhaps herself, if she couldn't get the baby out – hit her. The towels were all clean and fresh. In fact, everything in the flat was spotless. She had little else to do except clean and watch telly.

By early evening, she was rocking on the edge of the bath. The pain was intense. Then, suddenly, she had a feeling like nothing she had experienced before. Her body was bearing down and the urge to push overwhelmed her. She got off the bath edge and knelt down. The baby was coming and she had to do it alone. "Please, let it be all right," she said, over and over again. She pushed as hard as she could but it was no use. The sweat was running down her back and down her forehead, but the endless pushing was exhausting her. "Please,

God, help me!" she screamed. She lay down on the bathroom floor, trying to gather enough energy to get the baby out. The room was spinning and she felt faint, but she had to stay awake. The burning feeling between her legs made her scream. Her baby was there, but his head was stuck and it hurt like hell. She took a deep breath and with one last push she felt the head come out followed by the body. There was silence. She sat up to see her baby lying there with the umbilical cord wrapped tightly round his neck. She unravelled it and tried to rub his back. "Please breathe, please." She smacked his bottom, hoping he would gasp for breath. The baby was limp and lifeless. She smacked him again. "Come on, baby, please." The effort was to no avail: the stillness confirmed he had died.

She held him close in her arms and kissed his mop of hair. He was beautiful – he was perfect – but he was dead. Like a wolf, she held back her head and screamed. Howling like an animal, she rocked back and forth, clutching her baby boy. It wasn't fair; it was too cruel to comprehend. She would have given up her life just to save his, but he was gone. She never even got to see him open his eyes. The pain was unbearable. The Ruthers could lock her up, beat her, or even kill her, but not harm her baby. Nevertheless, they had, though; but for them he would be alive.

Bobby had decided to come home earlier than planned and as he entered the flat he could hear screams. They weren't normal cries; instead, they were alarming shrieks of terror. He dashed to the bathroom to find his wife clutching a baby, the cord still attached to her, with blood everywhere. The sight shocked him to the core. For months, he hadn't even looked at Gemma and what he saw now was so disturbing. She was wringing wet, her eyes were sunken, her face was drawn, and those thin scars were everywhere on her body. He could tell the baby was dead. The little mite was blue and lifeless. Gemma was still crying and rocking like a deranged woman.

He hadn't had a puff, a snort, or a drink, and yet his brain was reluctant to believe what he was seeing. Gemma didn't see him though, as she was too immersed in her grief, clutching her baby and willing him back to life.

Gripped by an overwhelming sense of guilt, he knelt down beside her and tried to take the baby. She almost snarled at him as she gripped the little body tighter. Her face said it all. He had never seen her like that. She would have killed him if she could.

"Come on, babe, give the baby to me. Let me help you."

Gemma looked at his face and suddenly snapped, "Get away from me! Don't you dare touch my baby!"

Bobby almost jumped back. The venom in her voice was unbelievable. She was like something out of *The Exorcist*. He paused and looked at the blood still oozing out from between her legs with the cord still attached. The afterbirth must be still inside.

"Listen, Gems, you have to give me the baby. There's nothing else you can do. Come on, babe, we have to get the rest out or you're gonna die." He had seen it somewhere on the TV.

"Get away from me, don't you fucking touch me! You did this! I hate you, I hate all of you!" She sobbed into her baby's face, nestling him under her chin and kissing him. She looked up and glared at him coldly. "May you rot in hell, Bobby Ruthers. May you be haunted by my baby for the rest of your life." Her tone was alarming. She had stopped the hysterics and was acting like a cold, controlled woman. Her words and the expression on her face stopped Bobby in his tracks. He was scared. This was more chilling than a horror film. He was silent for a moment and then he knelt down by her side. "Please, Gemma, give him to me. We need to get the afterbirth out of you. Please, Gem, I'm sorry, I'm so sorry."

Gemma was now in a different place; her mind was gone and only her body was in the bathroom.

She kissed her baby one more time and in resignation handed him over.

He pulled out a flick knife and cut the cord. She lay there watching; the tears were burning her cheeks. As she rolled over, she felt the afterbirth come away. The last part of her baby was gone.

He wrapped the baby in a towel and looked down at the perfect, tiny, round face, which was framed with soft blond curls. He knew he was the father and a tear left his eye and dripped on the baby's face. After he laid the baby on the bed, he returned to the bathroom. Gemma was on her feet but unsteady. He grabbed her arm and helped her into the shower. She was so thin. He hadn't noticed before but her arms were like bare bones. The warm bubbles washed away the blood and sweat. He stood by her side, holding up her frail body, and then he wrapped her in a towel, guided her to the bedroom, and helped her onto the bed. They both lay there in silence with the baby between them.

The tears continued to roll down Gemma's face. He pulled open the bedside drawer and retrieved two tablets. "Here, babes, take these. It'll help."

She hadn't noticed he was being kind. Too grief-stricken, she assumed he was handing her a way out. However, the pain of losing her baby was so great that she forced herself to swallow them. Eventually, the room became dark but not before she noticed the clock flashing 18:30 11 July 1997. She drifted into sedation, memorising her son's birthday. Bobby called his mother and told her what had happened. Her reply was harsh. "For fuck's sake, that's all we fucking need, some nosy quack digging around. Go and dump the baby and keep her sedated for a while. You can tell her that a doctor came and took him away."

Violet hadn't taken into account that Bobby would also be hurting and that it was his baby too. If he hadn't held Gemma prisoner, maybe the child would have lived. She would have called him, or an ambulance, and they could have saved him. Gemma wouldn't be so thin and not so sick. He had done this to her and all because his sister had said she'd been unfaithful.

Bobby knew his sister was a cruel cunt and did at times question her honesty but only in his own head. She had the family behind her and he couldn't go against all of them. His older brothers had been home for some time and were pleased with his work. He had maintained their business, pimping out the girls and running the drugs. But now they had another business — a bigger moneymaking racket. There was no place for soppiness. They were ruthless, he knew it, and yet they had clout and money, and he wanted the same.

He looked back at Gemma. Even as she slept, he could see torment and pain still etched across her sweet face. His heart ached and he knew he did love her. She was a kid when they had met and now she was a woman and she was a beautiful one too.

He called the doctor, ignoring his mother's advice. He could not just dump his own son.

The doctor arrived while Gemma was still asleep. He checked the baby over and concluded he was strangled by his own cord. "Why didn't your wife call an ambulance or anyone else?"

Bobby looked at the floor. "I mistakenly took her phone to work with me, and she didn't have time to get help. The baby came too quickly."

"I need to take the afterbirth as well."

Bobby led him to the bathroom where the body sac was intact on the floor.

"I'll call an ambulance to take her to the hospital."

"No!" snapped Bobby. "Err, sorry, I mean she hates hospital, and she's been through so much ... can't you check her over here?"

The doctor agreed and went to Gemma's side. "She seems very drowsy," he said, and glared at Bobby.

Bobby sighed. "Yeah, she's a drug user, I'm afraid. Not sure what she's taken."

"And those marks up her arms?"

"Self-harmer." His reply was matter-of-fact.

The doctor walked away, taking notes. He would make sure it was highlighted on the young woman's file that she was a drug taker.

A black ambulance arrived and took the baby away. Gemma was still drowsy and Bobby kept her that way for a few days. He cleaned the house, cooked her food, and tried to nurse her back to health, but she liked the tablets; they stopped her facing the reality of the situation. As the weeks rolled by, she got stronger. The vision of her cruel husband's face, when he'd pulled her hair, and thrown her to the floor, and when he'd sliced her skin relentlessly, eventually subsided. He was gazing with adoring eyes and kindness in his heart. He told her how sorry he was about the baby and how he wanted to try and get their relationship back on track.

Gemma had gone through almost a year of hell and was vulnerable, so she accepted his words and agreed to make another go of it. The weeks that followed were spent with Bobby overcompensating for the shit he'd put her through. But she never forgot her little boy and would still shed a tear now and then.

"Bobby, are you going to tell your family that we are … err?"

She didn't know what to call them anymore; what was she to him now?

"Yes, babe, I've told me mother that we are starting afresh. All that shit is behind us now. In fact, she said to come over Sunday for dinner. You can meet me brothers."

Gemma froze, as suddenly it hit her. He wanted to reunite her with his sick, evil family. She wasn't just married to him, she was married to the whole poxy lot of them.

"What's up, babe? You gone quiet."

"I … err … I don't know if I'm ready."

Bobby threw her a hard glance; she hated his expression of disdain. "They've forgiven you, like I have, so you ain't got any worries there."

Those words hit her hard. There was nothing 'to forgive', as she had done nothing wrong, but she had paid the ultimate price in losing her baby. She bit down on her lip and tried to contain her anger. She thought of the razor and headed for the bathroom: it was gone. She scanned the room: no blade. She frantically rummaged through the drawers: nothing. He had thrown them all away.

The reflection in the mirror was new. She hadn't looked at herself in months but she looked well. All except the scars had cleared up and make-up could cover those. The look in her eyes was new too: cold and hard. She wasn't the same Gemma, but how could she be? Life had dealt her too many blows. As a child, she'd had hope, and she'd allowed the past to be just that: the past. She'd looked to the future and to pastures new, with the wish for a happy ending to her dismal childhood. Now, as a twenty-one-year-old woman, she realised that this was probably an unrealistic expectation: life wasn't a fairy tale. Instead, this was it: it was harsh and unforgiving. She gave up on any expectation of playing on a sandy beach with her children building sandcastles or of her husband buying that little house in the country with dogs and chickens. The images of what her future life should be like were fading, and she knew that it was all a wild fantasy and one that was probably shared by most people. She was now living in the real world, the dog-eat-dog world, where only the famous and infamous really hold sway.

It dawned on her that if she didn't become part of his family again, she would be a prisoner forever. Her lungs filled with a fast force of air as she threw her shoulders back. There would be no more feeling sorry for herself. She was going to do whatever it took to live again, leaving no compassion whatsoever for another living soul.

Breaking away from talking to Francesca and Jamie, she remembered that time well. It was the moment her former life ended and a new one began. She'd resolved then to take down Bobby's entire family – every fucking one of them – and take over all their businesses for herself.

Sunday arrived in no time and she appeared from the bedroom dressed in tight jeans, a black jumper, and knee high boots. She covered the scars and added a small amount of make-up. Her hair, she pulled back into a tight ponytail. She didn't look the sweet child anymore, for now she had taken on a sophisticated air. Her once round face was different now. Her weight loss accentuated her high cheekbones and she was every bit a woman. It was the cold expression and confident stance that captured Bobby's attention. He stared longer than he normally would and Gemma noticed.

"Babe, you look … err …"

"Better," she replied, coldly.

"Yeah, kinda strong."

She smirked and gave him a sadistic eye.

Her new persona almost knocked Bobby sideways as he had never seen her like that before. She was so different that he was unsure, and he smiled nervously at her. What he thought was confidence though was in actual fact a woman with her soul ripped out of her – devoid of emotion. What could ever hurt her more than what she had been through? She felt she might still love Bobby, but she was distant now, and she wouldn't expect too much from him, not ever again. The trust had gone.

She'd thought that standing at the back door of Violet's house would send her into a panic but it didn't. She was just going through the motions.

The sight of seeing them all there, sitting around that extra-large wooden table, should have overwhelmed and even intimidated her, but she felt more than capable of handling herself now. They appeared to her like a bunch of animals around a watering hole, much like hippos. It was the first time that the three older brothers had laid eyes on her. George and Charlie had been out for almost a year, during the time Gemma had been locked in the flat. She knew little about them. But this was not the case with Jimmy, whose reputation with women was legendary and not in a good way either. He was now taking an interest in her, ogling her up and down in a sleazy manner. George smiled and sat back on his chair. "So this is Gemma? Well, she's a looker all right, Bobby boy." He laughed.

Violet and her daughters were looking uneasy *and so they should be*, she thought to herself. It was apparent they didn't know what to say and were probably surprised to see Gemma standing so tall and upright, albeit with a stone face, unlike the eager-to-please kid she'd been just twelve months ago.

Rita wanted to have a dig. She was even more jealous than ever, but she'd paid Gemma back big time and knew she should let it go.

Violet gave a tense grin. "You sit there, Gemma, next to Bobby. D'ya want gravy?" Her tone was stony but then that was her all over.

The table was covered in food. A huge joint of beef, two roast chickens, and a tray of Yorkshire puddings and stuffing, took pride of place on the oak table. The men were slicing and grabbing as if they hadn't eaten for a week. Rita looked away from Gemma, as she was too focused on the food and on her own thoughts. But Gemma wasn't hungry. Watching them eat, like a pack of wolves, turned her stomach.

Then Violet looked up and noticed that Gemma was pushing the food around on her plate. "What's up, girl? Not good enough for ya? Or are you on one of those fad diets?"

Gemma smiled almost sarcastically. "The food is wonderful, and no, I am not on a diet."

The others stopped shoving food into their faces and watched, trying to ascertain the emotional temperature of the two women. They just could not be sure whether Gemma was being funny or polite. She cut into a roast potato and serenely popped it into her mouth, looking at everyone in turn with a sweet smile on her face. Violet was lost for words.

Charlie was the first to make Gemma feel welcome. "So, Gemma, Muvver 'ere tells me ya made a good debt collector before you took sick."

Gemma wanted to laugh out loud. *So that's what she'd told them: I was sick.*

"Oh, I guess so," she replied flippantly, flicking her long fringe from her eyes.

"Well, girl, now ya all better, I may have a bit of work for you."

Gemma thought Charlie was a bit of a flash prick. He was dressed in a poncy suit and his other distinguishing features revealed a gold tooth and a glint in his eyes. George was almost identical, but his eyes were heavier and his movements slower. Jimmy looked like the backward brother he was and as Daisy had said – one real nasty and ugly bastard.

However, she didn't care what they thought of her anymore. In fact, she was past trying to impress this family.

"Oh, yeah? What's that, then?" There was a condescending tone to her voice.

Violet looked up and glared at Bobby. Bobby noticed this, but he pretended he was too busy looking down at his food, although the fact that his foot was tapping nervously under the table was a bit of a giveaway sign he was nervous. He knew she was acting oddly.

Charlie laughed. "Ya got gumption, girl, ain't ya?"

Gemma shrugged her shoulders; *it was another confident move, but how far could she go with this charade*, she thought? She realised she needed to tread a little carefully with this bunch of animals.

"I got some brasses living out of me flats up town," he carried on, "and Tressa ain't got time to collect the rent and poke. She has bigger fish to fry now, don't ya, Tress?" He winked her way and then turned to face Gemma. "So you can 'ave that job."

Gemma chewed the inside of her lip in thought. For a second, she wondered what the bigger fish were. However, it didn't concern her, so she switched her thoughts back to herself. "How much are we talking about?" she asked, brazenly.

George placed his fork down and sat upright. "You what?" he snarled.

Bobby grabbed Gemma's knees under the table to shut her up.

"How much are ya gonna pay me?" Now all eyes were glaring at her and Bobby was digging his fingers into her knees, but she was indifferent to their angry expressions. In fact, she was quite enjoying this.

Rita made a pathetic attempt at a false laugh. "I thought you was supposed to be part of the family again, ya cheeky cunt."

Gemma looked her directly in the eyes and replied, "Well, Rita, that's your choice, but it ain't mine to make, now, is it?"

Rita was dumbfounded that Gemma would dare to speak like that. It wasn't just the words; it was the proud tone of voice, which implied 'bollocks to the lot of you'.

"All right, I think Bobby's Gemma needs to learn how things work in this family. I'm fucking surprised at you, Bobby, for not

239

putting her straight. Ya see, Gemma, we don't pay you a wage. It don't work like that, does it, Bobby?" spat Charlie.

Bobby was hot under the collar.

"How does it work, then?" asked Gemma, sweetly, totally unperturbed by the tension in the room. Whatever they chose to do with her could never hurt as much as the pain she felt inside.

Violet put her cutlery down and slid her chair away from the table. "I don't like your cocky fucking tone. I'm surprised that you have the front of an alley cat to ask for wages. Who do you think you are, eh? Our Bobby keeps you in clobber, in a nice pad, and I gave you a cunting van, and now ya want wages!" Her voice was climbing up through the screeching pitches to a level that did her own ears in.

Gemma remained calm and replied, "I want to earn me own money so I can treat my husband to nice things. I want to come home from work with tickets to the theatre or a trip to Venice and stuff like that." She was lying, of course; she wanted to save up, so if things went completely pear-shaped again and Bobby turned back into the monster he'd been a few months ago, she could do the off.

Violet was angry that the girl had answered her back, but she was lost for words. How could she answer that? The undertone, however, was menacing, and she felt it.

Charlie grunted as he conceded, "Yeah, well, all right, you can go on the payroll. Let me tell you, though, that money you collect ain't for your pocket, got it?"

Gemma nodded. "Yep, I can be trusted, just you see."

Charlie laughed. "Good girl. Will five hundred a week do ya?"

Gemma nearly choked on another of her roast potatoes; that was way more than she'd expected.

Rita was livid and couldn't keep her mouth shut. "Are you on something, Charlie? I fucking earn that, and she … well, she ain't family."

"Correct me, Rita, if I am fucking wrong, but ain't she married, proper wed, to our Bobby? Because in my book that makes her fucking family," growled Charlie.

Rita pursed her pouting lips. It was always the same. The three older brothers called the shots and were always backed up by Violet.

"You better not let us down or Charlie will be collecting rent from you," stated Violet, cementing her role as head of the family. However, her queen-like status was short-lived.

Gemma still had the last word. "I didn't fuck-up before, did I? I intend to take me job seriously."

Violet grunted; she didn't like Gemma anymore and her cool front was really quite unnerving. The boys hadn't known her before and of course they just assumed this was who she was. In reality, the eager-to-please Gemma had gone and instead Violet was faced with a strong-willed woman and one with a tongue in her head. The kid she could order about had disappeared and without being in full control of her she was left wondering.

That evening on the way home there was silence. Bobby didn't know whether to feel proud of Gemma or livid with her. He decided, however, to show no reaction. Nevertheless, it wouldn't have bothered Gemma either way. She guessed that she had riled them up, but she would do as she'd promised.

241

Charlie picked her up the next day in his flash Mercedes. She dressed herself in dark clothes; the bright colours and sparkly jewellery had been pushed to the back of the wardrobe. They didn't reflect her personality anymore. The trip to north London was a nightmare as the traffic was heavy and Charlie was banging on and on about what she had to do, as if she had no brains to think for herself.

"So, Gemma, if any of the brasses act up and get lippy, ya tell them that they either hand the money over to you or Jim will come and collect it, and then there'll be interest." He laughed out loud. "That puts the fear of Christ up their fannies."

Gemma looked ahead, nonchalantly; she believed him, though. Jim was vile, a real creep, just as Daisy had described him. She hadn't thought about Daisy until now. If she knew what Gemma was doing for a job, she wouldn't be best pleased. She missed her friend, her soothing voice, and her cosy home. She would go and see her, but not just yet, and not when she was on a trial. She had to play the game and assure the family she could be trusted.

The first flat in the block belonged to Bunny Robins. Gemma assumed it was a fake name. Charlie banged hard on the door and instantly it opened to reveal a very attractive and heavily made-up young woman. Gemma guessed she was probably younger than she was.

Bunny cocked her head to the side. "I got ya money, but I had a bad week." She hoisted her dress up to show black bruises on her thighs and stomach. The fact she was revealing her fanny meant nothing to her. She had lost her dignity years before. "Got me gear, Charlie? I'm almost out." Bunny was shaking and fumbling. It wasn't nerves either. Gemma noticed the vacant look in the girl's eyes.

"Shut ya mouth and get inside!" he snapped back.

The girl lowered her head and turned around to walk through to the lounge. Charlie and Gemma followed. Gemma expected a room like Daisy's and was shocked to find a cold, miserable place. Wallpaper was peeling off the walls and mould grew from the floor up to the ceiling. She could smell the damp. The bed, however, was immaculate. A crisp white sheet edged the deep red satin duvet cover. The kitchenette was grotty and the sofa was shabby. Gemma clocked the needles neatly lined up alongside a black spoon.

"Don't ya ever discuss business on the fucking doorstep, got it, cunt?"

The girl was shaking more than ever. "Sorry, Charlie, I just need me gear."

Charlie put his hand out. "Where's me money?"

"Like I said, I didn't earn too much this week. That Charles Enright is a bit rough—"

Charlie grabbed her hair. "I'll only warn you once. Charles Enright can do what the fuck he likes. If you have a problem, then get ya stuff and fuck off. I got a list as long as me arm for this flat." He let go of the girl's hair and glared.

"Sorry, Charlie."

"You make sure if he wants your arse, ya treat him like God, and if I find out otherwise, then trust me, Jim will pay you a visit. You won't know what rough is when he gets his hands on ya." He tapped her face with his fat fingers.

She lifted up the well-worn rug and retrieved a wad of notes. "I got the rent and three hundred."

Charlie snatched the money and sighed. "Ya better make up for it next week when she comes to collect. She's got Jimmy on speed dial."

The girl looked at Gemma and nodded so much her head looked like it was going to fall off. Gemma's cold expression scared the shit out of the young girl. Little did she know that Gemma felt gutted for the poor wretch and was cringing inside. Gemma smiled ruefully to herself at the irony of the present situation. Hadn't she been in a similar position as this young girl, almost one year ago, in being on the receiving end of her family's violent threats?

As Charlie handed the girl a very small packet, her expression changed and she looked up with resigned sadness. The hope that she was getting enough heroin to see her through the week was gone. She would have to buy her own to top-up and that meant walking the streets too.

Gemma silently took it all in. Every one of the girls in that block was no more than sixteen and all were hooked on heroin. Charlie was harsh, sharp, and spiteful.

"Give 'em an inch, Gem, and they'll fucking take a yard. Ya can't be soft, now. They know what they're doing. What they don't appreciate is the roof over their heads and the punters sent to the door. They could be out on the street wiv no protection and then it's game over. They'd be dead in a ditch, if it weren't for us."

"Yep," was all she said. What else could she say? She was in up to her neck as it was.

The next five days were all the same. They visited blocks of flats and big houses converted to bedsits, all of which were run-down, damp, and cold. Gemma's job was simple: from Monday to Friday she collected their money and there was no margin for excuses.

On her first day on the job, she sensed someone following her and assumed it was planned. After all, why would they trust her anyway? Her first collection was Bunny Robins – she was the girl she'd met the week before.

She banged hard on the door and instantly the girl opened it.

"Ya got the money?" asked Gemma, with no feeling to her voice.

Bunny ran to the kitchen and returned with a wad. "It's all there and two hundred extra. Have ya got me ...?" She froze, remembering the warning from Charlie.

Gemma handed her a packet and the girl smiled. "Fanks, err, what's ya name again?"

Gemma didn't want to say her name because then they would be in a conversation and she didn't want to get involved with the girl. She had to remain detached. So she just shook her head and walked away. The next flat was Summer's. She was a tiny little thing with wild black curls and whiter-than-white skin. She could have been fifteen but the brown circles around her eyes had probably aged her by ten years. Gemma stepped inside the cold flat and shivered. Again, the bed was immaculate but what disturbed her was the presence of ropes, handcuffs, and whips. Summer walked towards the kitchen area and Gemma noticed the state of her legs as her dressing gown flapped open. She winced; the black bruises looked horrendous. Not only that but her ankles were covered in injection sites and she had scars like her own.

"'Ere, it's all there. Count it if ya want." She handed Gemma the money and sat on the ripped sofa. "Do you like your job?"

"Nope, but like you I have to earn money."

Gemma handed her a packet and left but not before she heard Summer mumble under her breath, "You're nothing like me."

She didn't challenge it. What was the point? It was true she was nothing like them, and she knew she was fortunate, as they were living a sad and manipulated life, with no hope.

For a year, Gemma continued to collect rent from the prostitutes. In that time, she watched the young women age rapidly and fall into a complete downward spiral with no way to ever return from the netherworld they were living in. She tried not to listen to their pleas for help or their excuses for their downfall in earning money. She stayed strong and took what they had, as she soon realised that the threat of sending Jim or Charlie over was enough to have them shitting hot bricks. The terror in their eyes was heart-wrenching, but Gemma had become hardened to it. She tried not to see them as kids, barely out of school, but more like animals, as this helped appease her conscience.

Violet was still a hard-faced bitch and so Gemma spent as little time as possible around the family. Rita was the worst. She continually made sly threats when no one was around just to keep Gemma on her toes, but in reality Gemma wasn't scared of Rita anymore.

Bobby was spending more time with Tressa, since they were both learning the ropes. What business they were up to, she never asked. Maybe it was because, deep down in her heart, she sensed that the men's business was more corrupt than the young prostitute racket she was now mixed up in.

Gemma tried to love Bobby like she had before, but there was always that doubt in her mind that he could go back to how he was in the months before the baby was born. She never truly forgave him

246

and she blamed him for her little boy's death. She had to keep up the pretence now, though; she was in too deep to ever escape their clutches. Bobby wanted to try again for another baby, but she'd secretly had a coil fitted.

The five hundred pounds weekly money was gradually building up to a nice little stash. She bought Bobby bits and pieces, and stuff for herself, just to show she wasn't hiding it. One Tuesday morning, Gemma got up very early and decided to go off to work and then spend the afternoon searching for a decent hairdresser. She arrived at the first flat in the block at five in the morning. The girls were usually up until ten and then they slept so they'd be ready for the night-time punters. The main heavy front door was a bastard to push open, but just as Gemma managed to squeeze through, she heard a blood-curdling scream and then muffled sounds, coming from Summer's flat. Gemma's heart was in her mouth; she had no weapon and had left her phone at home. She heard Summer begging for whoever it was to stop. Gemma couldn't listen to the sound anymore and was on the point of leaving when it hit her. She could not let a girl die – no amount of money was worth that. Not knowing who was inside, she ran to the door and banged hard and then hurried and hid around the corner. She couldn't risk getting caught interfering. Suddenly, the door opened and she just managed to catch the back of Jimmy Ruthers, running from the flat. She hoped he wouldn't look back and see her.

Summer was on the edge of the bed shaking uncontrollably. Gemma slammed the door shut and rushed to her side. "What the fuck happened?"

Slowly, Summer removed her hands from her face, and there, almost flapping away from her face, was her cheek.

"Jesus!" shouted Gemma.

247

The slice across her cheeks was gruesome, and with her hand away from her face, the blood began to pour. Gemma jumped up and ran to the kitchen, desperately trying to find a clean cloth, some kitchen roll, or anything in fact. She managed to find a tea towel and rushed back. She pulled the girl's hand away and pressed the towel against the flapping skin. "Hold that tight. Right, let's get you dressed and up to the hospital."

"No, I can't, they'll ask questions and I'll be—" She stopped abruptly, seeing the expression on Gemma's face. Gemma looked horrified. The girl couldn't be left like that – no way – or she could get an infection or, worse, die.

"Get dressed. Come on, I'll help you." Gemma pulled open the small wardrobe and grabbed a modest-looking dress. She tried to pull it over Summer's head without tugging at her damaged face. Summer was in shock. She didn't have the energy to argue as the pain was unbearable and the blood was still oozing down her neck. She was going whiter, if that was possible, and Gemma knew if she didn't get her in the van she would faint.

The journey to the hospital was a quick one. Gemma drove like a madman, screaming and shouting at people to get out of the way. Summer was holding the towel tight to her face, hoping the bleeding would stop.

"Right, when we get in there just tell them you wasn't looking where you was going and tripped into a broken window."

"Yeah, all right, but please don't tell Charlie, please," begged Summer.

"I ain't gonna, don't fucking worry. We'll sort this out," Gemma assured her. A car was dawdling along in front of her. "Get outta me fucking way, cunt!" she bellowed.

248

They pulled up outside the hospital in a 'do not park here' zone, but Gemma ignored the sign and helped Summer inside. The receptionist hurried her into a cubicle and within minutes the doctor arrived and peeled back the towel. Even he looked shocked. The edges of the flapping cheek were beginning to shrivel up, and he had to get the plastic surgeon down urgently or Summer would be seriously disfigured.

Gemma had to go as she couldn't risk being questioned. As soon as the doctor left the cubicle, she shoved a fifty pound note in Summer's hand. "I gotta get out of here. I'm gonna come over to yours tomorrow. Leave everything to me. Jesus, why would Jimmy do that?"

Summer lowered her face and whispered, "He's a wicked man. He's truly sick in the head. If you hadn't knocked ... Oh my God, he would have killed me. I don't know who is worse, him or Charles Enright."

"Who?" asked Gemma.

She paused and looked at Gemma with puppy-dog eyes. "Oh, never mind ... Look, I don't even know your name, but thank you. You probably saved my life. I may not have much of one now, but one day I might do, eh?"

Gemma swallowed hard to get rid of the lump in her throat. "Yeah, course ya gonna have a life, babe."

She fled down the hospital corridor and just managed to jump in the van before she was clamped. Everything had happened so fast, she didn't have time to think. Then it all hit her: she was a part of a terrible game.

Gemma forced her eyes to glaze over as she looked at Francesca. She realised that this interview and subsequent ones were crucial. She'd done plenty of planning in her cell in preparation for the day she would have to get her version of the truth over to Francesca – always assuming, of course, that the lawyer could be enticed into her web of deceit. She'd seen Francesca at work, so she had to be at the top of her game to ensure her story sounded convincing. So how did she feel now? *This little yarn would definitely have the barrister sucked in and rooting for her. In her mind, that story guaranteed Francesca would pull out all the stops to get her out of the nick as soon as possible. She had lain in bed for night after night, practising how she would throw in that curved ball about Charles Enright, if she ever had the opportunity. Well, now she just had, and boy, did it feel good!*

CHAPTER ELEVEN

Francesca stopped the tape. Jamie's throat tightened. He knew what Charles had done to Francesca and hearing Gemma describe the poor girl's ordeal sickened him. He held back a tear and reached for Francesca's wrist under the table. She felt his strong hand and turned to give him a reassuring smile. Gemma looked at their faces, knowing only too well that naming Charles Enright would stir their emotions; it was a masterstroke. She naïvely assumed that Francesca would be on her side now and hell-bent on getting her out of prison.

Francesca looked at the clock and turned the tape back on. "We don't have long. Please, carry on. We have to know everything."

Gemma breathed deeply and gave Francesca a brave little smile. She was enjoying herself, enjoying the story she was spinning, and enjoying reeling Francesca and Jamie in. And so the tale continued. She would pretend she was the young girls' knight in shining armour.

*

Gemma returned to the flats with a heavy heart. She'd distanced herself for so long and now it was as if she had woken up and realised she must do something about this atrocity.

Bunny opened the door and pulled Gemma inside. She looked dreadful and her shakes were worse than ever. Her lovely long hair was now thin and her skin was ageing. "I saw you through the window. What happened to Summer? Is she all right?"

Gemma could see the girl was nervous.

"No, she ain't. Jimmy cut her face. I've taken her to hospital, but we can't let the Ruthers know, okay? So keep schtum."

Bunny slowly nodded. "I thought you were a Ruthers."

"Yeah, well, technically I am, but by fucking marriage, not blood. Christ, I can't believe I've   been doing this!"

Bunny frowned. "What?"

"Collecting money from you girls. I should have been helping you. What was I thinking?"

Bunny rubbed her arm. "You might not know it, but you have helped. At least you don't hurt us. That Jim, he's a cruel man ... mind you, so are George and Charlie. And at least you don't ask for freebies."

Gemma laughed; it was so surreal. "How can I help? What the fuck can I do?"

Bunny smiled. "We don't know your name."

Gemma decided to tell her. "It's Gemma."

"Gemma, there's nothing you can do except come for our money yourself. They are dangerous people and it's better that you don't get on their bad side, or you'll end up here, like Jasmin did. Poor woman, she had it all. George was with her for a year. Then, when he was done with her, she ended up in the flat next door, out of her head on heroin. It was so sad."

"What happened to her?"

Bunny's eyes welled up. "She was stunning, you know? Long black shiny hair and the prettiest eyes. She could have been a top model. I guess she knew too much, so they made sure she was well and truly hooked on the gear. Completely off her face most of the time. Then, one night, that Charles Enright came with another one of our punters, a guy called Wiers. They must've liked a two's up or something, but after that she was never the same. She disappeared one night. I guess she made a run for it, but that serial killer out there got hold of her. So, Gemma, just do as they say."

"Tell me, Bunny, why don't any of you go to the police?"

Bunny laughed. "Some of the girls have tried, but the Ruthers are somehow protected. They have lawyers that get them off — the Enrights and that bastard Wiers. In fact, we have more judges and lawyers getting their bit of strange than the average guy on the street. I wish they were normal but they're cruel. Honestly, I'd be safer on the streets if that face-slashing serial killer weren't out there. It's on the news that he's killed five toms, but they don't know the half of it. So many more girls go missing, but we are nobodies and it doesn't get reported. Sad, really."

That afternoon, Gemma headed for Violet's house. As she passed Major in the garden, she handed him a pig's ear as a treat. He loved them and she loved the puppy, who was only a few months' old.

The back door was ajar and she waited, listening.

George, Charlie, and Jim were inside talking to Violet. It appeared that their new business was taking off.

"Muvver, we need an extra hundred grand. Alex has organised another run."

"Cor, fuck me, boy, a hundred grand? Those girls better be top dollar, no skanky-looking bitches."

"Nah, the last lot were good. Nice little clean classy bits they were. Jim gave them the once over, didn't ya, Jim?"

Violet laughed out loud. "That don't mean shit. Jim would fuck anything, even a pig if it had lipstick on, the dirty cunt!"

Gemma could hear them laughing. It was nothing to them. After all, the girls were just a commodity. It sickened her.

"So where are these girls going, then, George?"

"Alex has a new set-up. It's a fucking great big mansion away from London. Igor is making sure it is lock-tight. They won't be able to escape. He's proper mustard, is Alex. Cor, I wouldn't wanna take him on, let me tell ya," said George.

"Who's gonna run it? Only Bobby and Lenny are like a fart in a trance, the pair of 'em. I suggest ya stick Rita in there. She can take the food and ensure all the necessaries."

George snorted. "No way, Muvver, not Rita. No disrespect, but she ain't got the charm and could lose us business. Nah, keep Rita running the drugs. Charlie wants Tressa in the new mansion. She is good at all that stuff and she's also shown her worth over the last two years. Gemma's running the flats well enough. Tressa is well liked by the Russians, and soon we can shut the old villa lock-up and make a fucking mint with this one. Ya wanna see it, Muvver, it's huge and exclusive. The punters will love it."

Violet screwed her nose up. Rita was her favourite, but George and Charlie knew what they were doing.

"Anyway, this hunter idea is a fucking blindin' one. I got a couple of clients already interested." Violet's face looked a picture as her eyes registered the potential profits to be had.

Charlie laughed. "Ya don't fuck about, Muvver, do ya? So who ya got interested, then?"

Violet sat back heavily on her chair and smirked. "None other than Charlie boy and his cronies. Fucking amazes me. They're all rich and clever and still they love a bit of strange. It goes to show ya, there's many a wolf in sheep's clothing."

"I couldn't give a flying fuck as long as they're there with the readies," said Charlie.

"Anyway, boys, I got a parcel arriving very soon. Are two hundred stun guns any good to ya?"

"Muvver, ya have your hands in so many fucking pies, ya wanna slow down in ya old age." Charlie laughed.

"Oi, you cheeky muvver's ruin, I ain't old! For your information, I like to keep me nose to the ground, and any good deals going, I'm the first in the queue. Ya might wanna learn from that, divvy boy."

George stepped in. "Let me tell ya, the new business will bring in thousands. Ya don't need to be ducking and diving, selling knocked-off gear, or dealing in dodgy twenties or drugs. Ma, ya can put ya feet up in a nice luxury home by the sea."

"Fuck off, I ain't leaving me home. This is me. I like it 'ere, and that, me boy, will never change, if I am a millionaire or not."

The older boys had been telling her for years she could live anywhere. She had more money than any fucker in Streatham. She loved her life, sitting there with her three big boys. They were as

255

hard as nails and a right chip off the old block. She revelled in gossip and plans of criminal money-making scams. The idea that they were a Face kept her going. She was the queen of the underworld and lived for that status.

Gemma was grinding her teeth as she listened to the conversation. She'd heard no word about the mansion. This was the first she'd heard of it. Major barked and made her jump. She turned around to see Lenny struggling with a big cardboard box. She had to pretend she was one of them, and so she ran down the path to give him a hand. He was always quiet around her, as was Jimmy, but they both still had those creepy eyes, which raked over her, all the while undressing her. They carried an end each. Gemma pushed the door open with her foot and together they lifted the box onto the table. Violet was like a rat up a drainpipe. She jumped from her seat and ripped off the lid. "Cor blimey, these are gonna make a tidy few grand."

She pulled out a stun gun and turned it around. George laughed and helped himself to one. "Not bad, but how d'ya know they're gonna work?"

Jim was licking his lips, a bad habit of his, but then his whole life revolved around bad habits. The sores around his mouth added to his ugliness. "Major!" he shouted.

Gemma managed to stop the gasp leaving her mouth. She felt her heart beating so fast. *Please, no, not the dog.*

He snatched the gun from George and in a flash he'd rammed the two points into the dog's neck. Gemma didn't have time to intervene. The poor puppy made a high-pitched scream and then collapsed, convulsing like he was having a fit. The others looked on, totally unperturbed. Gemma jumped to Major's side and held his head to stop it from smashing on the tiled floor. She glared up at Jimmy, wanting nothing more than to grab that gun and ram it into his potholed face. The dog finally stopped shaking and then tried to get to his feet.

"Well, they work, then, Muvver." Charlie laughed.

"Yep, I reckon they are gonna go for a ton each," said George.

Gemma stared at them in amazement. They really were fucking cruel bastards with no conscience or compassion. She helped Major back outside and gave him a drink of water. His eyes looked dazed and his head was still floppy. She guided him into the kennel and helped him to lie down on his blanket.

"Gemma, leave the fucking mutt and get inside. Ya ain't left the money!"

Gemma bit her lip. She had the money in her bag. "Coming."

George, Charlie, and Jimmy were ready to leave. They stood up and each kissed their mother in turn. Jim was still giving Gemma the eye, which made her cringe. She hated him with a passion.

Lenny was upstairs and Violet was alone.

"Here you go. There's the seven packets. All paid the full amount and none owing."

"You wanna check yaself, girl. There's no room for soft touches in this business," Violet chided, a look of malice on her face.

"Wanna cup of tea, Violet?" asked Gemma. She wanted to find a way to get her hands on some of those stun guns. The box was packed; Violet wouldn't notice a few missing.

"Yeah, make it strong and no gnat's piss." Violet rummaged through the box.

Gemma placed the tea in front of Violet and sat opposite. She didn't really know what to say because she had made a point over the last few years not to make conversation.

"So, what is it, then, girl?"

"What do you mean?" Gemma cocked her head to the side.

"Ya never sit with me for tea, so what's fucking changed?"

Gemma sensed Violet was uncomfortable and that was probably a good enough reason to stay. "Well, there ya go. We don't really talk and maybe we should. After all, you are me mother-in-law. I never had a mother of me own. I thought I should make more of an effort. It's taken me a year to get over the baby. I guess I shut everyone out, and it's time I moved on and started to enjoy being part of the family."

Gemma could see that Violet was mulling it over, and she stared at her with those questioning beady eyes.

"About time, girl, 'cos I, for one, was getting royally pissed off with your miserable boat race. I don't know how Bobby put up with it. I lost two babies, but ya didn't find me crying into me cornflakes. You have to get a grip. It ain't like ya can't 'ave another one. I ended up with seven. Shame two were girls, but still."

Shocked and stunned by those words, Gemma spoke without thinking. "So ya only wanted boys, then?"

Violet laughed. "I ain't one for pink frilly dresses, tantrums, and being a namby-pamby. Rita was a fucking fairy when she was young, but I soon knocked that out of her. Now look at her. She's as hard as a lead pipe and a worker. I got no time for nonsense."

"What about Tressa? She's very feminine."

"Ya can be as pretty as ya like, but inside ya gotta be tough. The most successful people in the world are the fucking hard ones. It don't pay to give a shit about anyone, 'cos, girl, d'ya think anyone gives a fuck about you? Nah, everyone's out for themselves, and me and mine will always be one step ahead. Hit 'em hard before they hit you. Now, girl, that's a valuable lesson I just taught ya. It's one I taught me kids, and you, being part of my family, will be wise to learn the same."

Gemma smiled and nodded. Violet was right. No one gave a shit, especially the Ruthers, and she would have to be one step ahead.

Violet finished her tea and then as usual she needed the toilet. Her clumping up the stairs gave Gemma time to grab some of the guns and hide them in her big tote bag. It must have been fate because she'd toyed with taking a small handbag to work that day, but she'd grabbed the larger one just in case she went shopping. After seizing about ten guns, and throwing them into her bag, she zipped it up and returned to her seat. Violet was only gone a few minutes, but it was enough time for Gemma to pinch the weapons. Her heart was pounding though.

"So, girl, what ya up to today?"

"I'm going to get a nice bit of beef and make a casserole for Bobby. I was gonna get me hair done. It's looking scruffy. Oh, yeah, before I forget. I don't know if ya got punters lined up for Summer over the next few days, only the slut's got chickenpox. Smothered she is. Ya couldn't get a fag paper between the pimples. Just thought ya should know."

259

"Bollocks, that's all I need, a run of the lurgies. Yeah, all right, I'll take her off me list for a bit."

"Do I still go and collect from her?"

Violet snarled, "Collect what? The bitch ain't gonna be earning now, is she?"

"No, s'pose not. Anyway, gonna get going. Thanks for the chat."

Just before Gemma left, she checked in on Major; he was still dazed. As she knelt down and stroked his head, Tressa slammed the garden gate and marched up the path. She stopped and glanced at the dog. "What the fuck is the matter with him?"

Gemma stood up. "Jim tried out a stun gun on him."

"What? He never!"

Gemma stared coldly at Tressa. "He did. I think he's fried the dog's brain." She knew Tressa loved the puppy too.

"Cunt!" she said, through gritted teeth.

Gemma nodded in agreement and left. She was aware then that Tressa hated Jim, or she would never have called him that – not in front of her.

With money in her purse, and the guns in her bag, she drove over to the flats, stopping at Tesco on the way. She bought some basics: bread, milk, a couple of microwave dishes, a new fluffy dressing gown, and bed sheets. When she had run around Summer's flat, looking for a clean towel, she'd noticed the girl had nothing.

She knocked, hoping Summer would be back from the hospital, and luckily she was, but the poor bitch was in a terrible state. Not only did she look as though she'd just had a few rounds with Nicola

Adams, but she'd lost a considerable amount of weight, probably from all the stress of the last few days. Gemma sat next to her on the crumpled settee.

"Listen, I've stopped any punters knocking for a few days. I said ya got chickenpox."

Summer tried to smile but the pain was too much. Under the heavy wadding and plasters were twenty stitches, holding her cheek in place. Luckily for her, the plastic surgeon had been on call and managed to do a neat job although it would be some time before anyone saw the results of his expertise. They wanted to keep her in and call the police because her little story didn't match the injury, but she refused and left before they could convince her otherwise.

"Summer, I got a few bits." She pointed to the Tesco bags. "I got some kinda protection too. Here, take this." She handed her one of the stun guns.

Summer's eyes widened – even the left one, although it was badly swollen.

"Take it, and if anyone tries to pull a stunt like that again, you can zap 'em."

Summer knew then that Gemma was on her side. "I don't know what to say, except thank you so much. The men that come to my door may be rich and successful but they're animals. My God they're disgusting"

Gemma frowned. "What do you mean by disgusting? I'm so naïve when it comes to this stuff."

"And let's hope you stay that way. They like to humiliate. As if we don't feel degraded enough as it is. It's too sordid to talk about."

Gemma listened to the girl and noticed how well-spoken she was. She might be hooked on heroin and slur her words a bit, but she was well educated and smart. It was ridiculous that a girl like Summer could end up in a shithole like this. She was worse than a prisoner.

"Thank you, Gemma, you're like an angel right now." Summer lowered her eyes.

"Oh, yeah. Look, take this. I know ya gonna be fucked without it." She handed over a small parcel of brown powder.

Summer smiled. "This makes the days and nights roll on by and allows me to hang on. It takes the pain away."

Gemma rubbed her arm. "Take care, Summer, I'll see ya next week. Make sure you do what the hospital doctors told you, eh?"

Summer nodded. She was weary and needed to sleep. The painkillers would wear off soon and the pain would be back.

Gemma paid the other girls a visit, handing over a stun gun to each of them, much to their surprise. Bunny's eyes were like saucers. "Fuck me, Gemma, this is one serious weapon. I'll keep it under me pillow. Thanks, mate, I owe ya one."

Time was getting on, and she had to get home or Bobby would wonder what she had been up to. If she didn't have shopping bags laden with purchases from different shops, he'd question how she'd spent her day. Suggesting she'd gone to the library wouldn't cut it. Just as she went to tug on the main entrance door, it opened, almost knocking her over. She caught her balance and turned white with shock; standing there, looking like a bulldog chewing a wasp, was Jimmy. He didn't move but just stared, and then he curled his lip like he was snarling. Gemma tried hard to come up with an excuse as to why she was there at five o'clock in the afternoon. They all knew her rounds were finished by eleven o'clock. If he had been to his mother's, he would also know she was supposed to be shopping. There was an awkward silence as they both stared, not moving, and then he spoke. "You ain't s'posed to be here now, are ya?" He looked her up and down.

"I, err, thought I dropped me purse in the hallway. I can't find it, see." That was a feeble excuse. She knew it and so did he. In a flash, he snatched her bag and tipped the contents on the floor. "Let me help ya, Gemma." His tone was cold and intimidating and she was shaking. There on the floor, along with her purse, were two stun guns. Too horrified to speak, she tried to pick up her belongings before he noticed, but it was too late. He pushed her aside and snatched the guns. "So, what have we here, then?"

Gemma was shaking, and with her back against the wall, she crumbled. There was no excuse and certainly not one she could come up with quickly enough. He threw her belongings back into the bag and grabbed her arm. She assumed he was going to march her back to Violet's and grass her up, but he didn't. Instead, he dragged her along the hallway to the room at the end. It was an empty flat. He opened the door and threw her inside, and then he pulled out a key and locked it shut.

"What the fuck are you doing? Jim, I gotta get home. Bobby will be worried."

He laughed, showing his red large gums and tiny white teeth. He licked his lips again. "You got yaself a little secret, ain't ya? And I'm gonna have one too." He took off his jacket and undid his belt, sliding it out of his trousers.

"Leave off, Jimmy! I'm Bobby's wife!" she screamed.

263

Jim laughed again. "Yeah, that's why I'm gonna keep our little secret in the family, just you and me. Don't worry, I won't tell them about ya lie or the stun guns." He walked towards her, grinning like a deranged sicko.

"No, Jim!" she screamed at the top of her voice.

He lunged forward and dragged her onto the bed. He was so strong. The force winded her and then he climbed on top. His breath could have smoked mackerel. He pushed his sharp stubble along her cheek, licking her face.

"Get off me!" she screamed, as loud as she could. He made a muffled grunting sound, and then, without warning, he had his hand in her knickers. His penchant for pretty young things, and modus operandi of being rough and vicious with his victims, certainly extended to Gemma, who was about to get a taste of his brutality. "Wanna real man, do ya?"

She had heard those words before when her foster father had raped her. This ugly, vile creature was not going to do the same. She screamed, "Help me!"

"Shut it, tramp. No one will hear you anyway," he growled, through gritted teeth.

There was a banging on the door and Jim froze, and then he jumped from the bed and zipped up his trousers. He snatched Gemma's bag, unlocked the door, and almost ripped it off its hinges. Bunny was standing there with one arm behind her back. Jim pulled back his fist and backhanded her, knocking her flying, then continued on along the corridor and out of the main entrance.

Gemma helped Bunny to her feet. "Jesus, he would have raped me, the horrible cunt. Bobby's own dirty brother!"

Bunny was going to have a shiner, that was for sure.

"You best get home and tell your ol' man right away. I tell you, that is so below the belt, it wouldn't surprise me if your Bobby rips him a new arsehole."

Gemma was still shaken up but had to get home and tell him. She called a cab. Luckily, she had her mobile in her back pocket, but her van keys had been in her bag. This was going to split the family apart, but she didn't care. She wanted nothing more than to have Bobby all to herself, away from the others. This might do them both a big favour. They could be free from the Ruthers' clutches once and for all.

The cab turned in to the close and she noticed that Bobby's car was gone. She had no way of paying the cab driver. Then she saw Lenny pull up. She ran over to him and asked for a score. He frowned. "What's up, Gem?"

"Nothing, but can I borrow a twenty? I'll pay ya back."

Lenny handed over two tenners and she paid the cab driver.

"Gemma, where's Bobby? He was supposed to be here with a bag for me. The fucking divvy knew I needed it tonight."

Gemma shrugged her shoulders.

Lenny's phone rang. "I bet that's him," he replied.

Gemma watched as Lenny's face changed, and he stared at her as he listened. She wished she could hear what was being said to him. Then he smiled. "Yeah, he's on his way. Come on, I got a set o' keys."

None the wiser, Gemma followed him up the stairs and into the flat.

"What's he say, Lenny?"

Lenny was grinning, as he usually did, which Gemma hated. He looked a lot like Bobby, but his character and expressions were more like Jimmy's. He had his eyes as well.

"Oh, nothing, just he was running late, and he'll meet us here in five minutes. I'm parched. Any chance of a brew?"

Gemma was still shaken from her ordeal, but she managed to put the kettle on and fill the teapot with tealeaves without spilling any.

Lenny's phone pinged and she watched as he read the text.

"Is it Bobby?"

Lenny nodded. "He said he had to go and see someone, but he's on his way. Any chance of a cheese sarnie? I'm fucking starving."

Gemma was anxious to say the least. She tried to stay unflustered as she made Lenny a sandwich.

Just before he tucked in, Bobby burst through the door. Lenny jumped from his seat and nodded to him. "All yours, bruv. Shall I bring back a body bag?"

Bobby ignored the comment. He stood like a raging bull, his chest heaving in and out.

Gemma waited for the door to shut. "Jesus, Bobby, ya fucking brother, Jim. He's mental, he tried to rape me!"

"Shut it!" he bellowed.

Gemma gasped. He was supposed to pull her close, tell her it would be all right, go mad and threaten to kill Jim. But he didn't, though. Instead, he just stared at her coldly as if she were a piece of shit.

She grabbed both his arms. "Bobby, what's going on? Ya brother tried to rape me, didn't you hear me?"

Bobby pushed her away. "Ya dirty sly cunt. Ya think you can pull a stroke like that, eh?"

This was déjà vu all over again. Gemma watched in fear as her husband's face turned back to the monster's mask. He had to believe her; surely, after all this time, he would trust her now?

"Bobby, you have to believe me, you have to!" she cried. The hysteria in her voice and the tears that poured from her eyes were nothing he hadn't heard and seen before. She begged him to listen to her side. "He did, he dragged me into a room and tried to rip my clothes off. It was horrible. I was so scared. Please, Bobby, please, I am telling the truth."

"Shut the fuck up!" he screamed.

She stopped crying and looked at her husband, hoping he would listen and praying that he believed her. He didn't; it was then she realised he'd never loved her. His love was for his family and they were placed far above her and anyone else.

"The first time in my fucking life I have ever called my brother or any of my family a liar. I stuck up for you. I even had me hands round Jim's throat for saying what he said, and yet he weren't lying, was he?" screamed Bobby.

"Bobby, all I did was nick a few stun guns, to protect the girls from Jimmy. Your brother is evil. He tried to fucking rape me!" she screamed back.

"How can anyone rape you? You're a fucking streetwalker anyway. I should have fucking known. I ain't stupid. I've clocked how much ya spend a month, and yet ya still have a grand over to pug up somewhere. But I am fucking stupid though, ain't I, for trusting a whore? You're all fucking whores."

"What? No, Bobby, ya got it wrong. I ain't a whore, I keep money for——" She stopped. She couldn't tell him why because he would then realise she wasn't loyal to her family. It was her safety net, her escape fund, in case Bobby reverted to his vile and dangerous ways, and she was witnessing it right now. She knew she would have to get away. He had the look of a deranged psychopath, and this time she wasn't going to hang around. In a panic, she turned and ran for the door. In retrospect, that decision was a culmination of inept actions she'd made that day and it very nearly cost her her life. He was quicker than her. He snatched a clump of hair and dragged her back into the living room. With one almighty punch, he knocked her to the floor. She was dazed and seeing double.

He locked the front door and then he stood towering over her. "Jim said you was selling yaself. He said you was using the empty flat, and he caught you. I fucking wanted to kill him for even suggesting you would do that. But then he begged me to ask Bunny if you was in the flat. So I did. I wanted her to say no. I was hoping so much that me own brother was lying. So I asked her. Did she see you in the flat and Jim leave? One simple answer. 'Yes,' she said. That was all I had to hear." He was almost foaming at the mouth like a rabid dog. The second blow caught her cheek, the third her nose, and that was all she remembered. He had knocked her unconscious.

She didn't know what time it was, or even what day. Bobby was lifting her head, the room was blurry, and her skin was alight. The buzzing in her ears was loud.

"Drink this," he said, as he trickled some liquid into the corner of her mouth. She swallowed, too weak to argue. The pains were all over her body. Then a fuzzy gentle feeling enveloped her, and the agony eased off. She couldn't focus because her eyes were mere slits. She tried to speak, but her mouth was tight and her jaw was dislocated. She looked at Bobby's face, expecting through the blur to see eyes of sorrow or compassion, but instead she found evil grinning at her. The world grew black, and once more she fell back into a darkened world where sleep was a luxury compared to the last few hours of brutal terror.

The days must have turned into weeks – it was all much of a blur. She discovered that he had kicked the shit out of her. Her face was like a purple bowling ball, and her breathing was shallow due to the broken ribs. He must have gone mental, for every inch of her body was bruised. It was the constant daze that was strangest, and she thought maybe she had brain damage. His whole demeanour was odd. There was absolutely no expression on his face and no words except for when he would say 'eat this' or 'drink that'.

He was keeping her alive but for what reason? She wanted to die – she so wanted to leave this world which had imprisoned her into a world of violence, terror, and brutality. There was, she believed, no upside from this point forward.

The sickness she felt was easing off but the haze remained. Then, one afternoon, the phone rang and Bobby left. But just before he did, he told her to drink the orange he had poured for her. She wasn't thirsty and with him out of sight she threw it down the sink. The door was locked; it was happening again. Bobby didn't come home that night and by the morning she felt less hazy. Her thoughts were clear enough for her to realise he was drugging her. She searched the cupboards and drawers and there at the back was a bottle of Oramorph. He had been giving her morphine, so it was no fucking wonder she was out of it. She turned the TV on and checked the date on one of the twenty-four hour news channels. "Jesus!" she gasped. He'd had her drugged up for two solid months.

She would have to think quickly and make a plan. She was well enough to make a dash. If she hid behind the door, when he walked through, she could push him over and make a run for it. Either that or stab him whilst he slept. But the plan didn't work. He overpowered her once again and this time he upped his game with a nastier beating. She knew then she was powerless. If she ever tried to run he would kill her. So she ended just a downtrodden shell of her former self — too weak to fight back and too petrified to try.

CHAPTER TWELVE

Sandra knocked on the door. Francesca stopped the tape recorder and nodded for her to enter. The officer walked in, avoiding eye contact with those present.

"Yes, can I help you?" Francesca looked sharply up at Sandra.

Gemma was almost thankful for the interruption; her heart was racing and her head running in all directions. This was the pivotal moment because Gemma knew that Francesca was no idiot. She had tried to devise a plan and play Francesca like a fiddle. Yet now was the time to convince the barrister that for the next fourteen years she had been locked away. She swallowed hard and could feel the beads of sweat across her brow and hoped to God that Francesca could not see her perspiring. The first part had been easy because most of this was true, but now came the hard part – those missing years.

Sandra stood, uneasy. "Just thought I'd mention you only have thirty minutes left. Would you like refreshments?"

Francesca nodded and the officer left.

"My God, Gemma, this is awful. It's so hard to imagine that you went through so much, and then to end up here." Francesca shook her head. "Are you still okay to go on?"

Gemma nodded with a serious look on her face but inside she was smiling. The exaggerated story of being drugged and locked away for years had worked, well, so she thought, and she was now on a home run. The expression on Francesca's face gave Gemma enough reason to believe she'd achieved her objective. *Give me a fucking script, Tarantino, and I will win an Oscar.*

Francesca turned the recorder back on. "We haven't got long. Tell us about the girls."

Gemma rubbed her eyes. "If you think what was happening to me was bad, then think of the girls this way: some of them were only kids, twelve or thirteen years old, drugged like I was, but they were kept in awful conditions. I had the freedom of the flat and then the house. We moved, you see. Bobby bought a house in Surrey, away from London. It was a nice country cottage but sadly with bars at the windows, which came with the house. There were no neighbours to hear my screams if he beat me. Even the postman stopped at the letter box up the drive. Anyway, at least I had that and only Bobby climbing on top of me for a quick loveless shag now and then. Those poor kids, though, locked up in that cold mansion … chained up, they were." She sniffed back a fake tear and tried to hold it together.

Francesca and Jamie both noticed how her face changed when she spoke of the girls. She appeared to be less saddened. *Is she being truthful*, Francesca asked herself.

"How do you know all this? Did you see them?" asked Francesca.

"No, but the Ruthers enjoyed talking about their cruel antics. Over the weeks, I err … I mean years." She stopped and felt herself redden; she had nearly tripped herself up. Francesca's expression showed no sign that she had clocked the mistake, so Gemma carried on hoping that they were still believing her. "I listened and pieced it

272

all together. It gave me nightmares to think of how they must have suffered. God, they were just kids." She swallowed hard, exaggerating her sad look of compassion.

Francesca knew damn well that Gemma was lying, as being locked up for years made no sense – weeks she could believe, but she continued pretending to be unperturbed by the slip up. *Give a dog, no bitch in this case, enough rope ...* she thought. "What did they do to them, Gemma? I need to hear this from you, so please speak clearly into the tape recorder."

"Men paid a fortune just for the privilege of having them as a sex toy I guess."

"Do you know who was behind it all?"

Gemma nodded. "A Russian guy called Alex, his brother, and a man called Igor. And, of course, there were also the Ruthers. What I managed to fathom out was Alex was based in Russia. He sent the girls over, his brother took over from England, and Igor organised the rest. The Ruthers set up the mansion. They had two to begin with, well the first one was a big villa, a lock-up they called it until they closed it down to plough money into the second one to make it so grand, and they did everything to keep their clients happy."

Francesca chewed the inside of her mouth. "Was Charles Enright a client?"

Gemma nodded. "Oh, yes, he was their best customer, by all accounts. They loved him, but I got the feeling they feared him too. I remember hearing Bobby saying something like, 'Fuck being alone in a room with Charles Enright, the evil nut job.' But him and his mob were the top-paying clients."

Jamie took over. He could sense this was fazing Francesca. "How do you know? And can you remember any other names?"

Gemma cocked her head to the side. "Well, of course I do. It's all in the ledger. Everything is in there——" *This was it, the hook that would have them chomping at the bit to help her get out of here.*

Before she could finish, Francesca jumped in. "What ledger?"

Gemma frowned, exaggerating the look of confusion; and yet really she had snuck in that little nugget of information, about the ledger, knowing full well it would grip the two barristers. Yes, there was a ledger, but it was always kept at the mansion; it never left the place because it contained too much incriminating evidence, which would lock them all up for years.

Acting surprised, Gemma went on, "Didn't I tell you? The reason Bobby tried to kill me was because I was trying to steal the ledger. It had everything in it, literally everything, dating back years. Violet was a stickler for keeping notes and accounts. If she wasn't screaming and hollering, she had her head in that book. Like a fucking plutomaniac, she was. I heard that word on *Who Wants to Be a Millionaire*! It means someone who's obsessed with wealth – well, that's Violet all right! Anyway, I guess she recorded everything for those unlucky punters that didn't pay. If I could have shown it to the police, then it would have closed the whole operation down. I told the police, when they arrested me for knifing Bobby, but they thought I was just a nut job, especially when Bobby told them I'd been on drugs for years and was a self-harmer with tendencies to make shit up. They checked me records: it was all there, the self-harming, the baby, the drug taking. They had Wiers, their lawyer, on their side. I didn't stand a chance."

"What I don't understand is why you didn't try to run away sooner?" asked Jamie in a serious, cold tone. It was at this point he doubted her story.

She paused before continuing. Francesca observed Gemma's reaction and was concerned because she had a gut feeling that this woman was more devious than she appeared. The story was too rehearsed and the timings didn't add up. Francesca was adding up the years. For Gemma's version of events to be credible, she must have been kept a prisoner in the flat and the cottage for fourteen years at least; it made no sense at all. She could have escaped and Francesca wasn't buying into her lies.

"Well, I did try a few times, but every time Bobby managed to catch me, he gave me a beating, so I decided to just live my life the best way I knew how. I was so frightened of them. I was too scared to run away again, so I just played the dutiful wife, cooking and cleaning. Even the thought of running, terrified me. The beatings were too harsh and I knew that if I ever tried it again, I would end up dead. They would track me down and torture me." She paused, looking for signs that the barrister deemed her story credible.

"Then, one afternoon, Bobby was at home with Lenny. I was in the bedroom but I could hear them talking and drinking. They had a bottle of Jack Daniel's, and by the afternoon they were both out for the count, lying on the sofas. It was then that I thought, this is all wrong. I need to save those poor girls. I crept into the living room and saw the ledger. I picked it up and then, without thinking, I made a dash for the door. However, I was not prepared for what was to happen next. Lenny saw me and jumped up. He shouted for Bobby and before I knew it they had a hold of me. Then Bobby told Lenny to go to George's and fetch him over. I was so shit-scared because I knew that they would kill me. I remember the phone ringing and Bobby answering it, still gripping my arm. It was then that he got the rope and wrapped it round my neck. It must have been one of his brothers or Violet telling him what to do because he was like a fucking robot with the automatic switch turned on."

Her words tripped over themselves even though she had practised so long to get her fictitious story straight. Of course, she wasn't in the cottage for all those years, and Bobby didn't have the ledger. That ledger was kept in the basement of the mansion ready for when she took over the business. She just hoped that her little story was washing with Francesca. She tried to remain calm and keep the sorrowful look spread across her face. She had no way of knowing if the barrister had cottoned on to the fact that she was never kept a prisoner in the cottage.

Sandra knocked again, this time with a tray of teas and biscuits. "You have twenty minutes left before I have to take Gemma back."

Francesca nodded and waited for the door to close.

"Gemma, we need Daisy's address and the addresses of Summer and Bunny."

Her stomach began to churn because she'd never expected Francesca to act like a detective. She had to think quickly. "Summer and Bunny are dead. I heard George telling Bobby. My lawyer at the time, useless prick, tried to find Daisy, but she'd either moved away or died, so there is no address for her. See, all I have now is my story." She buried her head in her hands and cried, "I ain't never getting out! I'll be stuck in here and those poor girls will die!" She forced the tears, hoping the desolate tone in her voice was enough.

Gemma needed to put on an Oscar-winning performance to ensure Francesca believed her, praying that she wouldn't realise there was a big void in the story.

Francesca frowned. "I'm good at my job. We'll start an appeal as soon as I can find reason for one, but don't you worry, leave all that to me. I'll make some inquiries myself ... the reason I came to see you, though, Gemma, was to find out why Cassie was killed. Why would they want to kill her?"

As Gemma raised her eyebrow, her face took on a very different expression; it was a look Francesca had seen before.

"They are so desperate to make sure I stay, or worse, die inside. I think they shot her because she was my only link to the outside. You see, they know if I get out, I can expose them all."

Another lump wedged itself in Francesca's throat; poor Cassie.

Sandra appeared again. This time she had a resigned expression on her face and lowered her head when she saw Francesca staring.

"I'll make another appointment for next week."

Gemma smiled. "I can't thank you enough." She put out her arms to hug Francesca but was rudely stopped by Sandra.

The visit came to an end and Gemma was marched back to her cell.

Jamie walked on ahead, closely followed by Francesca. The outside was a light relief from the closed space and prison smell. Francesca noticed that Jamie was unusually quiet on the way back to the office.

"It's all very disturbing, I know, and you must be wondering why I haven't crumbled in a heap on the floor." She tapped his knee.

"Sisco, I'm used to you now. You've been through worse." He was silent again.

277

"What's the matter, love?" she asked in her gentle tone.

"I know that Gemma's story is tragic, and she's been through some horrendous things, much like you, yet … oh, I don't know. I guess I expected her to be more like you. Perhaps I'm talking a load of bollocks. It's just I know you're so much more intelligent than I will ever be. You're a brilliant lawyer, and yet you trust her implicitly. I'm not sure I do."

Francesca laughed. "What makes you so sure I do?"

Jamie shot her a sideways glance. "Your body language. You showed empathy. I know your expressions, Sisco. You bought into her story."

"Jamie, don't assume that me showing her sympathy, and going along with her without asking obvious questions, means I believe every word she said. There's one thing you need to learn. It's called a false sense of security. She perceived my empathetic gestures as a sign I was completely taken in. That's exactly what I wanted. Pardon the pun, but give her a rope long enough and she'll hang herself. If I had interjected, when her story seemed less than straight, then she would have probably clammed up."

Jamie took a deep breath and sighed with relief. "So, what do you think is really going on here?"

"That, my darling, I do not have the answer to, but for our Cassie's and baby Cass's sakes, I will fucking find out."

They stopped off at the office to make a copy of the recording and read over the case files. It had been a long day and her mind was spinning with wild theories. What she really needed was to have her brothers hear the story, but in the meantime she would keep her thoughts to herself. Before Francesca drove back to Dan's house she

278

said, "Oh, whilst I remember, could you look up Daisy's address and text it to me, please? It is in the Luciani case notes."

Jamie nodded and she left.

Her parents had left by the time she got there. She parked her car next to Sam's and awkwardly stepped out, stretching her legs. She had been sitting nearly all day and could feel them tighten.

As she opened the front door, she was surprised to find a strange man in the hallway, rocking baby Cass. He was smartly dressed, roughly sixty-five, and offered her a huge smile. "Oh, hello. I'm just taking my turn." He laughed.

Francesca cocked her head to the side. "Sorry, have we met?"

Maria walked in from the living room and offered to take the baby. The man straightened his suit jacket and held out a hand for Francesca to shake. "Yes, sorry about that. I'm Terry James. I was DI James."

Francesca nodded. "Of course. Lovely to meet you." They shook hands.

Terry blushed; she made him slightly nervous. He was unsure if it was the way she walked, spoke, or the look in her eyes, but she definitely had something about her.

"Did you have a pleasant journey?" she asked politely.

He was still entranced by her. "Yes, thanks. I came as soon as I could. Young Sam picked me up from the airport."

Francesca gave a pretty half-smile, somewhat amused by his term 'young Sam'.

"Sis," called Fred, "we're in here. How did it go?"

279

Francesca joined them in the living room. She sat serenely on the sofa and retrieved the tape recorder from her bag.

"I'm so pleased that Terry could join us. He might well help to answer some concerns I have." She looked his way. "Terry, may I ask why you want to get involved in this case? I'm sure retirement in Spain is more appealing than this?"

Terry looked at Sam and then back at Francesca. "Do you mind if I take a seat?"

Francesca made a hand gesture, inviting him to sit opposite her. Sam passed him a brandy and the others also took a seat. Terry watched the family dynamics change once Francesca was in the room. He had arrived an hour earlier, and after being introduced to all the Vincents, it became clear that the head of the family was Dan. But Francesca's arrival had put his earlier assessment in some doubt. It was quite obvious that everyone, Dan included, looked to her as their leader. They gathered around her like children. It was strange to see these hard men have so much respect for their younger sister. Clearly, she must have done some extraordinary things in her relatively short life to deserve this admiration and respect from her family.

"Fran, do you want a cold drink or a cuppa tea?" asked Dan. He was looking a little better than yesterday.

"I think I will join you in a brandy."

He jumped up from the seat and poured a drink.

"Terry, you were going to tell me—" Before Francesca could finish, Terry jumped in.

"Oh, yes, of course. When Sam called me, to tell me the devastating news, I knew I couldn't sit back and do nothing. For years, I hunted for the man who left my daughter for dead in that filthy flat. I didn't even recognise her when I had to identify her remains. I thought for a long time it was Charlie McManners, but when Sam called and told me what this Gemma girl had said, I was over here like a shot."

"I'm very sorry for your loss. It must have been difficult for you."

Terry nodded but didn't take his eyes off her. He felt like he was being tested. He would have to lay his cards on the table to gain their total trust and respect.

"It was a while ago now, but I'll not rest until I find the monster that did it. May I call you Francesca, or …?"

She laughed. "I'm called many things, so of course you may."

He put his glass on the coffee table and edged forward. "I know you have many names – Launa Enright being one of them."

There was stunned silence as every pair of steely-blue eyes turned to him and glared. They were like a pack of wolves ready to pounce.

"I would have denied it, but I won't insult your intelligence. Only my family and my husband's family know this, so I assume you have cleverly worked it out for yourself."

Terry nodded. "I'm telling you this because I want you to trust me. I joined the police force because I wanted to make a difference. I was going to clean up the streets of filth and reprobates, the real nasty bastards that had no place in society, and I'll tell ya this for nothing, it makes no difference. Yeah, okay, they might get arrested and have their knuckles rapped, a few months in the slammer, a few years, maybe, but it doesn't stop them. They just learn to get smarter. The sad bit about it was, I knew who the real nasty ones were, and most of the time my hands were tied. No disrespect, Sam, but it was like your ex-missus. We knew she was responsible for all those drugs being in your house, but because you took the rap, we couldn't go after her. The McManners — now they were another horrible lot. We picked up their tortured mess. Mostly they were young lads too shit-scared to grass. There were many more, and when I retired I looked back over those years and realised I'd been wasting my time. I have to admit, I got more satisfaction covering your arses than doing my job, and I have absolutely no regrets. Like I told Sam, I like you lot, and I always have. I know the truth about the McManners, and, of course, the O'Connells, and naturally as a DI, I was nosy by nature. I have to admit you fascinated me. Then I got to wondering what you were really all about." He stopped and took a swig of his brandy.

"Want a top-up?" asked Fred sedately, which was rather unusual for him. It must have been the tone of Terry's voice. They had nothing to fear from this man.

He nodded. "Yeah, why not. I'm laying my life on the line here."

Sam laughed. "You're safe here, mate. We know you looked out for us."

Terry nodded. "Not that ya needed it. It was only when the Met was asking too many questions, did I ever jump in. But anyway, I have to be honest. Like I said, I was fascinated. Then I watched you, Francesca, in the courtroom with Ruby the day you got Sam's wife locked up. I was intrigued, and in awe, to be honest. I knew the boys over the years, checking on the clubs, but I never knew you. Then I realised you didn't grow up with your family, did you? They were always around, but not you. That day in the court, I thought I recognised you, not so much by the way you looked but by the way

282

you moved and spoke. Things started to add up. I bet it was you that planted the drugs in Jesse's bag to get her banged up to save young Ruby and Jack. The McManners' disappearance happened soon after. Then, one day, Dan was talking about how he was going to run the club like his brother-in-law, Sergio Luciani. That name rang bells, of course it would. The biggest trial for years, a young man by the name of Mauricio Luciani, accused of the face-slashing serial murders, and a young beautiful barrister representing him. She was good. I was there, watching her elegantly walk around the courtroom. She had class and a rare demeanour. And then I saw that same walk, and that same class, years later, when you worked your magic in the courtroom with Jesse Right."

Francesca didn't move, and she barely blinked, listening to every word he said.

"Yes, Terry, that was me. I was married to Charles Enright, and I was supposed to make sure Mauricio was found guilty. They groomed me for that case. But I was going places in my career. I was young and eager to reach the top, and I worked hard to make sure he remained a free man. All I can say is, it didn't go down too well for the Enrights. I was not aware back then that it was all one big set-up and I was the pawn in the middle. They used me as part of their plan to ensure Mauricio would be found guilty of killing all those women. The real serial killer was my first husband. But I only discovered this after the trial, when he tried to kill me."

Terry knocked back the rest of the brandy. Her story was horrific, almost unbelievable, but he knew it was true.

"It's your face. That's why you look so different."

Francesca nodded. She looked at Fred; he was watery-eyed. She didn't find talking about it difficult, but in front of her family it was hard to see their look of pain.

"We all called her Dolly when she was little 'cos she looked like a china doll," said Fred. "We thought it was Mad Mick McManners that brutalised her. When she came back to us, sliced up like that, we really thought it was him, the mad cunt."

Terry watched as Fred's expression turned bitter. "Why would Mick McManners want to hurt you?" he asked.

Dan coughed and stood up to speak. "We were young then. Mad Mick thought our dad had grassed him up, but he never did. Mick made a threat to kill our Dolly because he knew that it would destroy our dad if anyone hurt her, so we sent her away to protect her. Fucking fifteen years we couldn't have contact. Fifteen fucking years is a long time to inflict that much fear for our Dolly's safety, so when I picked her up from the hospital, smashed to bits like a china doll, we naturally assumed he'd got to her. So I, for one, am fucking glad they are dead."

"I'm honoured that you've trusted me enough to tell me the truth, and I have to tell ya, I knew what ya did, but I never knew the truth behind it. It had to be a good reason, though, because you all have a moral standard. I know that." He turned to Francesca. "You are a remarkable woman. I remember the Enrights ... well, they were renowned in the justice system, and when William went to prison for killing his brother Charlie Enright, it shocked us all. Then, when Charles Enright just disappeared, I guessed there was more to it. Having said that, they were part of the Gentlemen's Club. They stood by each other and it was all a little too close for comfort. Personally, I could not stand that William Enright. He was a cock of a man – a real snotty-nosed, spiteful cunt."

"Well, now you know the background, I think you all need to listen to this recording," said Francesca. "Terry, I have concerns with the story you're about to hear, but I'll let you draw your own conclusions. It'll be interesting to see if we have the same doubts. I'll leave you alone while you listen. I need a shower. I hate the prison smell. It always lingers." Her face lit up. "And after that, I'm going to spend some time with our new baby."

Francesca slowly climbed the grand staircase, admiring Dan's taste in decoration. Maria was asleep in the rocking chair and Cass was purring like a kitten. She left and crept away into the bathroom. She stepped out of her dress and decided to have a bath rather than a shower. Her headache was slowly subsiding and soothing bath salts and muscle relaxants would help to take away the tense feeling. She tried to switch off from Gemma's story, but those vivid pictures kept returning. She was confronting her past: the Enrights, the McManners, the O'Connells, in fact the whole bloodbath, and now they were coming back to haunt her. She had thought she'd moved on with her life, as she rarely thought of Charles; only now and then would she wake up in a cold sweat. Life after that had been good, except for the episode with the O'Connells, which had been highly violent and bloody for her family, and which had nearly destroyed the *Palaces*, but she hadn't been so much involved with that. Her brothers had taken care of that situation in their own inimitable style.

*

Violet was just about to tuck into a large fry-up, courtesy of Tressa, when the police knocked at the front door. She slowly put the knife and fork down on her plate and looked at George, who instantly stopped chewing.

"Ol' Bill, it must be. No one knocks at the front."

285

George left the table and went upstairs whilst Tressa opened the door to find two burly policemen and a meat wagon outside.

"We've come for Bobby," the taller of the two said.

Tressa looked them up and down. "He ain't 'ere." Really she wanted to say, 'come in and nick the lot of them. I will give you a list of crimes they have committed', but she didn't. She was too afraid of the consequences. She hated herself for being such a coward, though.

"Sorry, love, step aside. We have a search warrant."

Tressa didn't argue; she didn't care. She opened the door wider and allowed them in. They went straight to the kitchen to find Violet eating her breakfast, totally unperturbed. She looked up. "What do you boys want? And ya better 'ave a fucking warrant, just walking in me place."

The taller police officer pulled out a warrant and showed it to Violet. "Yep, love, we do."

Violet didn't get up. "Oh yeah? What's it for?"

"Bobby. We've come to arrest him," he said.

Violet had to play it cool; she didn't know if they were after him for shooting the pregnant woman or for the burglary down the coast.

"What's he been up to, then?"

No sooner had she got the words out of her mouth, than someone she recognised marched in. Detective Inspector Spencer was after the Ruthers; they were at the top of his list. He hated them with an obsession, especially since Violet had made him look an idiot a few years back. He had taken a look at the amount of arrests made and dropped, and he'd suspected foul play. He set up a unit to have the

Ruthers put under surveillance, but it was obvious they'd had a tip-off and Violet had made a complaint, reciting all the human rights laws, so the judge had had no option but to stop the unit in its tracks. Spencer was pulled over the coals, and in not so many words, was told to leave well alone. They hadn't been found guilty of anything, and this was in breach of their human rights.

Violet smirked in his face. "Well, if it ain't Spencer. I thought you was told to fuck off, mate, and stop hounding me and mine."

"Oh dear, Violet, it seems that little card has just gone out of the window. Your Bobby's driving licence was left behind at a burglary. I have every right to pull him in."

Violet smiled to herself; so the lad was using his brains. That now had him out of the picture for the murder; he couldn't be in two places at once.

"I shouldn't have to remind you, but Bobby don't live here, so fuck off with ya search warrant and go to his place. I know me rights. You ain't supposed to be 'ere, are ya? Ya supposed to be at his gaff. A burglary don't give you the right to search 'ere, now, does it?"

Spencer laughed. "His driving licence has this address on, so I do have rights. Oh, and just so you know, and ya can tell Bobby from me, I don't fucking believe he was at the burglary. Ya see, I know what you lot are up to. I can write a list as long as my arm, from drugs to fake fifties. Small time robbery ain't ya scene, now, is it?"

With that they left. Violet pushed her food aside and shouted for George.

"That divvy brother of yours has fucked up again. That Spencer cunt knows Bobby planted that driving licence. Now they're gonna be sniffing around to find out why."

287

George was pacing the floor. "Right, I'm gonna call Igor. It's not safe for any of us to go over to the mansion. You're gonna 'ave to stop Rita going over there. It can run without us for a while."

"'Ere, hold up, who's gonna collect the money?"

"Muvver, fuck the money for a bit. They can't come here and we definitely can't go there. If the Ol' Bill are suspicious of anything involving us, we could lead them straight there. Fuck the money. I ain't getting banged up for that shit. I wouldn't see the light of day again."

Violet huffed. "I could fucking kill Bobby meself. All right, I'll let Rita know, but she ain't gonna be happy. She's besotted with that flat-headed Russian, Igor."

George was nervous of his mother and always had been. She ruled them with an iron rod and that fear never left him, but lately she was oblivious to the seriousness of their business. He knew he had to take control. "Muvver, I don't give a flying shit how Rita feels. She's gotta stay away. Igor don't want her fat arse anyway. She's like a lovesick teenager around him, it's embarrassing, and she only has half a brain on the job – the other half is on how she can get to suck his dick."

"Hold on a minute. Rita is as hard as you boys."

"Muvver, it ain't about being hard, it's about being smart, and let me tell ya, she ain't too clever. In fact, the truth be known, she's a liability. I dunno, Muvver, but the girls being sick and her feeding them, seems more than a coincidence to me. I would rather have Gemma back running the set-up, any day of the week."

Violet jumped up and threw her knife, just missing George. The anger on her face was the worst he had ever seen. Purple veins popped out of her forehead. "You dare mention that whore's name in this house! You would prefer a no-good grass and dirty tramp to ya own sister, would ya, eh?"

She threw her plate and George managed to duck just in time.

"Stop it, will ya? For fuck's sake, listen."

Violet was livid. Her chest heaved in and out like she was gasping for breath. She stopped with the tantrum and glared with pure hatred in her eyes.

"Let's get something straight, shall we? I know Gemma was a no-good grass. All's I'm saying is, when she did work, she was good, and it would do Rita a favour to take a leaf out of her book."

Violet was off again. "Good? Fucking good, was she?" Another utensil came flying at George's head. "That slimy mother's whore stabbed our Bobby, she tried to murder ya own brother, and you have the audacity to call her good! If I hadn't nobbled her fucking brief when I did, she would have had us all in the cunting slammer!"

All the screaming caused her to start coughing and she sat down to catch her breath. As George turned to leave, the pepper pot cracked him on the back of the head. He didn't stop to turn around; instead, he continued walking out of the house.

Meanwhile, Tressa sat on the back doorstep with Major. He was old now and probably wouldn't be around for much longer. She was smiling to herself; of course, she was hugely enjoying the volatile situation. They could all kill each other as far as she was concerned. What vile and sick bastards they were. She thought about Gemma, and although she hated to admit it, she was well aware she had been really good at her job. She had a swinging brick instead of a heart, just like her brothers.

The sky darkened and it was about to piss down, but she didn't care. Her life was one big looming black cloud. She contemplated running after DI Spencer and spilling the beans, but what was the point? They would all end up inside and one of their henchmen would come after her. She had seen at first-hand what happened to those who were foolish enough to front the Ruthers.

Tressa wondered, even fantasized, about her father, and she just wished for once her mother would do the right thing and tell her who he was. But Violet was too tyrannical to entertain the idea. She did hear rumours once that Violet had been a hooker herself and ended up running a brothel up at King's Cross. Perhaps it was just spiteful gossip. There was one incident that stuck in Tressa's mind, though, and that was the day their neighbour Carla came around in a right state. She was a pretty woman and married to big Terry Steward, a hard man himself. He often popped in to see Violet and chat over skulduggery.

Carla was hysterical and plonked herself down at the table with her head in her hands. Violet put the kettle on and sat down too. "Now, what's happened? Has someone died?" she asked.

"No, worse than that. Terry fucking raped me! He fucking threw me on the bed, and no matter how much I screamed, he wouldn't stop. I begged him. How could he do that to me, for fuck's sake? I can't go back there. He's a fucking nut job."

Violet had laughed. "Jesus, girl, I thought someone had tortured your baby, the drama you was making."

Carla looked up, and with a shocked expression on her face, she snapped back, "Vi, did you not fucking hear me? That cunt fucking raped me!"

Violet did not take too well to being shouted at and she stood up. "Now, you fucking listen to me. If you were keeping him happy in the bedroom, he wouldn't resort to helping himself. For Christ's sake, woman, get a grip. He only wanted to get his helmet wet. It ain't the end of the world. You might have enjoyed it, for all he knew. What ya wanna do, girl, next time he does it – demand he leaves a score on the side for a new top or something? Tell him, if he wants a whore in the bed, then he has to pay for it."

Tressa remembered the conversation as if it were yesterday. Her mother had been so laid-back and matter-of-fact, she'd had no sympathy whatsoever. It was as if she saw a fanny as a money-making goldmine. It sounded very much as if her mother was speaking from experience. If so, her suspicions that her mum had been a tom years before might be correct. Perhaps Violet didn't even know who their fathers were. Tressa snapped out of her daydream when Rita bowled into the kitchen dressed in a skin-tight black dress, high silver shoes, and a ton of make-up plastered over her fake tan. Tressa leaned against the wall and was amazed that her sister could look such a state. Surely she must have looked in the mirror? What the fuck did she think she looked like? And, whilst she thought about it, what the fuck was God on at the time he allowed herself to be born a Ruthers? In her own present melancholy state, she wished she'd never actually been born at all – but life can turn on a tide, and she was not to know then that there would be many more twists along the way for her.

"Rita, ya can't go over there tonight, not for a while anyway," said Violet. "The filth have been here after Bobby. That cunt Spencer is leading an investigation. He don't believe Bobby did the burglary, and if he suspects something fishy is going on, then he'll have us back under surveillance."

Rita flared her nostrils. "I hate Bobby. He fucks everything up. Well, I'll have to go tonight to let them know what's going on." She stood up to leave.

"Nah, you ain't, Rita. George will make all the necessary arrangements."

"It don't matter even if the police do raid the mansion. They won't find anything."

"What ya on about?" snapped Violet.

"The place is like a palace. Ya wanna see it. All the rooms are done up. It's stunning. They've installed this floor that covers the basement. It's completely soundproof and there's no way in, unless you have the remote control. The hallways have ladders and pots of paint everywhere and Igor's men walk around in decorator gear. If the Ol' Bill go rampaging through that house, all they'll find is a beautiful place being done-up. The girls can scream as loud as they like, but no cunt can hear 'em. It makes me laugh. George thought Gemma was good at getting a mansion up and running, but now he should tell ya about what I've done."

Violet smirked. "Don't get too carried away, girl, 'cos you ain't done jack shit. The fucking mansion's been running for fucking years before you got handed the job, let me tell ya. Strutting around, cleaning up after them, feeding them, and making sure they're clean ain't hard, is it? In my day they called that maiding."

Rita flared her nostrils again. "Yeah, well, what the fuck did Gemma do that I ain't?"

Violet glared at Rita. "I've told ya all before. I don't want that whore's name mentioned in this house again. But, for your information, that whore brought in business."

Rita was fuming. She wanted to be the head honcho, calling the shots, but she knew it would never happen. She hated Gemma more than anyone. She knew in her heart that Gemma had been good. She'd had the Russians eating out of her hand with all her fancy ideas. She'd been the go-between for the mansion and the Gentlemen's Club. She'd been responsible for selecting the girls and making sure they were up to standard. She'd even had her Igor eyeing her up and down and seen Gemma giving him teasing grins. Rita had wanted Gemma dead more than anyone – and she still did.

Tressa slid her legs under the chair. "Maiding, ya say, Mum. What's that?"

Violet laughed. "Gawd, girl, ain't ya learned anything? Maiding is where a young girl is on hand to clean the sheets and lay out the room for the next punter. They do other stuff too."

Tressa wondered again if her mother really had run a brothel years ago.

"So what's gonna happen if Gemma does get out and blows the whistle?" asked Tressa.

"She ain't getting out, and even if she does, what's she gonna say?" snapped Rita.

Tressa glared at her sister. "Well, she can put you inside for twenty years for a start."

Rita gawked at her mother. "Bollocks, can she!"

"Fuck me, will ya turn it in? I've had enough. She can sing like a canary for all the good it will do her. She has no evidence of anything, 'cos if she did have proof, we wouldn't be sitting here now. The Ol' Bill didn't believe her then and they ain't now. Ol' Wiers will see to

293

that. The old bastard has been having freebies for a good few years now, and he ain't likely to give up his bit of fun for the sake of her, now, is he? Besides, he has a sex addiction, just like the others, and that's what keeps our business going."

Plagued with guilt for her somewhat small role she had played in the beginning and riddled with shame for not grassing them, Tressa hung her head, now totally deflated.

Wiers was a high court judge – he had been a good friend of the Enrights and continued to be so with William. Weirs was the chairman of the Gentlemen's Club, in the city, and a regular frequenter of the mansion. He was never questioned and neither did he need an appointment. The guards allowed him to roam around and pick who he liked, along with the sex toys or tools he wanted to use. He wasn't charged either, as he was their guaranteed legal protection. The members of the club were also visitors to the mansion. They were hand-picked and trusted. If the operation were to be exposed for any reason, then so would they be. The more friends they had on board, the safer they were: it was a case of safety in numbers.

Wiers was the judge who had put Gemma behind bars.

*

After soaking her tired muscles, Francesca stepped out of the bath. She wrapped herself in a large fluffy towel and sat by the window, gazing out across the beautiful stretch of gardens. Dan had really settled down now. It was obvious he had taken married life seriously – no more lads' nights out and no more flirting with the customers. His money was going into his beautiful home he shared with his family, but, of course, now poor Cassie was gone. She grieved more for her brother and baby Cass, the two left behind.

It had indeed been a brutal realisation to find that Charles Enright, the first man she'd thought she'd truly loved, and his family, were worse than Mad Mick McManners. No wonder she had become a different woman, following her return from the States. The anger she had inside had changed her totally as a person. She wasn't the only one with a deep-seated anger. Those past events had shaped and changed all her brothers, too. They'd grown up knowing that she'd been sent away to her Aunt Anne's for her own safety and had hated all of the McManners family with a passion. The ordeal had made them strong and they trusted no one except each other. When she had returned, they were whole again, and they had taken out the McManners and the Enrights in a manner which would have made the Kray twins proud.

Francesca was clever and had her Italian family and her own brothers to help her. Her once kind and caring character, the young woman who wouldn't hurt a fly, was now a woman with two emotions: love and hate. She had no time for 'outsiders': people were either with her or against her. She was lucky that she'd had so much love returned to her, not just from her family, but also from the Lucianis.

Her dedication in the Luciani case would never be forgotten, and when Charles had left her for dead and she'd made that phone call to the States, she'd been relieved and surprised that they were ready to do anything for her. She'd fled to New York and had been welcomed with open arms by Mauricio's father, Roberto. He'd called her his daughter and had taught her so much. During that time, she'd helped Roberto and his family deal with another member of the Enright family, and the manner in which she had accomplished this had given her the strength and the power to go back and face her demons. But she hadn't had to do this alone. She thought about her husband Sergio, her rock, her lover, and her best friend. Even after years of marriage, she missed him when they were apart, even for a day, and he felt the same.

Cass was waking up; Francesca could hear his soft mumbling. She went to her room and dressed in a soft cream tracksuit and then quickly rushed to the nursery, where Maria was stirring. She was exhausted, the poor woman, and Francesca's heart melted. She scooped baby Cass up and held him in her arms, gently rocking him. He wriggled to get comfortable and gazed up at Francesca. He was too young to focus yet. She stroked his curls and kissed his forehead. He was just perfect.

As Maria stayed in her chair, watching Francesca, her eyes moistened with so much love for the two of them. Her heart went out to the woman. She would have made such a wonderful mother. There was so much devotion in her eyes as she nursed the baby.

"How are you, Francesca?"

Francesca turned to face Maria and smiled. "I don't know. I just feel like my head is a jumbled mess right now, but I have to get to the bottom of it, for Dan's and baby Cass's sakes. Then, I look at his tiny face and just want to forget all this is going on. Selfish, I know."

Maria stood up and placed an arm around Francesca's waist. "I understand, my dear. You have had enough grief and heartache to last a lifetime, and at a time when we should be enjoying a new baby in the family, it is tainted with so much sorrow. I am concerned for Dan, Francesca. He won't even hold Cass. This has affected him more than I realised."

"Give him time, Maria. It's only been three days. I'm sure he'll come around. It must be so hard for him. Maybe he'll start to bond with Cass once we find out who did this and then he can close this chapter in our lives."

Maria nodded. She admired how the Vincents always used the words 'we' or 'our'. They referred to Cass as our baby and now she was doing the same.

"Maria, do you mind taking Cass? I have to go back downstairs to talk to the boys."

Maria smiled. "You go and I'll keep Cass quiet. He needs a bottle."

Francesca entered the living room just as the recording finished. Her brothers all looked her way. Fred spoke first. "Are you okay, sis? Cor, blimey, that was a fucking story an' a half."

Francesca sat in the empty chair and nodded. She looked resigned and it didn't go unnoticed. Joe, who was usually quiet, stood up, walked around the back of his sister, rubbed her shoulders, and then kissed her cheek. "That must 'ave been hard, Fran, but I, for one, don't believe her story. Having said that, I know you lot are much cleverer than me."

Fran grabbed his hand. "Hold on, Joe, that's not true, love. You have a different way of looking at things, that's all, but you are clever."

"Well, my two penn'orth might not mean much, but if you went through all that shit, you would do anything to escape and run straight to the police, not wait fourteen years. I don't believe any sane woman would play the dutiful wife, knowing there were kiddies out there being … God, it's awful."

Francesca nodded. "Exactly, Joe."

Pleased with himself, he sat back down next to Sam.

"Well, I reckon we go and find these Ruthers and take 'em out, the evil, 'orrible cunts," urged Fred, who was white-faced and angry.

"No, Fred, something doesn't add up, and if you go in there, like a bull in a china shop, then we may never know the truth." She looked at Terry. He would know how to deal with all of this, having been a detective himself.

Terry grinned. "Oh, there is definitely more to this. The biggest issue is the timing. I worked out the dates. She married him at nineteen, worked for a couple of years, was locked up at Bobby's flat while she was pregnant, collected rent for a year, and then was locked up again by the family. After that, she was put in jail for eighteen months. The woman's about forty years old, so what happened in-between?"

Francesca got up to pour herself a drink. "Exactly. What was she up to in those missing years? The other concern I have is this ..." She paused and sighed. "She makes reference to the Enrights too many times. Now, I know that sounds mad, but there must have been hundreds of punters who frequented the flats, so why recall Charles in particular? To top it all, if you were locked up, listening to their conversations, you would cover a broader picture, regarding the Russians, the hideouts, the plans, anything, in fact, that would prove these girls were hidden away. So, if her overwhelming need was to expose them, why would recalling the Enrights be paramount in her recollection? I don't know, but it doesn't make sense to me. I have the strong feeling she wants me to be sucked in. What's more concerning, I suspect she knows who I am and about my previous connections with the Enrights." She raised her head and took a deep breath.

Terry was surprised at her ability to pick up on the psychology behind it all, but he had to agree that what she said made sense. "Tell me, Francesca, do you believe the part about her stealing the stun guns to help the girls?"

"Well, I watched her body language and the expression on her face, and so I concluded that she was raped, she had been initially locked away, and sadly she probably did give birth alone. I also believe she was telling the truth about the stun guns, but I don't believe she helped the girls like she insisted she did. You see, her words changed when she described how she helped Summer to the hospital. It was as if she had rehearsed them. I don't know, but I get the feeling she tried to embellish the story to toy with my emotions. She wants me to see her as a victim, like the young prostitutes – but I don't."

Suddenly, the intercom was buzzing. Dan jumped up. "Who the fuck would call at this time of night?"

Terry stood up. "I'd better be out of sight, in case it's the police. Best they don't know I'm here."

Sam walked him into the snug room just off the kitchen. "Wait 'ere, mate."

Terry nodded and shut the door.

The police had called to give Dan an update. It was Sergeant Sampson and he looked uncomfortable. "I'm sorry, Mr Vincent," he said, "but we've checked the cameras, carried out house calls, and contacted the prison to see if Cassandra might have been visiting anyone, but so far we don't have any leads. That's not to say we are not still trying. If you have any ideas, anything at all, please let us know. Here's my card."

He handed Dan a business card and turned to leave; the sight of the family glaring at him made him uneasy.

As soon as he went out of the door, Francesca said, "Fucking useless pricks."

Fred chuckled to himself. He loved it when his well-spoken sister used good old profanity.

"They may have checked the prison, but for fuck's sake, they're blind. Cassie might have gone in under her maiden name, but 'Cassandra' is not exactly common. I mean, how many Cassandras visited that day? Surely to God, you would check it out? Well, I suppose it's a good thing really that they are useless at their job."

Terry was back in the living room and heard Francesca. "Yes, it is a good thing, or you'd have them on your back too, and it would get complicated. Look, I can do some investigating myself. DI Neil Spencer worked South West London, and he's a good mate of mine. He would happily give me what he has on the Ruthers, no questions asked. I won't mention you or Cassie. He knows I've been searching for my Lindsey's killer, and he'll help me. Is that all right?" He looked at Francesca.

She smiled with compassion. "Yes, Terry, good idea, and I'm sure we'll find the scumbag who hurt your daughter."

Terry left with Sam that evening. So many emotions had been stirred up, but one thing was guaranteed: with the help of the Vincents, he would find his Lindsey's killer.

CHAPTER THIRTEEN

Sandra paced her lounge floor, biting her nails down to the quick. She poured another vodka and sat heavily on the new sofa, courtesy of the Ruthers. *Is all this worth it*, she wondered — *the redecorated flat, the new furniture, the holiday abroad, and the stash under the bed?* Her mind was in turmoil. The job was all right. She had power, being a screw, and yeah, she enjoyed it. But it didn't pay too well, and she wanted more in her life. Material things made up for the loneliness and the troubled past, but it was the fear of being caught out and ending up in prison herself. Things had changed. Gemma was different now although she couldn't quite put her finger on how her official legal visits had caused this transformation in her attitude towards her. She was acting all belligerent and very cock-sure of herself. It was disturbing. When she'd arrived at the prison, she was a quiet, thin, pathetic creature who wouldn't look at you. She had spent six months on remand and was now serving her sentence at Bronzefield in Middlesex. When she'd escorted Gemma back to her cell the afternoon after her first legal visit, she'd initially been in floods of tears, but as soon as the lawyers were out of sight she'd stopped crying. Today was strange too. She pondered over Gemma's stance; it was weird, even the sorrowful expression had changed. She'd opened that cell door and nodded for Gemma to go inside, but Gemma had smirked and raised an eyebrow with a look of defiance on her face.

"What you grinning at, Ruthers?" she'd barked.

"I'm grinning at a fucking low life scummy screw that's gonna go down for a fucking long time," she'd said, and then she'd laughed, taunting her.

Sandra was shocked at the girl's arrogance; this wasn't the fearful, nervous Gemma she was used to.

"Shut ya mouth, Ruthers, and get in ya cell."

"Oh gladly, Sandra. Looking at your boat makes me wanna puke. But thinking about how you're gonna cope in this stinking shithole is gonna make me smile."

It wasn't what she'd said that spooked Sandra, it was how she'd said it.

Sandra grabbed her mobile and decided she wouldn't rest until she had spoken to Bobby. She dialled the number and after one ring he answered. "What's up?" He sounded on edge.

"I'm out of it, mate. That wife of yours has something up her sleeve and now she has the lawyers on her side. They know I'm involved. The barrister warned me in so many words. She knows, and I can't end up in the slammer. The fucking inmates would torture me."

"What d'ya mean, lawyers? What fucking lawyers?"

"Yesterday two turned up for a legal visit and today they were there for the duration."

"What the fuck was she saying?"

Sandra was uncomfortable; she didn't have the answers. "I don't know, but the barrister was recording everything on a tape recorder."

"Fuck, fuck, fuck. Why didn't ya tell me yesterday?"

Sandra didn't know what to say. She wanted out and to have nothing more to do with it. "Look, Bobby, ya better get someone else to do ya dirty work. This is too close for comfort."

"Oh, yeah? Well, let me tell ya, if I go down, you're coming with me. Now make sure that bitch don't get to see the lawyer again. Got it?"

Sandra put down the phone and stared into space. Twinkle, the big black tom cat, jumped from the table and onto her lap. She stroked his silky fur and tickled him under the chin. "At least I have you," she whispered. She loved the cat; he couldn't bully her. The past had turned her into a person she despised. She'd been picked on her whole life by her wicked mother and the kids at school ... in fact, by everyone. She'd had to be tough and fight back, but the power it had given her had become an addiction. She would lose it all if she went to prison and the thought made her shudder. But what could they actually find her guilty of? Making Gemma's life a misery, goading her into killing herself, and threatening her with the rapist, wouldn't really amount to an arrestable offence. On the other hand, sending information to Bobby Ruthers might be sufficient, but could they prove it?

They'd never proved it was her who'd tried to poison Gemma although she'd been pulled into the governor's office and questioned. Luckily, Gemma's records showed a long list of accusations emanating from her court files, which could not be substantiated, so with her history of psychological problems, including self-harming, the issue had not been taken any further. All the same, Gemma must have had a cast iron stomach not to have keeled over and died that day.

The phone rang; it was Bobby. She let it ring and then thought better than to ignore it. "Look, sorry, Bobby, I just need time to think."

"Don't you ever put the phone down on me again. Who is the fucking lawyer?"

Sandra paused; she couldn't think of what to say. "The barrister is a woman called Francesca Vincent and the solicitor is Jamie Walker. They aren't fucking around, either. They're determined to get her out. They questioned her for hours."

There was silence for a long time. She wondered if he had put the phone down. "Hello?"

"Yeah, right, Sandra, you'll have to find a way to get rid of her. She must never make it to court. Do whatever you have to, but make sure she has no fucking voice."

The phone battery died and Sandra shook. This was a nightmare. Then it dawned on her. Bobby had her by the short and curlies. She'd made the call from the prison on her mobile the day Cassie was killed. The phone was in her name. There would be questions if he got caught. She hated him right now; he was a smooth operator with a wicked and cruel side.

*

Meanwhile, Gemma was rubbing her hands together. The lawyer had been reeled in hook, line and sinker, and she was going to be a free woman. She went over her story, hoping she had said enough to push Francesca into getting the ball rolling. After all, she had given her enough reasons to be on her side. Cassie's murder was a sufficient incentive on its own, and then the mention of Charles Enright – well, his name would stir emotions in Francesca. Gemma was confident

304

that no one could touch her now. She was going to take down the Ruthers and anyone else that stood in her way. But the gremlins inside her were saying that this might be a big if.

CHAPTER FOURTEEN

The morning brought with it black billowing clouds, and it was cooler than it had been. Francesca opened the window to let the air circulate. Baby Cass was rousing and ready for another bottle. The night feeds were shared by Maria and Francesca, both doting over the little bundle. She held him close to her face and kissed him on both cheeks. "Good morning, my precious little thing," she said, as Cass opened his eyes and tried to focus. The breeze made him smile and Francesca giggled.

She was in a world of her own with just her and Cass. She loved the baby so much and secretly she liked the fact that he was soothed in her arms. She looked out at the dark clouds and sighed. It was a lovely feeling to hold and nurse her nephew, but she must not get too close. It was the same with her nieces and nephews generally because although she loved them as if they were her own, they weren't. She would just enjoy the time she had with them and be grateful she had such a close and loving family. She kissed him again and gently stroked his soft hair. She heard some noise downstairs and assumed her parents had arrived. Her mother would be missing Cass and no doubt wanting a cuddle. "Ahh, well, our little miracle, it's time for the others to make a fuss of you. Auntie Sisco will have her turn later. Aw, I love you, my little blue eyes," she whispered.

Suddenly, a voice behind her said, "And I love you." Instantly, she whirled around to see her Sergio, standing there. Her eyes filled with tears; she had only been away for a week, but with the tragedy that had struck them, she'd missed him more than ever. He stepped closer and leaned across to kiss her face. He peered down at the baby and felt an overwhelming sense of sadness. His wife would have made the perfect mother, and yet she could only borrow someone else's baby. He had been standing there for a minute before he spoke, and his heart went out to the woman he loved more than life itself. She was the woman he could give almost anything to, except the one thing she truly desired.

"He is perfect, my bella, just perfect."

Francesca nodded. "A miracle. Hey, what are you doing here?"

"We are all here. This is such a terrible thing that has happened. So Mauricio, Roberto, and Dominic have come too. Families stick together."

"What? You are all here?"

Sergio smiled. "Yes, Uncle Roberto is at our house, and Mauricio and Dominic are downstairs with Dan and Fred."

She looked at her husband's face and she still melted every time she saw him. There was no man more perfect for her.

He stared back with sadness in his eyes. "Bella, I know you will want to find this person that killed Cassie, but we are not getting any younger. You cannot do this alone, not this time."

Tears filled her eyes and she bit her lip.

Sergio put his arm around his wife. "What is it? You never cry."

Maria came into the room with a bottle. She felt awkward when she saw they were having a private moment. "Here," she said, "let me take the baby." She held out her arms and Francesca carefully handed him over. Maria then swiftly left the room.

"What's wrong, Francesca?"

She gazed into eyes that showed so much compassion. "My past is filled with so much darkness, and just as we have happy times ahead, someone comes along and takes it all away, and again my heart is filled with anger and bitterness. It is selfish of me, but I just want to be happy." The tears flowed and she began to sob.

Sergio had never seen her so emotional and it ripped at his heart.

She held on to him until the tears subsided and then she sat on the edge of the bed. He sat next to her. "Is there something else, my bella, that hurts you so much?"

She nodded. "I'm afraid that the reason Cassie was killed may be to do with me, and I honestly couldn't live with myself if that were true."

Sergio frowned. "How?" He loosened his tie and removed his suit jacket.

"The girl who Cassie visited in prison, just before she was murdered, gave us her story, and she mentioned Charles Enright. It was as if she wanted me to take note that he was somewhere in the mix. I have no idea why. The story doesn't add up, yet some of it I believe, and I guess I have so many emotions surfacing right now with fear being one of them."

"We are here now, we are all together, and we will face it together like before. The Enrights cannot hurt you again. Almost all of them are dead and gone." He kissed her cheek and swept her long black hair away from her face. "You are so beautiful, my angel," he whispered.

She smiled, yet her heart was aching. *The Enrights might be dead, but are they really gone or are their ghosts ready to haunt me?*

When Francesca arrived downstairs, she was delighted to see Mauricio and Dominic, and, as usual, Mauricio was all over her with a huge hug and lots of kisses. He was very much like her brother Fred. She noticed Dan had a smile on his face for the first time in days. Her husband and his family were very close to her and her brothers and so being in the same room was a boost of positive energy. The night they joined together to take down the McManners was the real true test of faith and the Lucianis had not let her down. They had stood by her side as if they were her own flesh and blood and cemented their allegiance.

"It's lovely to see you, but—"

"Bella." Mauricio interrupted and grabbed her hand. "This is a time when we all need to be together. We will see to this terrible business." His Italian accent was sexy – Francesca had seen many a woman melt – but to her he was another brother. They had grown close over the months before his trial, and when Charles had left her for dead, Mauricio's family were there to save her.

Fred was now livelier than ever, having his other sidekick on board. "Right, ya need to listen to the recordings, Maury. I tell ya, when I get my fucking hands on this Bobby Ruthers, I'm gonna rip his heart out and—"

Francesca stopped him. "Fred, the recordings reveal a lot more than what she said, and I am not sure this is all about the Ruthers. I want to get to the bottom of it before you go charging in. I want the truth, and Gemma is not being totally honest. The information she has deliberately left out may hold the key as to why our Cassie was killed."

Dan jumped in. "Fran, I don't care why. I just want whoever killed her to pay."

Francesca nodded with sorrow in her eyes. "I know, Dan, and trust me, they will, but we must know the truth behind all of this so that we're sure there will be no repercussions. Our family is big and I don't want any more bloodshed."

The morning was spent with the family arriving, one by one, sharing breakfast. Mary was itching to get her hands on Cass, and so she spent much of the time upstairs with Maria, making a fuss of him.

Bill sat around the table with the men whilst they listened to the recordings again.

Francesca watched her father's expression. He looked young for a man of his age and she could tell her brothers would age well if they took after him. This wasn't the place for him. He should be sunning himself on a cruise ship somewhere, along with her mum.

"Well, I have to agree there's a lot that doesn't add up. I find it hard to accept that if this woman was locked up for a long time by her husband, and finally set free once she had lost a baby, she wouldn't go straight to the police. Good God, a young woman would have been screaming blue murder, not sitting down and drinking tea with such a vile family – and they are vile," he said.

"What? Dad, do you know them?" asked Fred.

Bill nodded. "Yeah, well, Violet Ruthers, who don't? She's a nasty piece of work. When I was a young man, she was a nut case. I used to drink with one of me pals over at The Mitcham Mint. She used to get in there, running the pub like it was her office. Tough as old boots, that woman was. I saw her take a meat cleaver to a bloke once. Luckily, the landlord grabbed her arm before she took his head off his shoulders. Her boys were just bits of kids then and they were just as bad. 'Orrible brats, they were. Mouths like sewers, and even as young as they were, they could ruck. She was like a man, but I have to give it to her, she could earn money out of a used piece of chewing gum, her. They reckon she ran the brothels at King's Cross, which didn't surprise me." He sniggered, "And her mouth could put a hot-headed lorry driver to shame."

"So, Dad, do you believe that Gemma could have suffered at their hands, or is this story just that – a story?" asked Francesca.

Bill chewed the inside of his mouth. "She may have suffered but her story still don't make sense. Not only that, but as you say, this woman, Gemma, is forty years old. Playing the downtrodden, dutiful wife don't cut it with me."

Francesca was pleased her father had surmised the same as her, and yet the Enrights, popping up in the story, still concerned her.

"Okay, we need to start to do some investigating ourselves. Fred, can you make some inquiries about the Ruthers? Ask Beano to do the groundwork. That man Beano is a genius. I'm going to find Daisy Burrows. I have a feeling she's not dead, and I think Gemma said that to put me off the scent."

"I will come with you, Bella," said Sergio.

Francesca shook her head. "I think it's better that I meet her alone. She might be more forthcoming with her information. You can come along for the drive, though."

Sergio didn't protest. As long as he was near enough to protect her, he didn't mind.

Francesca didn't wear a suit. She wanted to look informal, so she headed off in jeans and a T-shirt, with Sergio by her side. She knew King's Cross, and after taking a few short cuts, weaving in and out of the traffic, they arrived by the hotel. The side street had one spare parking space. She turned to Sergio and smiled. "This is going to be a lucky day."

He returned the smile and added a kiss. "Bella, be careful. Do you have … ?"

She laughed. "Always." She patted her bag containing her gun, disguised as a jewelled lighter. It was a gift Roberto had given her many years ago. She had used it in the past and prayed she'd never have to use it again.

The hotel was fairly quiet but it was midday. Gemma had mentioned the caretaker and that would be a good place to start, as asking for Daisy would almost certainly guarantee a no response. A receptionist sat behind a desk. It wasn't a grand hotel, to say the least; it was more of a grubby one star flea-free room, if you were lucky. The young woman looked Francesca over and just glared. "Yeah? Can I help you?"

Francesca nodded. "Where can I find the caretaker?"

The receptionist pointed to the staircase. "He's on level one, end of the corridor, room marked caretaker."

Francesca turned to leave. "Hang on, love, what do you want him for?"

"Personal." She tapped the side of her nose and left.

She gracefully walked away and up to the next floor. The smell in the corridor almost choked her. The lino flooring had just been bleached and small pools of water gathered in the creases. He must have just mopped the floor. She tapped on the door and waited. There was no answer, but if he was washing the floors maybe he was on the next level. She climbed the next flight of stairs, and there, at the end of the corridor, was an elderly man in a blue boiler suit. He was sweeping with the mop from left to right. He had a name badge on his chest. As soon as he saw her heading his way, he called out, "'Ere, love, mind ya footing, the floor's wet."

"Thank you, Stanley."

Stanley stopped mopping and tried to focus on the woman walking towards him. He didn't recognise her.

"Sorry, but do I know you?" he asked, leaning on the mop.

"No, you don't know me, but I know Daisy Burrows, and I was told you could help me find her." She knew instinctively he would be wary. It was the underground mentality. No one gave out information unless they were confident or money was offered.

"Oh, yeah? What do you want her for?" he asked, eyeing her casual but very classy outfit. She seemed important with her black briefcase.

"I'm from one of the wills claimant companies. She might be into a few quid, but without talking with her, I can't be sure."

Stanley looked her up and down. She didn't look like the police; she was a well-presented and attractive woman with a soft face. "I'll take you there." Stanley was pleased he could do Daisy a favour; he liked the ole girl, and she was good company to share a hot cup of cocoa with. He took Francesca to the next floor.

"There, that door. Give her a knock. I'm sure she's in."

Francesca was eager to get inside and find out the truth. The door opened and standing there, in an old tracksuit that was ready for the bin, was Daisy Burrows. Francesca recognised her from the court case. She had aged considerably over the years. She still had her hair dyed ginger and the familiar red lipstick was creeping out from the creases round her mouth.

"Yes, love?" she said, in her half-London, half-northern accent.

"Daisy, may I come in? I need to talk to you. I'm not the police or anything like that. It's a personal chat, if you don't mind."

Daisy stared at the woman for a while. She thought she recognised Francesca, but she couldn't put her finger on where she knew her from. "Okay."

Francesca stepped through the door and looked around the well-worn room. It was apparent that Daisy wasn't a dirty woman. She had made her home cosy and it was clean, but it was also obvious she didn't have two pennies to rub together.

"'Ere, love, take a seat. Would you like a cuppa tea or coffee, or a cold drink?"

Francesca deferentially sat on the sofa. "No thank you. I'm fine for the moment."

Daisy eased herself into the chair. "So, now, what's this all about, then? Sorry, I didn't catch your name."

Francesca wondered briefly whether she should give a false one but then decided against it.

"I'll tell you who I am, but I want to be sure first that what I tell you cannot go any further."

Daisy nodded and eyed Francesca up; she seemed so familiar. At the same time, Francesca noticed how sober Daisy was. The last time she'd seen her was in the courtroom as a prosecution witness in the Mauricio Luciani case. She had downed a few shots before she'd appeared on the stand and that had been obvious to everyone in the courtroom.

"Daisy, I'm Gemma Ruthers' lawyer. She's asked for my help, but I have to be honest. I am not sure I can help her. You see, the story of events she gave me, when I questioned her, doesn't seem to add up, and so the reason for my visit is to ask your advice." She was playing it cool, trying not to come on too strong; she was there for information, and looking at Daisy's expression, she knew she would get it.

"Well, I can tell ya this for nothing, I wouldn't trust that young woman as far as I could throw her."

Francesca smiled. "I'm so glad you said that. Only, I thought I was going mad. She told me this long story of how her life was so awful and how she was only defending herself when she knifed her husband. There were a few points that didn't add up to me, and so since she mentioned your name, and said you were a significant part of her life, I thought maybe you could help me."

Daisy rubbed her feet on the threadbare carpet; she looked uncomfortable.

"It's okay, I can promise you this much – whatever you tell me will go no further. I won't ask you to stand up in court, and your name won't be mentioned if, in fact, I do go for an appeal." Francesca was trying to put Daisy at ease.

316

Daisy stared hard at Francesca. "It's no skin off my nose, to be quite frank. The girl's a liar, and a cruel one at that. Look, I don't mind talking to you, but I feel funny not knowing your name."

Francesca smiled. "It's Francesca Luciani."

Daisy leaned forward to get a closer look. "It's nice to meet you. I'm sure we've met. You have eyes that I have gazed into before, I'm sure."

Francesca shook her head. "No, I don't think so."

"My dear, I may be old now, but I have a very good memory, and the name Luciani is one I'll never forget. I stood there in the witness stand, accusing a young man of killing my friend, and his name was Luciani. I remember it like it was yesterday." She paused and stared into space, as if she was reliving a poignant memory. "Oh my God, the blood. Everywhere it was. And that handsome young man in the car asleep, with the girl sliced to ribbons. Oh, that night still haunts me to this day. I used to drink back then, ya know. It all happened so fast. One minute, I was in a car, waiting for another punter, and I must have drifted off to sleep. The next minute, I was awake, and the police were surrounding me. I thought I had heard someone talking in Italian, but I suppose I got that wrong … Anyway, that's got nothing to do with Gemma, me rambling on is all."

Francesca was interested in Daisy's view of the event. "Go on, Daisy, you were saying."

"Oh, yeah, sorry, it's just you mentioning Gemma, and me thinking back all those years to the trial."

Francesca was captivated. "Please, carry on, Daisy. Tell me, was there a connection?"

Daisy took a deep breath. "Oh, I dunno, nothing, probably."

"It might not be nothing." Francesca was on the edge of her seat.

"Well, that was the last time I saw Gemma, just before that night. It was strange, come to think of it. So are you related to that man, Luciani? The one had up for all those killings?"

Francesca didn't answer. She was focused on getting information. "Daisy, you were saying something about Gemma and the Luciani case."

"Are you sure you don't want a cup of tea?" asked Daisy.

Francesca knew she had to keep cool and not push the woman too fast. "Yes, that would be lovely. Milk, no sugar, thank you."

Daisy eased herself out of the chair and walked to the kitchen. While the kettle boiled, she pondered those steel blue eyes and tried to remember where she had seen the woman before.

Francesca's phone rang; it was Sergio. "Are you okay?" he asked.

"Yes, I'm fine. Give me a while. I'm just having tea."

Daisy waddled back in with a tray. She placed it on the table and offered biscuits with it. McVities Plain Rich Tea biscuits were one of her favourites.

Francesca politely took one, and like Daisy, she dunked it in her drink.

"Yes, Gemma was like a daughter to me, ya know. When she was a kid, of course. I warned that girl to stay away from that Bobby Ruthers, but she wouldn't listen. I could never understand why such a pretty young girl as her would waste her life on that family. She married him and I thought that was the end of it. She came to see me

318

about a year or two later, and I did feel sorry for her. By all accounts, she had been raped by five men. She was only young then – twenty I s'pose. Anyway, I told her again then to stay away, they're nothing but trouble, but she didn't listen, and she went straight back. I didn't see her for a few years. Then I heard she was going around to all the young hookers, ones that occupied the Ruthers' bedsits. Shitholes they were, an' all. She was collecting the rent. I didn't want to know after that. It goes against the grain, yer see."

Francesca sat back on the sofa. She felt comfortable in Daisy's presence. It was obvious she wore her heart on her sleeve. The dated décor put her in mind of when she was young, at home, with her family. The seventies' patterns and colours were on the walls and the floor, and even the china was from back then. Francesca noticed the fur coat, hanging on the back of the door. It was the same one Daisy had worn the day she stood in the dock. It was well-worn all those years ago. It had stuck in her mind then that it was the sort of coat that looked like it would be used as a rug. Perhaps it was her only coat. Francesca suddenly felt very sorry for Daisy: the tired flat, the old coat, and a life of selling her body. She wondered what comforts Daisy had in life, if any. The tell-tale signs of an alcoholic were there. She had a red nose and purple cheeks. Her beauty lay in her soft caring eyes. They held no hidden agenda.

"So, ya see, dear, I didn't have anything to do with her after that."

"Daisy, did you know that Gemma was locked away by her husband and had a baby that sadly died at birth?"

"It's funny you should say that. Only me friend, Shirley, God rest her soul, she knew Gemma. She was there when Gemma also saw first-hand what the Ruthers were capable of. She saw one of the poor streetwalkers, a young girl who'd overdosed at their hands, and had crawled her way to our safe house, and bless her heart, she died. Yep,

319

died, she did, right there in front of Gemma. That should have been enough to warn her off."

Francesca had to tolerate with Daisy's story drifting off-topic. "So did Shirley see her again?"

"Oh, yes. Shirley was visiting one of the youngsters, a girl called Bunny, and there at the door was Gemma, all grown-up, a proper woman. Shirley said she was like a snow queen. She was very pretty, but her eyes were so cold. She didn't talk to Shirley, either. She just snatched the rent money from Bunny and left. So I said to Shirley that Gemma must have turned into a right bitch. But she said no. There was a sadness in her eyes, she said, so maybe she did lose a baby. I dunno, it was as if Shirley was describing another woman."

"Gemma mentioned a girl called Bunny and another called Summer. She said she helped Summer after Jimmy Ruthers slashed her face, and then she gave the girls stun guns for protection, but she was caught by Jimmy Ruthers. She said it was then that they locked her up for the second time."

Daisy raised her eyebrows and smirked. "Yes, I heard about it. Jimmy cut poor Summer with his ring. It was a nasty affair."

"Daisy, do you know how long Gemma was collecting rent? Only she said it was for a year, and then the Ruthers locked her away, after she got caught with the stun guns."

"I tell ya this for nothing, dear, that Gemma has spun you a right fucking yarn. The girls used to keep our Shirley up to date, ya see." She paused and looked in deep thought. "There was a time, come to think of it, when the girls thought she was on their side, and she dished out a couple of those zap gun thingies, but Jimmy caught her, and then she wasn't on the scene for a while – a month, I think. Yes, that's right. She didn't collect rent for a few weeks, and that's when

320

she changed. Bunny reckoned that she had faint bruises and was never the same after that."

Francesca frowned. "Only a month? She led me to believe it was years."

Daisy shook her head. "See what I mean? Gemma is an out-and-out liar. She blamed the girls for taking a hiding off her ol' man. Anyway, as I say, she weren't locked up for years, and when she did come collecting again, she was ruthless and the girls were petrified of her. Gawd, I don't know whatever makes a young woman become so bleedin' cruel. 'Cos that's what she was, ya know – cruel. It was like she had turned into a true Ruthers, warts an' all." She shook her head in disgust. "She was like a fucking pimp, collecting kids off the streets, and finding flats for them just to rake in more money, dirty money. She had no scruples, getting them hooked on that shit, so they were begging for top-ups." She paused and stared off into space.

Francesca held her hands to her face in shock. "My God, and she led me to believe she was looking out for them. She also mentioned a Charles Enright and said he was a nasty, cruel punter."

"Who?" asked Daisy.

"Oh, I see, sorry. Gemma gave me the impression that you all knew that the Ruthers could get away with anything because they had judges and lawyers on their side, even the police. In particular, she mentioned a family by the name of Enright."

Daisy nodded and sipped her tea. "Oh, yeah, I knew that, but I never knew their names."

Francesca noticed that Daisy looked tired; her face was gaunt and her eyes had glazed over.

"Look, I've taken up too much of your time. I should go."

Daisy shook her head. "I'm fine, honestly, lovey. If I can help, I will. It's only fair you know what you're taking on. Gemma is a conniving bitch. I could not believe how that sweet happy-go-lucky kid, with so much compassion for us kind, could turn her back so quick and become a fucking monster, excuse my French. So, as I was saying, she was as hard as nails, she was. They begged her for time to pay, but she wouldn't have any of it. Bunny said she was as wicked as Jimmy. It turned my stomach, hearing that, ya know. Anyway, I did hear, years later, that she stopped collecting rent and was seen driving around in a flash car. So, no, I don't think they locked her up. I thought she had left that Bobby and moved on because Shirley saw her with another bloke. Done up to the nines, she was."

"What bloke?" Francesca jumped in.

"I don't know who he was, but I did see him once … Yeah, that's what I was gonna say. That night the serial killer, well that Mauricio Luciani fella was found in the car next to me. That was the last time I saw Gemma."

"Daisy, please, try to remember everything. It might be really important."

"Oh, lovey, I can remember it. It was shocking, I can tell ya. I was walking the street opposite here. I had me own spot, and then I noticed this flash car. It was warm that evening, and this car had its top down, one of those convertible thingies. It was parked across the road, so of course I had a gawp, hoping it was some rich fella, ready for a piece of an ol' girl." She laughed. "Trust me, it takes all sorts. Anyway, then I spotted Gemma. She didn't notice I had seen her. I s'pose she thought me eyesight wouldn't be too clever at my age, but the funny thing is I still have twenty-twenty vision. Then I clocked her fella. He was a handsome man too. He was watching me. I turned me head to the side, but kept me eye on them. Just being nosy, really. I don't know what they were up to."

"Can you describe him for me?"

"Well, as much as I can remember, it was a good few years ago now, he had quite longish hair, sort of thick and wavy. He wore a suit and had a tan, really handsome he was, but there was something flash about him."

Francesca felt sick as the hairs on the back of her neck stood on end.

"Yes, it was odd because after they drove away, I got a punter. He was a young man who offered to pay well over the top, not the usual client. Strange thing was, he drove me to the *Violet Club*. D'ya know the one? It has an underground car park. It's funny because I used to go there. A few of us girls did. We'd hang around to pick up punters from the club and take them to one of the dumped cars. Anyway, this man drove us there. I did me deed, and he was kind. He gave me a bottle of vodka, saying he couldn't take it home with him. Then, next thing I remember, I was waking up in one of the dumped cars, next to the car with the dead girl in it. I did hear a voice, but I was still drowsy, to be honest. Then the police carted me away, telling me what I had seen. D'ya know what I mean? They were not asking me but telling me."

Francesca's mind was running away with her – surely the thought that Gemma was connected in some way to the Mauricio set-up was too far-fetched? She had to go away and think about things.

"Would you by any chance remember the car you saw Gemma in with this flash-looking man?"

Daisy smiled. "Oh yes, it was a red Jag, a really fancy one."

Francesca knew then that it was her former husband's car.

"Daisy, I'm so grateful to you for being so honest. You have really helped me."

Daisy smiled. "I hope you make the right choice because if that girl gets out she could rain hellfire on us."

Francesca stood to leave, gesturing for Daisy not to get up; she could see herself out.

"Oh, did Gemma ever send you money?"

"No, she wouldn't do that. She knew I would despise her after all she had done. Ha, and money. She paraded around, dripping in money, but she wouldn't give me any. By all accounts, Shirley reckons she was always done-up, in designer gear, flash bags, and stuff. To be truthful, lovey, if she knocked at me door now, I would probably kill her meself."

Francesca tilted her head to the side and said, "I'm sure there are many people who feel the same way. I wonder if I should throw the lamb to the wolves?"

"There was one other thing that Shirley told me. It may not be anything, but as I say, she was taking kids off the streets. Shirley told me something strange. She said that sometimes Gemma would take one of the young pretty girls away somewhere. One of the others heard her tell them they could stay in a big house with posh finery. Those that went never came back. Shirley said that a kid called Jody asked Gemma why the girls hadn't come back, and Gemma replied that they were living like princesses in a castle. Now, I thought that was odd. Perhaps those youngsters *were* thrown to the wolves. Who knows, bless them."

Daisy struggled out of her chair and put her arms out to Francesca. "'Ere, lovey, give us a hug. You're a lovely woman, and I know that because I know who you are now."

Francesca went cold.

"It's all right, lovey, you did the right thing. That poor young man, Mauricio, was never the killer, and if you hadn't proved his innocence, then gawd knows where he would be now."

"Daisy, please——"

Daisy put her finger over Francesca's lip. "You have my word, lovey."

Francesca's shoulders relaxed; she could trust Daisy.

"May I ask, this fur coat, err …" She stopped as she realised she couldn't say, 'Why do you keep the smelly old rag?' Instead, she said, "How long have you had it? I remember you wore it in the courtroom."

Daisy was grinning. "I know, sweetheart, it's a bit of tat, but when I go out with that coat on, I pretend it's a real posh fake fur, and it makes me feel a million dollars. That's my way, see. My mother, the wicked cow, she had a real fur, strutting around the place like she was the queen mother. I hated her, ya know. I hated that she wore a dead animal on her back, but I wanted to feel posh and classy, so I found that coat in an Oxfam shop. It looked all right back in the late Sixties, but it's old now. I can't bear to throw it out, though."

Francesca hugged her again. "It was so lovely to meet you, and properly this time."

"Yeah, I'm sober now. I have been for a few years, and it was a pleasure meeting you. If ya nearby, pop in and share a tea with me." Daisy smiled.

"Oh, indeed I will."

Francesca was clear-headed and fired-up. She hurried down to the car to find Sergio wide-eyed.

"Bella, I was worried. This place, the people, they are—" But Francesca got there first. "Yes, Sergio, you mean the salt of the earth. They've landed on hard times, and underneath all that mess they are damaged girls, fighting to keep their heads above water."

He smiled at her view of the world. She was such a lovely person who always tried to see good in others and respect them for who they were.

"We need to go to Knightsbridge. I have some shopping to do."

Sergio rolled his eyes in jest, but he knew she was on a selfless mission.

One of the classy designer boutiques, she had been to before, held an array of fake furs; she had only purchased one for herself a year before. The lady serving instantly recognised her and was ready to make another killing in commission.

"Good afternoon. How lovely to see you again."

Francesca was in a rush and had no time for being pandered to; she hated all that false pretence anyway.

"I'm interested in a full length fur in a size fourteen."

The assistant sensed her urgency and rushed to the rail which held the most expensive fake furs the shop had in stock.

"This one here is so effective you cannot tell it's faux. Just have a feel of the quality."

Sergio sat on the round sofa and watched; he stayed silent. His wife would take control.

"Yes, I can see. I'm looking for a traditional cut and style for a mature woman, but it's not for me."

"Oh, I see." The coat the assistant had in her hands was the most expensive latest design. The traditional cuts were less expensive, but she wouldn't argue with Francesca. She hurried back with two furs: one was a brown one, and the other, a jet black one, was almost blue when the light hit it.

Francesca felt the lining and ran her hands over the surface. She took it from the assistant to make sure it wasn't too heavy; she didn't want Daisy to end up with backache. However, it wasn't; in fact, it was light and just perfect.

"I'll take this one."

The assistant had had a bad week and was desperate to make a good sale to make up for it. "How would you like the boots to match?" she suggested. "They're trimmed with the same fur and are completely fur-lined."

Francesca nodded as she tried to remember the size of Daisy's feet and then she made an educated guess. "Yes, in a size five, please."

The assistant left to go to the back of the shop and Francesca noticed a loose-fitting cashmere dress; it reeked of quality. It was black with a subtle row of diamantes around the neck. *Very royal*, she thought.

She returned with the boots and Francesca smiled. They were perfect; not too high, warm to the touch, and they had so much class. "I'll take them, and that dress, in a size fourteen, please."

The assistant was in her element; she was clocking up the commission.

"Now, please can you box them up in your best packaging, tissue-lined, and have them sent by courier to this address?"

The assistant was like a nodding dog. She would have kissed the soles of the woman's feet if she'd been asked to. She took the address and placed her glasses on her nose. "Err ... is this the right address?"

Francesca snatched the piece of paper and checked herself. "Yes, it is. Is there a problem?"

The woman couldn't afford to lose the sale and quickly said, "No, not at all, madam. I'll organise a courier right now."

Sergio loved to watch his wife. She had an assertive way, which made people jump to attention, and yet she was a kind woman. As they left the shop, she turned to her husband and kissed him on the cheek. "Why don't we go out for a meal tonight – just the two of us?"

Sergio shook his head. "Bella, you do not have to entertain me. That's not why I am here. Your brother is my brother. He needs your help, and we are by your side. When this terrible business is sorted out, we can go out, maybe take a holiday, but for now you must concentrate on this."

She kissed him again. "I love you, Sergio."

He smiled because he loved her too.

Stanley was mopping the top floor when the courier arrived, struggling with the boxes. He knocked hard on the door, praying someone was in. He didn't want to have to struggle all the way back to the van with them. Stanley walked towards the man. "She's in. Just wait a moment. If she doesn't answer, I can take the parcels." Nothing had been delivered to Daisy's before, and Stanley was just as excited as she would be.

The door opened and Daisy almost jumped back. She gazed down at the packages and then up at the courier. "These ain't for me, are they?"

"If your name's Ms Burrows, then yep. Sign here."

Daisy looked at Stanley and then at the boxes. She scribbled her name and the courier left. Stanley then helped carry the boxes inside. He plonked them on the bed.

"So, what's all this then, Daise?"

"Well, I'll be buggered if I know. 'Ere, look at the name on it. That's a very posh designer clothes shop, that is. Aw, what if they got the wrong Burrows? Some poor woman may be expecting this. Perhaps I should call the courier back."

Stanley laughed. "Don't be soft, woman. It's got your address on, so it's got to be for you. Go on, then, open them." Stanley's heart melted when she opened the biggest box, and there, wrapped in tissue, was a stunning black fur coat.

"Gawd help us, would ya look at that, eh? A real fur coat!"

Stanley looked at the large label dangling from the sleeve. "No, it's a fake one, but you would never know. That's class, that is."

Daisy wrapped it around her shoulders. It was perfect: soft, light, and her size.

"Open the others, girl, I got floors to mop."

Daisy pulled the ribbon from the next box and retrieved a pair of boots. She slid them on and looked down. "Cor, Stanley, these are only fur-lined an' all. What did I do to deserve this, eh?"

Stanley had an inkling who had sent the parcels. It was probably the same woman who had pulled him aside on her way out and given him a couple of hundred pounds to take Daisy out for a special meal.

"Aw, and look at this posh frock. Jesus, it's only cashmere an' all. Feel that, Stanley. It's like a baby's bum, it's so soft. Hang on, there's a note."

She picked up a card that had the name of the boutique on it, and as she turned it over, she read the inscription as follows: '*For the Queen. I hope you can feel a million dollars.*'

Daisy felt the tears welling up; she put her hands to her mouth.

Stanley put his arm around her shoulders. "It was that lady that came to see you, weren't it?"

"How do you know that, Stanley?"

"'Cos, on the way out, she gave us some money to have a good night out, me and you. 'Ere, ya don't think she's after something, do you?"

Daisy smiled. "Yes, she was after the truth, and I gave it to her."

CHAPTER FIFTEEN

Whilst Francesca was out on her mission, Terry was on his. DI Neil Spencer had agreed to meet up. They were old friends and shared the same moral code. Spencer was sick of the red tape and witnessing how some of the worst criminals could get away with so much, especially the Ruthers. He had a deep-seated hatred of them, every one of them. He had his suspicions that Lindsey, Terry James' daughter, had been left for dead at their hands, but he never did discuss it with Terry. He had to have solid proof, but unfortunately the legal system was not going to back him in finding it. They could get away with anything because once that judge decided that they were being hounded and harassed, he placed an order, under powers given by parliament in the Protection from Harassment Act, 1997. *What a joke*, thought Spencer. In fact, what the judge had placed was a free rein for the Ruthers to carry on running amok all over South West London. And it didn't help that the Ruthers had so many judges in their pockets. The only time they were caught bang to rights was the cocaine run. Luckily for Spencer, the bent judge was not in court that day, and so they had to serve time. Even that was a joke: four years for enough powder to have half of London hooked; they should have got a seven stretch at least.

British laws make it too easy to get away with crime. Clever villains, like the Ruthers, work around them because they have the financial muscle to pay for astute solicitors and barristers to exploit loopholes in any law of their choosing. You only have to glance at some of the headlines these days to see some celebrity or high profile footballer getting off paying a speeding fine or avoiding a huge tax bill. So our so-called bright politicians, who make the laws for our law-abiding citizens of this country, are obviously not as effective as they should be. Perhaps they should pay the villains' legal teams to make the laws doubly secure instead?

Still, despite knowing all this, and having to accept it, he was determined to find a way around the system if it killed him.

The Ruthers' name was mentioned at every major crime but nothing ever came of it. For example, the little drugs factory they had going in Mitcham was raided and even one of the illegal immigrants owned up, confessed, and gave the police George's name and details. But it was all a bastard joke; he was questioned and released, evidence unfounded, end of. Spencer would love to find something on them, which they could never get away with. He knew his blood pressure was rising too quickly. He'd been to the doctors only the other week for stress. Okay, most of his colleagues suffered from this, but his problem was that things were becoming a little personal with the Ruthers after that bitch, Violet, had had the last laugh over the latest warrant to search her premises.

The cafe just off Lewisham roundabout, run by a mad Irish woman, was a spot where the men often met up and chewed the fat.

Spencer was bang on time and pleased to see his old mate, Terry. "Well, look at you, ol' boy. Spain must have treated you well. I wouldn't have recognised you, except you still have that same dodgy haircut." He gently punched Terry's arm.

332

"Good to see you, too, me ol' mucker."

They sat down in the corner of the café, away from flapping ears.

"So, Tel, what's going on?"

"I got a message that my girl's death might have been the result of the Ruthers' wrongdoings."

Spencer took a deep breath. "You're going to hate me. I had my suspicions, years ago, but I couldn't get the proof. I had to call off the surveillance and was told to leave well alone. Believe me, though, I tried my best to get to the bottom of it. So, who told you?"

Terry pulled his chair closer to the table. "I know we're mates, Neil, we go back a long way, but for the moment I can't say who told me. You understand, don't ya?"

"No worries, fella, I'll still help in any way I can. You have my word. Besides, I need a break, and Spain's done you all right." They both laughed.

They could have been brothers, their appearance was so similar — it was a hardness in the eyes and the confident posture that went with the job.

"So, tell me about the Ruthers. What do you know about them?" asked Terry.

Spencer rolled his eyes. "Where do I start? Every fucking one of them's dabbling in something. They run most of the whorehouses in London, and they run the manor in South West London. They have links with the Yardies, and most known faces have a link one way or another. But the one thing I'm sure of, and it grates on me, is they have so many officials in their back pockets, it's frightening. Prosecution lawyers won't touch me. I've seen with my own eyes

333

three judges dismiss their cases. Insufficient evidence, they said. My fucking arse!"

"Did you know Gemma Ruthers?"

The Irish café owner approached their table, singing along with the radio. She smiled and her whole face lit up. "Two big breakfasts, lads?" She had the pen and pad to the ready.

"Just an omelette for me," replied Spencer.

"Yep, I'll have the same," said Terry.

"Good to see you again. It's been too long." She looked at Terry and winked.

Spencer laughed. "You still have it, then, son."

"She was good to me after my Lilly passed away. Nothing in it, but she's good company. She's a kind woman. She's got a heart of gold, her."

Joan was still smiling as she walked away. She liked Terry and had hoped for more, but he was his own man, and she was probably a passing phase.

"Getting back to Gemma, yeah, I remember her. Now that was an odd situation, you know."

Terry frowned. "Oh? Why was that then?"

"Well, as you know, we had the Ruthers watched. It was not a full-on surveillance, but we kept an eye, like. The older boys were inside, like I said, and then this kid suddenly appears, running around in a van. She was doing Violet's dirty work, collecting her debts. A pretty kid, she was, but a youngster. Then, overnight, she vanished. I feared the worst, but for a year nothing turned up, so I assumed she'd just fucked off. Then, out of the blue, she re-appeared. I wasn't sure it was her at first, she'd changed so much. She had grown up with a real cockiness about her. I watched her driving around in a flash car. She used to run the whorehouses for George and Charlie, I know that much. Christ, they were a fucking miserable place, I can tell ya. Anyway, I used to pop my head in there sometimes, just to see if the girls were all right. I couldn't shut the places down because as far as anyone could tell they were just renting flats. We had nothing and the Ruthers knew it. But the stories I heard would make your blood boil. They were barely women, teenagers they were, mostly hooked on crack cocaine. I pulled a couple in to get them to turn informant, but they were too far gone. They needed their drugs more than a life. They were afraid of that Gemma, though, I know that much. She hurt them bad if they didn't pay up. A few years after that, just as we set up surveillance, and fuck me did I have a big team, I pulled in everyone, but we were stopped in our tracks. We knew Gemma was taking the drugs into the flats but we only managed to nab her in the hallway. My sergeant was rubbing his hands together. She had enough gear in that handbag to put her away. But the court case turned out to be a joke. It was over in a day. Her lawyer, Wiers, got her off. They said Gemma was collecting rent from tenants in the area and she found the drugs in an empty flat in an adjacent building that the Ruthers had only recently taken over to house a young woman who was moving in there. So Gemma had removed the drugs from the flat with the intention of taking them to the police when she had finished her rounds. Ha, what a fucking joke. I swear, the smirk on that bitch's face had me boiling. I wanted to wring her neck."

The Irish woman arrived with two huge omelettes. The cheese and ham were oozing out of the sides and the chips were piled high. "There you go. Do you want more coffee?"

The men nodded and stared at the overflowing plates.

"She must like you, mate. She never fills my plate like that." Spencer laughed, and then he tucked in.

"So why do they have so much protection?" asked Terry.

Spencer wiped his mouth and took a deep breath. "This is why I want out of the force because the fucking judges are more corrupt than the likes of the Ruthers."

Terry stopped chewing and placed his cutlery down. He was intrigued by this remark and by the hostile tone in which it was said. Clearly, Spencer was as sick of the way that the rich and clever criminals could circumvent the laws of this country as he had been whilst in the force. "When you say judges, who do you mean?"

Spencer looked around, ensuring there were no prying eyes or flapping ears. There was a squad of builders across the room, but they could sniff out a copper a mile away and chose to keep their distance. "There's this club. They call it the Gentlemen's Club. You see, behind the courts and in the chambers, they gather like a secret coven. Members include Wiers, Stevens, Davies, and the Enrights, although only William is a member now. There are others but they are the main ones. I followed them off my own back, and put it this way, they're into young women, and probably boys too, but I can't be sure of that."

Terry loosened his tie. "The Enrights, you say?"

"Yep, all of them were members: William, Charlie, and Charles Enright, but, as I say, it's just William now. The slimy bastards. That was what I was going to tell you about Gemma. She was having it away with Charles."

Terry felt his neck getting hot and so decided to loosen his collar. "How do you know?"

336

Spencer grinned. "I was following her for about two weeks, in-between other stuff, and then I saw her meet up with him outside the Dorchester, no less. They booked in under Mr and Mrs Enright. I asked to look at the books, and sure enough, they had this regular thing going on. I couldn't understand it, myself. I suppose they were both as bad as one another and maybe that was the attraction. I met his wife once in the courtroom. What a stunning young woman she was. Now, that's another story. She disappeared overnight. I swear blind he killed her, but no one looked into it. Tel, they are all so fucking corrupt it makes me sick, and worst of all, I can't do anything about it. I had to laugh, though, when Charlie Enright was found shot in that park in Kent, and William, his brother, was found to be the culprit. I know they were set up. Nevertheless, the evidence against him was too overwhelming, so he was locked up. Charles disappeared a few months later. I reckon they had too much on the Ruthers, or maybe someone else had them taken out or executed them themselves."

Terry grinned to himself; he knew exactly who had taken them out and was impressed at the intelligence and gumption of Francesca. He was, however, shocked that Gemma had been seeing Charles; it would probably knock Francesca sideways when she heard the truth.

They ate in silence for a while and washed the huge meal down with more coffee.

"Neil, why did you think the Ruthers hurt my Lindsey?"

"It had Jimmy Ruthers' name all over it. There were a few young girls found in and around those derelict buildings, spanning a year, just the same as your Lindsey. One of the girls we knew came from the Ruthers' flats. We pulled her in once. I remember that she looked rough. She had bite marks on her cheeks, a black eye, and she was fucked. They called her Blossom, but in the morgue she was another

337

Jane Doe with no family. She had told me she was afraid of Jimmy. He was visiting her on a regular basis, and he was seriously hurting her, the poor kid. She wanted out. I said I would help her. I put her into a hostel as it was a safe house. But the poor cow was so hooked on drugs, she went back, and the next night we found her dead. She had overdosed. I won't forget the state she was in when we found her. There were bite marks all over her skinny little body. She had been so badly sexually abused. There weren't much left of her genitals, either." He stopped abruptly, realising that Terry had gone white; of course, it could be his daughter he was talking about. He reached across the table and grabbed Terry's arm. "I'm sorry, mate. Fuck, you didn't need to hear that."

Terry bit his bottom lip to stop the tears. "Yeah, mate, I did. I've always wanted to know who did that to my girl, and I think we both know now, don't we?"

"Tel, a word of warning from an old mate. I may have grounds to call on another surveillance. We have a new police commissioner, so I might have a clean slate. I'll have to test the waters because I don't know these days who I can trust, but if I call it on, I'll let you know. You watch yourself."

Terry knew he was giving him the nod. "So what do you have on 'em?"

"Bobby Ruthers, he's one of the two youngest boys, the one married to Gemma, placed his driving licence at the scene of a robbery. I know the Ruthers and petty burglary ain't their thing. To place himself at the scene of a crime, which he could get bird for, means only one thing: he's committed an uglier crime and he's going to use it as an alibi. He isn't the sharpest knife in the drawer, unlike his brothers. That Bobby may be the good-looking one, and a flash charmer too, but he ain't got a patch on George or Charlie."

"When was the burglary?"

"Four days ago. Why?"

Terry shrugged his shoulders. "Just wondered." He knew then that Bobby had killed Cassie.

The Irish woman came over with the bill and her phone number. Terry was looking good; he had lost weight and still had a good tan. Spain had definitely helped his health.

"Don't leave it so long next time, mate," said Spencer. He handed Terry a card. "Here's my private number. If the surveillance is called on, I'll let you know."

Terry shook his hand and walked away with more to think about.

Neil Spencer watched with a heavy heart as his friend disappeared among the flow of people, heading to the train station. He'd known Lindsey since she was born. She was the same age as his own girl and that was one of the reasons he was determined to have all the Ruthers behind bars. It had become an obsession. He guessed that it wouldn't be too long before Jimmy Ruthers was six foot under or his body parts spread all over London. Terry was a good copper, not a bent one; he turned a blind eye to petty shit and was after the real crooks, the ones who were evil. The man had too much bitterness in his heart to let Jimmy get away with that. One thing was for sure: Neil Spencer would do everything in his power to protect Terry.

The train was packed with commuters, but Terry managed to find a seat tucked at the back by the window. He pulled a picture out of his wallet and stared at the pretty little girl with the golden hair and huge eyes – *his* little girl. In his mind, he imagined having his hands round Jimmy's neck and squeezing until the man's eyes bulged out of his head. *Fuck the law, and fuck the consequences, but I will have my day.*

Sam was waiting at Sevenoaks station, as promised. He opened the car door as Terry appeared on the pavement. "All right, Tel? Jump in."

Terry was quiet as they headed back to Dan's house until Sam spoke.

"Did you see DI Spencer?"

"Yep and he told me some interesting stuff. Not sure how your sister's going to take it, though."

Sam gave him a sideways glance. "She's a tough cookie, our Dolly."

Terry smiled; he remembered the story he'd been told about how Francesca got her nickname.

"Sam, it's pretty obvious to me how much you all care about each other. You're all so close, and it's good to see. Your sister, though, she is something else. She's smart!"

Sam nodded. "You have no idea of her capabilities, and she's the brains of the outfit. She got me kids away from their mother. Cruel bitch, she was."

Terry had been in court to witness Francesca destroying Jesse, Sam's wife. He'd really enjoyed the experience. She'd never had a chance to defend herself because there was so much evidence pointing to her guilt. He had wondered, at the time though, how much of that evidence was manufactured by the Vincent family, despite Jesse's cruel cunt stunt to run away, following a drug's raid on their marital

340

home, which had led to Sam serving time and his children abused grievously by his crack-addicted wife.

Terry was concerned by how Francesca would take the information. But he would hold nothing back. If they were going to find Cassie's killer, then they needed to know everything.

It was early evening and the family were all gathered at Dan's. Bill and Mary were fussing over the baby, but Dan still hadn't shown much interest. They congregated around the table as soon as Francesca appeared, which made her smile. It was like entering a courtroom as the judge. She sat at the head of the table and Sergio sat by her side.

"Right, Mare, let's get going," said Bill.

"Hang on, I was going to cook dinner, and little Cass needs his bottle."

"Mare, the kids have business to attend to. They don't need us here."

Mary looked at her family and knew that they would not discuss anything in her presence. They kept their business away from her, so she never had to worry.

"Okay." She handed Maria the baby. "The meat's in the oven and the veggies are all prepared."

Maria gave Mary a kiss on the cheek. "Thanks, love." They had been nattering all day, as they fussed over Cass and shared cooking ideas. Roberto had paid a visit and joined Bill, Mary, and Maria for a light lunch and a bottle of wine. Mary savoured Roberto's company; they shared the same love of food. Maria had been flirting with him all afternoon, which hadn't gone unnoticed by the ever-observant

Mary. She'd tapped her arm and whispered, "You can't go wrong there, love. He's a keeper."

Once Bill had escorted Mary out of the house, Maria took the baby upstairs – but not before Francesca gave him a cuddle and a kiss. They were about to discuss their findings, when Ruby came in. Mauricio jumped up and threw his arms around her, squeezing too tight, as he always did.

"Uncle Maury, I can't breathe."

He laughed and let her go. "Little bella, at twenty-one, you are not too old for a hug." He kissed her cheek. Sergio followed suit, giving her a warm welcome.

Ruby looked sophisticated, just like Francesca; gone were the days of her acting cocky and flash. She had grown into the woman she was destined to be. Her soft expression melted their hearts. She walked and talked with such elegance, and after ditching the trashy clothes, she now appeared as a woman with class. Her past antics were forgiven by all the family, and she had become once again the sweet little three-year-old with the infectious lisp they all adored.

In her arms were papers. She sat in the chair next to Dan. "I'm sorry to disturb you all. I have just been told that they can release …" She stopped, not wanting to say 'the body'.

Dan nodded. "Thank you, Rubes. Now, are you sure you're okay with organising the funeral? It's a lot to ask."

"Uncle Dan, it's absolutely fine. You know I'll do anything to help. I was thinking we could hold the wake at the *Purple Palace*. Only that was Cassie's favourite club and its seating is more appropriate for friends and family."

Dan nodded. "Babes, that's a lovely idea, she would love that. I'm guessing there'll be a lot of people wanting to pay their last respects."

The others were silent; it was so final now. They were making plans to lay Cassie to rest. Francesca felt guilty, as her mind was on finding the killer, and she hadn't given much thought to saying goodbye to Cassie; she guessed they all felt the same. This whole situation hadn't given them time to grieve.

"What flowers did she like?" asked Ruby.

Dan frowned. "Do you know, I haven't a clue. I always bought her pink roses, every Friday, but I never did ask her." He felt the lump in his throat.

"She liked peace lilies," said Joe, out of the blue.

Dan smiled at him. "How do you know that, Chubs?"

"She always bought Mum them for her birthday. She told me she loved the smell and how they stood out among all the other flowers. She liked the name, an' all: peace lily."

Fred laughed. "Gawd, mate, you are an old romantic, remembering that, but good on ya."

"Thanks, Uncle Joe. I want to make her send-off just perfect, just as she was." Ruby's eyes filled up.

"Yeah, she was perfect, weren't she?" agreed Dan.

They sat for a while talking about the past and how Cassie had been part of their family and the funny antics she'd got up to at work. It did them good to talk about her. It wasn't fair that her name wasn't mentioned because they had been too intent on finding her killer.

They raised a glass each and made a toast. "To a beautiful woman, inside and out, may you rest with the other angels," proposed Dan.

"To Cassie," they affirmed, acknowledging her as one of their very own.

Ruby left after kissing each family member. Their attention then turned to business.

Terry took a deep breath and started with the harsh news that Charles Enright had been seeing Gemma. He waited for a reaction, as did they all. It was shocking, and yet Francesca sat undisturbed and expressionless. She knew he had been carrying on with every Tom, Dick, and Harry and had sensed the connection between him and Gemma. She had deliberately mentioned his name and Francesca was certain that it was to get her attention.

"I don't believe that Cassie's murder was anything to do with you, though, Francesca. The fact that you were married to him was a coincidence," said Terry, compassionately.

Francesca nodded. "Yes, but I have a suspicion that she knows who I am. I think she knew I was married to him, but God knows how. No one recognised me when I returned from the States."

Terry gave her a sympathetic smile. "I knew, though, so I guess she could have worked it out. Think about it. If she was seeing him, she might have taken it upon herself to look into his life, including sourcing you out. Some women and men become obsessed, so she might have stalked you, for all we know. But, besides all that, what does it have to do with the Ruthers?"

Dan said, "Sorry, sis, I know it's shocking for you, but do we actually know who killed our Cassie? I need a fucking name."

All eyes were on Terry. "Not a hundred per cent, but the evidence does point to Bobby Ruthers, and the reason is because on the day of her murder he planted his driving licence at the scene of a burglary, miles away. My mate, DI Neil Spencer, reckons that was an alibi for a more serious crime. It's my guess it was him."

Fred joined in. "Well, I got our old mate, Beano, the tracker, to look into the Ruthers. You know him, the clever fucker. He knows everyone. Maury and me went to see him today." He looked at Mauricio and grinned.

Mauricio was so much like Fred. He was lively and animated when he spoke. It was a far cry from his behaviour the day Francesca had met him in the legal visiting room, years before. She had been assigned to represent him as his defence lawyer, and after the first meeting she concluded he was innocent of the serial killings. Their bond grew over the months, but little did she know at the beginning he was from one of the most notorious crime families in New York. Fleeing England to join them, she became heavily involved in their family. From then on, they were close: the two families joined as one.

"Yes, Beano, he is the best, and that's why I have had him on my payroll for the last twenty years," said Mauricio.

"He knew exactly who we were taking about. He reckons they lord it up in The Mitcham Mint. George and Charlie, the two older brothers, go everywhere together. They're mean fuckers, and not many would take them on. Then, there's this nasty cunt Jimmy, who's a bit of a loner, but always backed by the older two. He said they run Streatham. As well as them are Bobby and Lenny, the two younger brothers, who are both flash bastards. They're like rats on a hot tin plate. They think they're hard, but the truth be known, they are living off their brothers' reputation. No one wants to take 'em on, and those that have tried, ended up hurt bad. Still, I personally would love to have a go. See, in my book, if Bobby killed our Cassie, and the others backed him, then they all need taking out," said Fred. He suddenly glanced at Terry.

"It's all right, mate, I'm with you, all the way. I don't care if it was Jim Ruthers that killed my Lindsey because my bet is they were all in on it. It stands to reason."

Fred looked at Francesca. "Are you okay, sis?"

Francesca nodded. "Yes, I am, and I agree. However, there's more to all this and I want to know what it is. That Gemma has spun a story that in part is not true, although there may be some truth to it, and what concerns me the most is, if the part about these young girls being locked up is accurate, then I can't sit back and ignore it. In among all this evil may well be some kids locked up somewhere, and if the police haven't done anything about it, then I must."

There was silence; she was right. It was all well and good to take revenge on the Ruthers for the killing of Cassie, but if the sex trafficking stories were true, how could they live with themselves if they didn't rescue the girls?

"Imagine, that could be our Sophie or our Rubes. My God," said Joe.

That brought the reality of the matter home to all of them.

Maria appeared in the doorway. "Baby's asleep, so would you all like dinner?"

Dan hadn't eaten properly in days and he suddenly felt ravenous. "Yes, Maria, my angel, that would be great. I think we all need a break."

The aroma from the roast beef was enough to have everyone drooling. Mauricio and Sergio loved English roast dinners and fish and chips. Mary had prepared enough joints to feed the street and used the catering pots to boil the vegetables. Francesca got up and helped Maria dish up the food; she needed to take a breather and a little time to reflect on all that had been shared.

"Francesca, you are taking on too much. You should unburden yourself," urged Maria.

Francesca stirred the gravy. "Oh, Maria, I'm afraid that Cassie's death was somehow linked to me, and I'm angry that I can't unravel this mess. It's so frustrating. I don't know what to do."

Maria rubbed Francesca's arm. "I was in something similar when I was a young woman and I chose to run away, but I wish I'd had the wisdom back then to go to the heart of the problem and face it."

Francesca spun around and faced Maria. "That's it. I'm planning and scheming without all the facts. I need to go back and face my demons once and for all."

Maria had no idea what she meant, but the look in her eyes was something she had never seen before. The other Vincents had, though. Francesca was going to do what she was good at. The Enrights had been taken out one by one by her own hands. She had executed a plan to kill Charlie and set up William to take the rap. Her former husband, she had left for dead in the cold, unforgiving sea, and Tyler Enright she had taken out by chance. The only remaining Enright was William, but he was lost somewhere in the prison system, if he wasn't already dead by now. The cruel McManners family, who had ruined her childhood and for years tormented her family, were dead and buried. She'd had the strength and courage to take them all out, with the help of her family. This was the same. She would do it all again and this time she would take no prisoners.

CHAPTER SIXTEEN

Tressa poured herself a steaming cup of coffee and waited for her mother to leave the kitchen before she added a generous splash of brandy. Her heart was aching. Poor Major was dying, and her mother flatly refused to allow her to take him to the vets to end his miserable life. She hated Violet more as the months passed.

Rita appeared in the doorway just as Tressa closed the cupboard to her secret stash of booze. "What's up with you? Ya got a face like a fucking smacked arse."

"It's Major, the poor thing. He can hardly breathe, and Muvver won't call the vet out or let me take him there."

"Oh, is that all? Only I thought ya boyfriend had dumped ya … oh, yeah, silly me, ya don't have one, do ya!" She laughed as she sat her fat backside on the chair. "Make us a coffee," she growled.

Tressa wanted to pour the kettle full of boiling water over her head. "Can't you talk Muvver into letting me take him? She listens more to you."

Rita opened the biscuit barrel and shoved a bourbon in her mouth. "I'll put him out of his misery, if ya like."

"Oh, yeah? How ya gonna do that?"

Rita opened her bag and pulled out a pop bottle, then grinned, showing chocolate-covered teeth. "Give him this. It'll speed things up." She handed Tressa the bottle.

"What is it?"

"Never you fucking mind. Just pour it in his bowl. That'll do the trick. Then you might stop fucking snivelling."

Tressa took the bottle outside but it was too late. Major was gone – his frail body lay there lifeless. She knelt down and stroked his face. A tear trickled down her nose as she said goodbye. He had been her sanity over the last few years and a companion that wanted nothing from her except a cuddle now and then. It was a surprise that he had lived so long as eighteen years in fact. They were like two lost souls, who no one cared about. They'd both had their uses, once upon a time, but now they were throwaways. She looked at the bottle, removed the lid, and sniffed it. Suddenly, it hit her. Those poor girls who Igor said had been poisoned. Christ, it was Rita. She trembled at the thought. Locking the girls up was one thing but poisoning them was a wholly different matter. Her mind went into a panic. She would have to pretend she hadn't overheard the conversation and act oblivious to the poison.

She hurried back in. "'Ere, Rita, it's too late, he's dead. Besides, an alcopop wouldn't have finished him off." There, she had put the thought into Rita's head that she didn't believe it was poison.

Rita snatched the bottle back and laughed. "Nothing wrong with a few drops of alcohol to see ya on ya way!" She realised she had nearly fucked-up, but then she wasn't the sharpest knife in the drawer.

Violet flushed the toilet and clambered back down the stairs. She eased herself onto the chair and glared at Tressa. "What's up with you?"

"Major's dead. Shall I bury him in the back garden?"

"What? No, divvy girl, shove him in a black sack and then put him out for the dustbin men. Digging up me fucking garden? Silly prat!"

Tressa was disgusted; she would never do that and throw that poor dog in a bin liner and have him tossed into the refuse lorry. Her heart was beating fast and the blood rampaged around her body. She looked at the two of them; they were both fat self-indulgent pigs. They were so gross that right now she wished she had the guts to cut them wide open and throw them into the dustbins herself.

Livid, Tressa went upstairs to find a fresh towel and a blanket to wrap the dog in. Violet wouldn't know if she buried Major or not, as she never ventured into the garden anyway.

Tressa's bedroom was a real girlie place to be. It was always spotless and very small. It was so small you couldn't swing a cat in it. It was also the antithesis of her sister's pit. She needed the bed linen that was next door in Rita's room, when she stayed over. She entered the pig pen and had an urge to push open the window to get rid of the smell. Body odour and stale air were never a good combination. She rarely went into Rita's room when she was using it, but the spare linen was there so she had no choice. As she opened the slimline cupboard, just inside the door, a bottle of antifreeze fell out. She jumped back before it landed on her toes. *Shit! That was the smell in the pop bottle – antifreeze. Jesus, Rita's a fucking murderer,* she thought. Quickly grabbing an old towel, she kicked the bottle back in the cupboard and left. She decided to stay in her own room and then wait until they went to bed before she buried poor Major. She lay on her bed, hugging the towel as if it were the dog. A while later, she heard George and Charlie arrive. She contemplated staying in her room, but she knew that within minutes Violet would holler for her to come down and cook dinner.

She edged herself off the bed and headed down to the kitchen. Maybe George would agree to have Major buried in the garden.

The boys looked flustered.

"All right, George? S'pose Muvver's told ya that Major died?"

George looked at Tressa as if she were speaking another language. "Tressa, make yaself busy, will ya? I'll 'ave a cuppa tea."

She looked at her brothers and for a moment she was staring at two strangers; how could she ever be related to them? Their fat heads, gold teeth, and hands like shovels, were so far removed from her own slim-like appearance. Rita was like them in so many ways, especially in her appearance and in her evil ways. In fact, without the tits, makeup, and hairpiece, they could have been triplets. "For fuck's sake, drippy cunt, stop standing there and do the boys some grub," shouted Violet through gritted teeth.

Tressa turned into the robot she had been for the last eighteen years. Perhaps Jimmy raping her, as bad as it had been, had done her a favour. If she hadn't been stopped in her tracks from helping with the business, where would she be now? For she had been every bit as involved as the rest of her conniving family: what with running around for them, helping organise the kids, collecting them from the coast, drugging them, and locking them away for all and sundry to do as they pleased. She shuddered; whatever had she been thinking? Why had she committed such terrible acts to support her cruel, heartless family? Well, you didn't need to be a brain surgeon to work out the answer to that one! Living with a family of eight vile and violent criminals, she was treated like dog shit. Her so-called family would, in the blink of an eye, snuff her from existence, if they had the slightest inkling she had the strength of will to protest or even, God forbid, grass on them. Of course, she had a conscience: she knew what she was doing was wrong. But, in her mind, appeasement was the only option – at the moment. No, she would bide her time, look for an opportunity, and then, by Christ, she would find a way to take them out.

She looked at each of them and wondered what she had actually been born into. Her life was hell; she was born to the devil's bride herself. Even Bobby had slowly morphed into them. She'd once really loved Bobby and the age gap between them had been small enough for them to be on each other's wavelength. They had been good friends once upon a time. He always saw to it that she had money for a night out or a new dress. At one time, he would help an old lady across the road but not now. His brothers had got their claws into him and naturally he'd looked up to them, not having a father. They shaped him into the nasty piece of work he had become. However, she understood all too well how clever they were at manipulating people. She too had been sucked in: living the high life and having people shit themselves as soon as she gave them a look. Having that much power had been very addictive, but now she saw how much it had hurt people because she had become a victim herself.

As she peeled the potatoes, she stared at the knife. If only she had the strength to stab them all.

"Right, we've decided to close the business for a while, while the heat is on. Alex, the Russian, ain't happy. His nosy brother has informed him that some of the girls have been poisoned and apparently he has taken that personally," said Charlie. He waited for a comment from his mother.

Violet stayed silent.

"I don't know, I think we need to lie low for a bit. Christ, we have enough dosh to live like kings, so maybe we should just close the whole operation down. Alex can have his mansion back. If Wiers and his lot want to carry on with him, then we're out of it," said George.

Violet sipped her coffee and stared into space. The boys looked confused; usually their mother had a lot to say.

"Muvver, are you listening?" growled George.

"Who's Alex?" she asked calmly.

George and Charlie were shocked and stared at their mother. She was continuing to sip her coffee as if she were the only person in the room.

"Muvver, are you all right?" asked Charlie.

"Yeah, son, I'm fine. Why?"

"Muvver, you just asked who Alex was. You know exactly who he is."

"What you on about, divvy bollocks? Course I fucking know who he is. What about him?"

George looked at Rita, who just shrugged her shoulders. Tressa grinned to herself; she had noticed more and more lately that her mother was losing the plot. The last month she had been getting a few things wrong, and she had her suspicions that perhaps her mother was going senile. In her heart, she hoped it was true.

"George, can I go over there tonight? I ain't seen Igor and he'll be wondering what the fuck's happened to me," pleaded Rita.

"What? Shut up, Rita, no, you ain't going over there. Did you not just hear me? It's too hot. Bobby's fucked up and now that DI Spencer's having a nose around. So, unless you want us all locked up, stay the fuck away."

Charlie rolled his eyes. "Rita, Igor ain't fucking interested in ya. He likes young birds and half the size of you. Stop showing us up and acting like a proper stalker. You're a fucking embarrassment, you are."

"Shut ya mouth, Charlie. Igor and me have something special. It's a secret, and it's none of your fucking business."

George leaned forward and grabbed Rita's hairpiece, yanking her face close to his. "Now listen to me, you thick fucker. If I get wind that you have been anywhere near the mansion, I will personally stick my boot right up your fat fanny. Got it?"

He ripped the ponytail off her head. Holding Rita's pride and joy up, he said, "Next time you even mention Igor, this won't be your fake hair, it'll be your scalp. Cunt!"

Rita didn't move; she glared back with her beady eyes.

Charlie was staring at his mother – but she was off again in her own little world.

"Muvver!" barked George.

Violet snapped out of her trance. "What?"

"What do you think about shutting up shop? Give the racket a rest. After all, we've had our day. I'm too old for all this now."

"Ya got no fucking stamina, boy. The flats practically run themselves. You only have to collect a weekly payment. By Christ, I have raised a pussy!"

"Muvver, I'm not talking about the flats, I'm talking about the mansion!" bridled George. He hated more than anything to be called a pussy.

"What fucking mansion?"

There was an unholy quiet as they all turned to look at their mother.

"Best call the quack," suggested Charlie.

"Who for?" asked Violet.

"You, Muvver, you ain't quite half the ticket. Ya might need a tonic or something."

Charlie rolled his eyes and sighed. He realised then that his mother was now a liability. If she was going senile, then she could have them all locked up if her mouth ran away with her.

"Now, you listen 'ere, Charlie boy, I'm fine, and I don't need a quack. No poxy doctor's coming in my house. Got it?"

Violet continued sipping her coffee, totally oblivious to the rest of the conversation.

George and Charlie agreed to close down the business. It would mean leaving Alex high and dry, but they couldn't afford to get nicked. Two of the Enrights were gone, Stevens was knocking on a bit, and Wiers wouldn't be enough to keep them out of the nick if it all went tits-up. The one thing they had to do was make sure Gemma couldn't get released. She had to be silenced.

"Where's my Jimmy?"

"He's out and about with his ear to the ground. We need to know what's going on out there. The Ol' Bill have been busying themselves, asking questions about us," snarled George.

"Bobby has a lot to answer for," replied Violet, angrily.

"Right, George, come on, we have a few calls to make," urged Charlie.

"Don't worry about Muvver. I'll look after her," smirked Tressa.

But no one listened to her. They left the kitchen. The potatoes were boiling and the chops were frying and Tressa smiled to herself. She would take care of their mother – perhaps once and for all.

Rita tried to fix her hairpiece but the clips had snapped in half. "Cunt," she mumbled under her breath. "Where's the Super Glue?" she shouted at Tressa.

"In the end drawer," she replied. Her family were beyond anything that resembled normal. She continued with the dinner and watched as her mother stared into space and Rita fiddled with the glue, mending her broken clip.

The greasy pork chops, boiled potatoes, and mushy peas, which were all covered in gravy, were a sight that turned Tressa's stomach. She began to realise she detested everything that her family liked and now it was even the food.

"Want more gravy, Rita?" Tressa offered.

Rita looked at the plate and grunted a reply. Tressa poured the thick brown liquid over the food, completely covering the plate. Rita snatched up her cutlery and started munching, smacking her lips and snorting. Violet did the same. It was like feeding time at the zoo.

They were both too engrossed in their food to notice Tressa staring. She thought about the alcopop bottle again, the girls in the mansion, and Major. Poor Major, she had loved him more than her own family. Jimmy, she hated the most. She could never understand why her mother doted on him.

She thought back to Major; if she dug a grave big enough, then she could bury all of them together. She knew in reality, though, she had neither the time nor the strength to dig a grave which was sufficiently adequate for her family. She looked at the gravy, which was dripping from her mother's chin. She couldn't be going senile; her memory loss was too fast. A brain tumour, however, was a distinct possibility.

Rita was chewing the chop bone and the grease was all over her face, like a toddler eating a bar of chocolate. Violet was now doing the same. Animals they were! Suddenly, she thought back to the alcopop bottle and wondered if they had noticed the taste in their coffee. Her mind jumped to the girls in the mansion. When she'd worked there, the girls were older and she'd treated them well, but listening to snippets of conversation from George and Charlie, she knew things had changed. She knew Rita was a spiteful jealous bitch and was probably getting a kick out of torturing them. She'd done it to Tressa when she was a young teenager.

*

She'd been fifteen and Rita seventeen when Rita had carried out the ultimate humiliating stunt. Tressa was dressed up and looking much older than her years. She wore a tube dress that showed her figure and at fifteen she had the perfect shape. The low-cut neckline allowed her cleavage to be on show. With high-heeled shoes and her hair curled, she looked stunning. Rita was done up, too, but looked more like a dog's dinner. Her figure-hugging dress did her no favours and her make-up was so thick it appeared to be sliding off her face.

The local club was Rita's favourite haunt. She'd had her eye on a young man called Paddy, an Irish fella with bright green eyes and jet black hair. She wasn't the only one who'd had her eye on him as half the girls in the club did.

Tressa had been going to the local pub with her friends but they had changed their minds and all wanted to go to the club. Tressa could get in anywhere – her paid-up membership to the Ruthers' family ensured that no bouncer would argue. The other girls whined to Tressa to get them in, but they were careful not to push her too far. They were still wary. They arrived outside the club, excited and clucking like chickens. The bouncer sighed; he couldn't be bothered to cause a scene. He knew they were too young, but he let them enter anyway.

Rita stood by the bar, half-cut, trying her best to impress Paddy. She drank her whisky and coke through a straw and giggled in-between sips. Paddy had no interest in Rita but stayed polite because of her reputation. Suddenly, he turned to see the bunch of young girls heading his way. The club wasn't full and so anyone coming through the door was gawped at, especially by the men looking for fresh meat. Paddy stared and Rita turned to see who had caught his attention. She was infuriated when she saw it was her own sister. Tressa was confident; she strolled over to the bar with a sexy wiggle, flicking her long fair hair. Rita, though, was enraged with jealousy. Paddy's gaze was glued to her and without thinking he said, "Cor, who's that eye candy?" It sent Rita over the edge. She marched over to Tressa, and with a hard blow to the side of her head, she knocked her to the floor. As Tressa tried to focus and get herself to her feet, Rita grabbed the hem of her dress and in one fluid motion ripped the garment over Tressa's head. "That's my fucking clobber you have on, ya dirty tramp!" she screamed.

The music stopped playing and everyone stared. Tressa was totally naked but for a bra. She hadn't put knickers on because she didn't want a knicker line showing through the dress. Her friends stood back; they were all afraid of Rita, as most women were. Tressa sat on the floor, still stunned, and terrified to stand up because everyone would see her. Paddy rushed over, knocking Rita out of the way. He was wearing a long suit jacket and in a flash he had it wrapped around Tressa and was helping her to her feet. Rita was even more enraged and punched Paddy at the back of the neck. He wobbled but carried on helping Tressa out of the club. Rita hit him again and this time he fell. But it was Tressa she wanted to vent her anger on and she went for her, ripping her hair and flinging her around like a marionette. The bouncer finally jumped in and pulled Rita away. Paddy spat in Rita's face. "Ya fecking monster!" he screamed at her.

Rita threw the dress back at Tressa and left the club. The girls wanted to help their friend then, but the damage was done. She had been humiliated by her own flesh and blood, and her friends had stood by and done nothing to help. She locked the toilet door behind her and slipped back into her dress. It was meant to make her look pretty and sexy, but now she felt pathetic, ugly, and stupid. It was an hour before she came out of the cubicle. Her friends fussed over her and a few of them offered to clean the blood off her face. Tressa let rip now, beyond humiliation. She snarled at them, "Fuck off, all of ya. Call yaselves mates? Ya ain't no friends of mine. Go on, fuck off before I do ya meself!" The girls ran from the toilets, afraid of Tressa's anger.

She looked in the mirror and noticed the purple lump appearing under her eye and the blood still dripping from her nose. It wasn't the beating that hurt – it was the total embarrassment of being exposed like that.

Paddy was waiting outside the toilets for her to come out. When she finally did appear, he gave her a gentle smile and without a word he put his arm around her shoulder and walked her outside. The bouncer offered to call a cab, but Tressa wanted to walk. Paddy strolled beside her; he didn't know where he was going, but he felt obliged to walk the girl home.

"I can't believe ya own fecking sister would do that to ya. Ya mother's going to go fecking mental when she finds out."

Tressa stopped to face Paddy. "Nah, she won't. I'll get the blame somehow 'cos me muvver loves Rita more than me," she replied.

"Jesus! I can't see why. She's fecking nuts and you're … well, you're lovely."

"Yeah, well, me muvver ain't like most muvvers, see. She likes Rita 'cos she's hard, and she don't give a shit about me, like me bruvvers."

*

Tressa liked Paddy and would have loved to have seen more of him, but her brothers made sure she never would. He had spat at Rita and they weren't going to stand for it. No one disrespected their family. They didn't even listen to Tressa's side of the story. The last Tressa heard, Paddy had been given a severe going-over and was now back in Ireland. Suddenly, she let out an unexpected sigh: *what man would ever want her now? Was there a man out there, who harboured his own dark secrets, who would ever comprehend hers? No, surely not.*

361

She watched as Rita chewed the last morsel off the bone and followed it by a loud bellowing burp. Her thoughts returned to the alcopop and just how ruthless her sister was. She had read somewhere about antifreeze poisoning … or maybe she had seen it on a TV programme. It caused the hair to fall out and the skin to change colour. She shuddered, recalling how, a few years back, just before the incident with Jimmy, she'd felt sick for a while. Her skin had looked ashen and her hair had started falling out. When it had stopped, she'd assumed it had been the flu. She wondered if that large brandy she'd had earlier had exaggerated the thoughts in her head. Nevertheless, she wouldn't, under any circumstances, take a drink or any food from Rita again.

After she'd filled the sink with hot water, she removed the empty plates and slid them into the bubbles. Rita sneaked off out of the back door and Violet remained in the same position, staring at a blank wall.

"Muvver, are you okay?" Tressa asked.

Violet looked at her daughter with a vulnerable expression; it was one that Tressa had never seen before. "Err, I think I need me bed. I have got the worst migraine." She sounded old and different.

"Come on, then, I'll walk up with you."

Violet was doddery as she rose from her seat. "Christ, me vision's bad. I've a bastard of a fucking headache." She sounded so weak.

"Let's get ya up the stairs." Tressa placed her arm under her mother's but Violet instantly shook it away.

"I can fucking walk, woman," she spat, but she was still wobbly. She took the stairs one at a time, gripping the handrail tightly. Tressa followed behind, praying that her heavy mother wouldn't fall on top of her. As they reached the top, Violet grappled inside her pocket, searching for the key to her bedroom. It wasn't unusual. No one had ever been inside Violet's bedroom; she even checked outside before she left the room to ensure no one could peek in. Tressa used to wonder what her room was like but had given up thinking about it when she was around ten years old. It just became a way of life.

Violet tried to unlock the padlock, but her eyes were failing her. The headache was too bad for her to focus. Tressa took the key and Violet allowed her to open the door and help her inside.

It was the first time ever that Tressa had seen the room. Tentatively, Tressa's eyes took in the room, a section at a time. The shock made her gasp, but it went unnoticed by her mother, who was heading for the bed. She didn't sit gently either; she fell onto it like a sack of coal. Quickly, Tressa picked her feet up off the floor and spun them around so her whole body lay horizontal.

"Get me some tablets, some strong ones, and hurry up, will ya!" Violet ordered, her eyes now firmly shut.

Tressa was aghast at the sight; she couldn't take it all in quickly enough, but if she stood there any longer her mother might notice. Violet was in a lot of pain and in desperate need of tablets. Tressa fled the room and went into the bathroom where she found all sorts of different drugs in the cabinet. She hadn't noticed the collection of pills before. There was even a bottle of Oramorph, a liquid morphine, and sleeping tablets. She returned to her mother's bedside with her hands full and carefully she lifted her head. "'Ere, Mum, drink this. It's morphine, it'll stop the pain." She popped the sleeping pills on her tongue and gently poured the whole bottle of Oramorph down her throat. Violet didn't complain or question; instead, she just took the lot. There was silence except for a gentle purring; her mother was asleep in seconds.

Tressa now had time to absorb her shocking surroundings. It was as if she had stepped back in time to 1940: the old oak furniture, the war trunk at the end of the bed, the photos – there were so many photos around the walls. They were all black and white or sepia. The uniform, hanging from the side of the wardrobe, was from an army, but not the British army – it was German. Surely her mother wasn't into some kind of war fetish? She looked at the photos and in many of them was a big man dressed in that very outfit. He was hard-faced, with beady eyes, and beside him stood a frail, gentle-looking woman, similar to herself and Bobby. The children in the picture, all boys except for one, were big, like their father. They had miserable faces. They could have been George, Charlie, and Jimmy, but the photo was old. She looked at another photo and again they had the same expression, but they were older in this one and possibly in their teens. These must be her mother and uncles she had never met. She was told she didn't have grandparents, or any other family, except Violet. Looking at the pictures, she didn't want to know them either because they all had that sinister, spiteful look and a bitter, tyrannical stance.

The other pictures were of her grandfather and other army figures. She didn't know too much about the war or even what the uniforms meant, but she concluded that her grandfather was high-up just from his smart uniform. He was, in fact, a general. There, among the photos, was one of Hitler, shaking hands with the man, and clearly visible was the swastika sewn to the left arm of his uniform. That confirmed he was an important member of Germany's Third Reich. Tressa was disgusted and yet at the same time rather intrigued. She had no idea her family were German. She had always wanted to know where she came from, but her mother was so secretive and angry all the time, so she could never ask without receiving a clout. She had to find out – in fact she needed to find out – and here was the

364

opportunity. She peered over at her mother to see if she was still asleep. Violet was almost unconscious.

The big trunk, which looked very old, was at the end of the bed. It was deep green with brown leather trim. Leather buckles tied it down but there was no lock. Tressa knelt and quietly undid the buckles and then she lifted the lid. There, inside, were notebooks, a teddy with something German written on the scarf, and more photos. She slowly pulled out a carefully concealed wooden box, hidden among the papers, and opened that. Wrapped neatly in a bundle were letters; they were written in English but sent from Germany. The first one she concluded quite quickly was a love letter. It read as follows:

My dearest Violet,

I am writing in hope that your circumstances have changed. I trust you managed to secure work? I enclose some money, hoping that you will not need it, but it is a precaution. I have to stay longer as there are problems here. How are our boys? I miss them every day, but soon, my love, we will be together.

Love always

Wilhelm

The letter was stamped 1966, which was the year Jimmy was born. So Wilhelm Ruthers was their father. She opened more letters, hoping to find some information about herself, but after 1967 there were no more letters. She read the last one and was so surprised she just had to read it over again.

Dear Violet,

I am so pleased we have a daughter. I cannot wait until my next visit. I will be home for good and all will be well. I shall find work and we will be a family, once and for all.

Father is dying and he has left a small token for me, so we will have perhaps enough for a good home. The courts cannot question him about our mother's death, and I am sure, in any case, he will not be around long enough to face the consequences.

I cannot bear to think of him standing in public accused of poisoning his wife. It is too cruel to contemplate. He misses you and in his confused state he calls out for his little Rilla.

I will write again soon.

All my love

Wilhelm

Tressa looked for other letters but there were no more. She had to be wrong, surely? Wilhelm, her mother's brother, could not possibly be the father of her older siblings. She looked through the photographs and there was the proof: on the back of a family picture were the names Wilhelm and Rilla, brother and sister.

She should have been more shocked, but she wasn't; nothing about her mother surprised her. She looked at the newspaper clipping. There was a large picture, front page news, of her grandfather, and then a very frail elderly man. The headline read as follows:

Former Obergruppenführer (High Ranking General) Oscar Reuter is formally charged with the murder of his wife, Rilla Reuter.

Tressa read on to discover her grandfather was accused of serious war crimes as well as poisoning his wife. He was to be brought to England to stand trial for crimes against humanity.

She had read and seen enough. Her family had emerged from a past so dark it was unthinkable.

Carefully, she returned the paperwork back to its position in the trunk of sordid secrets. She closed the lid and tightened the buckles. Under the bed, she saw what looked like books and she slid her hand underneath and retrieved one. It wasn't a book, however, but a diary. Dust covered the outside but inside it was perfectly intact, as if Violet had put pen to the page that morning. It was dated 1968.

Her mother had written in it every day and there were accounts too. It confirmed Tressa's suspicions that Violet was once a prostitute.

Violet stirred and Tressa checked the time. She had been in the room for over two hours. She headed back to the bathroom, intending to top-up her mother's morphine. It was easy enough. As soon as she lifted her head, her mouth opened and in went the liquid. Violet didn't even open her eyes; she was out of it again. Tressa returned to the diaries, desperately trying to find out about the date she was born and any clue as to who *her* father was. She pulled up the faded wicker chair, placed it next to the bed, and stared at her mother, who looked so old when she was asleep. Scanning the diary again, she saw no entry for 8 July 1969. Her heart sank. Leading up to that date, there was no indication Violet was even pregnant. By that time, she was running a brothel, but at least she was not selling her own arse. So the rumours were true.

"So, Muvver dearest, or should I call you Rilla, you really were a dark horse, eh? I mean, I knew you were a hard woman, but it just goes to show, eh, you really loved someone very much. Well, it should shock me that the only person you loved was ya own brother, but ya know what, Ma, it don't. George, Charlie, ugly cunt Jimmy, and Rita, were all your dirty offspring, born outta fucking incest. I guess you were named after your dear Ol' Mum. Shame, 'cos in the photos, she looks really sweet."

She sighed and stared at her mother's chest heaving up and down. "I knew I was different, I knew I was only half of your sordid sick family and now I have the proof. Funny, really, Muvver, but I looked up to you 'cos really you shit the fucking life outta me, but not 'cos I was proud to have a muvver like you. Now look at ya, lying there asleep, probably dying and helpless – so fucking helpless you left yourself wide open for me to find out the truth about you."

She laughed aloud and reached down to have one more glance at her mother and her mother's brother, standing side by side in that black and white photo. "Well, Muvver, I often wondered if you were pretty when you were young. You weren't. I just thought I would let you know, I think you were one ugly, evil fat bitch. And while we are on the subject, I aint like you. I may have been pushed into stuff I was too frightened to turn away from, but deep down, Muvver, I aint like you, or any of ya, and I am glad about that. One day, God will know what was in my heart, and maybe he will give me a short life to pay for the horrible things I did. But he knows, really, I never meant to hurt anyone, and I will feel bad for the rest of me life. But, you, Muvver, you won't, will ya, because you were born from evil, you bred with evil, and you spawned from fucking evil. I am different to you lot! I know I am. I have to be because I feel sick with guilt. I fucking hate meself, but you don't, do you? None of you do."

Tressa got up and put the chair back against the wall. As she placed the photo back inside the trunk, she smiled. "There, Muvver, now wasn't that nice to have a chat? See, I like it, like this, just me and you, talking over old times. I think we should do it more often. Anyway, I must dash. I have a job to do – bury me dear friend, Major."

CHAPTER SEVENTEEN

Francesca arose the next morning, more determined than ever. She would take the bull by the horns and sort this whole mess out. It was nine o'clock, much later than her normal start to the day, but there had been so much planning for what to do next that it had taken her family through until the early hours of this morning to put together something that everyone felt happy with. To her surprise, Terry had been the most dedicated. He would go along with every inch of the plan and had added a few nuggets himself. First, she needed to face Gemma one last time. Jamie had booked a legal visit for the afternoon. The others, including Dan, were to track down the whereabouts of the Ruthers and watch their movements. The strategy included discovering where the secret mansion was and this was something that Francesca had insisted upon. Beano would lead the mission, although so far he'd come to a dead end when trying to find Bobby and Lenny. The plan was almost in place, but it would be a slow process to get it right. Francesca wanted the Gentlemen's Club exposed. Her hatred for those corrupt judges ran through her veins, but even having wiped out the Enrights, all except William, she knew she had only scratched the surface.

Terry was on his own mission and politely declined any offer from Francesca for some of Mauricio's men. This was one fight he wanted to take on alone. Beano had given them all the run-down on

Jimmy's movements. He wasn't a creature of habit, but he could be found in The Mitcham Mint most afternoons.

Terry would have quite happily gone in and put a bullet through his face, but that would have drawn too much attention, so he would have to lure him out of the pub and away from prying eyes.

Two fifteen in the afternoon arrived not a moment too soon and Francesca walked through the main gate of Bronzefield. Jamie was talking for England. He had spent hours going over the files and researching the judges and lawyers of the Gentlemen's Club, and he'd found there was a correlation between the defendants and judges in the various cases. It was soon apparent that they worked as a team, ensuring incarceration or release of any individual they wanted just to suit their own ends.

As soon as they were seated in the legal visiting room, Sandra appeared with Gemma. Sandra seemed agitated and looked tired, and her skin was ashen with dark rings circled around her eyes. Gemma, however, looked very well and had a confident grin spread across her face.

She positioned herself on the edge of her chair and smirked at Sandra. Francesca didn't miss a trick. Gemma's whole demeanour was upbeat and cocky. The slow, sluggish movements had been replaced with sharp actions; even her eyes were alive. Francesca stared, chewing the inside of her lip.

"I was well happy when they said I had another legal visit. So, any news on an appeal?" Gemma's eyes were wide, like a child's at Christmas.

"Tell me, Gemma, what is the main reason you want to be released?" asked Francesca.

Clocking the serious tone, she suddenly felt uneasy. "I have to get out of here because I have to save those poor girls."

Francesca remained without emotion. Jamie did the same. The silence was uncomfortably long.

"But you knew that, didn't ya? I told ya before," said Gemma, nervously.

"We have grounds for an appeal and I can assure your release. However, as you know, these things usually take months, and as you say, those poor girls are locked away in that mansion. As time goes on, God knows what will happen to them. So to guarantee your release, we need to prove this mansion exists or we only have hearsay. What we need is the address. So it's time for you to cooperate sufficiently for the authorities to believe your story."

Gemma swallowed hard and her eyes flickered from Francesca to Jamie, trying to gauge their train of thought. She could see where they were coming from: that much was very clear. But she desperately didn't want to give away the address: that was her insurance. She needed to get out and taste freedom, along with finishing what she'd started. Next time, Bobby would have a knife through his heart, along with the rest of the Ruthers, and she could finally take over the business. She didn't need the Ruthers, and she had Alex eating out of her hand, or so she thought.

"Err ... But I don't know where they are. I was locked up in the cottage. I only heard the stories from Bobby and his brothers. I've never been there." She couldn't give the game away and certainly not at this stage.

Jamie inclined his head to the side. Getting slightly frustrated with Gemma's hands-off approach, he said, "Okay, Gemma, but you know it's impossible for you to be released without proof that the mansion actually exists!"

Gemma had hoped that the lawyers had a plan to secure her release without her having to give anything away. Yet, now, she felt a tension in the air; the sympathetic look, which had been on Francesca's calm and pleasant face during an earlier visit, had vanished and was replaced with annoyance. Gemma tried to act sorrowful and she gave a weak smile. "So what do we do now?"

Francesca looked over her shoulder to make sure Sandra or anyone wasn't at the door. Suddenly, she spun around, grabbed Gemma by the collar, and pulled her to within an inch of her face. "Cut the fucking crap! You're going to tell me the fucking truth, or I will find so much more on you and have your sentence increased. If you want out of here, then you had better start being honest." She let her go and leaned back on her chair. "You see, it's like this. I didn't buy into your story, Gemma, because firstly, I am a damn good barrister, and I can smell a lie a mile off. Secondly, you underestimated me and that was a big mistake. I know the truth about you. So if you think you can try to fob me off with another load of shit, then, girl, think again, because I'm not easily fooled."

Gemma was physically shaking; Francesca was not a woman to be toyed with.

"Tell me the truth and I'll get you out of here sooner than you think."

Gemma paused before she spoke. How could she tell the truth? It was too shocking for words, and she had to keep to herself the mansion's location otherwise it would have all been a waste of time. Besides, she had to know what information Francesca had on her before she gave too much away. "I am sorry, Francesca. I'm not sure what part of what I have told you, you think is untrue. Please! You have to believe me." She exaggerated her look of confusion.

Francesca smirked and kept silent, just staring at Gemma, and then she cleared her throat. "You can keep up with the pretence and try to call my bluff, but I promise you, it will get you nowhere. You see, Gemma, I am good with faces, and expressions to be exact, and when I first met you with your pitiful look and sad eyes, I didn't recognise you. Then, yesterday, you smirked, and I knew then I had seen you before. I have this thing, you see, when I am in a courtroom. I survey the gallery. I always have. You, Gemma, were there at the trial of Mauricio Luciani, sitting in among all those men dressed in suits. Actually, it was funny because you stood out like a sore thumb."

Gemma's face said it all, and her expression was now one of utter shock.

"I am pretty good with dates too, so just to let you know. I am fully aware that you were not locked away in a cottage by your husband." She stopped and raised her eyebrow. "Because, Gemma, you were standing in the gallery watching me."

Suddenly, Gemma was in sinking sand, and the more she racked her brains to think of an excuse, the more she knew she would sound ridiculous. She couldn't claw her way to the surface with any credibility.

"Okay, I did try to kill Bobby. He was a monster. They all were." She tried to divert the conversation away from the court case.

Francesca nodded and tapped her foot. "And Charles? Was he a monster too?" she spat, her face white and angry.

Gemma paused; she had wanted to get Francesca's attention on the first visit by mentioning Charles's name, but that was all. Now, she didn't know how much Francesca actually knew. She couldn't risk stringing together another load of lies and having Francesca walk away, leaving her to rot in this snake pit. She would just have to exaggerate the truth instead.

"Yes, he was a monster. He was a cruel and wicked man." She thought about him, the one man she'd truly loved. She'd thought the feeling had been mutual, but it hadn't; he'd used her like he'd used everyone. "Everything I told you in the beginning was true. You have to believe that."

Jamie pulled out the tape recorder. "You had better tell us at what point the story became a lie then, hadn't you." He forcefully pressed the record button. "Interview Three: Gemma Ruthers. Please begin, Gemma."

Gemma's eyes narrowed and she glared at Jamie. She felt the tension rising in the room and needed to assert herself.

"I lost me baby. Being locked in Bobby's flat all that time was fucking true. Collecting the rent from the toms in the flats, that was also true." She was hesitant, though, to say any more.

"So I can assume, by your reluctance to say any more, that your tale about being locked away again and playing the dutiful wife was a lie?" smirked Francesca, coldly.

"No, not exactly——" Gemma was stopped in her tracks.

"Don't play fucking games. You either want out of here or not. Now, start talking, and if you think I won't class your leaving out information as lying by omission, you're wrong, because, lady, I fucking will. Do we understand each other? Or am I wasting my time?"

Gemma felt the threat; she didn't have to hear it. She nodded and lowered her gaze. "I collected rent from the flats, and then when Tressa was stopped from working, they had me take over her job in the mansion, but you've guessed that, I assume."

Francesca snapped; she was losing her temper. "I know a fucking lot more than you told me."

Gemma sat up straight. "All right, yes, I worked the mansion after the villa was closed down. It was good money. The girls were older. They were over sixteen then—" she lied. But she was interrupted.

"Aw, that makes it all right, then! Tell me exactly what you did. I want names, times, and places," demanded Francesca.

"I knew it was wrong, but I didn't have a choice. It was either that or be locked up meself. Alex Morozov is the main man. He's Russian and he's not the kind of person you fuck with."

Jamie wanted to laugh, but managed to hold it in, because she was now singing like a canary to save her own arse. "There's another guy as well: Igor. I don't know his last name. He's a big Russian, and he runs the mansion. They deal with the imports and the Ruthers get the business."

Francesca nodded. "You mean the customers from the Gentlemen's Club?"

Gemma nodded. "Yeah, they're all in on it, you name 'em – judges, lawyers, bankers, basically men in power." She was on a roll and would give Francesca anything now if it secured her release, except the whereabouts of the mansion.

"And Charles Enright. Tell me about him."

Gemma felt her heart beat faster. She couldn't lie, but it would be hard to admit everything. Francesca sensed her hesitation and said, "I know about him and you and your little visits to the Dorchester, but I want to hear it from your own lips."

Taking a deep breath, Gemma went on. "I met Charles when I was at the club. One of me jobs was to take pictures of the girls and show them to Charlie Enright, but this particular afternoon he was away in court, and I was met by Charles. I knew they were related, they looked so alike. He was a charmer, to say the least, and we ended up spending the afternoon together." She stopped, awaiting Francesca's reaction. But there was no change in her expression. "I loved him, ya know, I really did, but I guess he was just using me."

Francesca sarcastically raised her eyebrow as Gemma went on.

"I never knew he had been going to the mansion. They all had code names, you see, and I never knew his code name. I just assumed he knew about the game but didn't take part himself. He was too good-looking and much younger than the other men. We had a secret relationship away from Bobby and his family. I could meet him on the sly because I always had the excuse I was doing business at the Gentlemen's Club." She paused and looked up but Francesca was still stony-faced.

"I think you've missed out some information. You say Charles just used you, but, Gemma, you didn't say how. Like I said, I know what you did, but I want to hear it from you. So don't hide it. What did Charles use you for?" demanded Francesca.

"I loved Charles, and he promised me the world. He said that there was a court case coming up. A serial slasher was about to be captured, and they needed to make sure he never got out of prison. He said they had inside information that the killer was going to the *Violet Club* for his next victim, and they needed a witness if he did it again. I said Daisy would be good. I knew then that they would use her in a drunken state to say anything they wanted. He convinced me that the serial slasher was an Italian man called Mauricio Luciani. He had evaded capture so many times that this time they would be ready and have the evidence to lock him up once and for all. I didn't know exactly what he meant and how the operation would take place, but I loved him, you see, so I told him about Daisy."

"Did you think that Mauricio was guilty?"

Gemma nodded. "Oh, yeah, I really believed Charles at the time. I tell ya, he was so clever, and he used such long words that sometimes I was baffled, but I trusted that man with me own life. He was so loving and kind. I would have done anything for him and—"

Jamie interrupted. "Why did you go to the Luciani trial?"

Gemma was now embarrassed and visibly uncomfortable. "I was just being nosy. After all, I somehow felt part of it. Charles had gone on a fishing trip with his father and uncle, and I was annoyed. He was spending less time with me and I have to admit I was jealous. I know it was wrong, and I know I should have stayed away, but I was probably obsessed with him. Ya see, Bobby gave me money and bought me presents, but there was no passion as such. We'd just become more like friends 'cos we were so young when we'd met. I knew that Bobby was fucking other birds, I ain't stupid, and I guess he probably turned a blind eye to what I was up to. But Charles was different. He was passionate, and he interested me with his ideas for the future and the special places he took me to. So there you have it. I was blinded by love. Yes, I was used, by all of them."

"Tell me the real reason you went to the trial?"

Gemma knew what Francesca was getting at and decided it wasn't worth lying anymore. "I wanted to see what his wife looked like. I knew she was representing Mauricio because Charles had told me. I was hungry for his affections. And in those days, leading up to the case, he was distant. I had to see if his wife was an ugly, moany old bag, like he described her."

"And was she?" asked Francesca.

They all knew the answer but Francesca wanted Gemma to squirm.

Gemma shook her head and allowed a large tear to fall from her eye and roll down her cheek. "No, she wasn't at all. She was stunning and beautiful. She seemed kind and yet firm. I knew then I was no match and guessed I was just a bit of fun. But that was the problem. I loved him and wanted to be like her. I wanted what she had. But I guess he wanted neither of us because his mind was twisted and sick. He was a cruel bastard. What made it worse was I realised in the end that Mauricio was being set up and I did nothing about it because I couldn't bear to lose Charles. I was just a pawn in his sordid plan."

Francesca rolled her eyes at Gemma's pathetic attempt at playing the victim in this interview. "Go on Gemma, I want to hear more. I want the fucking truth." She tried to keep it professional, but there were still unanswered questions about Charles, which needed to be dealt with.

"One night, Bobby was feeling unwell. He'd been on a bender for two days with his brothers and was nursing a hangover. He had to take some cash over to the mansion and asked me to do it. I couldn't stand him when he was drunk, or worse, on a come-down from his cocaine habit, so I agreed. Igor was there, but the men were in the grounds. So I arrived at the mansion to give Igor the cash, and out of the corner of my eye, I saw Charles slip into one of the rooms. I thought I must be mistaken, and he wouldn't do that because he loved me. I entertained him in the bedroom. He was going to divorce his wife for me ..." She stopped dead, and like a rabbit in the headlights, she stared at Francesca, realising she had said too much.

"Don't look so shocked, Gemma. We both know I was his wife."

Gemma shook her head. "Anyway, I went to check on the girls, but the idea that he might be in there, not only with another woman, but our youngest girl, fifteen she was, was driving me mad. I had to find out for sure, so I went to open the door. One of Igor's men grabbed me arm and that was when I lost it. I kicked him, demanding he let go. With the other leg, I kicked the door open. It was terrible." She paused, swallowing back the tears. "The girl was naked and gagged. But what was more shocking was the cut down her cheek. I screamed and he leapt from the bed. Igor came running down the corridor and pinned me down. He tied me hands behind me back and held me down on the floor, whilst I watched Charles just run away. Then Igor threw me into the end room to get me out of the way because they had a chase on. It was awful." She said it so matter-of-factly as if Francesca should know what that meant.

Jamie looked up and held his hand up. "Stop a moment. What exactly do you mean by 'a chase on'?"

Gemma chewed her nail and then she took another deep breath. "The chase or the hunt is where they let one of the girls go and the client chases them. They can't actually escape so they get hunted

381

down. Igor's men join in, making sure the client captures the girl and then … well, you can guess what."

Francesca's blood was boiling. "No, actually, I cannot guess the rest. In fact, Gemma, I cannot possibly imagine what they would do to a defenceless child running in terror."

Gemma looked to the floor. Of course it was absurd. It wasn't normal by anyone's standards. "They could do whatever they wanted."

"Murder?" asked Jamie.

Gemma looked from one to the other. "I do know that some were taken away and never returned. But rape and stuff … I don't know the details because I only arranged them. I didn't take part. Fuck, no way, that's sick."

Jamie took a deep breath and exhaled through his nose, as if he was holding back vomit. The visions were so sickening, he just had to know, and not through morbid curiosity, either. He didn't want to overthink the atrocities and needed a clear picture in his mind. "Gemma, don't just skim over this. I want to know what the hunt is. What the fuck do they do? And you know what they do, don't you? You fucking know exactly what goes on!"

It was the first time Francesca had heard him sound so aggressive, but she wouldn't stop him. In fact, it was probably wrong to dismiss the real part of the sick story just to ease their own minds. She raised her eyebrows, sat back, and folded her arms as if to say, 'tell him'.

Gemma swallowed hard and her mouth went dry. She looked up to the ceiling and said in a resigned tone, "The client chooses the woman …"

Jamie jumped in, "Child … you mean fucking child!"

Biting her bottom lip, she nodded, "Yes, okay, child. They picked which one they wanted, dressed them in a ball gown or a pretty dress, got them made-up like a princess, and then would tell them they have five minutes to escape. Morozov's men are already ahead of the runner so there is no way they can escape. Then they handed the client two tools, a tranquilizer gun and …" She paused. Her mouth was running away with her, and she knew then that telling the truth was her only way out. Francesca was too good, and Gemma guessed that there was no point in holding back now.

"And what, Gemma, what did they have?" grilled Jamie.

"And … Jesus Christ! Does it matter? They get captured, and then they can have their fun!" she shouted back in frustration.

Jamie felt his temper rising and saw his professionalism shoot out the window. "What else do they have, Gemma? What the fuck do they do to those kids?"

"All right, all right, they give them a stun gun. You know, the ones used in the abattoirs."

"What, are these the same guns you gave to the girls in the flats and you were supposedly locked away for?"

Gemma knew then that they didn't miss a trick. "No, those were Tasers, but these were something else."

Jamie gasped and Francesca felt her head getting hot again. It was too disturbing for words but Jamie couldn't leave it. He had to know the rest. "What are they doing with stun guns? This doesn't add up to me. They are not chasing the girls for a quick fuck at the end of it. These people are hunting to kill!"

Francesca was in a daze. The visions were hard to take in, but he was right. They had to know.

"The truth, Gemma," she said with a bitterly cold stare.

"They would use the tranquiliser gun if they just wanted to slow the girl down. Once they are out of it, the men take them back to a room with the client. The stun guns are used only if the client captures the girl. It's hit and miss if they survive. The strong ones do and the weak ones don't. That's all I know."

A flustered look crept across Gemma's sulky face, reflecting her anger at being pushed into a corner, like a kid in a playground, being bullied for her sweets.

There was a long silence as both Francesca and Jamie tried to take it all in. It was too disturbing for them to naturally absorb it. It was like a slasher film – only this was for real.

"And the ones that die, Gemma? What do they do with them?" demanded Jamie.

It was then that Francesca saw the look of nonchalance in Gemma's eyes. "Some of the men prefer them that way."

The shock hit them both. Like a bolt, it was worse than a sick horror film – men killing kids and having sex with a corpse. The looming silence was long as both Francesca and Jamie tried to take it all in. Francesca was angry but she tried to keep a lid on it. She hated Gemma with a passion. Gemma was worse than the men; after all, she assumed now that Gemma had been orchestrating these sick games.

In the back of Francesca's mind was an image of those young girls – terrified and running for their lives. The vision of them dressed in some sick outfit and praying they would escape – only to be shot with a dart, or stunned with a gun, which would have splintered their bones and fried their brains to an inch of their life, was horrific. Yet there was Gemma telling them how it was so awful for her. But she hadn't been brutalised by a slaughterhouse stun gun. The level of contempt had reached its peak, and Francesca had to slow her own heart beat and continue to remain calm and not reach across the table and rip out Gemma's throat.

Jamie spoke up; he sensed Francesca was seething. "You can put it all right now, by telling us where that mansion is."

"I wish I could. If you can get me out of here, I can show you or the police."

Francesca knew she was lying; she would remember what was written on the signposts, at least. If you were unable to recognise the junction to come off, the only clue would be the sign. There was no point in any more questions; she wasn't going to get the answers.

"Oh, well, it looks like we've exhausted everything you know. The thing is, I'm not sure we can help you," she smirked.

Gemma jumped up. "No, listen, you have to help me. Please, I'm begging you. Don't leave me in here. I can't stand it. You have to get me out. I promise, I'll show you the way."

Francesca slowly got to her feet. "I told you I would help if you were honest, but for some reason you won't tell me where this mansion is, and that means I have no proof it even exists."

"All right, please, wait," Gemma pleaded.

Jamie and Francesca took to their seats again and waited.

"Let me tell ya what happened after they locked me up." Gemma was desperate now to gain sympathy and anything, in fact, that would have Francesca back on her side.

Francesca nodded.

"As soon as Igor called George to tell him what I had done, they closed ranks and left me in that room. I was so afraid for me life. I thought I was gonna end up like... well, like the other girls. They kept me there for a long time. That Rita took over, and I was treated like one of the whores, except they didn't have clients lined up for me, thank God. I was allowed a TV, fresh bed linen, and meals. Luckily, there was a bathroom in that room. I begged and pleaded for them to let me out. I promised them, I wouldn't say a word, but they ignored me, even Bobby. He came one night to have a chat. He laid it on the line with me. He said me being locked up was out of his hands, but he would work on them. The months dragged by, and Igor was the only one allowed to come in. He gave me clean clothes and decent food. He wasn't horrible to me, although probably, deep down, he despised me for my part in it all. He hated the job more than anyone, but he couldn't afford not to work for Alex because if he turned against him his whole family would be shot. Rita was livid that he was the one looking after me. In her fucked-up brain, she thought we were having it away. She talked George into her taking over the running of the house, including looking after me. I got sick shortly after and almost died. That's no word of a lie. I don't know what I ate, but I was sick for weeks. Me hair fell out, and me skin was full of scabs. At that point, I just wanted to die. Then something changed."

Gemma stared into space, trying to act as if she was reliving a sad moment, and yet it was only another lie to add to the drama. "I thought, in his own way, Bobby still loved me. He didn't fancy me, not anymore, but I thought he still loved me at least. I couldn't have been more wrong. One night, just as I was dozing off to sleep, I heard the door open. It was dark, and I couldn't see who it was, but I could see it was a man and his silhouette was frightening enough. Then, I saw another man, my Bobby. I knew it was him. Suddenly, a bag was put over me head. I thought they were going to kill me. They tied it tight, and then they handcuffed me to the bed. There was silence, and then I heard the door close. I lay there naked and terrified. The gag they shoved in me mouth was tearing at the corners, ripping me lips. The man in the room breathed heavily, and then he began grabbing at me body like a fucking animal. He made this creepy giggling sound, and I felt me heart go in me mouth because I knew then who it was: Jimmy! My husband had let Jimmy assault me and it frightened me. Not the assault because thankfully he didn't hurt me like he did the other girls. No, I was afraid because I knew then I had no one to help me, and I was being used and abused with no hope of getting out of the hellhole. Then, when he'd finished, the door opened, and in the distance I heard Bobby laughing and asking for the keys to his new set of wheels. He had sold me to his brother for a fucking car. I couldn't tell anyone because who the fuck would believe me?" *There, that would have the lawyers feeling sorry for her*, so she stupidly assumed.

Francesca was ready to laugh aloud, knowing that Gemma was a pathological liar, and yet she was frustrated with the continual bullshit, which kept spewing from her mouth. Sarcastically she asked, "So that's why you wanted to kill Bobby?"

Gemma nodded. "Yes, that was the start of it. However, it all changed overnight. Alex had turned up at the mansion totally unaware that they had kept me locked up in one of the rooms, and to save face, George let me out before Alex got wind of it. I remember George gripping me arm and saying just get back to work, and any other fuck-ups, and you will be locked up for good. He said to always remember what would be in store, if I tried any nonsense. He could

387

have taken me away somewhere else and locked me up, but he didn't. I didn't know at the time why he wanted me back working the front of the house as they called it, wearing me posh dresses and dealing with the clients. Then, one day, I questioned George about why he needed me back on show and playing the friendly host. He laughed in me face and said in a slow, creepy voice, 'Because, darling, the clients were on edge when you weren't around, and I can't have me money-making scheme go down the pan because the old fuckers are afraid you've turned against us and would grass us all up. So smile sweetly and do your fucking job'. But I knew really they were more afraid of Alex than anyone. They couldn't kill me because I was Alex's best asset and they knew it. It was nothing to do with the clients. George made me move into the mansion. He told everyone that it was my choice, so no one questioned it. Then, after a few years, I couldn't stomach it anymore."

She stopped and looked for any sign that they believed her, and yet Francesca was a master at the poker face, and so Gemma carried on. "I finally got the guts to leave. I pretended that I was going back to the cottage to collect the rest of me belongings. George drove me back there and watched me walk up the garden path before he drove away. They had it planned because as soon as I walked inside the house, Bobby was there and tried to kill me … and well, you know the rest." She looked down in resignation; she had no more to say.

Suddenly, Francesca clapped her hands three times, and then she laughed, "Well, Gemma, that was a nice try. You would have had a full jury fooled with that pathetic story, but not me. You see, I gave you the opportunity to tell the truth, but you just couldn't do it. Oh, I believe you may have been locked up, and I do believe it was because of Charles, and sadly I also know first-hand that he was capable of such horrific behaviour. But you were never locked up for fourteen damn years – fourteen minutes to cool off, maybe. No way did they keep you locked away and for Jimmy to rape you. Gemma, I also know that you have talked your way out of trouble, lying, coercing, and manipulating. You are so much like Charles, it's uncanny." She sat back on her chair and waited to see the panic rise in Gemma's face.

The cracks appeared in Gemma's story long before she had finished it, and she knew she couldn't beat Francesca, so she just glared at her with beady eyes in defiance.

"You see, Gemma, I listened to your taped story a few times, and then it occurred to me, you were proud of how you managed to get one over on Rita, sending her to the Rastas, after your horrific ordeal, knowing she could be dealt the same fate. You gloated when you told me how you brazenly asked them for wages that Sunday at dinner, knowing how nasty they could be, and it clearly demonstrated how cunning you were. However, do you know what clinched it for me?"

Gemma was silent and she tilted her head to the side, waiting for Francesca to answer.

"You cleverly devised a plan, using poor Cassie to get me on your case. You fucking knew damn well who I was, and yet only my family knew my past, so you had to be one devious, clever, and conniving woman. So there is no way someone as shrewd and ingenious as yourself would find themselves locked up in a mansion, playing host, unless you really wanted to."

Gemma knew that now she had to fight for her life, but all she could say was "I had no choice——"

A furious Francesca interrupted her. "Oh, yes, you fucking did, and even now you choose to save yourself and fuck the rest!"

Gemma was wary now. Francesca's face was white and tight. It was a far cry from the soft expression she'd worn on the last visit. But, she thought, *she could hardly explain the real reason she didn't go to the police was because she wanted to exact revenge on the Ruthers and then take over what they had built up*, could she?

"No Please! You have to believe me. I was kept in the mansion ..." pleaded Gemma.

"Shut it! You wouldn't tell the police where the mansion was because, one by one, you were going to take out the Ruthers and then run the business yourself. You had that racket sewn up: the chase, the mansion, the Gentlemen's Club, and the Enrights. They were all your ideas. You knew you could continue that set-up without the Ruthers. The one thing you didn't plan on was me investigating your cruel and vile actions. I had you sussed Gemma. The police report never mentioned you finding a ledger. In fact, Gemma, you never even spoke about Daisy to them or to your lawyer. You seriously underestimated me, didn't you?"

Gemma knew then she was fucked. She had thought her own motives would go unnoticed, but Francesca was good and that's why she had been her last chance. She was the only one who could get her out of the nick. "No, you got it wrong. I promise you, it's not like that."

"Shut up, Gemma!" shouted Francesca. Her anger was rising, "You could have got out of that mansion at any time, but the truth is you didn't want to. You stayed there of your own free will because it was your choice. You loved the life, the thrill, and the power. No doubt you had the Russians on your side because, Gemma, I have listened to you trying to manipulate me, and I have to give it to you, you are good. The Ruthers thought you were a liability but for the wrong reason, and in the wrong hands, you could have taken them all

390

down. Therefore, they probably did plan to take you out of the picture. The funny thing is they were as stupid as you because they had no idea what you were really up to, did they?" She paused and gave Gemma a look of contempt.

"I think what did happen to you in those early years was sad, and perhaps it did turn you into a monster. Who knows? But here's the thing. I don't know exactly what you did in those unaccounted years, although I can make an educated guess. But it doesn't matter now. I promised Cassie I would help, so I will, because, unlike you, Gemma, I am a woman of my word, and I will make sure you get out of prison."

Gemma only heard those last few words. She had done it. The lawyer was going to get her out. "Thank you, Francesca, I knew you would."

Francesca stood to leave, along with Jamie.

Outside, Sandra stood waiting to take Gemma back. "Oh, the visit is over, then?" she asked Francesca.

"Yes, but I want a word with you."

Sandra felt her bowels loosen and a sickness engulfed her. "Oh? What, here, or ... ?"

"No, Sandra, this is a private conversation between you and me."

Sandra was worried sick about Bobby and the mess she could find herself in, and now she had the lawyer on her back.

There was a second legal visiting room around the corner. She locked the room Gemma was in and showed Francesca the way. The room was identical; Sandra turned around and locked the door. "What's this about, Mrs Luciani?"

Francesca smiled. "Sandra, I have enough evidence on those tapes to have you and the Ruthers locked away for a long time. Do you understand me? I'm being completely honest with you."

Sandra's lip quivered. She was about to cry like a baby, since the pressure was too much, and when push came to shove, she really was shitting hot bricks.

"What do you want from me?"

Francesca smirked. "Sandra, I know you're a heartless bitch because I'm good at working people out. I also know that you are fucking terrified of going to prison. You'll find that most screws are. You are probably in over your fucking head with the Ruthers because it's my guess that you struck a deal with Bobby, and now you're lumbered with it, and the consequences for you don't fare well."

She paused and waited for a reaction. Sandra wanted to bawl her eyes out and confess everything, but she bit her lip and just nodded.

Francesca grinned and raised an eyebrow. "Okay, I can help you. That piece of scum in there is, by my reckoning, a dead girl walking. She has a record of self-harm and suicide attempts. But the truth is, she's a dangerous woman and an evil person, who should not be walking the planet. The Ruthers want her out of the picture, for their own selfish reasons, but she needs to be taken out for the safety of society. It's my guess, you can take care of that little accident for me, and it's also my guess that if the shit hits the fan, you'll call me to defend you – if, of course, it should go wrong. It's my promise that if it does, I will pick up that call, and I will make sure you never serve time."

Sandra stared in shock; she hadn't expected that. "Err … I don't know—"

"Here's the thing, see. You don't have a lot of choice really. Either she dies, or you serve time. It's your call, but I can guess which one's the better option."

Sandra took a deep breath. "She is suicidal, and as her lawyer, she did mention it to you, didn't she?" She was trying to sound clever.

"She did say she wanted to end it, yes, and I have that logged on a separate tape. So you have my word. If you get pulled in for questioning, you call me, and I'll take care of it. But I'm sure no one would be interested in her suicide. She has no family or friends, you see."

Sandra nodded. "No worries."

Francesca left with Jamie walking behind her. He waited until he was in the car before he asked what that had all been about.

"Sisco, are you really going to get Gemma out of prison? We don't have enough new evidence for an appeal."

"I promised her we would get her out, but I didn't tell her it would be in a body bag."

"How did you know she planned to run the business herself? I had no idea."

"Jamie, why would you hide a cream cake from everyone?"

He laughed. "I don't like cream cakes, but I'd hide a doughnut because I wanted it for myself."

CHAPTER EIGHTEEN

Gemma was escorted to the canteen. Sandra was silent, mentally planning Gemma's demise. Although she hated the sight of blood, she hated the idea of serving time in prison more.

Scarlet was leaning against the wall on the landing. She needed some puff and her supply had run dry. The other inmates were being taken down to the canteen, and as usual there was an air of excitement, but Scarlet wasn't hungry. She whistled over to Sandra.

Sandra walked over with a resigned look on her face, much to Scarlet's surprise, since normally she would be marching over as cocky as fuck. "What's up, San?" She was trying to appeal to Sandra's better nature, hoping for a backhanded parcel. She was so low that the thought of offering Sandra a quick muff dive would be worth a few joints.

Sandra smiled. "What do ya want, Scar?" She sounded sheepish.

"Err … ya can't see me all right for a bit of weed, can ya? I got a bit of free time and everyone's gonna be at dinner." She winked.

Sandra wasn't interested; she had too much on her mind. "No can do."

Scarlett was chewing her nails down to the knuckles, desperate for some escape. Heroin was scarce, and although she had her addiction under control these days, she still had a need to phase out of reality. She knew, in her heart, she couldn't do any bird completely sober. "Come on, San, I'm desperate, mate. I can promise you a good time, babe."

"Yeah, I'm sure you can, but I ain't got any gear, so another time, eh."

Scarlet was losing face; the prison was dry and the governor was strict and keeping a beady eye on things. "Listen, San, I'll do anything. Ya have to sort me out," she pleaded.

Suddenly, the penny dropped; Sandra seemed to snap out of her downtrodden mood. She looked up and down the wing and then whispered, "Anything?"

Scarlett nodded. "Yeah, babe, just ask and it's yours. I need some gear, though."

"There's a rumour going about that Gemma Ruthers is 'avin it with B wing. She's sorted them some gear, getting it off the legal visit. She has them on her side, and she plans to take you down," whispered Sandra.

Scarlet's eyes seemed to pop out of her head. "You fucking what?"

"Yeah, the screws down on B wing were saying how she's walking around the yard like she owns the place and even Big Izzy is licking her arse. You need to watch yourself. I shouldn't be telling you this, but Gemma has it in for you. She wants you out of the picture so she can run C wing – your manor."

"Bollocks. No one's said a word to me, and Big Izzy ... well, we're cool."

Sandra smiled; she saw the concern on Scarlet's face. "They're all playing a sick game. You think you're cool with that little lot, but meanwhile, sunshine, they're nicking your punters and plotting to take you out. Gemma ain't the shrinking violet you think she is. She's played you like a fucking fiddle. I'm only saying because, well, I like you. Ya know that."

Scarlet swallowed hard; her mouth was dry and dread crept over her. Big Izzy ran the prison, really, but she allowed Scarlet to call the shots on C wing as long as she had a small cut of whatever went Scarlet's way. If that mutual respect was gone, then she was a rabbit thrown to the hungry dogs. "I'm gonna kill that cunt, Gemma."

Sandra nodded. "Yeah, well I'm with ya. I found out she's one nasty piece of work. That fucking pathetic story she tells is a pack of lies. Truth is she had kids locked up for dirty old men to rape. Shocking, ain't it?"

Scarlet was seething. "Right, San, are you going to back me?"

Sandra nodded. "Yeah, of course, and tomorrow look behind the chest freezer in the kitchens. I'll have ya puff and a bit of Charlie for you."

Scarlet grinned. "It better be good gear. I ain't doing nothing till I've sampled the goods though, San."

"No problem. You make it look like a suicide and there'll be more where that came from."

Scarlet stayed in her cell; she was on alert. Big Izzy was a mountain of a woman and serving four consecutive life sentences. No one fucked with her as she had nothing to lose. Another murder would just add a notch to her belt. If Big Izzy did decide to take her, Scarlet, out of the game, perhaps she needed to take out Gemma more quickly than she had expected.

Sandra walked away, listening to the sound of her own heavy footsteps. She could wash her hands of it once and for all now. Perhaps she should leave the prison service and set up a chicken farm, now that she had the money.

Scarlet lifted the steel frame of her bed and tugged on a string hidden up inside the tubular leg, pulling on it slowly until the knife was visible. Suddenly, she heard footsteps; the girls were coming back from dinner. She shoved the knife and string back up the leg and let the bed fall. She wedged her cell door shut and lay on her bed, planning Gemma's death.

The anxiety levels had reached their pitch with Scarlet. It was fine agreeing to take out Gemma, and yet cold-bloodied murder wasn't really her style. The notion that Gemma was ready to take over her position in the rankings was one reason to do her in, but was it really enough? Standing in the doorway of her cell, she had a clear view of Gemma across the landing. Scarlet waited and watched, as she knew that Gemma had a journal, and often when she passed her cell she clocked the girl scribbling away. Something inside her, maybe guilt, or perhaps her conscience, told her to read that journal, in order to get to know the girl she was about to murder.

Gemma, feeling unsettled, took herself off to the shower room. She was clammy and sweaty; undoubtedly it was nerves and worry, which had left her hot under the collar. The landing was empty because the inmates were not back from their work places. Casually, she flicked her towel over her shoulder and swanned off down the wing.

Seizing the opportunity, and like a sly cat shooting across the corridor, Scarlet slid into Gemma's cell and began her search to find the hidden journal. She had little time to do a proper search, so she thought it would either be under her pillow, for easy convenience, or possibly under the mattress.

However, Gemma normally only hid it under her pillow, for besides, who would be interested in reading her thoughts? No one.

Scarlet's first attempt failed, but when she slid her hand under the flat bed sheet and felt a hard object, she knew she had what she was looking for. Grabbing the corner, she whipped it out, and there, in her hand, was the journal. After shoving it up her jumper, she fled the cell and hurried back to her own. With her old shoe, she wedged shut her door and sat down on her metal bed ready to read the book of secrets. She was intrigued.

As she turned the first page, the immediate thing that struck her was the feminine and artistic writing, as if it had been done with a scroll rather than a pen. It was written as a letter to a Francesca Luciani.

Dear Francesca,

My antenna was giving me pretty bad vibes when I last left you. Wow, you are one scary bitch! I got the feeling, as I left the interview room, that you had pretty well guessed I was lying through my back teeth for much of the sessions, and I kinda thought you had pretty well sussed everything out. But I don't know that, do I? I have to assume you are not as good as I think you are, and so the purpose of this letter is this: to give you everything you need to take down the Ruthers and half the judiciary.

So if you are reading this, then I am probably dead. I can live with the lies I have told, but I cannot go to the grave with them. I don't know; it just seems as if by writing down the truth, I somehow absolve myself. Perhaps it should be a letter to God really, or should it be to Cassie? I am praying you don't get to read this because if you do it will mean that I have left this world for good.

Where, I can remember them, I am going to give you some dates. It just might help you to follow what happened to me and those bastards, the Ruthers. In particular, as I am sure you will have worked out for yourself, there are so many years unaccounted for. Not even you, if you were in my shoes, could have thought of a plausible explanation for those! But you were a lawyer once: I bet you liked to leave no stone unturned! This letter will walk you through it all. And whilst I am on the subject of the law, I just wanted you to know that I am due my A Level in law result any day now. I needed something to focus on in this place, and I thought that I might be able to learn how a lawyer's mind works for when I hoped I would have to face you here at the prison. And, of course, it would have also come in handy when running my business in the future.

As you know now, my relationship with the Ruthers started in 1992 when I first met Bobby. I was just 16. Those first few years were good! Bobby treated me like a princess, and the family were impressed with me. Crime must run through my blood, I s'pose, although I wasn't involved in the business then.

The wedding, in 1995, when I look back at that time, was a kinda pivotal moment for me, I guess. The problem wasn't me or Bobby: it was Rita! She was jealous: of my looks, of my relationship with Bobby, and especially with my skulduggery skills! Now I was a fully paid-up member of the family, Violet got me into the debt-collecting business. I proved to be pretty good at that. In fact, I was so good that I began to get up Rita's nose. It wasn't too long before she had the angst and wow did she set me up: twice! She knew I would get raped by Riff and his pals, after she deliberately supplied them with dodgy gear, and she would have placed the gold watch of the mystery geezer in Bobby's flat, which, she alleged, had been left there by my punter. These were both pretty cunning examples of Rita's vindictiveness. On both those occasions, my body took one hell of a battering: inside and outside respectively. And, of course, what was worse was I did get locked up for nearly a year because Bobby believed the gold watch incident and thought I was whoring behind his back.

During my imprisonment in the flat, I became pregnant from a few loveless shags, I expect. The still birth was a real low point even when Bobby wanted to give our marriage one more chance because I knew then that Bobby loved his family, not me. Perhaps it was a guilty conscience, who knows? I know I should have walked away from them. But I also knew that I wanted revenge. I wanted to take on the whole family.

Working the flats at twenty-one was not pleasant, but I had to show my creds to the Ruthers. They had to think I was onside. The stun gun fiasco, though, showed that I was not really clever enough at that time to live in two worlds.

On the one hand, I still had a conscience, believe it or, and wanted to help the girls where I could — as in helping Bunny and Summer, for example, who had both suffered under Jimmy. So I did give the girls the guns. And I did get caught by Jimmy. You might be wondering about what happened to the stun guns (the Tasers) and his reaction when I stole them from Violet's house? Well, there was an agreement made between Bobby and Jimmy. Bobby would keep schtum about the attempted rape on me, and Jimmy agreed not to tell the family about why I had taken the stun guns. Bobby then went to each of the girls to retrieve the guns. I had to wait a while though, until my bruises healed up, before I could return to work.

But, on the other hand, I had to enact my plan for destroying the Ruthers and that made me like them, I'm sorry now to say. And this became the case when I took over from Tressa, who had been running the first villa in London since 1996, which closed down two years later. She would probably have kept on with the job had she not been raped by Jimmy, but her protestations of ill treatment — like mine over the years — were always going to fall on death ears, and she was tossed aside by Violet like an old bag of rubbish. I began in 1998 to run the successor to the villa (or first lock-up), which was located down in Surrey, known as the mansion. This coincided with when Bobby moved close to the new place, having bought his country cottage nearby. It was a sensible move for me, at least, as I was there working 24/7. So what prompted the idea of a grand house?

George's and Charlie's four year prison sentences took place between 1992 and 1996. And didn't they strike lucky! George had got in with a Russian man while he and Charlie were in prison. His name was Val and he was inside for helping immigrants get to England. Charlie was eager to learn more. The money was easy; in fact, it was too easy to ignore. It was his keen interest that led eventually to his meeting, on his release from prison, with Alex, the main man. They'd plotted an idea that would make them all very rich men. There was a lot more money to be made in getting in girls from Eastern Europe, and they had come up with some pretty sick and cruel ideas of how to exploit them. Anyone could source a young hooker, so they had to offer something different to their clientele. So that's how it all started. I didn't even know about it then; I was too busy, collecting money from the girls in the flats.

Anyway, getting back to me. When I was brought in, the dynamics in the family changed. Tressa was demoted to being a skivvy at home, so I took over. The first night George took me there, I was nervous, but I have to admit I was also excited. George wasn't so tough on me; both he and Charlie had watched me work hard in the flats and knew I could make good decisions. I even took some kids off the streets, ensuring that it brought the Ruthers in more money. Perhaps they had a little crush on me themselves — better them than Jimmy. The mansion was so beautiful; it was far grander than the first villa, being bigger, very luxurious, and more secluded.

I remember going down the wooden moulded staircase there and was surprised to see the corridor was lit up so discreetly. What was so striking, though, was that no expense had been spared in the construction and in the fittings. The whole effect was dramatically vivid, but it did in some ways scare the shit out of me. It was then that I entered a whole other world. It was shocking to start with, but the respect and power I was shown made it worth it. The Russians liked me because I was firm and stood no nonsense. I tried to be like them: to

402

be hard with no compassion. It was tough at first, but the more I worked with them, the easier it got. Now, at this point, you are wondering how the hell I could have been so cold. But, you are respected for your skills as a barrister, and I can bet my front teeth you are loaded. Well, that's what I wanted: respect for my abilities and a lot of money. But unlike you, Francesca, I didn't have an all-round education.

It wasn't long before I was on the payroll, doing the high-end part of the operation, as I was working with Alex now, organising the shipments, selecting the merchandise, and supervising the disposals. To me, though, these young girls were just work product. Now, there's a legal term!

It was around about that time that I met Charlie Enright. George had arranged a meeting over some legal issues and he wanted me to be present to get to know Charles senior or Charlie boy, as they referred to him. He was a good client, but more importantly, he was also their lawyer. The meeting took place in the mansion, in a room at the far end of the downstairs corridor. It was a grand office with leather sofas and chunky ebony bookshelves. I was a woman then and soon mastered the art of manipulation. After what I had been through, it seemed to me to be the only way to survive. Charlie was surprisingly handsome for a man of his age, with striking green eyes and grey hair. The only issue was that he was hooked on cocaine and was sometimes reckless. The meeting went well. With a few brandies and a line of Charlie, he was like putty in my hands. It was a piece of cake talking him into setting up a club, a very private club, which we later called the Gentlemen's Club, to draw in the serious deviants, who would pay money to have their ultimate fantasy with no fear of comeback. He would have a cut himself for every member of the club who signed up and the best cocaine money could buy. With a few winks and eyelashes fluttering, the deal was done, and before long I had a list of punters as long as my arm.

I knew I was destined for greater things, and my ambition was that one day I would devise a plan to run the game myself, without the Ruthers. Mad when you think about it, me having big ideas — but the fact is, I did!

403

My relationship with Alex was a good one and it became a profitable business, which I was determined at some point to take over. But towards the end of 1998, I met Charles Enright, and by God, I wished now I never had. His handsome face and seductive charm, along with his intelligence, captivated my attention. But, Francesca, I don't have to tell you this, do I? I presume he had the same effect on you. If only I had stayed away, if only I had never met him. I think, Francesca, we have more in common than you first thought. He was such a plausible bastard and I was a gullible young woman. He had me eating out of his hand to set up poor old Daisy to try and get Mauricio Luciani locked up, and then a few months later, I caught him with a fifteen-year-old girl in the mansion, having had sex with her and then slicing up her face. I was incensed with Charles's treachery, as I saw it then, and I tried to kill him myself, but Igor stopped me, and locked me up in the mansion. I never did see Charles again. As you so rightly guessed, I was kept locked up for several days to calm down. George thought it was a good idea to have Rita on hand to keep an eye on me and at one point my hair started falling out. I suspected I was being poisoned and the only person I could think of who had sufficient motive was Rita. So I stopped taking drinks from her. She was jealous for all the reasons I gave you. She even thought I was having it off with Igor. As if!

The following years proved lucrative. George and Charlie were getting earache from the punters, especially Weirs and William Enright, because Rita proved to be a real pain in the arse. She was sent home to continue with the debt collecting. You probably have never met her, but let me tell you, she doesn't have much class and is one ugly bitch. So, right up to the end of 2014, I was having a ball, and Alex was too because not only was he getting laid regularly by yours truly, but he and I were on the verge of planning a takeover. If only! I honestly thought you would believe the story about being locked up in the mansion with Jimmy raping me. I guess I underestimated you, or I was wrong to think I was a good actress.

And then it happened. My carefree life once again was responsible for my demise. I needed to go back to the cottage. Although I'd not been there for years, as Bobby and I were an estranged couple, I had been there the previous night. All of us had. It had been a night to celebrate Violet's seventieth birthday. It was a three line whip event, so I was told. For some reason, I had left my phone there, and so I went back for it the next evening. As I went into the cottage, I was met by one deranged Bobby who decided to have a piece of me. He attempted to strangle me with some rope but was so high on cocaine that he fell over in the attempt, and I was able to free myself. Why I made that decision to return to the cottage alone, I'll never know. Anyway, I went for a knife and said, "Goodbye, Bobby, you bastard. Enjoy your last breath." I stabbed him and left him dying. I then left for the mansion. Unfortunately, for me, wonder kid Lenny turned up soon after I left and managed to revive him. That was me in the shit, and I was arrested. I felt a right prat, I can tell you. To have fucked up over a tiny mistake!

So there you have it. That's the truth. Those missing years were not spent being locked away in a cottage playing the submissive wife. And if I had got out of here, then I would have carried on. I am more than capable of taking the Ruthers out, one by one. And if you knew how sadistic they are, then you would probably want to do the same, if you were in my shoes.

But, Francesca, either way, I will get my revenge. Whether I am dead or not, the Ruthers will suffer. You will find on the back page of this journal there is the map as to where the mansion is. You can take down the Ruthers, now you know the truth. Armed with this knowledge, you can destroy them, and I will have my retribution. I know you will want to avenge Cassie's killer.

Who better than me, for you to take them out.

Yours in another life.

Gemma R

Just as Scarlett reached the last word, she heard her door being thrust open. Unfortunately, for her, she hadn't managed to wedge the old shoe tightly enough, and after a few hard bangs the door was flung open. As Scarlet jumped to her feet, shaking, she dropped the journal on the floor, much to the horror of Gemma. With a swift move, Gemma gave Scarlett a forceful clump, sending her backwards and totally off balance. Another swing came and this time it cracked Scarlet on the bridge of her nose, causing her eyes to instantly fill with water. Gemma snatched the journal off the floor and waved it in front of Scarlet. "You no-good dirty thieving cunt! Did you not think I've had me eye on you, looking into me cell, every time you've walked past? Don't you ever fucking go in me cell again, and if I hear you breathe a fucking word, I swear to God I will slice ya throat when ya least expect it!"

The sudden entrance by Gemma and the subsequent shock rendered Scarlet paralysed. It was as if Gemma had been consumed by the devil. Never in her life had she ever seen such manic rage. How a woman so meek, mild, and frail could turn into a monstrous being with so much substance was beyond Scarlet. She snorted back the blood trickling down her nose and looked away. She didn't want to hold a gaze with such a sinister pair of eyes. She remained silent as Gemma walked away, clutching that journal. What she had just read and witnessed was so unreal she wondered if she had dreamt it.

Gemma left to pay the number one governor a visit and to give her the journal for safekeeping. Gemma explained to her that she was concerned for own safety and should she not survive her term in prison she asked the governor to send the journal to the address on the envelope – Francesca Luciani, care of Jamie Walker, Solicitor.

CHAPTER NINETEEN

Bobby was raging and Lenny sat in silence. He hadn't seen his brother like this, hopping around and almost foaming at the mouth. The bedsit they were staying in was basic and too much like hard work for Bobby. He was used to luxury, and he missed his country cottage with all its modern conveniences. Two beds, a settee, and a TV, just didn't cut it. The kitchen was so small that it couldn't include a washing machine. And with no DVD player and his favourite porn and horror movies, he was bored senseless. He was not a happy bunny.

"What the fuck is wrong with everyone? Muvver's not answering the phone, that cunt Tressa won't pick up, and Sandra, the fat lesbo, is outright ignoring me. I swear, when I get me fucking hands on her, I'll slice her neck open."

Lenny was nervous; his brother was pacing the floor like a caged lion.

"Look, why don't we go and get the fucking tapes ourselves? Then that bitch won't have any evidence, and it'll take that top hotshot lawyer out of it."

Bobby glared at his brother. "Look, lanky bollocks, why don't you do something useful and skin up a joint? Better still, go and get me some Charlie."

Lenny was anxious when his brother was on a downer. His habitual drug-taking had turned his brain, and he was making rash decisions and carelessly too. He put up with his brother's volatile behaviour because Bobby was all he had. The older brothers had no time for him and his sisters didn't, either. But Bobby was different; he didn't mind having him hanging around.

Lenny rolled a spliff, hoping that Bobby would calm down. "'Ere, bruv, have this. It'll help clear ya mind."

Bobby flopped in the chair and dragged on the fully loaded joint. After a few minutes, he was mellow and making plans with Lenny to steal the tapes.

"George reckons those Vincents are nasty pieces of work. He said he wouldn't want to mess with them. He said the bird we shot is Dan Vincent's wife and they won't let it go. Apparently, her funeral is on Friday, so George's mate, the bouncer at the club, reckons."

Bobby blew a smoke ring and then jumped to his feet. "That's it, bruv. If they're all going to be at a funeral, then that's our chance to nick the evidence. She ain't gonna take them wiv her, is she?"

Lenny grinned. "Cor, good thinking, Bobby. I bet George and Charlie didn't think of that. Do we know their address?"

"Nah, but I can find out. That ain't hard." He grabbed his phone and called *Dan's Palace*. Ruby was in the office, making preparations for the funeral. She'd ordered thousands of roses to cover the cars and the grave. She couldn't do much to help her uncle but planning a good send-off was in her power. The phone rang. "Hello, *Dan's Palace*, how can I help you?"

Bobby put on a well-to-do voice. "Hello, it's Steven Carter. I hope you can help me. I was friends with Cassandra many years ago, and I was hoping I could send a wreath, but I don't have an address."

Ruby was miles away, thinking about the catering, and didn't consider questioning the caller, so instead she reeled off Dan's home address.

"Bingo!" Bobby laughed as he put the phone down. "That's it, we're in, boy! As soon as they leave, we can search the place."

Lenny frowned. "Does this lawyer bird live there, then?"

Bobby grinned. "No, but she's staying there, so George's mate says."

*

Francesca arrived home, feeling drained and washed out. The house was quiet. Cass was purring like a kitten and Maria was asleep on the bed next to the cot. She crept away, not wanting to wake her. Not only was the whole Gemma situation making Francesca angry but Dan's face was haunting her. His sad expression ripped through her like a hot knife, and she wanted nothing more than to kill Cassie's killer with her bare hands.

When the men arrived back, some time later, they were none the wiser as to where the Ruthers' family's brothers were. Jimmy, who drank most days in The Mitcham Mint, had gone on the missing list. They made a decision to stay back and wait until after the funeral. Someone, by then, would have a clue as to their whereabouts. Mauricio and Sergio made inquiries about Alex and his name came up blank. Francesca concluded that Gemma had lied yet again. The Vincents were at a loss as to where the Ruthers were, and so they decided that if they didn't want to be found, then they wouldn't be.

Their only other option was to watch the house, but Terry had had a tip-off that the house was now under police surveillance. The commissioner had granted DI Spencer the time and budget to go ahead. Spencer had also informed Terry that the house was quiet; there was no one going in or out.

Friday morning arrived, along with the whole family. The day was sunny with just a few clouds in the sky. Mary was fussing over her son, shoving tissues in his pocket. They watched as Mauricio's men arrived in black limousines, followed by the hearse. The family lined up as the cars passed and the hearse stopped outside the front door. Dan bowed his head and cried. Mary rubbed his back as tears trickled down her cheeks. The coffin was covered in sentimental wreaths which brought home to them the reality of Cassie's death. A huge wreath, spelling out 'Mummy,' was heart-wrenching.

Sergio was hugging Francesca. He still had the love of his life and couldn't imagine what Dan was going through. Sam and Fred stood shoulder to shoulder, swallowing back the tears. Their tears were of anger and frustration, mixed with unbearable sorrow. Joe wasn't so quiet; his sobs were loud. As big as he was – the biggest of the brothers – he was the most sensitive. Sophie and Alfie held their father's arms as his body shook.

Bill had his arms around Ruby. "Ahh, babe, you have done us proud with the flowers," he whispered, in a cracked voice. Ruby squeezed his hand to say thank you but couldn't bear to speak as the tears would start to flow and probably wouldn't stop. Jack stood tall, like his father, the young Vincent, who looked identical to Fred. He winked at Ruby to let her know she had done a good job with the arrangements. Kizzy, his fiancée, was by his side, looking stunning as ever, although today a deep sadness swept across her face. She'd loved Cassandra – maybe not when they'd first met, but years later, when she was dating Jack. Cassie had taken her under her wing and befriended her, like a mother figure. They were the in-laws-to-be and forged a bond because they understood what it was like to be a member of the Vincent clan, but not by blood. They shared the same worries and yet they both felt honoured too. Jack and Kizzy had intended to announce their wedding date on the day of Cassie's murder, but under the circumstances, they'd decided they wouldn't do this. They still had each other whilst Dan was empty-handed.

Dan's wife was an innocent woman caught up in a war that wasn't of her own making, and she'd been left for dead in the street with a new baby she'd never even got to meet. No one present could have a dry eye.

Dan walked over to Ruby and hugged her. "Rubes, thank you. She would have been so proud." He pointed to the huge bouquets of pink roses and peace lilies. "I never thought I would put pink roses on her grave. I always gave her them on Fridays just to see her face light up." He kissed Ruby's cheek as she swallowed hard, fighting back tears. Maria stood in the doorway with a heavy heart, watching the proceedings and empathising with them. She had offered to stay with baby Cass, saying, "It's what Cassie would have wanted."

Roberto offered to stay with Maria but she insisted she would be fine.

As the hearse began its journey to the local church, the family got into the long stream of black limousines and followed. Dan sat in the first car, along with Bill, Mary, and Fred. Dan stared out of the window and allowed the endless tears to flow. *Poor Cassie, this should have never happened.* All he kept thinking about was revenge. He couldn't rest, or even allow her to rest, until he was sure the evil culprit was dead and buried. It was wrong; he should be grieving for her loss – not hungry for avenging her killer. There was silence all the way. No words could ever comfort him.

The local church was vast. It had survived two World Wars and stood tall and grand among a stunning array of heavily bloomed roses. Friends of the Vincents gathered outside in silence, awaiting the arrival of the hearse, carrying Cassie's coffin. For those who didn't know the extent of the family, watching the endless cortège of black limousines was shocking but impressive. The Vincents stepped out of the cars dressed impeccably. The women wore dresses and hats and the men wore black morning suits. It was obvious to anyone in the crowd who they were because their appearance was strikingly similar. The Italians, too, were present: the Lucianis and their men. Roberto, of course, went nowhere without them and insisted the same for his son and nephew Mauricio and Sergio. Dan, along with his father and brothers, carried his wife's coffin into the church, and the guests followed, taking their seats. There was not a dry eye in the building as the music played a sad song called 'In the Arms of an Angel'.

The service was long and personal. The priest had got to know Cassandra better after she'd discovered she was pregnant. She'd even spoken about a christening. After the service, the coffin was carried to the graveyard and the priest blessed the ground. Dan glared into the deep hole and felt his heart beat fast. He was especially scared for his wife who would be down there all alone in the dark. His sobs were loud and his body shuddered. Sam grabbed his shoulder and pulled him tight. He knew what Dan was thinking.

"Come on, mate," he said, "it's all right, she's up there in heaven, not down there. Be strong for Cassie. She'll be looking right down at you this very minute!"

After the burial, they all climbed back into the cars to make their journey to the *Purple Palace*, Cassie's favourite.

Francesca pulled Sergio aside. "I'm going to pop back to the house. Cass was restless last night and I want to check he's all right. I won't be long. You go on with the others and I'll get Ricardo to drop me off. Don't tell Dan. I don't want him worrying about the baby."

Sergio insisted he should go with her, but she explained if he wasn't there either, then people would start to become concerned, and that was the last thing she wanted today.

"But, Bella, Maria can look after Cass. If he is sick, she will call the doctor," he urged.

"Yes, I know she will, but I just want to make sure. He was fine when I fed him, but his chest sounded a little congested. I'll be back in an hour, so don't worry."

She crept off to the back of the long line of cars and found Ricardo, one of Mauricio's men. He was on his own, leaning against the last in the long queue of limousines, having a cigarette.

"Ricardo, please take me back to the house. I want to check on the baby."

Ricardo didn't argue; he stubbed out the cigarette and jumped in behind the wheel. The journey was short; he stopped at the gates, which were strangely open.

"Thanks, Ricardo. I think I will walk up to the house. It will do me good. You go off to the club, and I'll take my car back." Still emotional from the funeral service, Francesca didn't think to question why the gates were open.

Ricardo did as he was told and left Francesca by the gates. Not needing her key fob now, she walked slowly up the very long tree-lined drive to the house, admiring the layout of the borders and carefully tended lawns. She loved this walk and particularly in the spring when the pink cherry blossom was in full bloom.

She looked at the cars lined up; it was like a Jaguar forecourt, except for the odd Mercedes and BMW. There was a silver one, parked at an angle, which she didn't recognise, but then it might have been another one of Ruby's, as a present to herself. She smiled, thinking of Ruby; she was such a lovely woman. The arrangements for the funeral were perfect; she had done an exceptional job.

The front door was open and Francesca suddenly felt nervous; she held her breath and listened. She could hear voices coming from somewhere upstairs, but she wasn't sure where from or what they were saying. The house was so big that it was unusual to hear anyone upstairs. She thought perhaps Maria had called the doctor after all. Cass was screaming and it was a sound he had never made before.

She climbed the stairs and when she reached the landing she heard Maria say, "Please don't hurt the baby!"

Francesca's cool, calculating mind went into stark panic, and instead of sneaking away and calling for help, she ran into the bedroom to be faced by two men. One was holding Cass by his arm and the other had a gun pointed at Maria's head. She had a nasty gash in her temple and blood ran down her cheek.

"Where's the fucking tapes?" screamed the skinnier of the two men, who was holding Cass.

Maria's eyes flickered towards Francesca and suddenly both men turned to see her standing there.

"Please, put the baby down!" shouted Francesca.

Bobby was shocked to see someone else there. He pulled a gun from the back of his jeans and pointed it at Francesca's head. "Who the fuck are you?"

414

"Look, just put the baby down. Please!"

Francesca wanted to grab Cass, but with the men looking scared and both now wielding guns, she couldn't take any chances. Terrified the bigger man was going to hurt the baby, she pleaded with him. "Please, just put him in the cot." Her eyes remained on Cass; he was hanging by one arm, his head flopping to the side, and he was screaming. The two men were highly strung. Adrenaline must be pumping through their veins. The baby's cries were high-pitched, and there was now a gun at Francesca's head as well as one at Maria's. She sensed the fear in their eyes and knew that a situation like this was so dangerous they could kill Cass at any moment. All she could think of was Cass. "Put him down and you can have whatever you want."

Bobby dropped Cass onto the cot, which luckily was raised so he didn't fall too far. Francesca was raging inside; she wanted nothing more than to lunge forward and rip that gun from the bigger guy's hand, but she was powerless for the moment.

"Who are you?" Bobby demanded again.

"Francesca," she replied, knowing she would have to go along with whatever they wanted just so they wouldn't hurt the baby. "Please, let me hold him, he's screaming, and it'll draw attention. I take it you won't want that. I can stop him screaming."

Lenny's eyes darted from his brother to Francesca and then to Maria. This wasn't supposed to happen; they hadn't planned for this. But, looking at the situation before them, perhaps their off-the-cuff planning had been pretty crap to begin with.

"Bobby, what ya gonna do?"

"Shut it, Lenny. Find something to tie her up with," ordered Bobby, not taking his eyes off Francesca.

Cass was still screaming; he must have been in pain, being held up like that. Francesca looked at the baby; without waiting for permission to approach the cot, she stepped forward.

"Don't fucking move!" snapped Bobby.

"All right, all right, I just want to hold him. He's fucking screaming, you heartless bastard!" she shouted.

"Shut the fuck up!" He was nervous and on edge. Francesca stopped moving.

"Lenny!"

Lenny was lost. He was holding the gun to Maria's head and being ordered to find a rope or something.

"What do ya want me to do?" he shouted back.

Francesca realised she was facing Bobby and Lenny Ruthers.

"What do you want, Bobby?" she asked. Her voice was calm. Now she knew who they were, she would use her powers of persuasion, assuming of course they weren't too agitated and didn't act recklessly.

"I said shut it, and how the fuck do you know my name?"

"Let me hold the baby. I need to stop him crying and then we can talk." She calmed her nerves and tried to think rationally. Suddenly, Maria slumped into unconsciousness. Lenny shoved her with his foot to see if she moved.

"Fuck it, Bobby, she's dead!" He was scratching his head and looking uneasy.

Bobby was hopping from one foot to the other. Cass's screams were becoming louder and panic was setting in. "Shut the fuck up!" he screamed in the baby's face. Francesca was shaking; he was in such a frenzy, she thought he might shoot Cass just to shut him up.

"Please, let me hold him. He'll be quiet."

Bobby held the gun to her face. "Go on, then!"

Instantly, she grabbed Cass and held him close to her, rocking him. She noticed the first signs of bruising on his shoulder as his skin had started to turn red. Her heart ached. She'd never hated anyone more than she hated Bobby at that moment. She feared he had broken the baby's arm. She could only imagine what he had done before she'd arrived, but that soreness was enough to know he had hurt Cass. The screams subsided and his tiny body shook in-between the sobs.

Lenny paced the room whilst Bobby stared at Francesca. They needed to revise their original plan before anyone else showed up. This was supposed to have been easy. They'd had no idea anyone would be in the house.

"Where are the fucking tapes, bitch?"

Francesca looked up to see Bobby's pupils dilated and white foam at the corners of his mouth. He was on cocaine or speed. She was not going to be able to reason with him — he was too fired up — and she assumed Lenny was the same.

She knew what they wanted. "Look in the room next door. They are in the bottom drawer. They are the ones I used at the prison."

Bobby flicked his gun at Lenny, indicating he should go and look.

Cass had stopped crying and was now asleep. Francesca held him tight; they were not going to get their hands on him again.

Lenny returned, holding the tapes in both hands, revealing to Bobby his find.

Out of the corner of her eye, Francesca saw Maria opening her eyes. She didn't react.

Bobby nodded at Lenny. "Let's go."

Francesca breathed a sigh of relief but it was short-lived.

"Right, you're coming with us. Put the baby back in the cot and turn around," ordered Bobby.

"Where are we gonna take her?"

"The mansion."

Francesca carefully laid Cass in the cot and covered him with a light blanket. She was aware that once they had her out of the house, they couldn't touch Cass, and Maria would call someone. She turned around with her hands above her head and walked out of the room. Lenny was in front, running down the stairs, holding the tapes in his hands. Meanwhile, Bobby was digging the gun into Francesca's back, urging her to move faster. Lenny had the doors to the silver BMW open, and he jumped in, ready to go. Bobby pushed her into the back seat, still holding the gun to her face, digging the muzzle into her cheek. As they raced away, Francesca prayed that Maria was conscious enough to make a call and get the baby to the hospital. At least they were away now and the fear of Cass being hurt had gone.

"Fuck, Bobby, what we gonna do now? And how did she know your name?"

418

"Shut it, Lenny, just drive, will ya? Get us out of here before the others come back."

"Bobby, I don't know the fucking way."

"You stupid cunt. Just get to the M25. I'll fucking direct ya."

Lenny shut up and drove.

Bobby was shaking but he continued to hold the gun to Francesca's head. Adrenaline was pumping furiously around his body. He had cocked-up big time and the only thing he could think to do next was to take the lawyer to the mansion. His brothers were hiding there so they'd know what to do.

Francesca's cold, controlled poise worried him. She wasn't a skittish bird like every other one he'd met. She was different; having a gun to her head, didn't seem to daunt her. Perhaps the rumours about the Vincents were true. His brother George had warned him that they were dangerous fuckers, and yet he hadn't expected to be face-to-face with one of them.

"How did you know who I was?" he asked, grinding his teeth. The cocaine was wearing off and his jaw slid from side to side.

Francesca slowly turned her head to face the gun. She smiled. "Because, Bobby Ruthers, I know everything about you and your family. I interviewed Gemma, and now you have the evidence."

"But I could be anyone," he replied.

She smirked, thinking how stupid they were. She had heard them referring to each other by name. Their idiocy would either make them dangerous or provide an easy means of escape.

"You fit the description perfectly, and who else would want the tapes except you? Besides, you had the most to lose but the most to gain from the recording of the interview. Without them, I would have no case." She assumed Bobby was gullible, knowing full well that she wouldn't need the information; they were only for her benefit. But in his little mind, this was all the evidence she had.

"Oh, and for your information, the evidence you have now will lock Gemma away for a very long time."

"What?" Bobby had no idea what she was talking about.

"Did you think Cassie asked for my help to get her out of prison?"

Bobby was completely baffled and sucked in by Francesca's blank look.

"Yeah, what other fucking reason? Stop playing games, bitch, or this bullet will go right through your head. Lenny, play one of those tapes," snapped Bobby.

Lenny was in a trance, staring at the road. Beads of sweat appeared all over his brow, and he could feel some trickle down his back. He looked at the dashboard.

"It's only got a CD player."

Bobby flared his nostrils. "Right, you'd better start talking." He hated being in the dark and confusion was the emotion he feared the most.

Francesca was shocked that Bobby and Lenny Ruthers could have been part of a very sophisticated racket that had gone unnoticed by the authorities for so long. The Ruthers were clever gangsters; she knew that much. If they could execute a crime on this scale, with half the judiciary on board, then they had brains and a shedload of power

420

behind them. Yet these two idiots were on their way to taking them all down. She wanted to laugh out loud, but that gun was loaded and pointed at her head. It was strange because she should have been scared to death, but instead she was calm. Her biggest fear had been left behind in the house – baby Cass. She didn't care if they killed her as long as Cass was safe, and she knew he would be. Maria wasn't dead, she was merely pretending, and with any luck she would, by now, have called someone for help.

*

Back at the house, Maria desperately tried to stay focused, but the room was closing in. The blow to her head had actually been worse than it looked. Cass was silent, and in fear of him dying, she managed to get to her feet and reach for the phone. Her eyes couldn't focus to dial a number so she pressed redial, hoping that someone in the family would answer. The phone at the other end was ringing. *Please pick up,* she prayed.

The club was packed with people now. Suddenly, Sergio felt his phone vibrating in his jacket.

"Hello?" he answered.

"Help us, please!"

Sergio recognised Maria's voice but she sounded distant.

He ran towards the back of the club, pushing past people to get inside the office, so he could hear better. Fred noticed his quick movements as he barged past. It was nothing like the laidback Sergio he knew. Instinct told him there was something wrong, so he dashed after him. Dan was already in the office, away from the sorrowful mourners, and reflecting on the church service.

"Maria, what's happened?" he asked, which grabbed Dan's and Fred's attention. Dan was sitting on the edge of the desk, swallowing a large brandy; he jolted upright when he heard Sergio's words.

"It's Cass, he is not moving, and they have taken Francesca!"

"*Who* has taken Francesca?" His voice was serious and distraught.

"The Ruthers. Two men ... they have guns." Her voice sounded frail; she was losing consciousness.

"Where, Maria, *where?*" he screamed.

"The mansion," she whispered, and then she slumped into unconsciousness.

"Maria? Maria?"

There was only silence.

Fred grabbed Sergio's arms. "What's happened?"

Sergio shook his head. "I'm not sure. It sounds like Cass and Maria are hurt, and they're at the house, but the Ruthers have kidnapped Francesca. Maria said they're taking her to the mansion. Jesus, why would they? For fuck's sake ..."

Fred appeared faint with shock and he shook all over. Dan put down his brandy and took charge. He had buried his wife but he was not going to mourn his sister too.

Terry walked in and saw their expressions. Instantly, he grabbed Fred's arm. "What is it, son?" he asked.

Dan was gritting his teeth. "We have to find the mansion. Those low life scumbags, the Ruthers, have taken our sister there. They've fucking hurt Maria and the baby. Can you get Sam and Mauricio? Someone has to go back to the house, now."

Sergio dialled the house phone. It rang three times and then a faint voice said, "Hello?"

"Maria, it's okay," Sergio said, "we'll be there soon. Is Cass all right?" He was afraid to hear otherwise.

Maria tried to focus on the bundle in the cot. She saw him move and then heard him whimper. "Yes, he is okay. Please come soon ..." Her voice trailed off.

Terry ran back to the bar area of the club and found Sam and Mauricio together. He led them away from the mourners and into the office. They didn't question him. There was trouble written across his face.

Sergio and Fred were fraught with fear for Francesca, but Dan was holding them together. As Sam and Mauricio entered the office, they knew something was gravely wrong.

Terry headed back into the crowd to find Bill and Mary sitting with Roberto. He rushed over and leaned across the table. "Maria has been hurt and I'm not sure about Cass. Can you head back now?"

Bill and Mary looked at each other. "Jesus, what's happened?" asked Mary, throwing her hands to her mouth.

Terry didn't want to mention Francesca's kidnapping, not at this stage. Roberto shuffled to his feet. He nodded at Ricardo to come over.

"Ricardo, take Bill and Mary back to the house and take two men." He moved closer to his security guard and whispered, "Make sure you are armed." Ricardo nodded and escorted Bill and Mary to the car.

Roberto joined the men in the office. "Do we have any idea where these Ruthers are? Any at all?"

Dan shook his head. "We've had men with their ears to the ground and no one has a clue. As for the mansion, I've wondered if it even exists and isn't a fucking code name for something else."

"No, Maria said they were taking Francesca there," insisted Sergio in a panic.

Fred had to go into automatic pilot if he hoped to save his sister. "I'm going to their fucking house and holding that cunting mother – or anyone else who's there – at knifepoint. They'll beg to fucking tell me where the mansion is, by the time I'm done."

Terry grabbed his arm. "Wait, let me call DI Spencer. I'll get him to call off the surveillance for an hour. If you go in there, all guns blazing, they'll nick you, and then you'll be no help to anyone."

Fred took a deep breath. "Make the call."

Sergio looked from one brother to the other. "We have to get her back." His voice was low and distant. Dan saw the pain in his eyes and instantly became the big brother and the head of the family. Putting his arm around Sergio, he said, "We will get her back. You fucking watch us."

They had to make a plan, and soon, before it was too late. Fred didn't need a plan. He wanted to go in like a lunatic and gun down anyone who got in his way.

Then Dan gave the orders. "Right, Fred. You, me, and Sam will go to the Ruthers' house. Sergio and Terry, go back to my house. For all we know, the mansion might be closer to home. We have to get to Streatham."

Terry nodded and put his arm around Sergio. "Come on, mate, let's get back and make some more calls. They know what they're doing." He called Neil Spencer who agreed to pull the men off the surveillance for an hour. He would send them on a wild goose chase, allowing Fred to go in.

Meanwhile, Sam, who was the best driver out of all of them, was racing towards Streatham like a bat out of hell. "'Ere, have you got a gun on you?" he asked.

Fred smiled. "Of course. You?"

"Yep. I've been carrying mine since Cassie's ..."

They drove through the streets at speed, swerving oncoming traffic, with no time to waste. Sam knew the area, as it was not so different from the one he'd grown up in. In no time at all, they were there.

They parked a few doors up and ran to the house. Fred and Dan rushed to the back of the house whilst Sam went to the front. If any of the Ruthers tried to make a run for it, they would only have two exits, which were both now covered.

Fred didn't knock at the back door; instead, he kicked it open and rushed inside like a raging bull, holding the gun in front of him. Dan was one step behind with his own gun, pointing over Fred's shoulder.

Tressa almost dropped the pan of boiling water. Her heart was in her mouth; she thought it was the police.

"Put that down!" shouted Fred.

Tressa did as she was told. Fred looked around and noticed a big woman slumped in a chair; she was face down on the table. There was an eeriness in the air. The skinny woman with the pinny on was cooking dinner, the fat woman remained motionless, and the strains of a 1940s song drifted down from somewhere upstairs.

"Are you Ol' Bill?" the woman asked casually, as if having a gun pointed at her head was nothing. Dan walked past her and snatched the back of the slumped woman's hair, lifting her head. She was dead.

"What the fuck is going on here?" he demanded, looking at Fred.

"Who are ya?" Tressa asked again.

Fred moved a step closer and shoved the gun in her face. "Your fucking worst nightmare. Now, tell me where the fuck the mansion is."

Tressa smiled, totally unconcerned once she knew they weren't the Ole Bill. "It's in Surrey. Why, what ya gonna do?"

The music stopped; the record had finished.

Dan was looking around the room; it was odd. A dead woman was slumped at the table, and they were pointing their guns at the skinny nutjob, who was strangely behaving as if they'd been invited for dinner.

"Your fucking brothers have taken me sister to some poxy mansion, and I'm gonna do whatever it takes to fucking get her back," thundered Fred.

Tressa nodded calmly. "Ya need to take a fucking army, then. They have the place guarded. The Russian has his guards around the grounds and inside they're dressed like fucking decorators. Ya best bet is to take me with ya. I can show you the way." She giggled.

426

Fred bit his bottom lip as he thought *what the fuck is going on in this house, and who the hell is this weirdo?* This was too strange for comfort. "And what you gonna get out of it, eh?"

She smiled. "Me fucking freedom. I wanna make sure me brothers are all dead. It will be peace of mind, I s'pose. Don't worry, mate, I'm fucking about. I ain't got an army meself, or the guts really, but you have, and I'll fucking join ya. Besides, ya might need me help. I might come in useful."

Dan walked to the bottom of the stairs. "Who's up there?" he looked at Tressa.

"Oh, that's only Muvver. She's a bit under the weather. I should go and check on her before we leave. She might need her tablets topped up." Casually, she removed her pinny and climbed the stairs, closely followed by Fred and Dan.

The house was eerily silent; all they could hear were their own hearts beating fast. Fred felt as though he had stepped into a twilight zone. The door to the second room on the right was open. It was dark and gloomy inside. Tressa walked towards the bed whilst Dan and Fred stood at the doorway in amazement. There, on the bed, was a fat old lady. Fred's attention was first drawn to her feet. *Fuck,* he thought. Her feet had ballooned to five times their size. Then he turned to her face. It was bloated like a purple oversized aubergine. Tressa bent over, peering into her mother's lifeless face. "Muvver, d'ya want more painkillers? Only, I have to pop out."

Dan and Fred looked at each other in utter amazement. Was this woman so deranged she hadn't realised her mother was fucking dead? You didn't have to be a coroner to realise that. This really was like Norman Bates' bedroom from the film *Psycho*! But the thing was, Fred

427

was quite taken by the skinny bitch, although for the life of him, he couldn't work out why.

Dan clocked the German uniform and all the 1940s antiquity; he shuddered, and then realisation hit him. His sister had been taken away by this nutty family.

"She's dead now. Come on, you're coming with us," Fred said, in a loud but firm voice.

Tressa turned around and smiled. It was an odd grin that unnerved Fred, but she had a kind smile. "Right, don't shout. There's no need. I'm wiv ya all right," she replied.

Dan couldn't be bothered to question her. "Come on then."

The clock was ticking. He had no time to waste as he had to take chances.

They ran down the stairs and pulled open the front door. Sam was standing there, waiting, and looked surprised when Dan and Fred stepped out with a woman wearing a big smile on her face.

"Get her in the car. She's gonna show us where the mansion is," instructed Dan.

"Wait," she said. "Look, you can't get in the grounds in your car. Let me get the keys to Rita's car. It's got a sensor on it that automatically opens the gates."

Dan and Fred lowered their guns. Tressa ran back inside. She grabbed the keys from the table and glanced back one more time to register her sister was dead. "Right, come on, it's over there, the red Beamer." She nodded at the three brothers.

Sam was bemused, to say the least, but they had no time to question the woman, as she was their only hope.

"I'll drive. I know the back roads," insisted Tressa excitedly, as she started the car up. She seemed to have suddenly returned to reality. The silly permanent grin had left her face and her eyes no longer resembled the saucers they had been when Dan and Fred had first arrived.

The boys looked at each other; Dan shrugged but did as she said.

As soon as the doors were shut, she tore away.

"No fucking funny business or I won't hesitate to blow your head off," warned Fred, in his cold, grim voice.

Tressa rolled her eyes at Fred. "Listen, mate, I told ya. I want those brothers of mine dead just as much as you do. Me name's Tressa, by the way. It's a stupid fucking name, I know, but it is what it is. I was conceived by not-right parents. Now, I hope you three have a fucking good plan, 'cos that mansion is guarded by ruthless bastards. I've seen at first-hand what they can do and believe me, mate, it ain't fucking pretty."

Fred was in the front with Tressa, and Dan and Sam sat in the back.

Sam looked around the car. "'Ere, there's a satnav. Check it to see if this Rita has any postcodes saved."

Tressa laughed. "Yeah, good idea, 'cos my sister is one thick bitch. She probably has got it saved."

Fred leaned forward and turned the satnav on and then he searched the last destination. *Holy shit!* Sure enough, there was a postcode. Next to it, it said unnamed road. It was in Surrey.

429

"Surrey?"

Tressa nodded. "I know the way but not the address. I do know it's in Surrey, though, so that has to be it."

Dan dialled Sergio; the phone didn't even ring before Sergio answered.

"Any news?" He was on tenterhooks.

"Serg, mate, take down this postcode and get all the men ready. By all accounts, the mansion is guarded by a load of fucking ruthless Russians. If Roberto has any other men he can call on, get them to meet us there. I'll call back with a plan before we get there."

Sergio was back at the house with the rest of the family. Joe, Jack, and Ruby, however, remained at the *Purple Palace*. They would field any awkward questions from guests who may have been wondering why so many of the Vincent family were missing. It was imperative that no one should know what was going on.

Mary was seeing to Maria; it was like history repeating itself. She, too, had been knocked to the floor in similar circumstances. In her case, it had been by Mad Mick, when that evil bastard had kidnapped Ruby. She consoled herself with the fact that her family had rescued Ruby, and they would do the same for her daughter. She tried hard not to think about it; she had to stay strong. Maria was finally coming around, but her thin frame was doddery and she looked helpless.

"Oh, Mary," she said, "I tried so hard to protect Cass, but they hit me with a gun and held the baby up in the air by his arm. Oh, Jesus, they were cruel men. Cass was screaming, poor thing, and I couldn't do anything. Francesca somehow managed to talk them into letting her hold him. My God, Mary, I really thought they were going to kill him."

Roberto was cradling Cass. It was an endearing sight, seeing Roberto, the hard-faced Mafia man, rocking a baby. He didn't care, though; family was everything to him. Francesca was the daughter he'd never had and her family was his family.

He was an old man now, not as big as he used to be, but he still had his mental faculties, being clear-minded and in control. As head of the Luciano family, he very much looked the part: his dress sense was impeccable, his aftershave was strong, and his hair was neatly creamed back. Furthermore, his inner cunning and common sense made him a formidable adversary. So it had been intelligent foresight on his part to have options at a time of crisis. These would become clear to his family in due course.

Mary helped Maria onto the bed. "There, girl, we'll get you and Cass to hospital as soon as possible. You'll be fine, my love."

"I feel so bad. Those men said they had a gift from the funeral directors, so I let them in. Oh my God, I let them in. Oh and Cass. If you call an ambulance ..." cried Maria.

Mary rubbed her shoulders. "It'll be all right."

"No, they will want to know how the baby got that injury."

Roberto smiled. "You fell, you hit your head, and you dropped him. Accidents happen. Now, you let Mary get you to hospital. I am sure the baby will be fine. He's asleep. Look." He leaned over to show Maria that Cass was, as he said, quite content.

Sergio ran into the bedroom. "Uncle, do you have any other men we can call on? Dan is on his way to that place, but there are Russian guards. We may need more help ... Uncle, I am afraid for her. What if—?"

Mary gasped as the reality hit her, sending her into a panic. "My God! Oh, please, my girl, save her, please!" She gripped Sergio's arm.

"We will, we will, don't you worry," Sergio assured her.

Roberto carefully handed the baby to Mary and said, "I am coming, my son." Although Roberto's nephew, Sergio was seen very much as a son by his uncle, who had taken responsibility for him at a very young age.

The men headed back downstairs, leaving Mary and Maria alone with the baby; it would be better to conduct business away from the women who were totally focused anyway on Cass's welfare.

Roberto made some calls and arrangements were made. "My boys!" He called Mauricio and Sergio over to him. "I would rather you two not go, but I know that you will. Make sure you're armed and let my men go first. This is what they do, and they are paid very well for doing it. I have ten more men that will meet you there. These men, my sons, you do not know, but let them take control. They are bred for this and they owe me."

Bill stood, listening in admiration. He was helpless, and his only daughter, the love of his life, was in danger. However, thanks to Roberto, she probably had the best army possible behind her. He felt the prickle of tears as he thought how afraid she must be.

The men left and Roberto put his arms out to Bill. "They will get our daughter. I have faith. We must be hopeful and strong."

Bill nodded, but the tears still fell. With the exception of the sound of a siren, the room was empty and silent. The ambulance could be seen, heading up the drive.

As the paramedics entered the bedroom, they found Mary red-eyed and rocking Cass and Maria lying on the bed with blood still seeping from the wound in her temple.

"It's okay, we'll check the baby over," reassured the female paramedic. She was surprised to see two grown men and a woman so upset, but little did she know they had tears for other reasons.

Maria was seen to by the male paramedic who dressed her wound and checked her eyes.

"I fell and dropped the baby when I bashed my head. Is he okay?" asked Maria.

"Yes, he's fine. His shoulder is bruised, but nothing is broken and there are no marks on his head. He'll be all right. He just needs a cuddle." The paramedic's soft voice soothed both Mary and Maria.

The paramedic gave Mary a list of instructions to care for Maria, who insisted she was fine. The main issue was concussion, but they felt comfortable leaving Maria in the safe hands of Mary, as she knew the signs to look out for.

"Where are the baby's parents?" asked the female paramedic. Mary looked down and said in a sorrowful tone, "His father is attending his wife's funeral."

The young woman was shocked. No wonder they were all so red-eyed.

"Okay, we'll leave you in peace. If you have any other worries about Maria or Cass, please don't hesitate to take either or both of them straight to the hospital."

Roberto saw them out and headed back up the stairs to be with Maria. Bill and Mary took baby Cass downstairs, as by now he needed a bottle.

Bill sat with his arm around Mary. "All our girl has been through – never moaned, nothing was ever too much – why is her life so terrible? How does she cope with the past, Mare?"

Mary rubbed his arm. "'Cos, Bill, she has a family who cares and she knows that. She'll also know that her brothers and the Lucianis will come for her. She'll know, I promise you that."

"But what if …? I couldn't bear it, Mare."

Bill was the strong one. He was the man of the house. Yet, when it came down to it, it was Mary who would always hold them together. "Now, you listen to me, Billy Vincent, our girl is smart, she can outwit anyone, and she'll be bargaining with them as we speak."

Bill wanted to believe her because he couldn't bear to think of anyone hurting his Dolly. It had always been the same. That was why he had sent her away when she was eleven years old, just to protect her. The fact that she had been left for dead, not by Mad Mick but by her own husband at the time, had shaken him to the core, and he'd never got over it. He'd tried to make it up to her. She loved her father no matter what. She knew that he had lived many years in fear for her safety and suffered a deep emptiness that was only filled once she'd returned.

CHAPTER TWENTY

Lenny was nervous and not always the complete ticket, so it was only to be expected that he stayed true to his inner self when the pressure was on him: he missed the exit on the M25.

"You fucking prick, you stupid cunt, I should never have brought ya along! Christ, ya can't even do up ya own fucking shoelaces. Now, concentrate on the fucking road. Take the next exit. We'll have to find it from there."

Bobby was becoming more agitated by the minute. Francesca remained composed and said nothing. The more people like him who got in a state, the more dangerous they were. She knew this more than anybody from experience. Bobby had the gun cocked, so one false move and his sweaty fingers could pull the trigger. Her cool demeanour was intimidating him and Lenny sensed it, although Bobby didn't.

Francesca stayed calm and stared across the fields. Black clouds were looming and then she heard thunder. Lenny jumped. "Fuck, Bobby, we got a flat tyre!" He tried to veer onto the hard shoulder and just missed a car.

"Lenny!" screamed his brother, "it's thunder, you crank. Stay on the fucking road, will ya!"

Lenny was shaking like a leaf. Any loud noise was jangling his nerves. "I don't like this, Bobby. We should just drop her off and get out of here. That thunder is a bad omen, bruv."

Bobby was coming down from cocaine and amphetamines, and his head felt as though it were trapped in a vice. The constant buzzing made him angry.

"Shut ya fucking stupid mouth. Just drive, get us there, and George will know what to do."

Lenny stared at the road ahead. The rain began to pour and he flicked on the windscreen wipers and slowed down.

"Lenny, put ya fucking foot down will ya!" screamed Bobby.

"I can't fucking see, bruv. The rain's too heavy."

Francesca wouldn't look at either brother, so she kept her eyes on the fields on either side of the road. They were heading towards Camberley, she thought, as she looked at the road signs. So did Bobby. "Where the fuck are we? This is the wrong fucking way. You gotta go back. We need the A3, not the fucking M3, ya thick cunt."

Lenny was fraught with nerves. He was driving through a storm, with his brother screaming at him, and he was totally lost. He spun the car off at the next junction and headed back towards the M25. The traffic was building up and the rush hour queue had started to form.

"See? Now look what you've done. Now we're fucking stuck in poxy traffic!" yelled Bobby, anxious that anyone could see into the car and witness him pointing a gun at a woman. "Get on the fucking floor!" he yelled at Francesca.

Without looking at him, she knelt in the footwell.

"Now, don't you fucking move."

Francesca stayed quiet. The only sound was the windscreen wipers chattering to and fro.

*

Meanwhile, the convoy of black cars was on its way. They weren't lost; they were too sober and organised to make mistakes.

Tressa was like a racing car driver and she knew she had nothing to lose. Within a few minutes, they were on the M25. Fred called Mauricio. "Where are ya, mate?" he asked.

Mauricio looked at the sign. "Junction 8."

"Fuck me, mate, you must be hammering it!"

"I don't know what hammering it means, but we are on our way."

"Look out for a red BMW. I must be a minute behind you."

Dan looked ahead. "There, Fred, look, it's our cars."

Fred was still on the phone. "Mate, I can see you just ahead."

Tressa put her foot down to catch up with the black cars. "Cor, fucking 'ell, is that your lot?" She was shocked at the number of limousines and blacked-out Mercedes travelling almost in convoy. "Anyone will think the queen's being escorted somewhere."

"Nah, love, that lot is about to rescue our own queen. Now, tell me what ya know about this fucking mansion."

"It sits on acres of land. It's a massive plot, it is. There's an electric fence around the perimeter and two guards patrol it. They're dressed like gardeners, but they each have a shooter down their trousers. There's only one door. Inside is a huge entrance hall. The guards there are dressed as decorators and there's seven of them. Then, there're the rooms downstairs. I ain't been down there, but I do know there's a remote control which opens the floor to the basement lock-up bit."

"And cameras? Any CCTV?" questioned Sam.

"Nah, only a spy hole on the door. Mad, really. You'd think with that much security they would have CCTV all over the grounds, but as I heard it, those clients don't want any footage on them."

"So this car will open the gates, then. What opens the main door?" asked Sam.

Tressa chewed her lip. "Err, I dunno, to be honest. I only went there a couple of times when Rita asked me to drive 'cos she didn't feel like it, the lazy cunt. They were expecting her, I guess." She paused for a moment. "Oh, no, wait, there's a fucking code on the door. It's the intercom thingy. That's right. I remember now."

"Fuck 'em. Let's just shoot the fucking door open. There's enough of us to go in and take them all out," declared Fred. He was anxious to get his sister.

"Wait, Fred, we have to do this properly, so we can't risk them hurting her."

"So what do you propose we do, Dan? 'Cos I can't see any other way."

"We need to reach this place and size it up first," reasoned Sam.

Tressa was passing the stream of black cars with a malicious grin on her face. She knew full well that her brothers and those cocky

Russians wouldn't stand a chance. She thought about the mansion, trying to engage in a plan that would fuck the lot of them. "What if your mob could somehow surround the house? I could phone me brother to open the door. I could say … uhm … I could say …"

Fred was staring at this most unusual woman, totally intrigued by her offer to help.

"Ya could say your sister's dead." He raised an eyebrow.

"Oh, yeah, I could, couldn't I! I mean, it wouldn't be a fucking lie, either." She laughed.

Fred turned to face his brothers in the back seat. They both shrugged and grinned.

"So what's with ya dead sister, then, Tressa?" Fred's voice was calmer; he was beginning to trust her now.

"Yeah, well, I found out that the fat bitch was poisoning them girls in there. She thought her boyfriend – ha ha, I mean wan-him-to-be boyfriend – was eyeing them up or something. So the sick bitch poisoned them. I mean, there's wicked and then there's fucking insane. She wanted to poison me dog. I loved that dog, you know. He was me only mate. Anyway, I used her own poison in this alcopop bottle to make her a drink. I thought it was only fair, see."

Fred shook his head; it was strange because she reminded him of Francesca. She had killed a man because she thought he had killed Bear, her dog. That was the first day he'd realised his sister was a dangerous woman. "And your mother? Did you kill her?"

Tressa smiled. "No. Funny, really, she was dying. I just gave her morphine to stop her headaches. I might have given her too much, I dunno, but anyway, I probably would've killed her, one day. That woman was a sicko, a real fucking weirdo, and I had to grow up with that. I swear, if I'd known who she was and where she came from, I would have scarpered years ago."

Fred slid the gun down the back of his trousers.

"Tressa, I appreciate this, love. We have to save our sister. She's a good person."

Tressa laughed. "Oh, yeah? Didn't she murder the McManners?"

"What?" choked Dan.

"Me bruvvers are shit scared of you lot, ya know. I heard them telling me muvver you murdered the McManners. I heard Charlie say to George that the Vincents are the silent killers. I ain't scared, though. I don't think anything frightens me except knowing me bruvvers are out there hurting innocent girls."

"What? And you mean to tell us you were an innocent party in all of this?" Sam was not so easily convinced; he trusted no one. "You really want us to believe you played no part?"

Tressa was staring ahead; she felt really blameworthy for her part in those things all those years ago. "Yes, I did, a very long time ago, and I have no excuse for that. I should have been braver and gone me own way in life, but being one of the youngest, and dragged up by the family from hell, people expected me to be the same. See, the outside world viewed me as a dangerous, manipulative woman, when really that was just their expectations. They were so afraid of me bruvvers' and muvver's wrath that they treated me like I was some hard case and would shoot them in the back if necessary. I weren't like that. The truth is, I got used to the power, but I was also shit-scared of me family. They never liked me, none of them did. I helped with the first lock-up or villa, as they called it, because I was the only suitable

440

woman in the family. Rita's a bit thick, and no one likes her except me muvver and me bruvvers. They only used me 'cos the punters liked me. I hated it, really. Those young girls didn't deserve what those men put them through. But, like them, I was scared too, and like them, I had no one to turn to."

The Vincents were listening intently and they respected her honesty. Sam softened; he knew now he could trust her. "Tressa, what changed? Why do you want them dead now?"

Tressa took a deep breath. "Me bruvver Jimmy raped me and that changed me. Me muvver wouldn't have a bad word said about her precious boy." Her tone became bitter as she carried on talking. "The vile creatures are born from incest. They're sick cunts – all of them. Anyway, she turned on me, along with the rest of them. It was then, I s'pose, I realised they weren't just bad, they were evil."

Fred had his mouth open. It was shocking and hard to believe, but he was beginning to warm more and more to this woman and actually felt sorry for the sordid life she'd led. "Jesus!" was all he could say. He turned once more and noticed how attractive she probably was underneath the cloak of sadness. Whilst her body showed all the signs of stress and despair, she had a smile to die for and a body that would more than pass muster, in anyone's company.

The turning was just up ahead. They had left the A3 and driven along country lanes, and as they'd done so, the day darkened from the storm clouds as they began to gather and threaten the beautiful countryside they were passing through. Tressa slowed down, making sure she didn't miss the almost hidden road. Thick bushes lined the narrow drive. The unmade road was not lit up, and if you didn't know the way, you would never find it. But that was probably the point. The occupants clearly valued their privacy.

Slowly, she drove the car along the dirt track, easing over every bump. She turned the headlights off. After a quarter of a mile, she stopped. "Fred, over there, see? There's the mansion. The main gates are just down this lane."

"What's at the end of the lane?" he asked.

"Nothing. It's a dead end."

Fred called Mauricio. "Right, Maury, turn your lights off and follow us past the main gates. We can all park-up out of sight."

Tressa drove slowly towards the end of the lane and turned the car around. There was a field and beyond that there were woods. "Be careful! Those hedges might look safe but they're electric."

The black cars slowly followed suit and parked up behind Tressa.

The storm had darkened the skies but it had also camouflaged the black cars.

"Thank you, Tressa." Fred touched her hand. She looked at his face and wished for a moment, in this sick turn of events, that she had a man like him to care for her. He was so handsome with his thick dark waves and eyes that looked like the blue moon. She smiled. He would be nice to dream about after she'd, no doubt, ended up in a prison cell for many years.

The men stepped out of the cars and the Vincents met another group of men. They were all Roberto's men. Fred was taken aback by the size of them: they were huge, with faces that would scare the shit out of anyone. He was glad they were on his side. He felt a renewed sense of purpose by their presence, and he was also more hopeful of a positive outcome.

Mauricio and Sergio hopped out of their cars and walked over to Fred. "What's happening?" asked Sergio. He looked like he was about to be sick. He was full of fear for his wife and it was making him feel ill.

"We have to make a plan. I don't know what to do, to be honest." He nodded towards the men he didn't know. "Who are those fucking great giants?"

Mauricio grinned. "To fight a Russian, you need a Russian. It's a saying of my father's."

Fred didn't question it as he was well aware of Roberto's influence.

Terry clambered out of the second car. He wasn't as fit these days and it showed. "Fred, who the fuck is that?"

"That's our way in. She's on our side, mate. It's Tressa Ruthers. She's a bit nuts, I gotta say, but she's the full shilling, and I trust her. She wants the Ruthers dead as much as we do."

Terry stood with his hands on his hips and looked around. "How much do you trust her?"

"Put it like this. I trust her to help us get our sister back," said Dan.

Terry looked at Tressa, who was puffing away on a cigarette. He waved for her to come over.

Instantly, she jumped out of the car and joined them. "What do ya want me to do?" she asked.

Fred could see her properly now, and he was surprised she seemed to be more in control. Her body language gave off all the

443

right signals, she looked strong and confident, and her eyes were alive.

Dan felt a slight drop in focus from the group, with everyone distracted by these Russian giants, and so he decided that as head of his family, he needed to assert himself.

"Here's the plan. I think Tressa needs to go up there and get that door open. Now, as soon as they open the door, we could have a gun to her head, and then our men could run in from the sides and take over the guards. I'm betting on the surprise factor, and I think it will just buy us those vital few seconds to take 'em out."

Fred paced up and down. "I dunno, mate, what if they kill Fran? Jesus, this is like a fucking James Bond movie."

Suddenly, they noticed headlights coming along the lane.

"Fuck! Who's that?" exclaimed Fred.

One of the tall meat-headed Russians pulled a pair of binoculars out from his black combats.

"A silver 5-Series BMW," he said in heavily accented English.

"Fuck, that's Bobby's car," warned Tressa.

Fred went to march forward but Dan dragged him back. "Wait, boy, we need a new fucking plan. If that cunt has a gun to her head, then it could be game over in a second."

Tressa looked at the four giants dressed in black army trousers and black T-shirts. She assumed they were part of a Russian army.

"I can meet him at the gate with these four and tell him they're Alex's men," she said. "He won't think otherwise."

The lights were getting closer so it was imperative they had to act now. Terry nodded. "Just make sure you say whatever it takes to get your brothers to hand Francesca over to the men."

"Yeah, yeah, I got it."

Fred nodded to the Russians. "Make sure my sister don't get hurt," he said.

The tallest of the Russians, the head man called Kristov, grinned. "This is what we do." His voice was low and harsh. Fred, well built himself, felt insignificant in comparison to him.

Dan stood back with Terry, and Sam returned to the car with Mauricio and Sergio.

Tressa hurried towards the entrance with her own small army, hoping to stop Bobby before he went through the gates, using his own fob. Lenny was bouncing over the bumps. He was eager to get inside that mansion and in the care of his three older brothers. Suddenly, just before the entrance, he slammed on the brakes. The rain was easing off, and there, in front of him, was a bedraggled-looking Tressa with four men. She was waving for him to stop. Bobby was still on edge, but he leaned across the front seat to get a closer look. "Bollocks. What's she doing here?"

"'Ere, Bobby, are those Alex's men?"

Bobby looked again. "Yeah, looks like it. What the fuck are they doing outside the perimeter? I don't like it, Lenny, something's going on."

Lenny lowered the window. "What's up, Tress?" he shouted. She didn't answer. Instead, she walked towards one of the rear passenger

445

doors. She looked in to see Francesca kneeling on the floor with Bobby pointing the gun to her head. The Russians surrounded the car.

Bobby also lowered his window. "What's happening, Tress?" he yelled.

"Bobby, we have a problem at the mansion. Ya best get out the car." She peered down at Francesca and was surprised to see the woman looking so calm. "Is that Francesca?"

Bobby's eyes widened. "Yeah, why?"

"Good. Alex will be able to bargain with her."

Bobby looked at the Russians, surrounding the car, and then back at his sister. It was all too confusing. How did she know that was Francesca? And why on earth did Alex want to bargain with her?

"Tressa, ya better tell me what's going on." His breathing was fast and the hairs on the back of his neck were standing on end.

"It's the Vincents. They're in the mansion and they have George and Charlie at gun point. Alex wants Francesca to do a fair swap. That man there," she nodded to Kristov, "is one of Alex's men. He will take her to him."

Kristov leaned into the car and glared at Bobby. "Get out. Give the woman to me. Alex wants to talk with her now."

Bobby looked at the tall Russian and then back to Tressa and she nodded.

Francesca knew, then, that the Russians were on her side.

Bobby and Lenny stepped out of the car. One of the Russians opened a rear door, and holding a gun to Francesca's head he shouted, "Move!" Bobby breathed a sigh of relief. The tall Russian smiled.

"Thank you," Bobby said, and held his hand to shake the leather-gloved Russian's. As Bobby smiled back with relief and gripped the black glove tightly, he felt four prongs enter his skin and cocked his head to the side. Lenny now had a gun pointed at his head and didn't dare move. He felt something loosen inside him – he was going to shit himself. Not an educated bloke himself, he could, nevertheless, still see the irony of his predicament. *Was this how it felt to be on the receiving end of the Ruthers*, he thought?

Tressa watched as her brother's lips quivered. "What was *that?*"

Kristov smiled. "Oh, just fish sting. It comes from puffer fish."

As the toxin entered Bobby's bloodstream, his lips tingled, his hands cramped up, and slowly but surely he became paralyzed. He was still alive but unable to move.

The Russian grabbed Francesca's hand and ran towards the cars. Fred was the first to hold her. He was shaking and she could feel his body shudder. "Sis, sis, I thought they were gonna kill ya!" he cried, and then Sergio ran over, tears streaming down his face. They were all there to save her. Tressa watched as each brother hugged her: she was clearly a much loved and very special person. It was touching to see such warmth and concern for one of their own. She had never felt love like that. They really cared for their sister and she was their queen. Suddenly, she felt awkward and looked down at her scruffy boots. Francesca was classy and sophisticated. In comparison, she was just a thin and bedraggled daughter of Violet Ruthers.

Francesca was shaken but she appeared strong for all their sakes. "Is the baby all right?"

Dan looked at his sister and his heart melted; she had just been a dead woman walking and now all she cared about was Cass. He nodded. "Yeah, he's fine."

He held out his arms and she held on to him. His pain must have been so immense. Burying his wife, then seeing his baby hurt, and then, as if this wasn't enough, to find his sister kidnapped. "It's going to be all right Dan," she whispered.

Terry looked around. So far, this had been so carefully executed it put the police force to shame, but what happened later would shock him to the core.

Tressa quietly crept back to Fred. "So, mate, what do we do now?"

Francesca turned around and looked the woman up and down. "You must be Tressa Ruthers."

Tressa shyly nodded. "Yeah. Sorry about me bruvvers." She looked at Lenny, who had been injected with the same toxin. He was also twitching on the floor next to Bobby. "They gonna die, then?"

Francesca smiled. "It seems to me you don't care either way."

"Nope, you can blow the whole house up with them all in it, for all I care."

Kristov stepped forward. "They are not dead, but just out of action."

Dan stared at the bodies on the ground. "Tressa, who killed my wife?"

Tressa pointed to Bobby and Lenny. Their eyes were wide. They could hear and feel but the toxin had a paralytic effect.

Dan pulled out his gun and stood over them.

"Dan, wait!" shouted Francesca.

"What? I'm gonna kill the cunting mongrels! My Cassie lies in the ground and—"

"Dan, please, I haven't finished, we haven't finished. Tie them up and put them in the boot. I'll do what I promised to do. Our work has just begun."

Dan took a deep breath and nodded. In his heart, he knew that his sister would make Bobby and Lenny pay. He said no more and did what was asked of him. After all, wasn't she the alpha female in their pack?

CHAPTER TWENTY ONE

The rain was passing over, but Francesca and Tressa were already soaked through. They were hurried into the back of one of the stretch limousines to warm up. Terry poured them a hot tea each from one of the flasks.

Tressa was mesmerised by Francesca, not that Francesca noticed, though. She was solely focused on a mission and using all her energy to think straight and devise a plan.

"So, where did the Russians come from?" she asked.

Mauricio was his usual excitable self, now that he knew Francesca was safe. "Father has them on speed dial. Some time ago, we had some issues with a Russian mob, and he soon learned that they have their own way of dealing with business and we have ours, but it is better to fight a Russian with another Russian. They know what to expect. We are probably too forgiving, you might say. They are not."

Francesca sipped her tea and smiled. "And you, Tressa, why did you help me?"

Tressa looked at the floor. What could she say to this lady who seemed so much further up the social and moral ladder than her? "Well, I didn't plan it. It just happened that way. I guess I got in the zone. Me family ain't nice people, ya see. I ain't nice, either, but they're pure evil, and I decided it was about time they died. I couldn't do it on me own, but I sure as hell will help your fucking army."

"Good, because you are going to get us in that mansion. Are you up for it?"

Tressa looked up and into the eyes of a dangerous woman. What she saw there gave her goose bumps, but reassuringly, there was also a twinkle in them, which made her feel safe.

"Can I ask a favour, though?"

Francesca nodded.

"When you kill me, can you make it quick, please?"

Fred, Dan, and Terry all looked at each other, and then their eyes turned to Francesca. They hadn't even thought about what to do with Tressa. She had kept her word and helped them save their sister.

"Why, Tressa? Do you want to end your life? Or do you want a new one?"

Fred smiled. "You don't honestly think we are like your brothers, do you?"

Tressa shook her head. "Nah, there ain't anyone out there as bad as them. A new life sounds good, to be honest."

The plan was swiftly arranged. Francesca was eager to get inside the mansion and save those girls, but she also had unfinished business.

Tressa drove Rita's car towards the gates and they opened automatically. As soon as she drove inside the perimeter, the two guards appeared, dressed in groundsmen's green boiler suits. She stopped the car and stepped outside. They knew who she was and dropped their defence. This proved to be a fatal mistake, however, as two Russians, hiding low in the back seat, slowly pointed their guns and fired through the gap in the window, shooting the guards dead. Silencers muffled the bangs. As soon as they were on the drive, all but one of the entourage of cars drove past the mansion and parked at the rear. Tressa got out of the car in front of the mansion and dialled George's number. Men gathered either side, ready to rush in and take out the guards.

The phone rang. George was downstairs with his two brothers and Alex, discussing business. It was all a front because they had decided to call it quits and do a runner. They were just too afraid to tell Alex all of this to his face.

"Tressa, what the fuck are you doing, calling me?"

"George, quick, I'm outside." She put down the receiver.

"For fuck's sake, that was Tressa. She's only here! I fucking hope the Ol' Bill ain't followed her, the silly bitch. I bet something's happened to Muvver."

Charlie rolled his eyes and Jim said nothing. Alex, however, stared with an expression of displeasure.

George marched up the stairs and glared at the guards who were playing dominos and drinking beer. "Ain't you lot seen who's at the fucking door? Me sister's standing there and you ain't even seen her. A fat lot of good youse are!"

The two huge double entrance doors were metal framed and hard to pull open. His anger made him careless. As the doors eventually opened, he stood totally exposed and facing his sister, unaware that on either side of the door were armed men.

"What the fuck are you——?"

He didn't get to finish his question. Mauricio lunged at him and pulled him to the ground. The guards jumped to their feet but they were not quick enough to pull out their weapons. The Russians, working for Roberto, had them gunned down in seconds.

There was silence as Tressa watched in stunned amazement at how fast and silent the ambush was. She had seen movies, but this was for real. The white marble floor was soaked with claret. A tinkling sound almost echoed as the last shell casing fell to the floor.

Francesca appeared, escorted by Sergio and her brothers. George was face down in the mud, held there by Kristov, no less.

Francesca nodded to him. Kristov lifted George to his feet and shook him. George was a big man but a midget in comparison.

"I have a present for you," grinned Francesca.

George stared at the woman, trying to place her face. He didn't have a clue who she was.

"Who the fuck are you?" He was still cocky. The Russian gave him a dig in the ribs.

"The lawyer your silly little half-baked brothers tried to kidnap."

George looked around and was amazed to see so many armed and dangerous men.

"Vincents?"

Francesca nodded. "Yes, that's right, but your lot saw to it that one of us is missing. Your family took one of our family, and in my book that means——"

He tried to finish her sentence. "You take one of my family."

Francesca laughed. "No, that means I take *all* of your family, unless of course you want to help me. I have a proposition for you."

Fred and Dan looked at each other; this wasn't part of the plan. Sam looked at Terry and frowned whilst Terry just shrugged his shoulders.

"Sis …"

"Sam, wait."

Sam shut up instantly. Francesca walked towards George. "Do you want to live?"

George tried to gauge the woman: that cold exterior and eyes of steel. She was not a big woman and not mouthy or cocky. She was too calm and collected though for his liking. She wasn't messing.

"Yeah. Wha'd'ya want?" he replied reluctantly.

"Let's go inside. We're going to have a party. I want you to lock up the downstairs."

George had no idea what she was up to but he was sure of one thing: if he didn't go along with it, he was a dead man. He turned to his sister and realised that she wasn't being held at gunpoint, so she was in on this. He spat at her but the phlegm missed and her eyebrows raised along with her confidence.

Kristov marched George inside. "Lock the downstairs," he demanded.

George was trying to think on his feet, but after a few shots of Alex's vodka, his brain wasn't so sharp. Every hope he had of Alex or his brothers hearing the commotion was dashed because the Russians had used silencers on their guns. The entire professional operation had been done with precision and in relative silence. The remote was hanging on the wall; as he reached for it, the tall Russian pushed his gun into George's face. "If you want to live, you'll be clever and do exactly as the good lady said."

George pressed a button and they all watched as the door slid across the floor, concealing the entrance.

Francesca stepped forward. "Right, now this is what is going to happen. You will call every fucking member of the Gentlemen's Club and get them here. I don't care how you do it, but do it," she ordered.

"But they won't just come here 'cos I tell them to. They choose when."

"Then you had better make them an offer they can't refuse," she smirked.

George looked around the hallway and realised that there was no escape; he had to think of something and quickly, too.

He pulled a phone from his pocket. Francesca snatched it and looked at the directory. She wanted to laugh; he hadn't even used his brains to hide the names. She scrolled down to Wiers. "Here, call him. I want him here tonight."

George was sweating. The beads gathered on his nose and his red shirt was already soaked under the arms.

He dialled the number and took a deep breath, unable to take his eyes off Francesca.

"Hello, Wiers, I've got a special batch for you to try out. Yes, I'm sorry, I wouldn't normally call, but we have them for one night only. They're on a stopover. They are three young virgins who are eleven years old."

He watched as Francesca's face took on the look of the devil.

She couldn't hear what Wiers was saying but could guess by George's reply.

"Well, bring them over and we can carry on the party here. You won't be disappointed, I can promise you that."

She snatched the phone back. "Who's coming?"

George flared his nostrils. "All of them. There's a party at the club, and they're gonna finish it here. Now, lady, are you going to let me go or what?"

Francesca laughed. "I said I wasn't going to kill you. I didn't say I was going to let you go."

George tried to shake off the Russian. "Ahh, you no good cunt!" he screamed at Francesca.

Tressa cringed; she knew the Russian was going to give him another dig. She heard the rib crack as George collapsed to the floor in pain. She didn't care; if she was honest, she was getting a kick out of it.

Dan pulled Francesca aside. "What you doing, sis?"

"I want to finish the corrupt legal system once and for all. I can't stand by and ignore what's going on. We could burn this place down, but those bastards would just find another source, whereas without them, there'll be no need for this sick business. Besides that, Dan, I was married to an Enright, who was backed by the Gentlemen's

Club, and it's my job now to make sure they can't carry on playing God with people's lives."

Terry walked over and put his hand on her shoulder. "We can call the Met in and let them sort this mess. You don't have to get your hands dirty."

Francesca smiled sweetly. "With all due respect, Terry, I've seen at first-hand how those slippery, slimy bastards get away with murder, literally, and they need to be taken out of the system permanently."

He slowly nodded. Of course she was right. He'd worked hard for years in the force and time and time again had come up against dead ends, all because the corrupt judges called the shots. Good men were leaving the force because their hands were always tied. He had nothing to lose and so much to gain, knowing if they pulled this off, there would be less corruption and sex trafficking and his little girl's murder would finally be avenged. "Your call, Francesca."

Kristov grinned; he liked Francesca. He knew who she was, of course. Roberto had told him to do whatever it took but to make sure she was rescued unharmed. Kristov was indebted to Roberto and he had a great deal of respect for him. The relationship between him and Roberto went back to his own father, when he was a boy. The help Roberto had given, all those years ago, had saved his father's life, and so Kristov and his small army would jump through burning hoops to help. He was a hard man, trained in the army, but he was vicious and fast. Luckily, he was in the country when Roberto called and was eager to pay back the debt; not that it was expected, for it was just the honourable thing to do.

*

Sergio was half-laughing and half-crying when he phoned the house. Roberto was fussing over Maria as the phone rang. He answered with his heart beating furiously and almost screeched like a child when he heard the news. He kissed Maria and ran down the stairs to Bill and Mary. "They have her, she is safe!" he yelled.

Bill jumped up and hugged Roberto. "Thank God, thank God!" he cried.

Roberto laughed. "No, thank the family."

Mary began to sob. The tears she had tried so hard to hold back flowed and the two men went to her side.

Roberto took her hand. "Mary, you are so strong. Our Francesca gets that trait from you. She is one hell of a woman and you must be proud. No more tears unless we are celebrating. This family needs to live with joy in our hearts." He looked down at baby Cass and gently stroked his cheek. "He is our future and he has the most amazing teachers. This boy will be lucky. He is born from tragedy but he will live a special life. We will make sure of that."

Mary choked back the tears and nodded.

Roberto stood back up and smiled. "I must get back to Maria. She needs me."

As he left the room, Bill sat with Mary once more and whispered, "We are so lucky, Mare. We have all our family and we have each other. Roberto's lost a lot in his life – his brother, his wife – but I've got a sneaky suspicion he might just gain someone special."

Mary giggled and nudged him in the ribs. "Ahh, Bill, stop it. Next, you'll be arranging their wedding."

"Well, why not? Haven't you noticed that little spark between them? I hope he does settle down with her. Think about that, eh. The multimillionaire Mafia man marries a housekeeper."

"Bill, it don't matter where you come from, it's where you're going that matters."

Bill laughed. "Now where have I heard that before?"

"It's your favourite saying. Even our young Jack says it. I think you instilled it deep in all the boys."

"Yep, it's my guess little Cass here will hear it, too."

*

Alex and Charlie heard the dull groan of the floor closing and instantly jumped to their feet.

"What is going on?" Alex glared at the two brothers.

"I've no idea. Fuck, perhaps the filth did follow Tressa," responded Charlie.

Jimmy remained seated and continued sipping his vodka.

"Call George. And where is Igor?" Alex's accent was harsh and demanding, which was so typical of the Russian's attitude.

Charlie shrugged his shoulders. "I don't know. I haven't seen him all evening."

George's phone rang and Francesca snatched it from him and looked at the screen. "It's Alex. Where is he calling from?"

George looked at the floor. "Down there." He knew he had to cooperate. He sensed she called the shots, so his life was in her hands.

The rumours about the Vincents were clearly true. He looked at the men and could have easily guessed who each member of the Vincent family was from the descriptions his friend, the doorman, had given him. He had to admire them. Unlike him, they were clean-shaven, smart, well-kept, and smooth. He guessed who Dan was. He looked older with just a few wisps of grey in his neatly swept back hair. He walked slowly and deliberately and had a hardness in his eyes. The taller brother he assumed was Sam. Then there was Fred. He was clearly the fiery-looking man with the face of an angel. He'd been warned not to be sucked in by those round baby blue eyes, though, because Fred was reputed to be a right fucker. But his friend had never prepared him for the power the sister had. She was the leader of this pack of wolves; it was clear she was the governor, the alpha female, who the others obeyed. His mother was the same: she ran their household. Francesca was different, though; she wasn't ruling with an iron rod. She led because she was a master at it and they respected her, not out of fear, but out of love.

Tressa looked at the staircase that ascended the left-hand side wall. Her eyes followed the landing and then they followed a matching staircase on the right-hand side wall. She had never been upstairs. The guards lay still in the entrance hall at their posts. They had been caught off-guard this evening, though. She looked at the slumped bodies and the pools of blood. The mansion was a master set-up, but the Ruthers were just not cutting the mustard enough to have this foolproof. She looked again at the guards and noticed Igor was not among them.

"Where's Igor, George?" she asked.

George glared at his little sister and his jaw protruded in anger. "He ain't here."

"Lie and you're dead!" challenged Francesca.

Kristov was holding George to the floor with his arm twisted at an awkward angle which left him unable to move. Suddenly, a man appeared on the landing; he held his hands in the air. All the guns were pointed at him in an instant.

"May I come down and join you?" implored Igor.

Francesca stared; she was bemused that the guard had his hands in the air and yet had asked to join them.

"I want to speak to Kristov."

"How do you know my name?" Igor made to descend the stairs.

"Don't you move!" Kristov shouted.

Francesca looked at Mauricio, then at Kristov, and suddenly she felt her neck heat up – was this a double cross? Her eyes widened and she nodded to Sergio; instantly, the Italians pulled out their guns.

"Who the fuck is this, Kristov?" asked Mauricio.

"No one. I do not know this man."

Igor nodded. "It's true, he does not know me, but I know him."

The Italians kept their guns pointed at Kristov and Igor.

"Get down here!" ordered Francesca.

"I know you are a very dangerous man. I know you have hunted the man that never blinks," said Igor, as he slowly walked down the stairs. "I also know where he is right now."

Kristov remained relaxed and held the gun at Igor's eye level.

"Do not worry, Kristov. I am not your enemy."

"Who the hell is the man that never blinks?" demanded Francesca.

"Here, he is known as Alex, but that is not his real name. He is a Russian and wanted in many places," replied Igor.

"So where is he?" asked Francesca. It was a test; George had said he was downstairs.

"He is downstairs," said Igor. "I tell you this because he is armed. Be aware; he carries two pistols."

Francesca looked at George. "So you thought that by leaving out that little nugget of information he could save you? Fool."

"Fucking traitor, Igor, you no good cunt!" screamed George. Alex had been his only hope.

Igor nodded. "Yes, I am a traitor, to everyone. I have a family, wife, and two daughters, and they are held in Alex's home. If I do not do as he tells me, then they die. Yes, I get paid well. Yes, I wanted – no, needed – the money, but I cannot live with this anymore. So, Kristov, you can shoot me, and I know you will shoot Alex, but please, I beg of you, make sure my wife and daughters are safe."

Kristov lowered his gun. "I make this promise," he replied.

Francesca silently sighed with relief.

The doors were closed. The groundsmen, the two dead soldiers they had shot earlier, were hidden out of sight and they waited for the men from the Gentlemen's Club to arrive.

George's phone rang once more and again it was Alex. Francesca handed George the phone. "Tell him you had company from the police and had to lock the floor, but he can come up now they've gone."

George screwed up his face and his beady eyes were glittering.

"Try anything and they'll shoot you and your brothers. Trust me, I don't make promises I can't keep," she said, her eyes boring into his soul.

"Alex, it's okay, I had to lock the floor. Tressa was followed by the police. They've gone now. You can come up. It's all clear." George ended the call and threw the phone on the floor.

Francesca was surprised at how convincing George sounded. The guards took their positions as the floor slowly slid back, revealing the stairs down to the basement. Within a few seconds, Alex appeared, unaware that standing around the room and against the walls were Mafia men and Russian military intelligence.

As soon as his head was above the floor level, he froze; there were so many guns pointing at him. He put his hands in the air and continued to ascend. One of the Russian men grabbed him and patted him down. Pulling two guns from his back pockets, he slid them across the floor.

Alex acknowledged Kristov out of respect. "So, you have found me at long last. I must ask how?" He was calm and collected, and certainly a well-dressed man, but with scars that showed he had a nasty history.

Kristov didn't answer. Instead, he nodded to the guard to handcuff Alex.

"I thought you would be man enough and honourable enough to shoot. You have planned this for a long time."

Kristov laughed. "I didn't plan this. You are just a bonus."

Alex looked around the room. Except for George, Tressa, and Igor, he knew no one.

"Fetch the others," ordered Francesca.

Terry's heart was beating fast. He was finally going to meet Jimmy Ruthers, the monster who had killed his girl, and he hoped to achieve closure for his precious daughter. His jaw tightened and the blood pumped like fury through his veins.

The Russians headed down the stairs. They were armed and ready to fire. The entrance hall was quiet; no one dared moved. Alex and George looked helplessly at each other. The two hard men were fucked. There was nowhere to run and no gun to shoot.

"Your family are dead, Igor. I will see to that," warned Alex, in a resigned but still defiant tone. He knew he was never going to be able to carry out his threat.

Kristov stepped forward; he grabbed Alex by the face and squeezed. "You will make sure his family are free to leave unharmed, and I will allow you to die without pain. If you don't, I will cut out your tongue." He threw him backwards.

Alex snarled and narrowed his eyes.

The shouting downstairs came from Charlie. He hated to be manhandled and anyone trying to rough him up pissed him off, especially if they touched his new suit, or dirtied his shoes. Jimmy was quiet; he was a man of few words at the best of times. Francesca took a deep breath and waited for the last two to appear.

As soon as Jimmy had two feet on the hall floor, Terry knew it was him. The description fitted perfectly: the crater-face, beady eyes, and big gums with small teeth. He lunged forward and grabbed Jimmy by the throat, dragging him to the floor. The Russian stepped back and Terry choked the man near to death.

"Stop, wait!" shouted Francesca.

But Terry didn't listen. He was on top of Jimmy now, squeezing the life out of him. The Russian tried to pull him off, but he was in a blind rage. His overwhelming anger and hate had consumed him. He wanted nothing more than to see those evil, dark beady eyes pop out of Jimmy's head. The Russian finally managed to pull Terry away as Jimmy rolled on the floor, red-faced and foaming at the mouth.

"Let me kill him!" he screamed.

"No, wait, Terry, please!"

Sam helped him up off the floor and whispered, "No, Tel, not yet, mate. You'll have your day."

Terry wiped his mouth and calmed his breathing without taking his eyes off the monster who had hurt his beloved little girl.

Jimmy was practically unconscious, but he was still alive.

Francesca looked at Kristov. "I'm going downstairs. There are young girls down there and they might be afraid if they see you."

He nodded and pulled Charlie away from the stairs. The men were held against the wall at gunpoint.

"Please, let me come with you," Igor said to Francesca. "I will show you where they are."

Fred, like a coiled spring, jumped to her side. "Fuck off, mate. I'm going with her."

Tressa was nervous. She looked at her brothers and then at Igor. She still didn't trust him. "Hey, shall I come with you?"

Francesca nodded.

Descending the stairs to the basement almost competed with the luxury that Francesca was accustomed to, and she looked in amazement at the opulent corridor. Like Gemma before her, she was astonished by the contrast from upstairs. Although that was modern, clean, and well appointed, it couldn't compete with what she saw in front of her. Here, there was a high ceiling along which four champagne-coloured chandeliers were suspended. Everywhere was painted in brilliant white except for the skirting boards, architrave, and doors, which were finished in a high quality oak effect. The corridor had twelve rooms altogether, six on each side. Each door had a window looking into the room and a sophisticated key card locking system was installed. Panic buttons had been fixed along the walls. The corridor was carpeted in a thick pile in a deep blue colour, embedded with gold diamonds. On both sides were displayed large paintings from the Kama Sutra. But it was at the end of the corridor that caught her attention. Here an enormous portrait was displayed of a stunningly beautiful young girl who was completely naked, save for the diamond-encrusted silver necklace worn around her neck. She was surrounded by caricatures of men, of all ages, holding instruments of torture. Francesca was sickened but at the same time intrigued by what she was seeing and what she expected to find. She spotted that the doors to each room were industrial in quality and stronger even than any prison cell she had seen in her previous life as a barrister. This huge underground void was surreal and yet a master-minded arrangement.

They stopped at the first door and she inserted the key card she had been given upstairs. It was something similar to what she was used to in hotels but it looked different somehow. She turned to face Tressa. "Why do I need this special key card?"

Tressa sighed. "Each room is locked only from the outside. This isn't a hotel!"

Fred stood to one side and Tressa the other as Francesca slowly opened the door. She was afraid of what she would find within. The door swung open and Francesca gasped, throwing her hands to her mouth in horror. There, huddled in the corner, was a girl barely fifteen years old. She was completely naked and shaking with fear, as she tried desperately to back further into the wall when she saw them. Fred instantly took off his jacket and handed it to Francesca, who slowly approached the poor wretch in front of her, so as not to frighten the child. Francesca's face was full of concern and her body language accommodating and fearful for this wreck of a human being. Fred wanted to cry: it was beyond comprehension. Even Tressa was horrified because years ago, when she worked at the villa, the girls were never as young as this. *Gemma, you fucking heartless bitch* she thought to herself. Placing the jacket around the girl's slight shoulders, Francesca wiped the tears from her face and stroked her thin, matted hair. "Hey, it's okay now. You're safe," she whispered to the child through quivering lips.

The girl looked terrified; she didn't understand. But how could she?

Francesca and Tressa helped her to her feet and saw the unimaginable marks covering her fragile body. The deep septic sores around her neck, where something had been tied or clamped, were horrendous. That's when Francesca slowly turned her head and saw the heavy metal medieval neck brace bolted to the wall. This was worse than any caged animal. Francesca bit hard on her lip and drew blood; her anger was now overwhelming and the hate inside her was fast building into a crescendo. She couldn't remember feeling like this since that day she walked into the scout hut to confront those vile women who had attacked Ruby, all those years ago. And she had been upset then – very upset. It hadn't gone well for those vicious bitches and someone was going to pay for their crimes today. That was a given.

The room was a cruel place for anyone to be locked in. The bed had a clean sheet and beside it was a plastic chamber pot – basic facilities. But on the wall there were whips and handcuffs, hanging from hooks. Also, she could see that there were no windows looking out and the lights were high in the ceiling. They had thought of everything; there were no weapons for the girls to use for means of escape and of course no dignity whatsoever. They had been stripped of everything. She just could not conceive that anyone could inflict such cruelty on such young girls. How could grown men do this to anyone, let alone a young defenceless girl?

This was being done for rich, arrogant bastards like Weirs to get off on: to get their kicks.

Francesca swallowed back the bitter taste in her mouth. Her mind once again focused on the reality of the situation in front of her. Tressa went to the bed and ripped the sheet off the immaculately made bed and wrapped it around the child.

Francesca and Fred hurried to the next door, unlocked it, and pushed it open. "No!" screamed Francesca.

Sergio and Mauricio heard the scream and ran down the stairs. They stood in the doorway with Fred to see Francesca trying to lift the head of a small naked girl strapped down on the bed. It was abundantly clear, however, she was grey and lifeless. Francesca looked back at her husband and shook her head. The tears just streamed down her face as she stroked the dead girl's heavily made-up face. *My God, Gemma was right — they even kept a dead child for their warped pleasure.*

Fred didn't wait; he rushed to the next door and hurried inside. Luckily, the next girl was alive. She was handcuffed to the bed and staring up at the ceiling. It was clear she was beyond fear, for her soul had left already. He grabbed the small keys from the floor and unlocked the cuffs. She didn't move; she just stared. He gently wrapped his arms around her battered and bruised body and helped her to sit up. She seemed to snap out of the trance when Francesca walked in.

The young emaciated girl, who looked no older than thirteen, although appearances might deceive those present, was dressed in a black sequined dress, torn at the edges, and her make-up was thick and similar to that of a doll. As she sat on the bed, Francesca realised she was just going through the motions like a mechanical robot. Her heart ached when she saw the child-like eyes look up in resignation as if they were there to perform some sick, twisted game.

"Oh, my darling, we won't hurt you. You're safe now. What's your name?" The child blinked and in a soft gentle whisper she said, "Anya". Slowly, Francesca knelt down by the bed and pulled the child into her arms. "You are safe now. I promise you."

Tressa was unlocking the next door, and the next, but only to find the same sight: young, traumatized girls, naked or dressed in ball gowns, who were absolutely terrified.

Francesca and the others were shaken by the sight and they were angry. But anger didn't really cut it. What emotions do you experience when you see such bestiality? The great British public don't see such scenes and neither should they. They are normally

470

cocooned with *The Sun, EastEnders,* and reality television for their thrills. The twins didn't say anything: for once they were speechless. It was all too shocking for words. They gathered the girls up and led them to the room at the end, which was a large office with couches and chairs.

"Fred, Sergio, make them comfortable. Tressa, find some clothes, drinks, food, whatever." She was treating Tressa as part of her own family now. She had gathered very quickly that unlike herself Tressa had never had anyone to rescue her, and in some ways she now understood the woman better. Ultimately, they all had a secret and their crosses to bear. The difference was that Francesca had always had the support of her loving family.

Back upstairs, Francesca found the Ruthers and Alex handcuffed and sitting on the floor, their backs against the wall, with Russian guns pointed at their heads.

"Kristov, could you escort them downstairs, please? We have accommodation for them. I'm sure they won't mind for the moment sharing a room. Oh, and you can remove the cuffs. I'm a fair woman and it's only polite to allow our guests to feel comfortable," commanded Francesca.

Kristov showed no emotion as he removed the handcuffs and led the men downstairs. Following Francesca's instructions, he locked them in the first room and then he trailed Francesca to the office where the girls were. His hard demeanour changed as soon as he gazed in horror at the seven children.

Sergio was helping to pass around the brandy. The girls were in shock and probably had been for weeks. "Kristov, speak to them. They don't understand us. It is quite possible they are Russian."

He was shaking and he could see the girls were terrified. A strong man, so used to human cruelty, the scenes here in this underground section of the main building had nevertheless shaken him to the core. His usual hard-man expression, used for his enemies, had transformed into a softer countenance at the flick of a switch. He could be almost human when he wanted to be.

"Are you from Russia?" he asked gently, in his mother tongue.

They nodded and one of them murmured a name.

Kristov looked at Sergio and gasped. "My God, these girls are from my home town." He turned back to the girls and said to them in their own language, "It is all right. You are safe now. No one will hurt you. I will see to it that you are returned to your families."

One of the girls, the smallest, fell to her knees and sobbed. Sergio knelt on the floor and held her as she cried, rocking her like a baby. Some of the other girls held on to each other, sobbing. Kristov, normally devoid of emotion, was teary-eyed and didn't care. He had never seen anything like this. Tressa was on a mission and quickly found the girls' clothes locked in a cupboard, along with their passports.

Francesca couldn't face the girls again; she had a job to do and it was making her sick to think what they had been through, but one thing was for sure – they would never go through it again.

Terry was livid; he wanted to kill Jimmy, and he wanted his day, but Francesca had taken that away. He paced the floor and then marched downstairs to come face-to-face with her. "Why?" he snapped.

She patted his shoulder. "That man left your daughter for dead, and how she suffered we'll never know. But I promise you this: how they will suffer before their final demise, we *will* know. Terry, I'm a fair woman, but the horrors I have just witnessed are beyond revulsion. I would have had them all shot dead, but not now. No, now I want justice for the victims, and I will get it. They will suffer as those girls did."

Terry's shoulders slumped and she faintly heard him cry. Putting her arm around him, she pulled him close and whispered, "You will avenge your daughter's death – that I can promise you."

He looked up with tear-filled eyes. "I'm sorry, Francesca, I didn't mean to—"

"Hey, it's all right, so stay strong, Terry. We haven't finished. Can you organise a couple of limos to take the girls to a safe hotel? Then we can arrange for them to go home. Ask one of the Russians to go, too, so they can explain what's happening. I'll join them later with money to help them on their way. By God, how they'll ever get over this … they'll be scarred for life. The least I can do is to make their future bearable."

Terry hadn't seen the girls and was mortified when he did. He thought of his Lindsey and started to shake. Francesca was right. How these poor girls would ever come out the other end normal was beyond him.

The arrangements were made. The members of the Gentlemen's Club were on their way, but there wasn't enough time to clear up the bloody carnage in the main entrance.

The girls were driven to a country hotel. Francesca had the remaining cars moved away from the mansion and put out of sight. Francesca directed the men to their positions. She strategically placed some of the Russians by the door and had Mauricio and Sergio standing by with trays of drinks, like butlers. She had to make it look like they were hosting a party. She tidied herself up and stood at the door, ready to receive her guests. The others were inside the mansion; they were all armed and ready to swing open the gates of hell.

She stood like the gracious host with a glass in one hand and a cigarette in the other.

The first car appeared along the drive and then she saw the headlights of a second. Her heart was beating too fast and she took a drag of her cigarette to soothe her nerves.

The Russians stared ahead; like those inside the mansion, all were armed but with their guns pointing down. It would look normal to their unsuspecting guests. Suddenly, she saw two more cars appear behind the first two. She was nervous because she had no idea how many to expect. She would have to be cool and wait for everyone to arrive. If they made a move now, any other cars joining them would spin around and take off.

Wiers was the first to step out of the car. He was half-cut and that was his stupid mistake. Fred kept a beady eye; one false move and he would gun them down. He was on edge, having witnessed the carnage downstairs.

"Hello? What is all this?" Wiers laughed and helped himself to a glass of champagne.

Francesca smiled. "Welcome. Please ask the others to come over. We have a real gem of a surprise for you." She gestured for him to join her.

Wiers eyed Francesca up and down. She looked ravishing and he fancied her for himself.

"And you are?"

Francesca bowed her head shyly for his benefit, removing her steel expression. "I am your host for this evening. Alex has asked that I make sure you and your friends have a wonderful time, and you can be assured that there will be lots more like this to come."

Wiers was admiring her sophisticated dress and air of class, unlike George's sister.

"I see Alex has provided the perfect host. I'm pleased to make your acquaintance." He took her hand and kissed it. She smiled back.

"Let's celebrate with a glass of champagne for all your guests." She gestured to the four carloads of men.

Wiers had aged, but he still had the same cocky expression that Francesca remembered seeing in the courtroom all those years ago. She hated him. After the Mauricio case, he had been one of the men who had tried to ruin her career. He, along with her father-in-law and husband, had ridiculed her, mocked her, and turned her into a shell of the woman she'd once been. They were all the same, bullying their way through life, using their power to manipulate and control people. They'd turned her from being a top lawyer, winning case after case, climbing her way to the top as a fair and just barrister, into someone suddenly stripped of work, dignity and – as they'd thought – her life.

Wiers beckoned the men to join him and he passed around the champagne, laughing along with the others. Francesca recognised them – all of them. They were the same close friends of the Enrights. She had to keep her cool and execute things to perfection. Suddenly, her heart went in her mouth; she froze for a second, when the last man climbed out of the car. He, too, had aged. But for a man who had served time in prison, he looked fit and well. She thought he

475

might have died in jail. She was mistaken, however, for standing there, as large as life, was William Enright, her ex-father-in-law. She had no reason to think he would recognise her. No one had ever done so after her surgery – not even her own family.

"William, here, have some champagne. This is your night and what fun we will have. Happy birthday, old fellow," Wiers said, raising his glass.

The men were out of the cars and gathering by the door. The Russians walked to the back of the group, whilst Fred, Sergio, and Mauricio stood on either side. After placing the trays on the ground, they slowly put their hands behind their backs and gripped their guns. Francesca tapped on the door and swiftly stepped away. The men were laughing and talking and eager to go inside and get the real party started.

The doors were suddenly ripped open and there stood what looked like an army of Italians and Russians. Wiers stopped in his tracks when he saw the dead men slumped on the blood-stained floor.

"Put your hands up!" commanded Kristov.

"What is this?" asked William, wondering if, in some way, they were witnessing part of the evening's entertainment.

Some of the men turned to run back to their cars, but they were stopped by Fred and Mauricio and herded into the house. Sergio was now by Francesca's side and they followed the group in. The men looked at each other with total dread on their faces.

Seeing they were all unarmed and had their hands above their heads, Francesca stepped forward. She was surrounded by dead Russians, and live ones were pointing guns at her audience.

"Well, hello, William. Fancy seeing you here," she said sweetly, although her expression belied her true feelings.

William stared, unnerved. There was something uncomfortably familiar about the woman – it was the commanding way she spoke and the confident way she moved.

"Who are you?" he asked, in an authoritarian tone.

Francesca ignored him. "Take the men downstairs," she said, "and see they are comfortably accommodated."

Terry glared at all the familiar faces and cringed. The thought that he had worked hard to rid the city of villains, only to get them to court and find himself up against the worst perpetrators possible, boiled his blood. He shook his head and Wiers glanced his way.

"Oh, it's you, DI James. I think you'll find that you have overstepped your position. You can't arrest us with firearms. We're unarmed. By Christ, I will have you for this!" spat Wiers.

Terry laughed a loud false laugh. "I'm not arresting you. In fact, I don't work for the Met anymore. I've given up on that load of red tape bollocks. Justice? With you lot in power, mate, justice is never served."

Wiers' hope that he was just being arrested went out of the window. He watched as his friends were marched downstairs. He knew then there would be no escape. He was well aware what was down there. But he couldn't fight. He was too old and had too many guns pointed at his head. He looked back at Francesca; she was the one in charge of this little set-up. What concerned him most, though, was that for all the familiar actions, he didn't know who she was.

Kristov grabbed William's arm to take him away, but Francesca stopped him. "No," she said, "not him."

William shrugged the big Russian off and stared, trying to work out where he had seen the woman before. Those eyes were so familiar.

Sergio and Fred were next to her and then Mauricio appeared. William shot him a look and his eyes widened.

"Recognise me, William Enright?" he demanded, as he glared back.

"What are you doing here? What the hell is going on?"

Suddenly, William looked old. Fear consumed him as he was faced with his arch enemy, the son of the man he'd spent years trying to break. Even so, the woman was the one he couldn't take his eyes off. The men by her side had the same hard, cold expression with identical steel eyes. They were her brothers, that was certain.

"Sam, could you fetch me two chairs, please? I think Mr Enright here needs to sit down."

Sam smiled at his sister and walked over to the wall where he seized two grand high-backed chairs. He pushed one into the back of William's legs and placed the other beside his sister. Mauricio was glaring with malevolent eyes. He hated William Enright with a passion. William felt it, too, although it was no surprise how the Lucianis viewed him. It was true: he had spent years trying to take the family down. He had started the process by having Roberto Luciani's brother executed by a contract assassin. However, try as he might, he had never managed to take them all down. All it would have taken was one false move and Roberto or Mauricio would have been in prison, and the three-hundred-year-old legacy would have been rightfully his. He could have been the richest man in France. But it was too late; his daughter-in-law at the time had seen to that. Their last chance to have either Roberto or Mauricio behind bars went out of the window. By the look in Mauricio's eyes, he assumed he now knew the truth about the past: his mother's killing, his uncle's murder, and of course, the set-up.

Francesca slowly seated herself, facing William. She was surrounded by her brothers and Sergio, all pointing loaded guns at William's head. So many thoughts ran through his mind. *How did they find me? Who is this woman?*

"So, William, I never expected I would be having this conversation. I assumed you had died in prison. At least, that's what I was led to believe. But, then again, how ridiculous would that be? You, the founder of the Gentlemen's Club, surrounded by your friends, the judges. Of course, it would have been absurd that you would remain in jail."

She sniffed the air and looked around. "I thought perhaps I would torture you to get the truth, discover what you have been doing all these years, you and your stinking family, but …" She took a deep breath and smiled. "I don't think I could deal with your past."

William smirked. "Torture me? You're nothing, young lady. You are a mere fucking woman with ideas far above her station. Like most women, you live in a dream world. There are no women with more power than I have."

Francesca saw for the first time how deluded he really was, as the words leaving his mouth were almost childish. She looked at Kristov and nodded. In a flash, he snatched William's hand, and with his diver's knife, a cruel, unforgiving weapon, he tore his index finger clean off. William was horrified as it all happened so fast. Then he clutched his hand, his body shaking with shock and pain, rocking back and forth. Kristov threw the finger on the floor. Francesca stared at William, with cold, hooded eyes, watching with no remorse as he was writhing around on the chair in pain. He slowly stopped rocking, and holding his hand to his chest, he tried to sit upright, ready to pay attention.

"Sorry, William, you were saying how I have ideas above my station."

Tressa was standing in the corner cringing; she had never seen a woman with such class be in so much control and so utterly ruthless. She realised just then she was witnessing something incredibly powerful.

"I would like to know the name of every member of the Gentlemen's Club. You are going to give me that information, and if you do, I will let you keep the rest of your fingers."

Igor was listening intently. He went to walk towards the stairs but was stopped in his tracks.

"Where are *you* going?" snapped Francesca, looking over to him with hostility.

Igor was tall and had a head like a medicine ball with an ugly square jaw. He was toned for an older man, wearing a snug-fitted shirt. His eyes were wide and he almost held his hands in the air. "I maybe have something you want to see. It's in the office."

Francesca looked at Sam. "Will you go with him? Watch him."

Sam nodded to one of Kristov's men to follow him. They escorted Igor down the stairs into the office.

William shot a spiteful glance at Mauricio. "Who told you, Luciani?" His face was like stone.

"No one. It was by chance that we found this devil's cauldron," growled Mauricio.

Francesca held her hands together. "It's funny, how evil finds evil. We didn't expect to find you. You see, the scumbags who run this sordid set-up kidnapped me, but I guess they had no idea who they had messed with. And, William, I come from a close family. We would die for each other. Oh, yes, and my husband," she nodded to Sergio, "is Sergio Luciani, Mauricio's cousin. They are another close, loving family."

William snorted. "I am well aware of who the Lucianis are."

"So different from your family, as I know only too well. When you went to prison, your dear son wasn't bothered by that, or the fact that both his uncles had been murdered. All he cared about was who he was going to abuse next – who he could manipulate, slice up, and kill."

William stared in horror and amazement. She knew so much, but how could she?

"Oh dear, William, I fear you have just faced power at first-hand and from a mere woman. Knowledge is power, wouldn't you agree? Right now, I know so much about you and yet you know nothing about me."

"Who are you?" He cocked his head to the side. The smart upright man in the very expensive suit was now feeble and old, totally powerless, and far too weak to confront this formidable woman.

"You, William, are a very clever man. I'm sure you can work it out for yourself."

Suddenly, she tilted her head and gave the look of an innocent child with soft round eyes. William sat upright and glared, his eyes flickered from left to right, and then his complexion dulled.

"Launa?"

"Oh, the penny has finally dropped, has it?"

"But you're——"

"Fish food?" she said for him.

His mouth was open; he was shocked beyond belief.

"Actually, no, I am Francesca Luciani. I was born Francesca Vincent, but I had to change my name to Launa Matthews because of another evil man like yourself. I grew up as Launa, and I have to say, William, you were good. You groomed me to be a barrister who would do whatever you said. I was proud to be your daughter-in-law. I was proud to be working in your chambers, and I believed in you. I truthfully did. Youth and innocence does that, you see. But, when I went against your wishes and worked hard to prove an innocent man not guilty of the deviant crime of serial murders, murders that your own flesh and blood committed, you tossed me aside. You all tried to take me out of the system, and then you allowed your son, my former husband, to get away with murder. But he didn't get away with it. He may have left me scarred and ..." as she paused, she felt the lump in her throat almost gag her "... and without the means to have my own family ... to have my own baby ... but he didn't kill me. I'm too strong for that." She spat the final words at him with venom in her voice. Dan gripped her shoulder. He felt her pain: they all did. They remained still and silent as this was her call. This was her past and it was his fate.

William remained still; he was open-mouthed and glaring. The words rambled around in his head, but the pathetic woman called Launa Enright was gone and in her place was a woman with more clout than he had ever seen.

"What do you mean, he didn't get away with it?" William had assumed that his son had run away from it all to start a life in another country.

"Oh, he died." She smiled.

"What!" he shouted.

"He may have thought I was weak and pathetic, just a girl, but William, you and your family turned me into someone else. I came back from hell and vowed to take you, your brothers, and your vile son there, and so now it's your turn. You'll know what it feels like to be trapped, helpless, and terrified – like I was – and I think it's only fair I tell you what also happened to other members of your disgusting family."

William began to cry like a baby. He wasn't crying for his brothers or his son, though: he was crying for himself.

"Your brother, Tyler, tried to rape me, and he hurt my dog, so I plunged a knife through his eye. Awful, I know, but then you lot are all the same. You're sex-driven, violent savages. Then I killed your brother, Charlie, but I let you take the blame for that." She stopped and watched the fear on his face.

"And your son, the serial killer ... it was funny because he admitted it all to me, about the women he'd killed, I mean."

William threw his bloodied hand to his mouth, assuming she had tortured his son too.

"He sat there on the edge of the cliff – you know the one, it's at the end of my garden – the one he threw me off, after he'd slashed my face and cut out my fucking womb."

Fred felt sick. He couldn't cope with the thought of his sister experiencing such pain and cruelty, and up to this day, he had never actually been told by his twin what had happened to her. Dan bit his lip, holding back the tears, whilst Sergio could only stare on in horror.

"Well, he tried for the second time to take my life, and like a fool, he underestimated me and took a bullet in the stomach for it. He did walk with me to the cliff edge. I think he wanted to die because he certainly didn't struggle when I pushed him over. So I guess he really did end up as fish food, don't you?"

There was silence except for the raspy sound of William crying.

Tressa was crouching on the floor in bewilderment. She had watched thriller movies and gangster series, but this was for real. She thought her family were bad, and they were, but dangerous didn't come close to this woman's wrath. It was actually like watching a tower block being demolished, such was the destruction she had witnessed in less than an hour. She wondered about the fate of her brothers. What was Francesca going to do about them? The omens weren't too good, judging by this performance.

Igor came back up the stairs, holding a thick leather-bound book. He had a smile on his face. Sam and the Russian followed. He marched towards Francesca. "Here," he said, "I have found it." He presented her with a large ledger.

She looked up and frowned. "What is it?"

"It is the Ruthers' book."

Francesca realised this must be the book Gemma had mentioned, so she opened the ledger. As she turned the pages, she found the names of the members of the Gentlemen's Club, and more besides: the girls who were available, how much had been paid for them, and even sick, sordid photos of the customers abusing those young girls. She snapped the ledger shut.

"My God, this has to be the complete work of the devil!" She allowed the book to fall to the floor and then the contents fell out. The men in the room gasped. They had seen many things in their time, but those photos really were beyond the realms of anyone's imagination. Terry crouched to see them and then he sobbed. He sobbed for himself, he sobbed for his daughter, and he sobbed for the life that he could have given his Lindsey. His daughter would have been exposed to brutality such as this, and the reality of seeing the photos brought him to his knees.

"William, you never had a real family. You all pretended to care for each other, but really you needed each other for protection. I'm lucky, I have a family. I may never know what it feels like to have my own child, but I know how it feels to be loved. Kristov, please remove the vermin."

Kristov had to help the old man to his feet. William had noticeably and suddenly aged ten years.

Tressa slid up the wall. "Uhm ..."

Francesca shot her a look. "*What?*"

"Bobby and Lenny are still in the boot of the car."

Francesca nodded to one of the other Russians. "Bring them in."

Sam helped Terry, who looked utterly bewildered and so old, up off the floor. "Come on, mate, it's over. Let's go home."

Sergio placed his arm around his wife and kissed her forehead. "Bella, I love you so much. Your work is finally done."

Francesca gazed around the room. The house of the devil.

Igor bowed his head and felt awkward; he had expected to die, and he sincerely hoped it would be quick. Roberto's men, the Italians, were quiet and awaiting instructions.

"Can those men downstairs escape?" She looked at Igor.

He shook his head. "No, never. The rooms are made of steel, the small window in the door is welded in, and even if they broke it, they could never get out. It is soundproof. It was built to hold people in."

She smiled. "Then we must go and leave this place. It takes two weeks to die with no water – if, of course, they don't kill each other first."

Terry looked at Francesca and grinned; he had wanted to torture Jimmy himself, but her plan was so much better.

"I'll stay here and watch to make sure no one finds them," he said, hoping that Francesca would agree.

Igor shook his head. "There is no need. If you take that remote, no one will ever know there is even a basement. The floor locks so tight, it's soundproof, and only the remote can open it." He took the remote from the wall and threw it to Terry. The small object, the size and weight of a television remote control, was in his possession now. He would take it to bed each night for fourteen nights and imagine the torture those men – especially Jimmy – were going through.

The Russian returned with Bobby and Lenny, looking an inch from death. He held them up by their collars.

Dan's heart was racing. He had taken all he could and wanted nothing more than to kill Bobby Ruthers. Like a madman, he screamed and snatched the diver's knife from Kristov; then, he ran the jagged blade down Bobby's face. The Russian dropped Bobby to get out of the way of Dan. Francesca wanted to stop him but didn't. In fact, she knew that Dan needed to rest his demons. So she stood there and watched as he set about releasing them. He shredded Bobby's face just like grating cheese, and then, with one fast movement, he ran the blade across his neck. Lenny was paralysed with fear. But he didn't suffer; instead, Dan plunged the knife deep into his chest and he died in seconds. Sam pulled Dan away and held him close until his breathing calmed down and the red mist had subsided.

"It's time to go now," said Francesca. She turned to Kristov. "Would you see those two are thrown in the room with their brothers, please?" He nodded, and she took her husband's hand and walked, serenely, down the steps to the waiting limousines.

CHAPTER TWENTY TWO

Two weeks later, DI Spencer was pouring the last of the cat food into a plastic bowl whilst Ginger, his daughter's cat, got under his feet, crying for his breakfast. Long strands of fur had caught on the cuffs of his new suit and he didn't have time to brush them off.

The phone rang and as he reached across the kitchen counter for it, trying not to trip over Ginger, he knocked over his coffee. "Damn it," he growled to himself.

His wife was still getting dressed upstairs and she tutted; she hated him swearing.

"DI Spencer." His voice wasn't full of joy this morning. There was silence. "Who is it? I ain't got all day."

"Take down this address and you'll find all your eggs in one basket."

Spencer wrote down the address he was given. "Who is this, please?"

The phone went dead.

Sam patted Terry on the shoulder. "All done, my friend."

Terry nodded and lowered his head. He was finally free from the torment he'd carried for so many years. He decided to go to the graveyard one last time and lay a wreath of peace lilies at his daughter's grave. Over the past two weeks, he had ached with grief, deeply disturbed, after looking at the pictures in the book at the mansion. He knew his daughter had been through all of that and had then been left in a derelict flat to rot. He took solace in the notion that he had helped rid the world of some of the evil that had once been free to roam. All those years in the police force had never once given him this level of satisfaction. His last job and one he'd cherished had been to go back to ensure they were all dead and leave the gates of hell open for the world to see.

Spencer was hoping he hadn't been sent on a wild goose chase. He decided to take just one squad car with him. They almost missed the turning since the bushes had grown so wild with all the rain. He drove his new Audi up the long drive, hoping not to scratch the sides, but he couldn't avoid the bumps and dips in the unfinished road, which also threw the car left and right. He cursed for the second time that morning.

The main gates to the mansion stood open. He stopped for a minute and surveyed his surroundings. This was so well hidden. It was such a huge mansion, sitting proudly on a landscaped field. There was so much land, yet every inch of it was contained by a high fence, which was partially hidden by bushes and saplings. He drove slowly along the drive, heading towards the building. He shuddered as he looked ahead of him. The main door, in fact the only door he could see, was wide open. There was stillness as the last of the morning mist left the ground. He stopped the car directly outside and waited for the officers in the squad car to join him. The entrance hall was clearly visible. It was a beautiful room, large and ornate, and yet immaculately white and clean. To the left, he noticed a decorator's ladder and pots of white paint, suggesting perhaps that the house wasn't lived in at the moment and was being tidied up, ready for sale. But this thought was immediately contradicted by what he saw next. There, ahead of him, he saw something very odd indeed – a staircase going underground. As he stepped forward, indicating to the officers to stay back, the smell hit him, and he gagged and clamped a hand over his nose and mouth. Turning around, he waved his free hand at the officers, telling them they should go back.

"What's up, guv?" asked the youngest officer, looking very concerned for his boss; he looked like he was barely out of nappies.

"Oh, Jesus!" he said, as he too smelled the pungent odour of death and cupped his hands over his mouth.

Spencer pulled the officer away from the entrance and then leaned in through the car window and retrieved a pot of Vicks VapoRub. He rubbed a smear under his nose and passed it to the others, who followed suit. "Right, lads, follow me, but don't touch anything. Judging from that smell, there's a dead body down there, but it might just be a dog."

Gingerly, he stepped down the stairs, amazed by the décor, and particularly by the grandeur of the basement. He stopped at the bottom and scanned the corridor. This was either the work of an artist or a nutcase. The doors, leading off the corridor, were painted like front doors, yet they were metal. An electronic key card – it looked to be like one of those master key cards used by hotels – lay on a table on which dead flowers sat. He pulled on a pair of latex gloves and turned to face the other officers. "Put your gloves on." He had a really bad feeling about this – in fact they all had as they glanced at each other. Moments like this thankfully didn't come around very often, but when they did, they tended to be remembered for ever. He had to take a deep breath to stop himself from gagging; the smell

491

was unbearable, and even the Vicks couldn't mask its pungency. As he inserted the key card, a green light flashed quickly on the door of the room. He edged the door ajar and the smell immediately intensified. Spencer had to put his hand over his mouth and nose.

Pushing the door open, he recoiled in shock. Five men lay there, dead, with twisted expressions of pain and fear frozen on their faces. He stared without going inside and recognised one of them. George Ruthers lay on the floor with his fat head turned to the side, eyes wide open, and tongue hanging out. He stared harder at the others and recognised two more because of the connection: Charlie and Jimmy. Then there were two smaller men who were in an even greater state of decomposition, with skin blackened and faces unrecognisable. One had had his face ripped into strips; it was also apparent that one of his eyes was missing and his earlobe was hanging off. His clothes were bloodstained from what must have been a violent assault. A shiny diamond was left intact in the partially severed earlobe. This, surely, had to be Bobby, and if his suspicions were confirmed, then the other man next to him must be Lenny. Spencer shut the door. He wanted to laugh but the sight was too shocking and this was no time for humour. It turned his stomach to witness this horrendous scene and made him want to gag again. The grotesqueness of dead bodies always got to him. But this, though, was on a wholly different scale from what he had seen so far in his career. The young officer had already hurried back up the stairs and outside, where he immediately threw up a decent fried breakfast.

Spencer looked at the other officers. They were all relatively young and he guessed that this was their first house of horrors investigation. He had enormous sympathy for what they had seen. However, they were all here to do a professional job and they would do this. "You lot stay back for a moment," he said. "God knows what's behind those other doors."

Spencer moved to the next door and again used the same key card to enter the room. Neatly lined up on the floor were men, and judging by their appearance, he guessed they were decorators. That was what he immediately thought because of their white boiler suits. Their white clothes, though, were stained red, and then, on closer inspection, he noticed how each of them had a bullet hole planted neatly between the eyes. The palms of his hands were sweaty; this was a contract job, an assassination. Whoever had done this was a pro: SBS, SAS, KGB, CIA, Mossad, or a hit man. He looked again: seven men were all lined up on the floor, all with precisely-placed gunshot wounds.

No one in the first room had been shot: Bobby had been torn to ribbons and Lenny had been stabbed in the chest, but the others didn't have a mark on them, so this hadn't been done by the same people. He took a deep breath, opened up the next room, and was shocked to the core. The small window looking into the room was covered in blood, obscuring his view. *Could this get any worse*, he thought? This surely had to be a political assassination, and yet the men were not marked. There were no gunshot wounds and no stab wounds. In fact, there was nothing to give him a clue as to what had happened, except for their finger nails ripped away from their desperate attempts to claw their way out. They all lay in different positions: some were bloated and some were yellow, and there were some he recognised. Then he saw photos had been placed neatly upon each man's chest. He stepped inside and carefully retrieved one with his gloved thumb and forefinger. What he saw made him sick. He had to look for a while, to take it all in, as his brain just didn't want to process such vile images. He looked back at the smartly dressed men and slowly shook his head. It was unbelievable. These were men who commanded respect, men believed to be of integrity, men who were supposed to keep their country safe by locking up the guilty. It was more shocking than he could have ever imagined.

493

As he glared closely, he recognised more of the men: all were judges, every last one of them. The photos said it all. It was ironic: they couldn't be tried and convicted, as they were dead, but they probably would have got off anyway. There, on the floor, among the carnage, was a leather-bound book. Spencer crouched down and opened it and saw it had it all: the names, dates, times, more pictures, and even bank details.

The smell at that horrific scene of death didn't stop him from smiling. He had all he needed now – no one could ever deny these judges were corrupt, cruel, and evil. The papers would have a field day: this story would run for weeks, and he wouldn't try to stop it. He sent the squad car away. At long last he had had the last laugh. What was that saying, he thought to himself? Oh yes, *what goes around comes around*. Well, never had truer words been said in the case of this lot of bastards. It was important now to deal with this in a way that wouldn't get covered up by any of his superiors, of whom some, no doubt, would have an ulterior motive for hiding the truth. For the truth had to come out. He wanted there to be no one to stop the reporter he'd just called – and he was exceptionally good at his profession – from gathering everything he needed. He, himself, might get fired, but right now he just didn't give a shit. No way would this ever be covered up. This had to be exposed for all to see. He was going to take down every last one of them.

The next day, people in this country and the rest of world were reading the details of the house of horrors. Every newspaper and all the news channels were full of the 'crime of the century' as the anchor woman at Sky HQ reported. In fact, Sky TV, helped by a tip-off, were first to the location and even ran the grisly scenes of some of the rooms before they were stopped by an injunction at the High Court. Yes, thought DI Spencer, there were still people in so-called authority who made it their life's mission to pretend to the world that

494

the United Kingdom was a bastion of civilisation. He suspected, in this case, that the devil this time was some politician and that the issue had gone as far as the Cabinet Office. Anyway, they couldn't do much about it. *'Raw Justice'* was the most popular headline, which had more than 3 million web searches in the first 30 minutes alone for people around the world attempting to seek further details of this despicable crime.

CHAPTER TWENTY THREE

The September morning sun suddenly lit up Dan's house, streaming through every window. The family had all arrived to wish the Lucianis a safe journey home. They gathered around the table for breakfast. Francesca was the last to enter; she had Cass dressed in a beautiful teddy bear outfit and he snuggled under her chin, gripping her thumb, which lately, had become quite a habit. He couldn't settle unless he was on her chest. He was awake and gazing into her steel blue eyes with his own pools of blue. She looked up at her family and felt the urge to cry. She was always torn between living in England and the States, but America was her home now and had been for years. Even so, her heart had always belonged in England. She had managed to flit between the two countries on a regular basis, an arrangement which had worked for years, but now something had changed. She peered down again at baby Cass and a lump lodged in her throat. She would miss him so much. She couldn't help the enormous tear that trickled down her face.

Her family watched the pain in her face and they knew. Dan stood up from the head of the table and pulled out a chair for her to sit on. Sergio's heart was breaking; his wife was so broken inside, and yet for all their sakes she always held it together.

Suddenly, she let the floodgates open, and in front of her entire family, she sobbed. They had never seen her cry like this; her body was rocking as she broke her heart with endless, relentless tears. Sergio tried to comfort her, but she couldn't stop herself.

Mary took the baby and Bill went to Francesca's side, held her like a child, and then rocked her. They all felt her pain because every one of them knew what she had been through. She had been their redeemer, their angel, and she had saved them all. Ruby and Jack had been rescued from their evil mother's clutches, her brothers had been saved from the McManners, and Bill and Mary were free from the pain of not having their daughter – and it was all down to her because she had done that; she had been there to save them all. Even the Lucianis, she'd protected when their need was at its greatest. She had saved Mauricio from a life in prison. And now she had rescued those poor young girls from God only knew what and probably saved a lot more from the same fate. And what did she want in return? Nothing, absolutely nothing.

They cried and thought of their own lives and how she had affected them for the better. Terry cried too, for she had saved him from a life of not knowing who had killed his daughter and effectively safeguarded him from a life of misery. Closure does that to people.

"Fuck it! Let's sell the clubs, sell our houses, and we will come to the States with you, sis!" Fred was both sad and angry that his sister was crying; he hated it, and he would die himself rather than see her in pain.

"No, Fred," she said, wiping her soaked cheeks. "I'm so sorry. I shouldn't cry. I guess it was all too much. Growing up alone, I always wondered if you would remember me. I wondered if my memories were fake because I felt so loved and cherished. I thought maybe I wanted to believe that, and then the day I returned to you all, I knew it was true. I knew you hadn't forgotten me, and even after all these years, I thank God we have a family who care so much. I was born privileged, and as the years go by, that never changes. We've had our wars with some right bastards in our lives, and we've always done this together, side by side, but this fight was something you should never have been dragged into. I should have fought harder, I should have known what they were doing, but I didn't, and I turned my back. If only—"

Bill put his hand over her mouth. "Shush, you could never have known what they were about. It wasn't your place to know." He looked at Terry.

"He's right, Francesca, it was our job to have looked into it, not yours."

She shook her head. "I hate it that you have gone through so much heartache."

Roberto shuffled his way off the chair and he cleared his throat; the man of wisdom was ready to speak. "My child," he said. He always called her that and it would invariably put a smile on Mary's face. Bill never minded, either; Roberto was, after all, like a father to her, and he was a good man. "You have walked a cruel path for many of your years, but for those times when it has been hard for you and you saw only the black dark fog of unearthly memories, you have also brought great light and bright futures for so many people. We would not all be here, enjoying life, if it wasn't for you and for all you have done. Those young girls would not be able to go on to have careers and families if it wasn't for your persistence in rooting out the terrible evil they were forced to endure. So, my child, do not think of those who may have suffered a little along the way. Think of the bigger picture and the tears you cry from now on must only be tears of joy."

Francesca stopped crying and smiled through quivering lips. "Thank you, Roberto. I know we are lucky to have each other, but Cass should have the right to have his mother here with us and Dan should have his wife."

Mary knew then it was grief that was flowing through those tears. They hadn't had time to grieve.

Dan nodded. "I've lost my Cassie and she'll always be in my heart, but I know she would want us to live and not grieve for her. Roberto is absolutely right: you have changed for the better the future of such a vast number of lives, some in our own family, so you mustn't cry for that."

"Yeah, sis, I would fucking do it all over again," affirmed Fred.

"Me too, sis," agreed Sam.

Joe hadn't been part of that evening's events. He was the most sensitive and had been left in charge of the funeral guests. He sat with a tear-stained face and now wished he could swap places with his sister, just to take her pain away.

Dan looked at his mother, nodded, and smiled. She smiled back. It had all been arranged.

The cars arrived to take them to the airport. Roberto had a private jet and although they rarely travelled together on one flight, for reasons of safety, he felt that after all the family had been through, which now seemed a lifetime ago, he somehow wanted them close this time.

Francesca kissed each member of her family and then she went up to Terry and embraced him warmly. It was so hard this time to say goodbye even though she knew she would return next month. But it was Cass she found the hardest to part from. As she walked to the front door, with Sergio's arm around her shoulders, she saw Maria at the foot of the stairs with two suitcases. Francesca frowned. "Are you coming for a break, Maria?"

Maria shook her head and looked at Dan.

Francesca noticed her mum and dad holding each other with tears of compassion in their eyes.

Dan took Cass from Mary's arms and handed him to Francesca. "You've forgotten someone."

Francesca looked at all the smiling eyes and then she glanced down at Cass; he had a piece of paper tucked inside his blanket. "What's going on?" she asked, totally bewildered.

Dan hugged her and Cass. "You've forgotten to take your son, Fran."

"But ..." she looked at her husband, who was smiling through tears, and he nodded.

"We cannot ever give you what you deserve, we can never replace those lost years, and I cannot give the love and care to Cass that you so obviously can. He needs a mum, sis, he needs a loving home, and Cassie would not want anyone other than you to be his mother. The passport and birth certificate have yours and Sergio's names on."

Francesca bit her top lip to stop the endless tears, which had reddened her eyes.

"But ..." she repeated. She didn't know what to say.

"Fran, I can't be a good father to him. I run nightclubs, for Christ's sake. I'm not the fatherly kind, but I will be the best uncle. He has your Vincent blood running through his veins and I'll get to see him grow up. It's what I want, too, sis."

She looked at her husband. "Did you know?"

He nodded. "We all knew." He turned to Dan. "I will make a solemn vow to you that I will be the best father possible to Cass. He is my son and my first priority."

Dan nodded and shook his hand. "Serg, I know you will."

Francesca stepped into the limousine with her son to begin her new life as a mother. It had once been a dream of hers – a dream that she never imagined would ever come true. She quickly realised that Dan's decision hadn't been made on a whim. He had planned it a week ago. The baby's car seat was already in the car and Maria had her own and Cass's bags packed. She was going to be Francesca's nanny, if, of course, she could ever get her hands on the baby.

As they approached the church, Francesca stopped the car and jumped out. She walked to the back where the graveyard was, and where, covered with pink roses and surrounded by peace lilies, Cassandra's grave lay. Dan had made sure it would always be covered in flowers. She knelt down and whispered, "I promise you, Cassandra, I will love your son as if he were my own. Please watch over him while I sleep because that will be the only time I can't."

CHAPTER TWENTY FOUR

Terry was packing his suitcase. He was looking forward to the trip back to England, as it had now been a year almost to the day since he had last seen his old friends. He had lost more weight and was looking the pinnacle of good health. His face had softened and in some lights he looked much younger.

"Right, love, are you ready? I don't want to miss the flight."

"Gawd help us, Tel, you ain't gonna miss the plane. We got three hours before we fly. I can't get me poxy jacket in the case."

Terry rolled his eyes. "Tressa, just carry your jacket. We're only going for a week!"

Tressa was still trying to squeeze the last bits in. Finally, she sat on top of the case and managed to zip it up.

Terry stood at the doorway to her bedroom. "Right, are we ready now?"

She smiled. "Yep, come on, then, you ol' fucker, let's get going."

Terry grinned. "Tress, listen love, I know that you want to impress young Freddie, but I think you need to work on your language. There's no need to swear, and you should think before you speak, as it might somehow improve your chances."

Tressa glared back. "Leave off, Tel, I don't fucking swear ... err ... that much. Anyway, how do I look?" She stood up and smoothed down her simple but elegant dress.

He smiled. "Like a debutante, but like I said, all that goes out the window when you open your trap."

"A debutante, you say?" Tressa grinned to herself. She had been working hard to change her appearance and so far it had worked. She had no need for her daily shot of brandy or the odd dose of sleeping pills. Her hair was back to its former thick and shiny waves and her perfect skin positively glowed. The Spanish sun had given her a tan and the healthy eating had padded her exquisite figure. She had changed, there could be no argument about that, and Terry's kind offer of a home to stay in with him had been snapped up. She'd promised to make amends for her past and had got stuck in with real enthusiasm for doing this. The local Spanish school had been set up to accommodate disabled kids and Tressa helped out four days a week. She was good company for Terry too. He wasn't bored anymore. How could he with a livewire like Tressa for company. She had a unique sense of humour and always made him laugh, and although not a churchgoer, he thanked God he had found a family who wanted him. The maxim there's no gain without pain had an unfortunate context for him personally, but he felt he could now move on with his life, and he had those around him who loved him and would help him along his journey. He looked over at Tressa. It was hard to imagine someone with a past so dark that they could rise above it. But she'd done this and had become a pillar of society. And with her friendly and genuine personality, many people had naturally warmed to her.

"Anyway, Tressa, you've no need to bleedin' worry. How many times a week do you spend on the phone with young Freddie? I mean, he is a busy man. He wouldn't waste time if he didn't like ya, now, would he?"

"I know, I know, but he is so fucking handsome, and I am well …"

"Stunning!" replied Terry with a sweet and generous smile.

"Ahh, give over, Tel."

"Babe, you have always seen yaself as ugly but that came from the inside out. You are different now and he will fancy the bleedin' pants off ya. Anyway get a move on, or we're gonna be late."

*

Mary and Bill were fussing out in the marquee. The food had arrived and she was checking that all was in order. Roberto had arrived a few days earlier with his granddaughter Angelina, the real apple of his eye. She was eighteen and stunning and a very good-looking Italian woman, much like his poor dead wife. Mauricio and his wife Kathy were visiting her mother Nellie and would arrive just before the christening. Dan had arranged the parking for all the guests and Fred had helped with security. They were all in good spirits. It was so different from how things had been the year before.

The limousine pulled up and Fred waved as he ran over like a child. Dan followed him, full of smiles, and excited to see his sister and Cass. The driver opened the door and Francesca passed the baby to Fred, who held him in the air. "Look at the little porker!" He looked at Dan, laughing.

"Here, come to Uncle Dan, chubby boy," Dan said, as he took the baby from his brother.

Cass was squealing with excitement. "Ahh, look at those dimples, sis. He really has your smile, don't he, Fred?"

Francesca laughed. "He doesn't stop smiling, the cheeky boy." She squeezed his chubby legs.

Sergio was talking with Fred about the casino, and Dan, carrying the baby, walked with his sister. "You look so well, sis."

She smiled. "Do I? With Cass, I haven't got time to grow old. He keeps me on my toes."

She radiated happiness and had a look on her face he had never seen before. It was a look of completion, satisfaction, and peace.

Suddenly, Mary came running down the stairs with her arms out. "Here he is!" she shrieked. Bill was still at the back of the house in the marquee with Roberto, when he heard the shriek. "I guess the baby has arrived," he chuckled.

Roberto was used to Cass, for he saw him every day back in the States, but he knew he would have reacted in the same way as Mary had he not been so fortunate to have Cass in his life so much.

Sergio graciously helped Maria out of the car. Dominic, the driver, Francesca's bodyguard and bag carrier for many years now, lifted the boot lid and shook his head. There was so much, it would need five trips to the house to unload the endless baby holdalls.

Mary clocked how fresh and smart Maria looked and she smiled to herself.

The guests began to arrive in their droves. This was one christening they wouldn't miss. Each was greeted with a glass of champagne. The waiters paraded around with canapes whilst guests mingled and fussed over Cass. Francesca kept looking at her brother, wondering if he regretted his decision, but he winked back and smiled. Fred had stayed in London, helping Dan with the clubs, and making sure his big brother was happy, and the regular phone calls to Francesca assured her that he was living his life and not moping around.

Sam arrived with Terry and Tressa. He had picked them up from the airport and everyone was surprised to see how well they looked. Tressa had filled out and looked radiant, and Terry was in his element, having a woman to look out for – although someone more like a daughter than a wife.

Francesca sat in the garden, talking to her mother about Cass, who of course was really the main subject of conversation in the last year. Mary watched her daughter's face – it was so alive and full of happiness. She noticed how her steel blue eyes were warm now and the cold glaze, which had clouded her expression so often in the past, had now gone. She was once more the eleven-year-old girl, her Dolly, that she had said goodbye to all those years ago. Just as Francesca went to say that Cass was cutting a tooth, she stopped dead and stared over her mother's shoulder. Mary whirled around and jumped to her feet along with Francesca. "Anne!" squealed Mary.

Anne, Mary's sister, was the woman who had raised Francesca from the age of eleven. She had put her through a good school and university, and she had also given her the tools to become the sophisticated woman she was today.

Anne hugged both Mary and Francesca. "Well, I'll be blowed. Look at you both!" Anne held them away from her and looked them

507

up and down. "I can't tell you how happy I am to be back on British soil *and* with my family. Now, where's our baby?" she asked.

Francesca absolutely adored Anne, for she had done her best to give her a good life and for that she was truly grateful. Despite the fact she wasn't her mum, she was the next best thing. Anne had changed over the years. The hardness in her eyes had softened appreciably and she appeared different too, looking so much more like Mary.

Sergio walked towards them, laughing, with Cass in his arms. "Bella, our son has definitely cut a tooth. He is a wolf cub, biting on my chin."

Francesca smiled, watching Cass with his hands either side of Sergio's face and his mouth firmly gripping his chin.

Anne clapped her hands together and reached out to hold the chunky bundle. Cass stared up at her and a huge smile spread across his chubby face.

"Ahh, Dolly, look! He has your dimples. He's your double!" exclaimed Anne.

Mary pinched the baby's cheeks. "Yep, he sure is. I have to say, he's the image of our Dolly when she was a baby."

Cass turned to face his mother and in-between dribbling he called her name: "Mummum."

Mary's eyes welled up but not from Cass speaking his first words; instead, she was overcome by the look of complete joy on Francesca's face.

Terry and Tressa headed straight for the garden to greet Francesca. Tressa was still nervous, for she had seen at first-hand the strength and power Francesca had and would never forget it. She had absolute respect and admiration for the woman, but she was unsure if Francesca had forgiven her for her part in the Ruthers' nefarious businesses. Francesca hugged Terry, thanking him for flying over, and then she turned to Tressa who had her eyes to the ground. She hugged her and tilted her head up with her finger. "Thank you for coming, Tressa. It's really good to see you. You're looking remarkably well, and I hear you are spoiling those less-privileged children over there."

Tressa looked up and smiled. She was so warmed and comforted by Francesca's soft, soothing words. She had no reason to feel worried any longer. The look on Francesca's face said it all. Fred came bounding over, still as lively as ever, and Tressa, usually very gobby, smiled coyly.

"Come and join us for a beer, Tel, and you, Tressa, fancy a glass of bubbly?"

Tressa smiled, showing bright white teeth, courtesy of Terry. He had noticed how hard she was trying to look her best and had paid for her teeth to be sorted out as an early birthday present.

"You're looking good, babe," Fred whispered in her ear. She felt his freshly shaven skin just brush past her face and inhaled the aroma of his expensive aftershave.

"Thank you, and you look good, too, Freddie Vincent," she giggled back.

The little flirtation didn't go unnoticed. Francesca clocked everything. The way Fred placed his arm around Tressa's waist, guiding her, said it all really. She had often wondered what sort of woman Fred would eventually settle down with. It had to be someone extraordinary and with a personality to match his. Tressa, with her attractive new appearance and lively eyes, was perfect for him, and she already knew he was smitten.

The gathering was a hive of activity with everyone laughing and pleased to see each other. She then saw Jamie approach her with a beautiful smile; he was as charming as ever. "Hello Sisco."

She got up from her chair and embraced him. "It's lovely to see you and how is everything in the new offices?"

He winked. "Just perfect ... oh, by the way, there is a letter from the prison for you – it's in my pocket – but, hey, let's celebrate today." He smiled and diverted his attention to something more interesting.

Francesca noticed Ruby, showing off in front of Jamie. She smiled to herself; her niece and Jamie – now that would be a perfect match. "No, Jamie, let me read it, and then hopefully we can put the past behind us and then celebrate."

Jamie handed her the bulky envelope, placed it in her hands, and then he turned to face Ruby who had been trying to catch his attention.

Francesca opened the envelope and found inside two letters. The first was from the governor at Bronzefield and the other, also addressed to her, but handwritten, was inside a sealed envelope. She read the governor's letter first.

Dear Mrs Luciani,

Please find a letter addressed to you. It was given to me to pass on to you in the event of Ms Gemma Ruthers' death, while serving her sentence at HMP Bronzefield Prison.

I regret to inform you that this is indeed the case. Ms Ruthers was found dead in her cell three days ago. The circumstances are still under investigation. However, all I can tell you at present is that one of my officers, Sandra McFee, found her hanging from a makeshift rope. We are assuming it is suicide.

Please feel free to call me if you would like any further details as I understand you were her barrister.

Yours sincerely

Victoria Marshall, Governor HMP Bronzefield.

Francesca breathed deeply and then she smiled inwardly. She then checked the date on the letter, placing it in her pocket. She decided to read the second letter, which appeared to be very bulky, when she had a private moment. She put this in her handbag. Searching for her family, she headed back to the table.

The men had made their way to the huge bar area inside the marquee and the women gathered around Francesca, all excited to see her. Suddenly, Sergio came bounding back, holding her phone. "Bella, it's for you!"

She took the phone and straight away recognised the number. "Hello, Kristov, and how are you?" She could hear excitable voices of the girls in the background.

Kristov's voice was softer. "Hello, Francesca, I would love to say I am good and not stressed, but as you can hear, I am surrounded by girls, but as you say in England, it is like herding cats. They are too excited anyway. We wanted to wish you a happy christening, and I have someone who wants to talk to you. She thinks her English is perfect now and much better than mine." He chuckled.

Francesca's face was alight with joy. "Hello, Anya, it's good to hear your voice again, and how are the English lessons coming along?"

Anya could hardly breathe with excitement. "Yes, yes, very well, thank you, Francesca. We are all here at the airport, and we wanted to wish you a good day, and to say thank you for everything."

Francesca could hear the flights being called and she smiled to herself. Those poor girls had lost a great deal of their childhood, and she was making it her life's mission to ensure they regained at least a small part. "I must go, Francesca, but I will see you soon. Disneyland is calling. I love you. Goodbye!"

"I love you too, Anya. Have fun and I will see you in two weeks."

Mary swallowed hard. There was no end to her daughter's kindness. She knew the story of the poor wretches and wasn't surprised that Francesca had ensured their safety, with help from Kristov. Francesca had also paid for their education and of course their holidays to destinations fit for young girls. Mary smiled with pride, through her tears, at her daughter's selflessness.

Her eldest nephew, Jack, the apple of her eye, appeared with a face bursting to say something. Kizzy was as stunning as ever with her long waves tumbling down her back and dressed in a simple but elegant summer dress. "Aunt Sisco, Nan, I have some news. I know it's our Cass's day, but I can't wait to tell you."

Francesca looked at Kizzy. With her radiant face and the glow across her cheeks, she guessed. "You're going to have a baby!"

"Yes, due in about six months," laughed Jack, excitably. He was eaten-up with pride.

Francesca was elated. "Oh, my goodness, that is such wonderful news. Baby Cass will have a buddy." She held out her arms to embrace her nephew and then Kizzy.

Mary was hopping up and down like a child. "Oh, Jack, this is the icing on the cake. Ahh, Kizzy, I can't wait ... another baby."

"Errm, no, not exactly."

Francesca and Mary frowned, their heads to the side. "What?" asked Mary.

The grin on Jack's face said it all. "Not a baby but two babies. Kizzy's carrying twins!"

"Well, it does run in the family." Francesca laughed.

The church was full to the rafters and the priest was elated to celebrate the christening of Cass. It was such a different affair from a year ago when he'd laid Cass's mother to rest. Cass wasn't too impressed when he had water dripped down his face, though.

"Please, would the godparents step forward," the priest instructed.

With a huge smile, Dan stepped forward and held Cass, kissing his face, and then Mauricio and Kathy stepped up. Kathy winked at Francesca, her dear friend.

Francesca felt the lump in her throat again, but if the tears should fall they would be happy ones from now on.

Roberto was holding Maria's hand. "He looks wonderful. That gown was Sergio's, when he was christened. I have saved it for this day, and I am so pleased that he has a son to wear it. That baby will be the most spoiled and loved baby ever born." He squeezed her hand.

513

As the church proceedings came to an end, the guests departed to join the celebrations back at Dan's house. The sun was out and the churchyard was alive with bees and butterflies, flitting around the mass of rose bushes. Francesca held back with Sergio and Dan. She plucked a pink rose from one of the bouquets and carefully removed all the thorns, and then she placed it in Cass's hand and carried him to the grave, which was covered in peace lilies. A huge angel statue stood towering over the flowers. She placed Cass on the ground and went to hold his hand. He was learning to walk but he still needed to hold on to something.

Dan watched in amazement as Cass took his first step, completely unaided, towards the lilies, and then, unexpectedly, he took two steps more and dropped the pink rose to fall among the sweet-smelling flowers.

Francesca let the tears fall as she thanked the woman who had given her a son, her future, and her life.

The End

515

Printed in Great Britain
by Amazon